PUBLISHER'S NOTE

This is a work of fiction. Any names, characters, places, and incidents are the product of the author's imagination or are used fictitiously, and any resemblance to actual persons, living or dead, business establishments, events or locales is entirely coincidental.

The scanning, uploading, and distribution of this book via the Internet or via any other means without the permission of the publisher is illegal and punishable by law. Please purchase only authorized electronic editions, and do not participate in or encourage piracy of copyrighted materials. Your support of the author's rights is appreciated.

www.sacredforestpublishing.com

P.O.Box 280

Moyock, NC, 27958

Digital ISBN- 978-1-941315-29-3

Print ISBN- 978-1-941315-30-9

Sacred Forest Publishing

MY
WARRIOR

BEWITCHED AND BEWILDERED

ALANEA ALDER

DEDICATION

~Omnia Vincit Amor- Love Conquers All~

~Thank you for waiting~

PROLOGUE

❦

Three weeks ago

THE IMAGE OF HIS MATE'S soulful brown eyes looking up at him in resignation before leaving, ate at him. It was three o'clock in the morning, and he was awake, again. He didn't even need to look at the clock; he'd been waking up at the same time for weeks.

In his dream she always turned from him to pick up a gun and walk away.

Was she in danger and choosing to leave to keep him safe? Did she feel like she had no other options? Growling, he rolled over onto his side and prayed for dreamless sleep.

CHAPTER ONE

ᘓ

ARI MADE HIS WAY DOWNSTAIRS, rubbing his face. For the past week he had been
training with his commander and the unit leaders
of the Gamma and Beta units. Never in his life
did he think that their enemies would ever find
a way to not only make themselves invisible,
but also gain entry to Éire Danu. The protective
measures created by the fae queen to reach their
city were supposed to be impregnable.

When he reached the dining room, he was
surprised to see that both his parents and older
brother had made it downstairs before him.
Then again, he was probably the only one being
plagued by nightmares, which caused his sleep
to be brief and restless.

Not to say that being an Elder was without
problems of their own, but he was feeling especially prickly this morning due to broken sleep.
No doubt Jedrek and Rex Lionhart would handle
this sort of thing in stride, yet he found himself
getting irritated over the smallest of things. He
wished he were more like his mother. Catherine Lionhart only lost her composure when

something happened to one of her sons. He was nowhere near her levels of aplomb.

"Good morning, darling," his mother said, tilting her head for him to kiss her cheek. Smiling, he could no more refuse her than he could refuse to breathe.

He dutifully bussed her cheek and inhaled her perfume. She smelled like pride, and the perfume she wore was one she had been using since before he had been born. He would always associate it with his mother, and it never failed to calm him.

"Good morning, Mother. May I say that you are looking exceptionally beautiful this morning."

His mother's eyes twinkled as she lifted a hand up to cup his face. "It's because I have two of my boys home."

Rex chuckled. "You'd be just as beautiful even if I weren't visiting."

"Well said, son," his father replied gruffly, lifting his coffee cup to his lips.

Ari sat down in the empty seat by his mother. "Any updates?"

Rex shook his head. "Meryn said she'd text me with any news regarding the queen. But between the two of us, I think she's at a snapping point."

"Meryn or the queen?"

"Meryn. She, Darian, and Oron have tried broaching the topic of ferals many times and have been completely shut down each time. The people are getting restless, something has to be done."

His mother nodded. "If anyone can ferret out what is wrong with Queen Aleksandra, it's that tiny typhoon."

Ari sat back in his chair. "Can you believe she is second in line for the throne?" he asked no one in particular.

Rex shrugged. "Yes and no."

Their father eyed his eldest son. "What do you mean by that?"

"I know you believe her to be flakey and prone to outbursts, and it's true she does tend to cause chaos around her naturally, but she also has to be one of the most brilliant minds I have ever witnessed in action, except for Declan of course."

"Of course." His mother confirmed.

Jedrek shook his head. "She has no respect for tradition or decorum."

Ari watched as his brother's eyes narrowed. "Do not judge her so quickly. She just about single-handedly saved Noctem Falls from a magic-borne virus and courageously jumped into a transport tunnel to save Kari from certain death. Her mind simply works better without social constraints, and her bravery helps her to speak up and make changes that benefit everyone."

Ari felt as shocked as his father looked. Rex, in all the years he had known him had never gainsaid their father.

Jedrek recovered quickly. "You have spent more time with her than I have." He rubbed his jaw. "I have to admit, even Magnus had nothing but glowing things to say about her. I will be guided by you in this, Rex."

His mother's smile was partially hidden by her teacup. "Probably a good idea, dear," she murmured.

His father gave his mate a wry look. "That human has wormed her way into your heart as well?"

"Half- human," Rex corrected.

Jedrek simply nodded his acknowledgment and looked to his mate for an answer.

She set her cup down. "Doing something simply for the sake of tradition without reason or purpose is asinine, doing those things repeatedly and expecting different results is insanity. I find it refreshing that Meryn can see into the heart of matters and ask questions that allow those around her to see beyond our traditions."

Jedrek's mouth dropped. Catherine's words rang with truth and conviction. It was quite stunning to behold. Jedrek's eyes shifted to a tawny color. "Darling, what do you have planned after breakfast?"

Smiling, she looked down at her plate before lifting her heart-shaped face to grin at her mate. "Nothing that cannot be rescheduled."

Rex chuckled. "And people wonder how you two have been blessed with so many children."

Their mother blushed, but laughed at his words. "We're tame compared to Byron and Adelaide McKenzie."

Ari snapped his fingers together. "Speaking of

the McKenzies, is it true that Aiden challenged every level of Noctem Falls?"

Rex's grin turned evil. "It most certainly is true. An impudent tunnel escort's words had a devastating effect on Meryn. If Aiden had not challenged the city, I'm pretty sure Magnus would have." He winked at Ari. "Etain told me that Aiden started on Level Five and worked his way down. I swear his recounting of the tale has grown with each telling. If it hasn't been immortalized in our history books yet, it's only a matter of time."

Jedrek chuckled. "That boy most definitely takes after his father. Slow to rile, but once their bear is enraged, watch out."

"Good morning, Ari," a familiar voice called out in greeting.

Ari looked up to see Leo, his parents' squire, breeze into the room carrying a steaming carafe of coffee. He immediately came to his side and poured him a cup.

"Good morning, Leo. Do we have any eggs today?"

The squire shook his head. "No, a cold breakfast was prepared. We have a selection of fae fruits, bread, and cheeses available in addition to yogurt and granola." He looked him over. "You've been training more than usual, haven't you?"

He grimaced. "Yes. Our commander has Lorcan running us through blind man bluff drills."

Leo set down the carafe next to his cup. "Give

me a few minutes, and I'll whip up some eggs. You need the extra protein."

Ari sighed in relief. "Thank you, Leo."

He simply inclined his head and returned to the kitchen.

"Yeah, you're not spoiled at all," Rex taunted good-naturedly.

Catherine turned to her eldest son. "And who was it that complained that they hadn't had in fresh fae fruit in years?"

Rex blushed. "I wasn't angling for special treatment."

Ari was about to tease his brother mercilessly when a familiar chime echoed through the house.

Catherine frowned. "Who on earth could that be? We don't have any appointments scheduled until this afternoon."

Ari shook his head as a male voice reached them. "Baby, I told you that we shouldn't just drop in."

Ari rose as his commander and Meryn, with Ryuu and Pierce were escorted into their small dining room. His father and Rex rose as Meryn entered the room.

"Rex!" Meryn hurried over to his older brother. "Do the arm thing," she entreated, ignoring everyone.

Grinning from ear to ear, Rex brought his arm up and flexed his bicep. Ari watched in amazement as Meryn hopped up and swung from his arm. "So hot," she said, laughing.

Grumbling under his breath, Aiden walked over and plucked his mate off of Rex's arm.

"What did I tell you about using the Elder as a jungle gym?"

Leo had to turn his head to hide his laughter. He coughed once into his fist and faced them, his mouth twitching. "Commander, would either you or your lovely mate like to join us for breakfast?"

Meryn turned to him, her interest piqued. "Breakfast?"

Leo nodded. "We have a selection of fruits, breads, and cheeses available."

Meryn sighed. "Oh. Fruit. Again."

Aiden covered his face with his other hand, his ears turning pink. He dropped his hand and looked out over the room. "Meryn is still getting used to fae cuisine that is rich with fruits and vegetables."

Meryn shrugged. "It's okay for a day or two, but not all the time. I swear I'm going back to the goblin village for more boar."

Jedrek leaned forward. "Boar?"

Meryn nodded slowly. "Oh, yeah. Roasted on a spit and everything. They cut huge chunks off with, like, a machete and hand you whole body parts. It was awesome."

Jedrek leaned back. "Well, well."

Rex was licking his lips. "Maybe we should arrange a visit."

Leo placed his hand over his heart and gave a short bow. "I'll see what else I can whip up."

Meryn looked surprised, then she frowned. "You don't have to make anything special for me."

Ryuu ruffled her curls. "I will assist him, so don't feel bad."

Leo smiled at her. "Don't worry yourself a bit about it. Now, please sit down and rest."

Jedrek indicated to the empty chairs next to Ari. "Please make yourself comfortable, dear."

Meryn looked up at her squire, scowling. Ryuu sighed. "I promise that he won't be put out cooking for you."

Meryn gave a short nod and sat down next to Ari, much to her mate's chagrin. Aiden took the seat next to her, and Pierce stood behind them, leaning against the wall.

She looked over at him, and her eyes became slightly unfocused. "Stars, no, not just stars, berries and flowers. Stars? Or bells?" She tilted her head. "So, you're like a fruit basket?"

Aiden rubbed her back. "Good job, baby. You didn't even need Kendrick or Law to help you that time."

Ari blinked. How was he a fruit basket? "What?"

Meryn pointed to her chest. "My empathy thing does images, so that they can be processed quicker and not give me headaches. You're stars and berries and flowers."

Rex guffawed across the table, and Ari shot him a sour expression. "And I suppose you're something manly."

Rex shrugged. "She hasn't done me yet."

Meryn shrugged. "I can't really control it yet, at least not all the time."

Catherine turned to Meryn. "As much as I am pleasantly surprised at your visit, dear, was there a reason for your stopping by?"

Meryn's eyes widened. "Oh yeah. We're here to give an update regarding the queen." She turned in her chair to face Pierce. "Can you do the thing?"

Pierce nodded and reached into his pocket, retrieving a brass ring and key. Carefully, he moved the key until it was hanging within the ring. Around them the air pulsed, then settled.

Jedrek stared. "Did a jaguar-shifter just cast a soundproofing spell?"

Pierce winked. "A present from a certain archivist. He got tired of us asking for them all the time."

Aiden opened his mouth like he was trying to pop his ears. "He copied a prototype that Kee-lan invented to install a permanent spell in my father's study. I think it only cost Marius three of Keelan's favorite pies."

"That's ingenious," Jedrek said, looking very impressed.

Meryn spun back around. "So, the queen is stuck on being stubborn stupid."

"Meryn," Aiden chided.

"What? It's true. She's smart enough to realize that what we're reporting is accurate. She's just wallowing in guilt and pity, and it's making her obstinate."

Aiden gave her a flat look then pointed around the table. "She is still their queen."

Meryn crossed her arms over her chest. "Well,

she's my aunt, so I can say what I want cuz I'm family."

Catherine sat back, cradling her tea. "If it were for any other reason, I would say she's more than earned the time to process, but we're already fielding concerns from cat and bird shifters alike." She looked at them, sadness in her eyes. "They want to leave Éire Danu."

Meryn's nostrils flared. "She has one tiny hiccup, and they're ready to abandon ship?"

Jedrek shook his head. "Meryn, if she told us to fight and die defending Éire Danu, we would, to the last man. It's the blatant denial that has everyone spooked. They're afraid that when the time comes, the city won't be prepared to face what may happen."

Leo and Ryuu came in carrying heavy platters. "I thought it got quiet in here. Soundproofing spell?" Leo asked.

Rex nodded absently before turning to Meryn. "Is there any way you can convince the queen to send out a public message. Even something as simple as she's looking into the matter could make all the difference in the world."

Ari sighed happily as eggs and bacon were piled on his plate. He had just taken a huge bite when Meryn gasped loudly, causing him to almost choke.

He pounded his own chest as Meryn grinned wickedly around the table. "I know what I can do! In times like this, you're supposed to help family. You know, give them encouragement and stickers." She frowned. "Or something.

Ryuu's been helping me understand familial dynamics." She looked around the table. "But more than stickers, I know what I can do to help Aunt Aleks."

Ari was terrified to discover what this ticking time bomb was planning.

Aiden looked absolutely sick as he stared at his mate. "What's that, baby?"

"I'm gonna take over Éire Danu."

Boom

"Oh gods above, please give me strength," Aiden prayed fervently.

Meryn sat back, looking positively pleased with herself.

Ari looked over at Rex, who was convulsing with laughter. "Can she do that?" he whispered.

Rex wiped his eyes and reached for the spoon to the bowl of fresh berries. "Brother, you will quickly learn there isn't much this amazing child can't do." He turned to his father. "I'll be at the palace if you need me. I wouldn't miss this for anything in the world."

Aiden looked over to Ari. "After breakfast, get Tau assembled at the palace ASAP. I'm going to need back up."

Ari just stared. "We're going against the queen?"

Aiden shook his head. "No, we may need to bodily remove my pint-size terror of a mate from the palace quickly."

Meryn popped a piece of bacon in her mouth. "Yeah, good luck with that," she said, chortling.

Ari shoveled his eggs into his mouth as quick

as he could. Gods only knew when he'd get a lunch.

☾

It had taken them nearly an hour to finish breakfast and assemble the rest of the Tau unit. The men followed them, smiling. He couldn't bring himself to tell them what was about to happen. He'd let them remain blissfully ignorant for a bit longer.

He watched as Aiden, Rex, and Meryn, along with her squire and Pierce walk into the queen's chambers. He hung back, and his men paused alongside him. "No matter what happens in there, follow Aiden's orders," he said, in the barest of whispers. He felt like he had kicked a puppy when the happy-go-lucky-smile slid from Kincaid's face to be replaced by a look of sheer terror.

They stepped into the room and closed the door behind them. They silently moved to stand against the wall. Around the small dining table everyone smiled at Meryn and Aiden.

"Meryn, darling, where were you at breakfast? We missed you," the queen said, smiling at her niece.

"I was making some hard decisions," Meryn replied, in a serious tone.

Gods! The little nut was going right in!

Aiden exhaled, and the men around Ari tensed.

The queen frowned. "Is there anything I can help with?"

Meryn nodded. "Yup. You can step down as queen, and let me take over." She looked over at

Darian. "You don't mind if I skip ahead of you in line for the throne, do you?"

Darian just blinked and slowly shook his head, clearly confused as to what the hell was going on.

The queen stood sputtering. "Wha…wha…what?"

Meryn just nodded. "I've been thinking. You never really had heirs and stuff before, so you've never been able to take a break. Therefore, since you're throwing a temper tantrum regarding the ferals, I'll step in and help." She looked at Cord. "We're gonna make some major changes, especially to the menu."

The queen pressed her lips together. "That is enough, Meryn, you've had your fun. What you speak of is treasonous."

Meryn shook her head. "It's only treason if I was a citizen, but I'm from Lycaonia, so this is a…" She paused. "Like a friendly sedition minus the rebellion."

Cord nodded. "I've been thinking we could do with a change in the dishes served."

The queen simply stared at her squire. "What?"

Meryn looked at her aunt. "It's simple. You want to avoid the truth and cover your ears like a child being told no. So, I'm going to put you in time-out, and I'm gonna be queen."

The queen inhaled sharply looking mortally offended. Darian stood. "Meryn, maybe this isn't…"

Meryn held up her hand. "During my reign, you may address me as High Queen Meryn."

Darian gave her a flat look and sat back down, frowning fiercely.

"How dare you!" the queen screeched, inventing new octaves.

"I dare, because I love you. Your people want to abandon the city because they are afraid. They are waiting for their queen to take action, any action! If you can't, then I will. I won't let everything you've built crumble to pieces."

"They would never…" the queen started, then turned to Rex, who nodded.

"The only thing that has kept them here is the visible efforts of the Unit Commander. The fact that he is now related to the royal family and staying in the palace have most feeling that he is acting on your orders, so they are patiently waiting for word on what is going on, but that patience has almost expired," he reported gravely.

Meryn's face softened. "They are afraid."

The queen straightened her shoulders. "There's nothing to be afraid of."

"There are freaking ferals popping up in shadows all over the city!" Meryn shouted.

"There are not!" The queen stood, her back ramrod straight.

"Are too!"

Ari could not believe that he was watching Meryn and the Queen of the Fae scream back and forth at each other like children. He glanced to his left. Gage and Priest were watching with wide eyes, completely riveted to the scene before them. He looked to his right. Poor Kincaid looked pale. Then again, nearly everyone sitting at the table looked a bit wan and shocked, so he was in good company. Had he not known ahead of time what The Menace had planned he'd probably be freaking out as well.

"Are not!"

"There are!" Meryn shouted. "And if you can't or won't do something, I will. So, go stick your head in a flower bush and continue to ignore the problem, making everyone anxious and walk on eggshells around you, and I'll be figuring out how they're getting in so we can fry the bastards!" Meryn's words rang through the room as she breathed heavily.

The queen stared and sat down slowly. "There can't be ferals in Éire Danu," she whispered. She looked up at Meryn. "Because if that were true, then I've failed to protect my people."

"The only way you can fail them is if you continue to do nothing, my love," Brennus said, taking her hand. "Meryn is right. For thousands of years, you had to rule alone, but that's not the case anymore. You have me, my brothers, our sons, their mates, and one courageous niece who did the one thing no one else could, despite being scared to death that she would anger an aunt she just discovered after living an entire life with no family."

The queen looked up at Meryn and saw her clenched hands and trembling lips. "Oh, my sweet darling, I'm so very sorry."

"I'm fine." Meryn protested. Ryuu massaged her back soothingly. Aiden looked completely wrung out as he brought her hand to his lips for a kiss.

Around the table everyone exhaled explosively.

"Gods! You can't do that to me, Meryn," Kendrick complained, clutching at his chest.

The queen stood and hurried to where her niece stood. She took the small woman in her arms. "You're right. I'm so sorry I pushed you to do this. You should be taking it easy." She led her over and sat her between herself and Brennus. Ryuu walked behind Meryn's chair to keep a watchful eye on his charge.

Brennus looked absolutely lost as to what to do. So, he reached across the back of the chair to squeeze the queen's shoulder and rubbed Meryn's knuckles with his free hand.

Aiden sat down in the empty chair beside Kendrick and looked at Cord. "A shot of whatever you have open."

Cord simply leaned down to kiss the top of the queen's head in way of an apology and nodded.

"Aiden, it's eleven o'clock in the morning," Micah reminded him.

Aiden sat back, closing his eyes. "You're right; Meryn has the whole day in front of her. Cord, make it a double."

Cord chuckled. "Of course."

The queen kissed Meryn's temple. "You're the only one who could have possibly gotten through to me."

Meryn sniffled. "I know."

"Is it because she's your niece?" Law asked,

then pointed to Darian and Oron. "Wouldn't they have worked?"

The queen shook her head. "It had to be Meryn, because I know for a fact that she would never, ever want to take the throne. The absurdity of the whole scenario got through my anger, defenses, and guilt."

"Aunt Aleks, we have ferals trying to get into the city," Meryn said, leaning back to look up at the queen.

Aleksandra sighed. "I know. Of course, I know. I've known from the beginning. I just cannot fathom how."

"That's where we can help," Aiden said, opening his eyes. "We've been dealing with these kind of scenarios for months now."

Meryn sighed. "There's something else we need to figure out in addition to the portals," she said, leaning to one side to rest her head against Brennus' shoulder.

"There's something else?" Kincaid asked incredulously. "Isn't that enough?"

Meryn shrugged. "I'm not making the rules here."

Brennus kissed her forehead. "What have you figured out now?"

Meryn glanced at the queen, then looked around the table before staring down at her hands.

The queen placed her fingers under her chin and lifted her face. "No matter what you say, I won't be angry," she promised.

"Ferals and reapers trying to get into a pillar

city to wreak havoc is kinda normal now, right? First in Lycaonia then in Noctem Falls."

Thane winced. "I hate that that is normal for you."

"Go on," Kendrick encouraged.

"Well, them trying to get into Éire Danu makes sense." She looked over at Oron. "What I don't get is, if his family murdered Darian's family like thousands of years ago, how come they aren't drooling insane ferals? Aren't the necklaces kinda a new thing?"

Ari felt his heart constrict. How had no one caught that?

Meryn continued. "The queen said they should have faded honorably, which means they weren't a typical feral back then, right?" She eyed her aunt. "I woulda killed every single one, but that's just me."

The queen grimaced. "They were all mated, Meryn. I would have been sentencing innocent women to insanity or death. The men were bound by magic to be docile, so they could be handled by their mates. Over time, the women's lights would dim, meaning they would have had time to fade honorably, taking their mates with them."

"Obviously that didn't happen. How did Oron's dad regain and keep his mind intact?"

The queen sighed and collapsed against the back of her chair. "I have no idea; it should have been impossible."

Meryn gave her a wry look. "Y'all really need to work on redefining your sense of impossible, because that shit is happening all over the damn place."

Ain't that the damn truth, Ari thought as the whole room nodded in agreement.

Chapter Two

(◟

"I WANT TO APOLOGIZE TO YOU, Ari," the queen said, with a pained expression.

"For what, Your Majesty?" he asked, bewildered.

"You've been doing so much to protect the city. It must not have been easy."

Ari pointed to Aiden. "Your nephew is the one you should be thanking. He made arrangements to get unit warriors from Lycaonia here to train us on how to fight invisible ferals." Ari decided he'd take this opportunity to get the queen caught up, especially if she was in a forgiving mood. "Kendrick and Thane have also been teaching our unit witches how to use sweeps to combat the enemy in large open spaces, as well as creating distant early warning spells all along the Border City perimeter."

The queen blinked. "You've all been busy."

Brennus coughed into his fist, looking somewhat contrite. "All for you, my love."

Meryn looked at the queen. "So, back to the other major shit storm. Are the non-feral fae a reaper thing? Or do we have some new mystic mojo going on that we don't know about?"

The queen turned to Meryn. "As far as I know, there should not be a way for them to be whole. If they did not fade honorably, they should be feral."

"Great! Just what we need, new shit we don't know." Meryn sat back in her chair, looking disgruntled.

Ari didn't know which aspect horrified him more—that there was a way for these murderous fae to avoid turning feral after killing or that it had been going on thousands of years and no one knew. He looked over at Aiden. The unit commander was pinching the bridge of his nose. Ari had a feeling most of them would have headaches for the rest of the day.

Meryn sat forward, shaking her head. "Until we know more, there's nothing we can do about it." She looked over at her aunt. "I think you should make an announcement. Maybe something directly from you. That would go a long way in making everyone feel better." The queen rose and walked over to the table that held her summoning crystal. She tapped it lightly and then began to pace the room, her arms wrapped around her body. She turned to look at her consort. "How could any of this happen?"

Brennus stood quickly and strode over to his mate, taking her into his arms. "It happened because someone in the shadows is working very hard to orchestrate these nefarious deeds." He tucked the queen's head under his chin. "We are not the only ones affected, my love. Lycaonia and Noctem Falls have had similar attacks."

There was a knock at the door, and Kincaid went over to open it. Portia walked in and frowned when she saw her queen. "Your Majesty, is all well?"

The queen rubbed her forehead. "No, all is not well. Portia, I would like to arrange an announcement from me to the entire city."

Portia's eyes widened. "I think that would be best. Everyone desperately needs to hear your voice."

The queen gave her wan smile. "I know, and I'm sorry for taking so long to do my duty."

In an uncharacteristic show of emotion, Portia crossed the room and placed a hand on her queen's shoulder. "Everyone understands. Their love for you knows no bounds." She eyed the table of visitors. "And with your new friends and family, you should easily be able to handle these daunting tasks." She hesitated before adding. "I know you may feel like you face these things alone, but you haven't been alone in a very long time." She pointed to Darian, Oron, Cord, and Brennus. She reached into the satchel at her side and pulled out a parchment scroll. "I had a few of these made up last week, just in case. As long as they are written by your hand and then sealed with a drop of your blood, this spelled scroll will project the announcements in your voice to all of Éire Danu."

The queen looked slightly less harried at Portia's words. "You are right. I haven't been alone in a long time." She took the scroll, a look of determination on her face. "It's time to start tackling this problem." She looked around the room. When her eyes fell upon the Tau Unit, Ari straightened. He placed his fist over his heart, the men did the same, and they bowed as one. When he straightened, he smiled at his queen. "You have only to command us, my queen." He gave her a sly smile. "You won't even have to slip us any candy this time," he said, in a joking manner.

The queen's eyes widened before she gave a musical laugh. "Oh, Ari, I had nearly forgotten you used to do that." At the table, Rex began to chuckle.

Meryn looked from her aunt to Rex. "What? Forgotten what?"

The queen pointed to him. "The littlest Lionhart, the baby. He would sneak into the palace and offer to do small chores in exchange for candy. It'd been hundreds of years since Darian and Oron went to Lycaonia. And it was nice to have a little boy in the palace again. He always made me smile."

There was a knock at the door, and Kincaid, once again acting as page, opened it to allow Molvan to step inside.

His expression caused the smile on the queen's face to disappear. "What? What is it?" she asked.

Ari instinctively placed his hand on his side-arm.

Molvan looked devastated as he swallowed hard. "Your Majesty, we have the preliminary reports of the number of fae returning to Éire Danu." He hesitated before continuing. "So far, only half of those known to be living outside of the city have made contact with us."

The queen gasped, a hand going to her throat. "How many are missing?"

Molvan's hand clenched at his side. "Nearly five thousand," he replied.

Brennus and Portia supported the queen as her knees gave way and helped her to the closest sofa.

"What?" she whispered. She looked between her mate and Molvan. "Are we certain that many fae were living outside of the city?"

Molvan opened the portfolio he was holding. "There are an estimated thirty-thousand fae living in the country. Of those thirty-thousand, nearly one-third have made their homes amongst the humans in the past couple hundred years. Modern technology has proven to be a tempting draw to our people, more have chosen to live with humans because of it. Of the estimated eleven-thousand living in human cities, we've only had fifty-seven hundred reply."

At the table, Aiden stood. He turned to Kendrick and the Ashleigh brothers. "Can you work with the queen to find a way to track the missing fae?"

Kendrick nodded. "Of course. It shouldn't be too difficult, considering we're working with the Queen of the Fae. Her blood and magic would make it an easy task, since she is connected to all of her children."

Aiden turned to the Tau Unit. "Gear up, we're starting in Monroe. We'll be doing a full sweep of the city. Any missing fae from the register has to be accounted for."

Ari already had one hand on the walkie-talkie that Meryn had ordered for them. "Just the Tau Unit?" he asked.

Aiden grimaced. "Yes. I want to leave the rest here to maintain perimeter sweeps. But, I'm calling in the Vanguard of Monroe to assist." Ari pointed to the door, and the Tau Unit began to file out. He looked back at Aiden.

"Your first call should be to Cameron Rathais. He's been the sheriff of Monroe for the past ten years. I know he's in the process of aging himself out, but he should be able to get us access to all public records and reports."

Aiden looked at his mate. "Meryn, if we got you the names of the missing fae, could you plot their last known location on a map, like you did for the missing shifters around Lycaonia?" he asked.

Meryn nodded absently, looking spooked. "Of course I can. I just need the records that were updated for Beth's census. I can do the whole country in one go."

Aiden walked over and kissed her gently before straightening. "You do your magic tap-tap. I'll be relying on you to tell us men where to go."

Meryn smiled sadly. "I almost hate doing my magic tap-tap anymore. I always find out something horrible."

Across the room, the queen took a deep breath. "The more we know the better," she said with a shaky voice. "Our people, all of our people. Shifters, vampires, fae, and witches, we've all become too lax. Complacency has allowed an unknown enemy to grow unchecked." Her expression hardened, and she stood on steady feet. "But all of that stops now." Around them, the walls began to crack. Snaps, pops, and the groaning of wood echoed around them in the walls, ceilings, and floors, as the trees themselves seemed to undulate to the waves of the queen's anger. "I want my children. I want my children found. And if something has taken them from me, then I personally want to judge and punish the ones responsible."

Meryn smiled wickedly. "Kick ass," she whispered.

Anne turned to Molvan. "I don't know a lot about public works, but I can help assemble the records that Meryn needs. Just point the way."

Kendrick turned to the Ashleigh brothers. "We also have work to do." Thane stood, cracking his knuckles, and Law and Justice exchanged vicious grins.

Ari turned to Gage, Priest, and Kincaid. "You heard our queen, gentlemen. Move out."

€

As they were getting ready, the queen's announcement went out to the citizens of Éire Danu. In walking to the portal, he could see the effect her words had on the people. Along the street, vendors and families alike looked relieved.

He shook his head. It seemed impossible to imagine an enemy so great going unnoticed for so long. He thought back to what his mother said that very morning, how Meryn questioned everything and, in doing so, uncovered so much.

It didn't take them long to head through the portal to wait with the other warriors outside of Monroe. He stood with the rest of his unit, next to the volunteer Vanguard, by the portal from Éire Danu waiting on Aiden's team to join them.

Liam walked over to them. "Do you all need a fifth?" he asked, pointing to where Ilar Ri'Mierlan stood watching them. When their eyes met, Ilar gave a short nod.

Ari shook his head. "We're good. We've been operating as four for so long, adding someone in would probably hinder us more than help us."

"Must be tough to share your unit leader with palace duties," Liam sympathized.

Ari shrugged. "We've known nothing else, so it's hard to say."

Liam blinked. "That's right. Aren't you all the youngest unit amongst the four pillar cities?"

Ari tried to hide his grimace. He must not have done a good job, because Liam clapped him on the shoulder. "I don't mean anything by it."

"We know that the Éire Danu units are sometimes called 'Advanced Training' units." He sighed. "And up until recently, I could see why. With the city being in its own pocket, parallel plane, our greatest concern was fighting boredom, not ferals."

Gage stepped up beside him. "Who is having the last laugh now?" he asked, raising an eyebrow at him.

Ari had to chuckle. Both he and Gage knew for a fact that their placement with Tau was due to their families' requests, mostly to keep them safe. "Our parents must be getting anxious now that we're actually doing missions like regular units."

Gage rubbed the side of his nose. "Priest and I have a running bet as to how long it will take Jedrek to have sudden need to send you to another country to check on 'Lionhart' business."

Ari groaned. "Don't jinx me."

Liam pointed a finger to Gage. "You mean similar to the letter the queen will receive later today asking for your reassignment?"

Gage paled. "How do you know if the queen has not even received the letter yet?"

Liam smiled slyly. "I have friends everywhere, including House Géroux."

Gage simply shook his head. "I will call home when we get back."

"Time to snip those apron strings," Liam sang.

"You mean burn the damn apron," Gage muttered.

Liam placed a hand over his heart. "Ahh, the problems that come with being beloved and the babies of your families."

"Liam! Stop torturing the Tau Unit and get

your ass over here! The Unit Commander and his team should be here any minute," Cadoc Baines, the Vanguard leader, barked out.

"Coming, dah-ling," Liam called back.

When Cadoc glared at him and turned to face the portal, Liam winked at them. "He hides how much he loves me."

Ari kept a straight face and nodded. "We can see that."

Liam gave a final wave and jogged over to his unit leader.

Kincaid turned to him. "Will we be okay?" he asked quietly.

Ari knew exactly what the witch meant. Not that they personally would be okay, but that they wouldn't cause problems for the other warriors due to their inexperience.

Ari nodded. "Aiden himself has said on more than one occasion that he's pleased with all of Éire Danu's units. He isn't the type of commander that would say something he didn't mean, especially with so much at stake. Have confidence in yourself, Kincaid. We're doing more at our age than any of these old geezers ever did." Liam, without looking, simply raised a middle finger, causing them to laugh.

Gage was about to respond when the portal lit up, and their commander stepped through. Accompanying him were Kendrick, Micah, and Ben. Around them, to the man, the Vanguard straightened.

Aiden noted the change and gave a short nod. "As you were." He waved them over. "Gather round, men." They formed a loose circle around Aiden. "According to my mate's research, there were nine fae families living in Monroe, most included multiple generations. We're looking for approximately seventy-five people." Aiden pointed to Kendrick. "Kendrick Ashwood, Alpha's acting witch, will explain how we'll be tracking our missing persons."

Kendrick stepped up to stand next to Aiden. Those closest to them unconsciously stepped back. If Kendrick noticed, he gave no indication that he saw it or that he cared. He held up what looked like a cross made of gems, dangling from a chain on a key ring. "I, along with the Ashleigh brothers, have created this to act as a compass." He tapped the clear center stone. "Queen Aleksandra has provided some of her light to track her children, since she is tied to them all it shouldn't matter which human city we search." He pointed to the surrounding stones. "I have charged each gem with my own elemental magic. Emerald for North, topaz for East, ruby for South, and sapphire for West. The gems will react with the queen's light in the center diamond and light up accordingly. There will be widely spaced blinks of light if the fae are farther away, rapid blinks as we get closer, and a solid light when we are within a hundred yards. The center stone's color itself will give us a direction. For example, green for North, but greenish yellow for Northeast." He smiled down at the device. "Kinda genius, really," he marveled.

"Kendrick," Aiden murmured quietly.

"Right. In the event we don't get any readings, we have this." He held up a tiny vial. "This contains the queen's own blood. Blood will give us a wider range, but there may be some interference if any in this area are descendants of the fae who made their home here. So, we will primarily be relying on the center stone's stored light." He grinned evilly as Ilar groaned. "This gentleman has figured out the one true flaw to this approach." He pointed to the gems in his hand. "All fae Vanguard must be magicked so they won't interfere with the Divining Compass."

Ilar scowled. "Witch magic messes with my equilibrium."

"It's a small price to pay," Kendrick retorted, not looking in the least bit sorry.

"Fae warriors, line up," Aiden ordered. Ilar and Kyran Li'Alriden moved to stand in front of Micah and Kendrick.

Ari noticed that Kincaid's eyes had yet to leave the compass. "What?" he asked.

Kincaid stepped close. "Look around, Ari, I'm not the only one staring."

Ari looked around the clearing. Every single witch unit warrior's eyes were locked on the compass. "What?" he whispered.

"You don't get it because Kendrick explained the compass so casually, but what he's holding could be considered a once-in-a-generation national treasure. He's treating it like a cool keychain." Kincaid's voice held awe and frustration. "He also just confirmed that he has mastered all four elements, something no other witch has done. He just threw it out there that he charged the compass using all four elements like he simply charged his phone." Kincaid looked up at him. "I don't think there's anything he can't do."

Ari snorted, but then saw the truth in Kincaid's eyes. He looked over to the strange witch. "He's just an archivist, right?"

Kincaid exhaled. "Maybe that's all he's allowed us to see."

Gage eyed Kendrick as he and Micah finished warding the fae. "Glad he is on our side."

Priest nodded. "No lie."

When Micah stepped away from Kyran, Aiden looked to Kendrick. "You're up."

Kendrick held the compass. "*Invenio.*" He frowned when nothing happened.

Micah smirked at his friend. "You did remember to charge it right?"

Kendrick glared at the other witch. "Of course I did." He looked around. "How far are we from town?"

Liam pointed to the west. "Monroe city limits are about ten miles thataway."

Kendrick scowled down at his compass. "That should easily be close enough." He tapped it harshly, causing every witch to groan at its rough handling.

Aiden pointed to Kendrick's pocket. "Maybe you should try the blood."

Kendrick stared at the commander. "Didn't you just hear me explain that we would only try that in the event we don't get any readings."

Aiden raised an eyebrow, and Kendrick

blinked. "Oh." He pulled out the bottle and very carefully released a single drop on the center stone. It immediately began to blink rapidly, in a blue light. "Son of a bitch," Kendrick muttered.

Aiden looked down. "If it's blinking rapidly, that means there are fae close by, to the west of us, right?" Kendrick just gave a short nod. Aiden pointed to the diamond. "Then why didn't the light work?"

"I have no idea. Then again, this type of compass did come into existence this afternoon, there may be a learning curve," Kendrick replied acerbically.

Aiden shrugged, then pointed westward. "Move out."

☾

"Are you sure this is right?" Aiden asked for the fourth time, pointing to the large, generic-looking warehouse.

Kendrick looked like he was about to reach over and throttle their commander. "Yes, I'm sure!" he hissed. "The stone is a solid blue color now. It looks more like a sapphire than a diamond."

Aiden reached up to tap the comms unit in his ear. "On my signal," he said quietly.

Aiden, Kendrick, Micah, and Ben would be joining the Tau unit when they entered the building. The other ten Vanguard split into two teams. One would be entering from the back of the building, while the other would enter from the side.

Aiden peeked around the corner of the building of the adjacent warehouse. "I don't like this. Why would fae be in here?"

Kendrick stepped out into the open, heading toward the front of the building. "Only one way to find out."

"Arrogant bastard," Aiden growled. He reached up to his ear. "Go!"

Ari's heart was pounding as he ran alongside Aiden to enter from the front of the building. They fanned out, clearing each of the small offices before moving to the door leading to the main storage area. When the door opened, he fought his body's urge to gag. "Gods! What is that stench!"

"Gods, no," Aiden whispered, as he ran forward.

They quickly joined the other two Vanguard teams standing in front of a large clothing pile.

"Why do those clothes smell so rank?" Kincaid asked.

Kendrick turned to him with uncharacteristic kindness in his eyes. "Look closer, Kincaid, it's the bodies that smell, not the clothes."

Kincaid paled so fast Ari moved to wrap an arm around his waist. In seconds, Gage was on Kincaid's other side.

Their warrior brother shook his head. "I'm sorry," he whispered.

"It's not just you," Ari replied, as the sound of retching reached them. Across the room, Liam was bent at the waist, emptying the contents of his stomach.

Cadoc walked up to Aiden. "We need Cam.

His crime scene investigator is a vampire and does double duty as the medical examiner. We may miss something if we start moving bodies."

"Call him," Aiden replied, his eyes never leaving the stack of deceased fae. "Kendrick, would you estimate that to be about seventy bodies?"

Kendrick closed his eyes and nodded. Aiden ground his teeth together. "I think we just found the missing fae of Monroe."

It was as if his words released the men from their shock. Ilar turned to the nearest wall and began to pummel it. From the crunching Ari heard, he was certain the fae's hand was shattered. Cadoc went to him and struggled to pull him away from the wall. Despite being a bear shifter, he could barely keep the fae from hurting himself. "Monty! Some help!"

Montgomery Sandalwood, Cadoc's Vanguard witch, raced forward. "*Sopor!*" Moments later, Cadoc was lowering the sleeping fae to the floor. "Godsdammit!" he exclaimed, clearly upset at Ilar's pain.

Kyran collapsed next to Ilar. "I will watch over him. Please help my people," he begged, unable to look at the bodies. His request seemed to give Cadoc an avenue for his anger. "I swear I will do all I can for them." He walked over to where Manon Decker, his squad's vampire, was already on the phone with Cameron.

Ari knew that Aiden, and even Cadoc, was treating this as a crime scene, but his mind was racing forward. "Aiden, can you call Darian here?"

Aiden's eyebrows shot up. "You would have me call him here? With this?" He pointed to the bodies.

Ari nodded. "Yes. We need his ability to open a portal directly to the palace." He lowered his voice. "We can't carry seventy body bags thru the portal to be paraded through Éire Danu."

Aiden looked ill. "I hadn't gotten that far yet. Thank the gods you're with us." He painstakingly typed out a message for a few moments then tossed him the cell. "I texted Darian a brief sit-rep and told him we had injured that needed to return. "Call whomever you need. I'm putting you in charge of getting them home without causing mass panic."

Ari caught the phone. "You got it."

He jogged back to where his men waited for him. Kincaid looked a lot steadier on his feet. "What can we do?" he asked.

"We need to arrange the logistics for getting them home." He turned to Gage. "Can you call the fae you know from Houses Orthames and Liordon. Have them report to…" He looked around. "Micah! I need your mate's phone number."

Micah glowered at him. "If you think for even one second about asking her to come here—"

Ari shook his head. "No, I need her to act as a point of contact in the palace along with Amelia in arranging support." He pointed to Ilar and Kyran. "They will be treating cases of shock and dealing with the aftereffects the grief will cause."

Micah frowned. "I'm not sure that's much better. I'll tell her myself, so don't worry about getting her up to speed." He turned to Aiden. "If Serenity will be using magic to treat loads of people, I need to head back."

Aiden didn't even hesitate before waving him off. "Darian should be here any moment; you can return via his portal."

As if Aiden's words conjured it into existence, a glowing portal appeared, and the fae princes stepped through, immediately followed by the Ashleigh brothers.

Thane looked around until he spotted Ilar and Kyran. He whispered a few words, and the sleeping fae rose and headed toward the portal. "Since Aiden's text mentioned injured, Serenity is standing by to treat him."

"Kyran, you're to return with Ilar to Éire Danu and stay with him until we get back," Aiden ordered.

Kyran nearly sagged forward with relief. "Sir, I…"

Aiden's expression softened. "That's what warrior brothers are for. I support you when you need it, and you help me do the things I cannot. It all balances out. Now, go."

Kyran was too choked up to respond; he simply placed his fist over his heart and followed Ilar thru the portal before it closed.

Ari watched as the Ashleigh brothers walked over to Kendrick as Darian and Oron moved to stand next to Aiden, they all looked sick at the sight before them.

"Right." Ari turned back to Gage. "So let Houses Orthames and Liordon know that Serenity is on standby at the palace and to report in to her." Gage nodded and walked a few feet away to make his calls.

Ari looked at Priest and Kincaid. "I'm going to call my brother to mobilize the Lionharts so we can help those who may be affected by so many deaths. Can the two of you stay close to Aiden? There's no way in hell I'm facing Meryn if her mate returns with so much as a splinter. Kincaid, if he gets even a paper cut, heal him."

Kincaid gave him a sour expression. "You're just saying that because you know that healing is the only spell I don't fuck up."

Ari lowered his voice. "And it will keep you close to Kendrick and the Ashleigh brothers. You may not get many more chances to watch them at work."

Kincaid blinked. "You're right." He practically ran back to where Aiden was standing with the witches. Ari winced at Kincaid's enthusiasm. Priest clapped him on the shoulder. "I got him."

"Thanks, Priest."

Ari watched his unit brother walk away and dialed the one number he knew he could always call, no matter what.

"Hey, baby brother. How's the mission going?" Rex asked when he answered the phone.

"I need your help."

"Where are you?" his older brother demanded.

"I'm fine, I promise. In fact, there wasn't even

any fighting, well, at least on our end." He eyed the bodies.

"What do you need? I can come to you."

"I need you where you are." He thought about where exactly that could be. "Are you at home or at the palace?"

"Home, why?"

He swallowed hard. "They're all dead, Rex. All the people we were sent to find," he whispered.

"Gods!" Rex exclaimed. In the background, he heard his mother demanding to know what was wrong. "The palace will need us," he said, ignoring her for the moment.

"I knew you'd figure it out. There's over seventy dead fae here, Rex. Gods knows how many generations. This will impact a lot of people. The palace will need the Lionharts to provide steadfast strength through this ordeal."

"I assume Darian is there."

"You'd be right."

"I'll arrange for one of our meeting houses to be used for storage and identification. I'll need one of those freakishly powerful witches that I'm going to assume, again, are standing within ten feet of Aiden McKenzie."

Ari shook his head in wonder. His brother was amazing. "Again, you'd be right."

"I'll need them to spell the room to lower the temperature and possibly preserve the bodies." He paused. "How bad are they?"

Ari gulped and walked closer to the stack. He hissed at the smell, before backing away. "I'm no expert on how fae decompose, but there's a fair amount of bloating, but they aren't blackened yet. Most facial features should be identifiable."

"I hate that you are there," Rex growled.

"I'm a unit warrior, Rex. Where else would I be?"

"Safe, at home, with your family," he responded.

"I'll be home soon enough." He hesitated, then continued. "Can you tell Cord, maybe something light tonight. Not a lot of meat?"

"Of course. Don't worry about a thing. I'll handle everything concerning the receiving of the bodies. You just focus on getting them to us. Tell Darian it's the meeting house on Maple Street."

Ari felt relief at his brother's words. "Thanks, I will."

"Come straight home, Ari."

"What was that? Do my job diligently?"

"Brat," Rex replied before disconnecting.

Ari looked up, and Gage was waiting on him. "How'd it go?"

"They're heading to the palace. I heard the last part of your conversation and let them know that Rex is setting up on Maple Street. He is a genius to think of converting one of the rooms to a freezer."

Ari smiled. "That's my brother."

Together, they walked over to where Cadoc and the others huddled around Aiden. When they approached, Aiden looked to him. "Set?"

"Yes, though, I'll need one of the Ashleigh brothers to meet up with Rex at the Lionhart meeting house on Maple Street. He wants to convert one of the rooms into a large freezer to preserve the bodies."

"Thank the gods for your brother." Aiden scrubbed his hands over his face. "Cadoc, can you let the men know we'll be starting as soon as Cam gets here."

Cadoc nodded. "Yes, sir." He was about to walk away when the door opened. The men turned as one to see who had disturbed them, only to see Cam, in his sheriff's uniform, walking toward them, a dark-haired man striding behind him. Cam took one look at the bodies and grimaced.

"I didn't want to believe you, Aiden. I didn't want to face the truth that this happened in Monroe, right under my damn nose." Cam's jaw clenched.

The dark-haired man went immediately to the pile, pulling out a camera. When he began snapping pictures, Cadoc turned a deep red color. "What in the hell do you think you're doing?" He reached for the camera, but the man just batted his hand away.

"I am River Carlisle. I am the medical examiner who works with Cam and the other Vanguard in Monroe. Humans take pictures of crime scenes so that the act of moving the bodies does not completely destroy possible evidence. These pictures may preserve some small detail we overlook."

Cadoc calmed slightly. "Just let us know what you need," he said, slightly mollified.

Ari stepped closer to Cam. "How good is he?"

Cam gave a wry smile. "He's a vampire, and that makes him very good at his job. I bet you he's already picked up on something we'd miss."

"You would be right," the light voice called out. "Have one of the witches check for a barrier of some kind. There is bloating, but no sign that they have been ravaged by either pests or insects."

"Son of a bitch," Cadoc whispered under his breath. "Okay, Doc, you're in charge here."

"I appreciate that. Now, help me start lifting the bodies out so they lay side by side," his crisp voice ordered.

"Yes, sir."

Ari turned his head as they began to pull bodies out of the large pile. He couldn't get past the fact that they were fae. Growing up in Éire Danu, he'd always associated fae with being eternally beautiful, ageless, immortal.

To see them thrown together in a trash heap of rotting flesh, discarded, and unequivocally dead, disturbed him on every level.

A gut-wrenching cry had them all turning to where Darian knelt on the ground beside Liam, who was lifting out a tiny body. Ari gasped. Not even the children had been spared. Oron physically pulled Darian back until they both sat on the cold hard concrete. Oron cradled his younger brother as Darian just shook his head. "I'm so sorry, Darian," he whispered.

"It's not your fault, none of this is your fault." Darian replied, hanging his head.

"Found something," Kendrick called out, pulling Ari's attention away from the suffering brothers. He, Aiden, and the others jogged to the far wall where Kendrick was running his hands over the wall.

"River is a genius. Even I missed the lack of insects." He let his hands drop. "There is a barrier."

Thane whistled and held up his hand, palm side facing the dull gray wall. "It's so damn subtle."

Kendrick nodded, looking pissed. "I should have caught this."

Aiden simply placed a hand on his shoulder. "We were all distracted by the senseless tragic deaths of the fae. You would have found it when the immediate demands were met and you were allowed to think."

Thane grunted. "One of us should have seen it."

"What is it exactly?" Ari asked. He didn't really care who saw it; he didn't know what 'it' was.

Kendrick pointed. "There is thin barrier in place that uses the walls, ceiling, and floor as guidelines."

"Explain," Aiden demanded.

Thane continued. "The barrier follows the natural lines of the room, but aren't dictated by them. For example, it extends across the door's threshold, but isn't broken by the door being opened and closed."

"Can you take it down?" Ari asked.

Kendrick nodded. "Easily, but should we?" He turned to Thane. "Thoughts?"

Thane, then Justice sighed as they both frowned, before they began to glow with the color of their magic. Justice surprisingly spoke first. "There are no ties to any other components to trigger any traps," he said, his magic glow fading.

Thane's magic dimmed and he looked up at the ceiling. "It's not blocking sound or smell." He pointed upward to the skylight. "Light is able to pass through."

Kendrick tapped his lips. "So, what is it for?"

Aiden shrugged. "Unless you want to stay here and study it, as long as you don't think it poses a threat, take it down and find out."

Kendrick glared at their commander. "Meryn's brutal practicality is rubbing off on you."

Aiden just grinned. "She is the best part of me."

"Thane, if you would?" Kendrick pointed to the barrier, then stepped back to close his eyes.

Thane reached up, touched the wall, then stepped away. Everyone turned their attention to Kendrick who opened his eyes. "I sense nothing."

Ari let out the breath he didn't even know he had been holding. Moments later, his phone rang, he saw it was his brother. "Hey, Rex."

"Are you safe!" Rex demanded immediately.

"Yes, why?"

"Gods! Fae are wailing in the streets, there must have been more killings."

"Rex, calm down!"

Aiden and the rest of the men went on alert. "What's going on? Is the palace secure?"

"Rex, is the palace safe?"

"Yes, hold on." Ari heard muffled voices before Rex returned to the phone. "Portia is getting preliminary reports in now from Molvan who has taken charge of this crisis. She is saying the newly slain are from families from Monroe. The fae in the city are all saying the same thing. Their family trees changed all at once, registering the deaths of whole families. Multiple branches petrified, some of the Spirit Guardians have gone into shock."

"Shit!" Kendrick exclaimed. "The barrier masked their deaths, not from humans, but from the fae."

"Why?" Thane asked.

"River! Move faster. I want us out of here now!" Aiden began barking orders.

"Rex, we're moving now. I think the deaths that are registering are of the dead we discovered. I'll explain later, but Aiden wants us to get ghost."

"Then you get ghost, little brother, all gods be with you," Rex said, before disconnecting.

Ari pocketed his phone and joined his unit brothers in bagging up the dead. They moved quickly, sensing Aiden's urgency. In truth, Ari agreed. If the enemy took great pains for them to discover the dead here and possibly be distracted by them, then the last place they needed to be was in this warehouse.

"Freeze!" a female voice yelled out.

"What now?" Thane grumbled.

Ari turned and time seemed to slow. There, in the middle of the warehouse, in a deputy uniform, with her gun trained at his commander, was his beautiful mate.

CHAPTER THREE

❦

"BRIE, PUT THE GUN DOWN," Sheriff Rathais ordered gently.

Brie took in the scene before her. Men were moving body after body into large, black body bags. "Sir?" She took a deep breath and steadied the hand holding her weapon.

"That's an order, deputy," her boss repeated firmly.

"But…" She watched as River continued to process the scene. The ungodly large pile of bodies became her main focus. "Why didn't you call this in?"

"Why are you here?" he asked.

"You and River tore out of the office, of course I was going to follow." She loved the Sheriff like a second father. He had trained her and helped her become the law enforcement officer she was today. She knew in her heart that he would never have anything to do with so many deaths. "Sir?" she asked again, feeling lost.

Rathais walked over and placed a hand on her shoulder. "I need you to go back to the office and forget you ever saw any of this."

"Well, that does not sound super sketchy," River murmured.

"What he said," Brie pointed.

Rathais sighed. "There are things you don't know. Things I was going to tell you when you took over as Sheriff."

"Things? Pile of dead bodies kinda things?" she demanded.

Rathais blinked in surprise. "Actually, no, this is not normal, even for us. Brainless ferals attacking fae, shifters, vampires, and witches, is the usual norm."

River snickered. "Gods, you are terrible at this."

Brie felt her eye begin to twitch. "What?"

"It may be faster to simply show her," a gorgeous blond said, as he walked up to them pulling off his clothes.

"Sir, I'm gonna need you to stop," she said, trying to keep her voice even. One, she had no idea why he was getting naked, and two, he was absolutely breathtaking, and three, he was getting naked!

"Gods above, Ari," Rathais exclaimed, shaking his head.

Brie's eyes never left the beautiful man before her. Seconds later, it felt as if her entire head became wrapped in cotton. Her hearing was muffled, and she knew she was going into shock, but who wouldn't? The runway model was now a freaking lion!

"Sir?!" she yelled.

"Stand down, Brie, we can explain," Rathais

started. When she turned to face him, her body moved along with her head, and she now had her gun pointed at her boss.

"Brie, it's okay, honey, just put the gun down," Rathais continued.

Movement out of the corner of her eye had her swinging back to face the huge lion. "S-s-top," she ordered.

She felt Rathais move closer to her, and the lion began to snarl viciously. When her boss wrapped a comforting arm about her shoulders, the large feline roared loud enough to hurt her ears. Without thinking, she fired off a warning shot, her normally perfect aim skewed by her own shaking hands. When the lion collapsed, she was horrified. "I didn't mean to hit him!" she said, looking up into her boss' kind eyes.

"We know, honey. He had to go an act like an idiot. He should have known better than to approach someone holding a gun when they're spooked." Rathais easily pulled the gun from her hands. "Shift back, Ari, you're upsetting my deputy."

It wasn't until the men around her began to look concerned that she realized something might be really wrong.

"Ari?" Aiden called out, kneeling down next to the lion. He pushed back part of the mane and inhaled sharply. "He can't shift, the bullet looks close to the spine. If he shifts back to human, it may cause irreversible damage."

Brie felt her knees go. "I didn't want to hurt him," she whispered.

"I know, hon, you're a huge cat lover," Rathais easily supported her weight.

Aiden grabbed his phone. "Rheia, I need some advice."

"Who's Rheia?" she asked.

"A surgeon who lives with Aiden," Rathais answered.

Aiden ran down the series of events, explaining that they now had a four-hundred-and fifty-pound lion laid out with a bullet near the spine.

"I'd love to help, Aiden, but I've never operated on a lion before. If he were human, I'd say bring him straight here, but we're talking a completely different anatomy."

"Shit," Aiden exclaimed.

Brie stepped forward on wobbly legs. "I know someone who may be able to help," she offered.

Aiden looked relieved. "Who?"

"My father. He's a retired vet that used to work with big cats at a rescue sanctuary."

"Excellent idea, Brie!" Rathais looked over to where three other men stared down at the cat, looking anxious. "Gage, Kincaid, Priest, let's find something sturdy to transport him into my SUV. Brie, call your father and have him prep for surgery."

Brie reached for her phone, looking around the room. Not one man glared at her. Shouldn't they be upset that she shot their friend? Shouldn't she be getting led out of here in cuffs? What was going on?

One of the men stepped forward and placed a

hand on her shoulder. Suddenly, she felt as if she could think again.

"What was that?" she asked.

"Something I recently learned from an old friend. I simply negated a bit of shock is all. I know that a lot is coming at you fast, but hold on a bit longer. Unless I'm mistaken, the man you shot will be the one to stay by your side and explain everything. We just need to get him back on his feet."

"Thank you...." she stared up at him.

"Kendrick. Kendrick Ashwood. While you get Ari healed, I'll be helping to get these poor souls home." He looked her in the eye. "They were murdered, Brie—make no mistake about that—but they did not die at the hands of anyone in this room. The men you see around you represent the protectors of our kind. You couldn't be safer."

"Why aren't they mad at me?" she whispered.

Kendrick just smirked. "You're not the first female to shoot her mate," his head nodded toward Aiden.

Aiden glared at him. "Meryn said it was an accident," he grumbled.

Kendrick leaned down. "He says that to make himself feel better. We all know his mate, Meryn, is a sharpshooter."

"What's a mate?" she asked, that lost feeling edging back in.

"Cam will explain on the way," Kendrick said, gently pushing her toward the door. "Call your father in the car."

"Thanks a lot!" Rathais yelled back.

Brie jogged after the group of men struggling to carry the large lion to the SUV. As they were lifting him into the back, Aiden ruffled her hair. "Don't worry; he's at fault here. He never should have scared you."

She felt her mouth drop. "I shot him."

Aiden nodded. "Getting shot by human females is quite common."

"It is?" Behind the large man, her boss and the three other men were shaking their heads.

Aiden smiled wide. "My mate is human," he frowned. "Sort of."

"In the car, Aiden," Rathais called out.

They all piled in, and she called her dad.

"Hello, my beautiful baby girl. What are you up to?" Her father's voice sounded so normal she found herself clutching her phone.

"I shot someone!" she exclaimed.

"What did they do to you?" he demanded.

"He scared me."

"That son of a bitch! Wait. That's it?"

"And he turned into a lion."

"Baby girl, where are you? I'm grabbing my keys now."

"No! You have to stay there. We're coming to you."

"We who? Should I get my gun?"

"No, your scalpel."

"Brie Victoria Wilson, if you don't start making sense…"

She winced. She hadn't heard her middle name since high school. "I shot a lion, Dad. We need you to remove the bullet."

"Why in the hell would you shoot some poor lion?"

She rolled her eyes. "What happened to defending your baby girl?"

"How far out are you?" her father asked, ignoring her.

"A little under twenty minutes. We're coming from the warehouse district."

"Please tell me you didn't find some exotic animal dealer hoarding animals. Is the lion the only one that needs medical attention?"

"No, nothing like that. It's just the one lion," she looked around the car. "I think."

Aiden grinned at her. "Bear."

Priest bumped her shoulder from the seat beside her. "Eagle."

Rathais caught her eye in the rearview mirror. "Wolf."

"Bastard," she muttered.

"Brie?"

"Just the incoming lion, Dad."

"Okay, I'll get the table ready. Head straight to the back."

"See you soon." She hung up her phone, then kneed the driver's seat. Rathais grunted. "Seriously?" she demanded.

"Yes, seriously. I told you, there are things you don't know, the existence of shifters is just one of them."

"You also said something about fae, witches, and vampires."

"Let's focus on Ari first, then I'll lay everything out for you," he promised.

She rubbed her chest. She felt as if her heart was breaking. She had a hard time swallowing around the knot in her throat. "His name is Ari?"

"Ari Lionhart, lion shifter obviously." The youngest looking of them answered from the back where he was keeping Ari mobilized. He pointed to his own chest. "Kincaid Bayberry, witch."

The man on right gave her a small salute. "Priest Vi'Aerdan, harpy eagle shifter."

The man on her left nodded his head. "Gage Fabre, vampire." He winked at her, making her smile.

"Okay, let's get him well, then I'll face everything else." She heard her own voice break. "What in the hell is wrong with me?" She hunched over a bit, trying to ease the pain in her chest. Behind her, she heard a low growl.

"She's fine, Ari, just reacting to your injury and the pull. She's your mate, isn't she?" Kincaid asked.

A happy purr filled the cab. She found that the very sound eased the tightness in her chest, allowing her to breathe easier.

"I would say that is a yes," Gage said, a smile on his face.

"What is a mate?" She had a feeling she knew what they meant, but needed to hear their definition.

"In human terms, it's like a soul mate. Someone picked out just for you, the one person on this entire earth you're meant to be with," Priest explained.

She exhaled, that's what she thought they had meant. "How can he possibly feel that way toward me, we don't even know one another?"

Aiden shrugged. "I have no idea how it works, but when I met Meryn, my entire world suddenly became centered on her smile. Her scent drove me insane, and every minute I wasn't near her was almost painful." He half turned in his seat to face her. "Paranormals can live for a long time, and the thought of spending so many centuries alone is terrifying. I think that Fate or the Powers that Be know this and gift us a mate to make the long years bearable. They give us a reason to get up in the morning and someone to hold at night."

"Are all of you mated?"

Everyone but Aiden shook their heads. Priest patted her leg. "We hold on to the unspoken promise that if we can endure without losing our souls, we will eventually be blessed with our own mates."

"How would you lose your soul?" she asked, officially feeling as if she was in over her head. Was this conversation really happening? Can people really lose their souls?

"A paranormal loses his soul when he or she harbors an evil intent in their heart and act on it. Most say it's the act of killing, yet there have been many, many instances of paranormals killing and yet they are still whole," Aiden explained.

"Like self-defense?" she asked. This was somewhat familiar territory.

"Exactly. But on the flip side, I've had to put down a feral that had never killed, yet his accumulated crimes were just as heinous. We don't know exactly what tips the scale, we only deal with the aftermath."

"That other man, Kendrick, he said you were the protectors of your people. You deal with the criminals?"

Every man nodded. "We do," Gage said. "Everyone in the car except for you and Cam are what we call unit warriors. There are six units assigned to each pillar city, and there are four pillar cities. Lycaonia, the shifter city in the North Carolina mountains. Noctem Falls, the vampire city in New Mexico, Éire Danu is where we serve," he continued, pointing to himself, Priest, Kincaid, and Ari. "Éire Danu is the city of the fae. It exists in its own small pocket universe, but has an entry portal in Monroe. The last city is Storm Keep, the city of the witches, located in the Pacific Northwest."

"And when one of your citizens commits a serious enough crime, they lose their soul and you put them in jail?"

Priest shook his head. "There is no coming back from turning feral. It's our job to eliminate them."

"Right," she whispered.

"Brie, honey, we're here," Rathais said, putting the car in park.

She took a deep breath. Right now, she'd focus on making sure the poor lion didn't die, then she'd deal with everything else. She hopped out and met her dad at the back of the car, where he was already waiting with a large flatbed style gurney.

He opened his mouth to say something, then saw the men as they poured out of the vehicle. "I was wondering how we were going to get this guy out of the car, but I think they can handle it." He eyed Aiden. "Damn, son, what do you eat?"

Aiden grinned as his cheeks glowed. "Just about everything."

"I imagine so." Her father's attention immediately went to Ari as the men gently lifted him onto the wheeled gurney. "Let's go, gentlemen. Straight ahead to the back. It's where my personal clinic is."

They quickly got Ari slid onto the operating table, and her father shooed them out.

Rathais rubbed the back of his neck. "Rex Lionhart is gonna skin me alive."

"Who's Rex?" she asked.

"Ari's extremely protective older brother," Priest answered, giving Rathais a shit eating grin.

"Oh, god."

Gage waved off her distress. "He's gonna love you. You're his new baby sister. But he'll be super pissed at Cam that you shot Ari."

"But, I'm the one that shot him."

They all nodded.

"That makes no sense."

"Your actions are a reflection of my leadership. Plus, he's going to spoil you rotten. In his eyes, you can do no wrong," Rathais said, sounding resigned.

Aiden chuckled. "He'll probably be upset with Ari, too, for scaring you."

Rathais brightened. "Oh yeah. This was his fault too."

"So, everyone is at fault except me, who actually fired the gun."

"Yup," Kincaid said.

She turned to her boss. "I'll turn in my badge when we get back."

"Like hell you will," Rathais fussed.

Aiden cleared his throat. "Actually, that may not be such a bad idea. Ari will want her by his side in Éire Danu."

She watched as a stream of emotions crossed Rathais' face. "Son of a bitch! I'm losing my replacement!"

"I don't mind resigning for shooting an innocent, but I'll be damned if I turn in my badge to keep a man happy." Brie crossed her arms over her chest. The men just eyed one another. "Not happening," she repeated. If these men thought she'd just suddenly become Suzy Homemaker, they had another thing coming.

𝒞

Ari felt the Doc poke around his wound.

"Not just a lion, are ya?" Brie's father asked.

He huffed loudly.

"Didn't think so. I'm Doctor Chris Wilson, Brie's father. I've helped quite a few shifters over the years. Brie is gonna have a fit."

He just purred at the sound of her name. His mate was more beautiful than anything he could have imagined. Her skin reminded him of milk chocolate, and he intended to lick every inch of her to find out if she tasted as sweet.

"Like my Brie, huh?"

He just continued to purr.

"She did shoot you."

He huffed again, and her father laughed. "She yours?"

He tried to move his head, but felt a gentle hand on his muzzle. "Don't move just yet, just purr if she's your mate."

He purred loudly.

"I thought that might be the case. Never seen my baby girl go all to pieces like that before, figured something else had to be going on." He stepped back. "We can go about this two ways. One, I sedate you, extract the bullet, and wait for you to come around. Or I dig it out, numbing the surrounding tissue."

He huffed twice.

"Suit yourself."

Ari grit his teeth as Brie's father quickly pulled the bullet from his back. The second it was gone, he shifted back to human. Brie's father nodded while looking him up and down. "Damn fine body you got there."

Was his mate's father hitting on him?

"Got anything I can wear?" he asked.

Her father placed a stack of worn scrubs on the bed. "Help yourself." He gave him a devilish grin. "Want me to tell them I neutered you?"

Ari grinned back. "I'll even wear a cone of shame to sell it."

"I knew we'd get along. Now shift back."

Ari shifted back and closed his eyes as his future father-in-law hid the scrubs. This should be good.

☾

Brie stood as her father walked through the door wiping his hands. "He came through like a champ. No lasting damage from the bullet and the surrounding tissue isn't swollen."

Gage slumped back against his chair. "Thank the gods."

"I even took advantage of the anesthesia to neuter him for you. No sense in having to put him under twice for the second procedure."

Brie gasped. "What!" she screeched. She looked around the room, every single man was the color of milk.

Her father blinked. "What? It's the law. Unless the animal has paperwork from a zoo, they are desexed to keep aggression to a minimum."

"Ari!" Priest yelled, running into the room, Gage and Kincaid right on his heels.

"Oh Gods, no!" Kincaid wailed.

Brie walked in and could only stare. Blocking the view of his mane was a giant cone. "Oh, oh, oh." she repeated.

Rathais and Aiden stood in the doorway, staring at the large lion in shock.

"His brother is going to murder me," Rathais whispered dropping to his knees, looking as if he was about to vomit.

"Ari," she whispered.

The large lion lifted his head and yowled piti-fully. She rushed forward. "It's okay. You're alive; that's all that matters," she said, rubbing her hands over the soft fur on the top of his head.

Gage wheeled on her father. "How could you!" he raged.

"I don't understand." Her father looked so confused.

She sniffled, then stopped. There was no law that said exotic animals had to be neutered. She turned to look at her father. The second their eyes met, a mischievous twinkle appeared in his.

"I hate you!"

Priest wiped at his eyes and went to her side. "He's still Ari," he said brokenly. "Don't be angry with your father; he didn't know. This is our fault."

When her father began to chuckle, she tried to reach past Priest to whack him upside the head. "You're evil!"

"I couldn't help it." Her father simply shrugged.

At her side, the lion shimmered and there in *all* his glory was her supposed mate. He was laugh-ing as he pulled off the cone. "Sorry, but he was right; it was too good of an opportunity to pass up."

Rathais pulled out his sidearm. "Just one more bullet," he said, growling out each word as he stood.

Gage, Kincaid, and Priest, however, took more direct action. Their fingers were twisting and pinching at lightning speed. Ari yelped then hopped off the table to pull on some scrubs. He looked over his shoulder and saw that she was still staring. "You can inspect them later to ensure that they're still attached."

"Man, I wouldn't let her anywhere near my balls after that stunt," Kincaid said, glaring at Ari.

As the material covered up his firm ass, she sighed.

"Yeah, I don't think that's gonna be a problem," Priest said, sounding tired.

Ari looked at Aiden. "Any word on the transfer?" And just like that, the mirth in the room died. She had forgotten the mass of bodies they had discovered.

"What transfer?" her father asked, noticing the change in the room's tension.

"Doc…" Ari began.

Her father held up a hand. "Chris. Doctor Chris Wilson. You can call me Dad, the others can call me Doc, Chris, or Doctor Wilson."

Ari looked surprised as a shy smile appeared. "Dad, when Brie found us, we had just discovered the bodies of close to seventy-five of our people stacked up in a warehouse. The transfer refers to getting them home."

"Éire Danu?" her dad asked.

She simply stared. "Was I the only one who didn't know?"

"Sorry, baby girl, but this kind of secret is on a need-to-know basis. My name has been down as a paranormal-friendly doctor ever since I graduated. My college roommate was a wolf shifter," he explained.

"Un-fucking-real."

"I was going to tell you," Rathais said, pointing to his badge. "As Sheriff of Monroe, you'd have to know."

Ari smiled at her. "You're a sheriff?"

She shook her head. "Deputy."

"I was training her up to be my replacement for when I aged out," Rathais complained.

"Aged out?"

Her boss blinked. "Oh. Yeah." He placed his hand over his badge and whispered words she didn't understand. Suddenly, she was looking at a much younger, virile version of the boss she had always had a bit of a crush on.

"Damn," she exhaled slowly, her eyes never leaving Rathais.

Rathais winked, and Ari began to growl low in his throat. "Mine!" he snarled, pulling her so that her back was flush against the front of him. Through the thin fabric of the scrubs she could feel his flesh, hot and hard.

"Okay. Right. Come on, Dad, let me show you the SUV," Gage said, maneuvering her father out of the room.

"You better not hurt my baby girl, Ari, or I really will neuter you," her father threatened, though he was laughing the entire time he said it.

When the door shut, she was spun around to face him. "Mine," he growled again.

"Yeah, the whole supposed mate thing. Does

that mean you're mine too? Or do you expect me to wait at home while you prowl?"

She watched in fascination as his eyes shifted to a bright honey color. "I am yours, and you are mine. Fate has chosen you just for me. I will never forsake you, never betray you, and always place your whims, wants, and needs above my own. There will be no other for me, but you."

"If I truly am yours, then you better kiss me, because I think I may die if you don't."

"We can't have that," he said, before swooping down to take complete possession of her lips. She thought that the kiss would be hot and hard, like him. But his feather light touch and playful nipping was driving her insane. When Ari stepped back, he had a satisfied smile on his face.

"I'm sort of sorry I shot you."

"And I am very sorry I scared you."

She thumped the tip of his nose. "I'm getting you back for that horrible neuter prank."

His eyes lit up. "I can't wait."

CHAPTER FOUR

B RIE DIDN'T KNOW WHAT TO think as they made their way back to the warehouse. The men were quiet and somber. She had argued for five minutes outside the SUV with her father about him returning with them. Finally, he swayed the men by stating he wanted to get to know Ari better since he was mated to his daughter, and none of them could argue that point.

Both Aiden and Rathais agreed that since her father had been a point of contact for their world for years, him coming to Éire Danu to see where his daughter would be living was completely reasonable.

She looked up at Ari's profile. Just like that, every single person in this car, except for her, accepted that the two of them were together. What if he expected her to change, give up her job, or become more 'feminine'? God, what if he was a mouth breather? She watched him closely: his mouth was closed, and he was breathing. So far, so good.

He looked down at her and raised an eyebrow. She shook her head. Anything she wanted to say, she wanted to stay between the two of them, not the entire vehicle. This was not a group project.

"Ari, have you called your parents yet to let them know you've found your mate?" Gage asked.

Ari shook his head. "No, I'll let them know after we arrive. I imagine they are up to their ears in helping Rex get the body identification process organized."

Aiden tucked his phone into his vest pocket. "The queen is requesting for Tau to have dinner at the palace tonight, your parents and brother, of course, will be there."

Ari sighed and let his head fall back against the seat. "I was seriously looking forward to a quiet, light meal tonight."

She nodded absently. That sounded really good to her too.

"Ari, not only are you a Lionhart, but you are essentially the city's ranking unit leader. You won't have a moment of peace until this entire mess is behind us." Aiden turned in his seat to give him a sour look. "Trust me, I've been bouncing from shit storm to shit storm with Meryn in tow for months. I dream of a day where we aren't facing a worldwide catastrophe."

Brie stared at Aiden. "Meryn, spelled m-e-r-y-n, right?" He nodded. "Her last name wouldn't be Evans, would it?"

Aiden now looked spooked. "Why?"

Brie just smiled. If Meryn was who she thought she was, dinner was going to be interesting.

"Brie?" Aiden pleaded.

She simply smiled at him, then turned to look out the window.

"Godsdammit," Aiden muttered, pulling out his phone. His large fingers moved carefully. After a few moments he turned back to her. "She says she doesn't know a Brie Wilson."

She beamed at him. "She doesn't know me, but I know of her."

He paled. "Gods."

Ari pulled out his phone. She looked down and saw that he was texting someone named Leo, and he was advising him to have something called Forbidden Fruit on hand for Aiden. She gave him a questioning look.

He opened up the notes section of his phone.

Paranormal whiskey. Created by the vampires, probably the only thing that can get us drunk.

She held out her hand, and he passed her his phone.

Make sure he has a few bottles.

Ari's eyes widened, and he shot off another text.

Why?

She ignored his question and resumed looking out the window.

"Gods," Ari whispered, under his breath.

☾

When they entered the warehouse, her good mood evaporated. They were still gently photographing, lifting, and bagging bodies. She understood that the pace was brutally slow so that evidence wouldn't be missed or destroyed.

Aiden and Rathais immediately went to the

side of a pair of extremely tall blond men. Her father, along with Gage, Priest, and Kincaid went over to relieve the warriors who had been lifting the bodies into the black body bags. She watched in amazement as her father comforted the warriors around him and took over the process.

The second she had him alone, she was going to ask him how he got wrapped up in the paranormal world and especially why he wasn't freaking out at the sight of the bodies. He was just a vet, wasn't he? Feeling like she didn't know up from sideways, she wandered over to River, Ari glued to her side.

"Hey, River."

"Hey, Wilson."

"Anything I can do?"

"My camera is over on the table. You know what to look for. Can you start taking pictures of the entire room, starting from the perimeter, then moving closer to where they were piled?"

"Yup, you got it." She went to the table and picked up the camera.

Ari placed a hand on her arm. "Are you okay doing this?"

She pointed to her uniform. "It's my job, Ari."

He sighed and gave a single nod. "I know, the reason I ask isn't because I don't think you're capable, but something like this can't be a normal scene for you. Hell, it's not even a normal scene for us."

His explanation made her feel better. He wasn't worried because she was a woman, but because the scene was *that* bad. "You're right; this entire room is horrid. It's very difficult to keep my emotions in check, but it's not their fault." She indicated to the dead. "They deserve us at our very best so that we can find their killers. Later, I may fall apart, but right now, I will do everything I can to help them."

Ari simply leaned forward and kissed her forehead. "I'm so proud to call you my mate. I'll be with Aiden and Cam if you need me." He walked away, leaving her feeling even more confused. She had expected for him to put up a huge fuss over her work.

"Mate?" River asked, looking up at her surprised.

"Evidently."

He smiled as he nodded slowly. "You know, he may be the perfect match for you, Brie. He will not get his dick twisted because you are a badass the way your ex did. In fact, you being a badass is going to seriously work in your favor."

"How so?"

"He is a lion."

"Huh?"

He shook his head and went back to the small plastic bags he was organizing. "You will see."

She decided to leave the entire mating thing alone and focus on her job. She slowly made her way around the room, making sure to take extra care where River had left red markers indicating something was found there. As she worked, she couldn't help but think about who could have possibly done this and why. Why so many all at once? Why leave them here? If they were meant to be a statement, why were they left in an abandoned warehouse where the possibility of going unfound was high?

Before she knew it, the men had finished the transfers, and Ari was once again at her side. "It's time to go."

"Why do you look sick at the idea of going home?"

He just wrapped his arms around her, resting his cheek on the top of her head. She expected the caged in feeling to kick in at any moment, but surprisingly, it didn't. Not only was she taking comfort in his embrace, she also felt relief that she was able to soothe him.

"When we walk through the portal, we'll be going to the storage house for the dead in the city. Family members may be onsite to identify their loved ones and will, more than likely, demand answers from all of us—answers that we just don't have," he explained.

"The sooner we go through, the sooner we can get that dinner over with, and we can relax, right?"

He stepped back and smiled down at her. "I knew you'd be perfect for me. Yes, that's the plan as of right now."

"We're heading back to the station," Rathais said, walking up with River. "He needs access to his lab, and I'll be going over public records to start the process of getting their homes settled. That's a lot of property and personal belongings that need to be settled and transported to Éire Danu."

"What about me?" she asked.

Rathais ruffled her hair, the same as he always had done, but she blushed now that she could see how handsome he was. He tweaked her nose. "It's still me, Brie. I understand that it may be more difficult to see me as the father figure you once did, but that doesn't change how much I care. I'm just more like an older brother now."

"My mate," Ari growled.

Rathais ruffled Ari's hair much to the lion's astonishment. "And you just got another older brother."

Ari's mouth opened, then closed. He looked away but not before she caught his pleased expression. "Whatever," he murmured.

"On that note," Rathais turned back to her. "I know that right now you're focused on the job. You jumped in to help process the scene, mostly out of reflex. But who and what we are, your tie to Ari, none of that has hit you yet. You're about to go through a portal to an entirely different world, so please be easy on yourself. It's okay to get overwhelmed and upset. It will be completely understandable for you to ask for help." He pointed to the men standing around eavesdropping. "Brie, these men are now your brothers in arms. I trust them with my life and yours."

She exhaled. "I wish you were coming, but understand why you're not. Besides, my dad will be there, so as soon as I kick his ass and figure out how he's okay with all this, he can help me process."

"Hey!" her dad protested.

Rathais nodded. "I'll be checking in on you soon. Consider yourself on paid leave until the dust settles."

She glared at him and opened her mouth to protest. He held up his hand. "You're assigned this case, Brie, you'll just be working it from that side." He pointed to the portal.

She sighed. "Fine."

Ari took her hand. "Come on, hon, let's go."

She let him lead her through, not entirely sure what waited for her on the other side.

☾

Chaos.

Chaos waited for them on the other side of the portal.

The second they stepped through and the people saw who had arrived, questions, demands, and accusations began to fly at a rapid rate. Aiden was trying to answer as many questions as he could, but he and every other man looked like they were in way over their heads.

She looked around and spotted a standard folding table. Using a chair, she climbed up on top, placed her fingers to her lips, and let out a piercing whistle. The quiet was almost deafening after the panicked cacophony. All eyes were suddenly on her.

"Can I get everyone with a question to take two steps backward please?" she asked.

The people looked at one another then stepped back.

"Thank you. Now, I know all of you have questions regarding today's tragic findings, but the men before you and I are still looking for answers. I want to assure each and every one of you that we will not stop searching until we find those responsible."

"Why is a human involved?" one of the taller blond men sneered. "We were pulled from our homes to return to Éire Danu, only to find that our loved ones have been massacred."

"Your name please?" she asked calmly.

"Tyrien Ri'Aileanach."

"Tyrien, you have returned to the city from where?"

"The Hamptons."

She blinked. Of course, he was from the Hamptons.

"How long had you lived there before coming back?"

"I don't see how—"

"How long?" she asked again firmly.

"In that location, fifty years."

She pointed to her chest where her badge was very much on display. "Then you should know what this badge is and what it stands for. I have been trained to protect my people much in the same way these fine men have been trained to serve. I'm not sure what education goes along with such training here, but I have put in years studying to get different degrees to help me in doing my job." The man opened his mouth to speak, but she kept going. "I not only have a degree in Abnormal Psychology but also Forensic Science. That means I am specially trained to not only figure out why a criminal is committing these atrocities but also how. Now, I may be new to your world, but it sounds like you need someone exactly like me, human or not."

"Gods above, she is right," a woman whispered.

Tyrien went to protest, but the woman glared at him until he looked away. "My name is Kyla Vi'Aileanach, it was my"—she swallowed hard—"sister and her mate who were found."

Brie nodded. "I am very sorry for your loss."

"We know that the warriors don't have all the answers, but"—she paused again—"they represent the last tie we have to our loved ones. Any information they have is desperately needed."

Brie gave her a sad smile. "The type of information they have to give you, trust me, Kyla, you don't want. Please, I know it's very hard right now, but you must be patient. As we assemble more facts and piece together exactly what happened, we will share as soon as we can."

Brie saw the exact moment her words registered with the poor woman. Her face crumpled as she nodded and spun to collapse into the waiting arms of the man behind her.

"Now, to keep everyone moving forward, these rooms are, as of immediately, off limits to everyone not working this case. All family members will be directed to a secondary, undetermined location to work with the warriors that will help you in identifying, claiming, and releasing your loved ones to you." Immediately, the crowd began to protest.

"Quiet!" she roared. When the people before her were somewhat quieter, she began again. "What if, in your grief, you make a mistake?" she asked, and the crowd quieted further. "What if, for whatever reason you think, you recognize a family member, and it's not them? What if they are actually still missing, but now no one is looking for them? I know what you're thinking, 'that could never happen' 'who could make those kinds of mistakes?'

"I'm going to be blunt, and you may hate me for it, but right now, I am serving your loved ones. The unattended dead get harder to identify the longer they have been missing. That is why each family will be working with a single warrior, will be getting time alone with the body without the distraction of others, to help in identifying your loved ones, so that no mistakes are made and these poor souls can finally go home."

"What do we do?" a small voice asked. Brie looked until she saw a pale female clutching her golden shawl about her shoulders.

"Go home. Rest. Be there for your loved ones and your neighbors. We will let you know when we're ready to proceed with the next step."

"I refuse to obey orders from a human." Tyrien protested.

The low rumble began almost immediately. Brie smiled, she didn't know how she knew, but that was most definitely Ari.

"If my mate knows what's good for him, he'll let me handle this," she said pleasantly.

The rumble lowered but didn't dissipate.

"Mate?" Tyrien asked, looking nervous.

"Yes, but if you're more worried about offending him than me, then you're not that bright. Ari may be a lion, but I can assure you I'm just as dangerous."

"A Lionhart," he sneered. "A bunch of savage animals that ingratiate themselves to our queen for a place in our city. His brothers are just as useless as he is."

Every single fae in the room stepped away from Tyrien, including Kyla.

"Shit!"

"Grab him!"

A deafening roar had her covering her ears. Her gaze swung around the room, looking for Ari. He now stood over eight feet in height. His facial features had changed to look more lion-like. An insanely long mane hung past his shoulders and down his body.

"Ari?" she whispered.

He stalked forward, literally dragging Gage, Kincaid, and Priest with him as he snarled at Tyrien.

"Someone get that fool out of here!" Darian ordered.

When the surrounding fae reached out and began manhandling Tyrien out of the building, Ari roared again.

"Even living amongst the humans, he should have known better," Oron said disgustedly.

"What?" she demanded.

Oron pointed to Ari. "He's the ranking warrior for a reason. Look at his mane."

Her father stared. "I've never seen a mane that dark or so long." He turned to Brie. "If it means the same thing among shifters as it does in the wild, it means he is extremely strong."

Oron gave a short nod. "And he's undefeated."

"Damn it, Ari! That hurt!" Priest growled, then kicked Ari in the back of the leg, causing the lion-man to snarl. "Rein your shit in!"

"So he gets into lots of fights?" she asked. Was he some kind of psychopathic bully?

Everyone shook their heads, and Oron answered. "He has a very specific trigger. You never, ever say anything bad about his brothers. Ever. We all learned that when he was a cub. Everyone in the city knows this, looks like Tyrien forgot."

Brie remembered how the fae all stood back immediately at Tyrien's words.

"That's kinda sexy," she admitted.

The snarling stopped, plunging the room into silence. Then a low purr was heard.

Gage sighed. "Thank the gods. Brie, say that again."

Brie stayed on the table top. "Ari, come here and let me see you in this cat-man form."

Ari shrugged off his unit brothers and loped over to her.

When she ran her hands over his soft fur, he began to purr. His new form just meant more muscles to ogle. "I like."

"That's the fastest he's ever calmed down," a fae in the crowd observed.

Ari slowly shrunk back to his normal height. "Not too weird?" he asked lowly, the scrubs he wore now tatters about him.

She shook her head. "Remember, I was raised around big cats. Looks normal to me, honestly."

Ari looked around the room. "Where is Tyrien?" he growled.

"Probably at home compiling his complaints," Kyla said sighing. "He's my mate's brother, and frankly, I like him much better when he isn't at home." She pointed to the man with her. "This is my older brother Nylan. Tyrien is especially upset that my mate has asked him to oversee the Aileanach household while he was away. So please don't take his ire personally. He shouldn't be complaining now of all times."

"If you have any complaints as to how this is being handled, you can direct them to the palace, but please know that this young woman has my full support," a clear voice rang out over the crowd.

Kincaid handed Ari a bag. He quickly pulled out his clothes and began dressing.

"Your Majesty," the people replied, and moved as a single entity as they parted and bowed, making way for the ethereal being that had just spoken. The gorgeous woman made her way to the table and gave her a wan smile. "I was listening from outside. Thank you. Thank you so much for taking care of my children." At first, Brie thought the woman was referring to the crowd. It wasn't until the elegant being began to walk between the rows where the bodies lay did she realize that she had been speaking of the dead.

A tall uniformed man walked behind the woman, a steady presence and barrier between her grief and the crowd.

Brie turned to the people. "You may go. We'll be contacting you soon."

No one argued. In fact, it seemed as if they couldn't leave quick enough. Brie realized it wasn't because she had dismissed them and everything to do with giving this woman privacy to grieve.

Ari finished buckling his vest and stepped forward to help her down, his eyes still blazing gold. She placed both hands on his chest and felt his muscles relax a bit. It shocked her that she had such an effect on him. "Let it go. He was upset."

Ari simply growled and pulled her close. A gasp and low cry had them both turning to see the woman sink down to lay a pale hand on one of the smaller bags. The man in uniform scooped her up into his arms. "Enough, Aleks, this isn't your fault."

"Mother, let us return to the palace," one of Aiden's tall friends suggested.

"We can't leave them," the queen said brokenly.

The uniformed man turned to her. "What should we do?"

Brie looked around and saw that everyone was looking to her for some direction. "Keep the temperature low and seal the room. No one gets in unless escorted by an officer,"

"Warrior," Ari interrupted.

"Warrior," she continued. She took in the woman's distraught face. "Let's leave a candle burning for them, so it won't be so dark in here."

The woman exhaled and rested her head on the man's chest. He looked at her and mouthed, 'thank you'.

She nodded and everyone made their way outside.

Aiden turned to two men she didn't recognize. "Ben, you're in charge of security here. Work with Brie to create the teams that will be assisting the people in claiming their family members."

The man nodded then turned to her. "I'll meet up with you tomorrow morning at breakfast. I'll have a full roster by then." He clapped Aiden on the shoulder then walked away.

"Aiden, I'm returning to the palace with Aleks. I'll be advising Cord that dinner will start a bit late tonight, around eight." He simply looked down at the woman in his arms, and Aiden nodded. "Understood Brennus."

Brennus looked at everyone else. "Cord, Leo, and Ryuu have assembled drinks and light hors d'oeuvres in our personal dining room. Feel free to assemble there before dinner." He, along with Aiden and a small group of men, headed up the hill toward the large brightly lit building.

Beside her, Gage, Priest, Kincaid, and a man

that looked a lot like Ari stood around them looking tired.

She nudged Ari then pointed to the older looking version of the man that was supposedly her mate.

Ari smiled. "Rex Lionhart, I have the incredible honor in introducing my mate, Brie Wilson. Brie, my eldest brother, Rex."

Rex blinked then a wide smile broke out over his face. He swept her up into a fierce hug. He looked over at Ari, affection shining in his eyes. "I see you still defend the Lionharts down to the depths of your soul."

Kincaid snorted. "Lionharts? Yeah, to some degree. But you know it's when anyone says something derogatory about you or Declan that sets him off."

Rex swelled with pride. "I have the most incredible baby brother and now a new baby sister. Gods! I thought Kari had a hard time when she first discovered Declan was her mate. How are you holding up?"

For some reason his genuine concern had tears prickling her eyes—the day seemed to be catching up to her. "Well, all things considered, I'm okay, I guess." She looked around for the familiar head of light brown curls of her father.

"I'm right here, baby." And suddenly, she just couldn't stand anymore. She let her father support her as she buried her face in his chest and breathed in his familiar scent of Ivory soap and coffee.

"Is she okay," Ari demanded.

"She will be. She just needs to rest." Her father kissed her hair. "I'm so proud of you, baby girl. Just hang on a bit longer." She looked up and nodded.

"Bring her," Rex ordered imperially. "We're heading straight to the Lionhart estate. Mother and Father will want to meet her, and we can ensure she will get the rest she needs." He walked away without looking to see if they were behind him.

Ari smiled. "He means well, but he is the eldest and used to his orders being followed." He gave her a wry smile. "Better get used to being smothered lovingly."

She pushed away from her father until she was steady on her own feet. "Doesn't sound so bad at the moment."

Ari looped his arm through hers on the left, and her father did the same on the right. Gage ruffled her hair, and Priest and Kincaid brought up the rear.

One thing at a time.

&

"Mate!" The one word was screeched and reached them before they approached the door.

Ari began to chuckle. "My mother," he said, by way of explanation.

Moments later, a tall, blonde woman was barreling toward them. "Ari! What's this about a mate?" she demanded, practically yanking her away from her father and Ari.

"Mother, this is my wonderful mate, Brie Wilson, and Brie's father, Chris. Brie, this is my mother, Catherine Lionhart, and the man standing next to Rex at the door is my father, Jedrek Lionhart."

She was suddenly wrapped up in a soft hug. It had been years since her own mother's passing where she had experienced the kind of comfort only a mother could give. When she sagged against the woman, she was gently led toward the house. "Idiots, every single one of them. Insensitive morons! Come this way, darling. Let's get you into a hot bath, and you can tell me all about your horrible day." She glared at not only her own son but Brie's father as well. "Between the two of you, could neither of you see how worn out she is?"

"I've asked Leo to start a bath for her, Mother," Rex said when they walked into the large estate.

"I've also sent up some treats to perk her up," the older version of Rex added brusquely. If Ari aged like these men, she was one lucky woman.

"Thank you. Now, we'll be upstairs getting ready for dinner. Ari, send out for some robes for your mate and your new father." She led her up the stairs. Once they were ensconced in a large steam filled bathroom, the woman rolled her eyes. "Males!" She turned her back to allow her to undress.

Brie eyed the bath longingly. Without a second thought, she began to strip out of her uniform and stepped into the bubble filled bath. "Ahhhhhhh." The foamy layer of vanilla scented bubbles rose to her chin when she sat down. She had never been in a tub deep enough to truly soak, this may become an addiction.

Catherine took a seat on the elegant lounger against the wall.

"How bad was it?"

"War crimes bad. The bodies were stacked up in piles. I've never seen that many dead in one place."

"We only had rumors for most of the morning, the only concrete information coming from Ari via Rex. Once the branches began to petrify on family trees, that was when things began to get really bad here in the city."

"Branches?"

"You poor dear, you were literally thrown into the deep end with none of those adorable floaties babies get nowadays while learning to swim."

Brie shrugged, the warm water moving across her skin. "Ironically, the only thing that has me stuck on stupid is this whole mating thing." She groaned. "How messed up is that? Dead bodies everywhere, angry mobs, and I'm more anxious about possibly meeting my soul mate."

"It makes perfect sense, dear."

She turned to look up at Ari's mother. "How so?"

"You didn't know anyone who has died, but Ari is tied to you directly. Of course, it's making you nervous."

"I never considered that."

"Now, let me get you filled in on what's been going on in our world."

"I thought this was relaxy time for me?" she countered.

Catherine laughed. "That was for the men's sake. You and I both know that most bathroom breaks women take are simple 'fall back and reassess the situation' procedures."

Brie chuckled. Her own mother had told her something similar growing up. "Okay, lay it on me while the bath water is still perfect."

Brie sat and listened as Catherine not only introduced her to the different aspects of the paranormal races, cities, cultures, and history, but also the growing and alarming threats they were currently facing. The sheer number of names she was learning was astounding. If she didn't have a near photographic memory, she would have been sunk.

When she was officially a prune, she let Catherine know she was ready to get out. Catherine stood and retrieved a large fluffy towel for her. She handed it off before turning around once again.

"So, these reapers are killing pregnant women and stealing the soul of their unborn child to use as a container for the magical ability of their shifter parent, and they are more organized than anyone realized," Brie recapped as she dried off. Though she had just had a ton of heavy stuff thrown in her direction, the bath itself had done wonders in keeping her relaxed so her mind could focus.

The treats that Jedrek had arranged were small chocolate truffles that kept her alert and able to process so much information. Ari's parents had practically worked a miracle in getting her up to speed so she felt as though she was standing on solid ground. Sometime during her bath, her clothes were handed off, and two glasses of wine were given in exchange. She couldn't tell what helped more, the chocolate or the wine.

She watched as Catherine nodded and popped a truffle in her mouth. "Exactly. Meryn McKenzie has been invaluable in compiling information to track patterns to try to ascertain the killers intent."

"I bet," Brie murmured. If their Meryn was the same one she had heard about, they might actually have a chance at catching these killers.

There was a knock at the door before it opened slightly, and a masculine hand shoved an emerald green robe through the crack. "This is for Brie, Mother." Catherine gathered it and passed it back to her. Brie secured the towel around her body and stared down at the beautiful gown.

"Thank you, Ari, we'll be down in just a moment. Can you tell your father to arrange the carriage?"

"He's already seen to it."

"Perfect. Be down in just a few minutes, darling."

The door closed as Brie turned the material over in her hands. She normally lived in her uniform, but it wasn't lost on her that this must have cost a small fortune.

She looked up shaking her head. "I can't wear this."

Catherine looked back confusion on her face. "Why ever not?"

"It's too expensive!"

Catherine simply laughed. "Ari has more money than he could ever spend in ten lifetimes, and even if he didn't, we, as his parents do a few times over. As his mate, you will never have to worry about money again."

"Yeah, no. That's not gonna work for me. I like my job and having my own money."

Catherine nodded. "Naturally. You just have his money now too."

"That's not what I meant," she argued.

"Let's shelve it for now. After a few days, you'll see what I mean. Now, let's see what he chose for you," Catherine clasped her hands together excitedly.

"He didn't really…"

Catherine nodded. "Of course, he chose it himself. You'll find that Lionhart men, more than almost any other lion shifter are extremely dominant and possessive, but in a good way."

Brie didn't see any buttons or zippers.

"Up over your head dear." Catherine pointed out, turning back around.

Brie lifted the material and let it fall over her naked body. Seconds later, the dress began to move and tighten around her. She yelped, causing Catherine to giggle.

When Brie looked in the mirror, she gasped. Her hair, make-up, and jewelry all complemented the dark green material.

"Are these real?" she whispered, pointing to the emeralds.

Catherine nodded. "It's the upgraded version of dress robes. Ari has always had impeccable tastes."

"Wait right here, darling, I'm going to go change my robes, and we can go down together."

She just nodded absently as Catherine went to change. She turned this way and that in the mirror. She had never looked so pretty.

Just a few short minutes later, Catherine poked her head through the door. "Ready?"

Slowly, they made their way down the stairs. When they reached the bottom, the men rose from the lounge chairs where they had been waiting.

"Catherine, you steal my breath away every time I see you," Jedrek said, kissing his mate's hand.

"Brie, honey, you look amazing." Her father leaned down and kissed her cheek.

Ari simply stared. When she walked up to him, he wordlessly held out a small velvet box. "I had it commissioned when I heard we may be getting mates."

As she took it from his hands, she noticed that they trembled slightly. She squeezed his hand before opening the box. She stared down at the intricate broach. She tilted her head. "This almost looks like a military medal."

Ari grinned. "It's a platinum replication of my unit warrior tattoo, except, because you are my mate, I had it inset into a knot work heart to represent our mating. The tattoo shows my unit, city, and family name. I know it's not the most romantic thing, but I wanted you to have something of mine."

"I love it!" And she did. It was simple, but represented so much. She looked down, frowning. She didn't want to poke holes in her new robe.

Ari rubbed the back of his neck. "Yeah, I thought of that at the last moment." He held up a long piece of material. "This sash is made from the Lionhart tartan, you can attach the broach to this." He pointed to where a familiar bit of metal gleamed. "I added your badge as well, since it's also important."

He not only added her badge to his, but considered it just as important as his own achievements. Without thinking, she threw her arms around his neck and leaned forward to capture his lips. His arms tightened around her as they thoroughly enjoyed their kiss.

A throat cleared behind them. "Good work, son, but we really do need to get going," Jedrek said, grinning from ear to ear.

Ari stepped back and took a deep breath. "Allow me?"

She nodded, and he draped the sash across her chest and tied it at her waist. "Let's go," he said, taking her hand.

CHAPTER FIVE

B RIE WALKED THROUGH THE PALACE gates with Ari at her side. She moved a bit closer to him as they moved past the unblinking guards. Everywhere she looked surfaces gleamed and sparkled in golden hues. When they came to a large wooden door, Jedrek rapped on it twice, and they waited. Moments later, a handsome fae with dark blond hair opened the door.

"Welcome. Everyone has assembled in the queen's outer chambers before dinner." He stepped back, allowing them to enter before closing the door behind them. He looked first at Catherine, then at her. "Ladies, what can we get you to drink?" He indicated a long side table with trays of poured drinks. "We have red, white, and rosé wines, and of course, Forbidden Fruit whiskey."

Catherine smiled at the urbane man. "White wine for me, Cord, with my thanks. It has been a most trying day."

Cord nodded, a deep sadness in his eyes. "This has affected Aleksandra deeply. I took her a glass of her favorite white earlier." His attention turned to her. "And for you, miss?"

"What about the guys?" she asked.

Cord blinked then chuckled. "The men usually serve themselves so us humble squires can spoil you lovely ladies more."

Jedrek returned to where they stood two glasses in each hand. He offered one to Rex, one to Ari, and one to her father. Gage was right behind him, handing off glasses to Kincaid and Priest.

"Ummm." She wasn't used to this. She didn't even know anyone with servants.

Cord's expression softened. "Ryuu said he ran into a similar situation with Meryn when she first arrived in our world. Humans these days aren't used to being served, are they?"

She shook her head, and he continued. "My bringing you a drink is in no way disrespectful to me. I love my job here in the palace."

It still didn't feel right, and she was about to tell him so when a short woman with a pixie wearing sweats and a hoodie, walked up. "I got this one, Cord," the woman offered.

Cord placed a hand over his heart and gave a slight bow.

The woman turned her green eyes to her. "Don't think of them as servants, think of them as Super Moms. Like, they always make sure you're comfortable and have food."

Brie thought about it for a moment and turned to Cord, who was nodding. "Little Meryn has on more than one occasion called squires Super

Moms. It has to be the highest form of a compliment we can receive."

"In that case, it does feel a lot less weird." She looked around. "Do you have a squire?" she asked the infamous Meryn.

"Yup! The gorgeous Japanese one is mine. His name is Ryuu. He kicks all kinds of ass."

"Cord, could I please have a glass of rosé?"

Cord beamed. "Of course." He immediately left to retrieve their drinks.

"Meryn, is it?"

"Yeah, Meryn McKenzie."

"I thought it was Evans?" Brie asked casually.

Meryn shrugged. "After I mated Aiden, I took his last name…" Her voice trailed off as she stared up at her. "How did you know my maiden name?"

"I sat through a training class once about cyber-terrorism; your name came up quite a bit."

Meryn paled and took a step back. "I totally squared up with the government!"

Immediately, Aiden and her squire Ryuu were at her side. Aiden looked over at her. "What's this about?"

Brie laughed. "Meryn, calm down. I'm not going to haul you away in cuffs. You were actually mentioned as a good example—an exasperating and annoying example—but a good one."

"Government?" Aiden asked, his eyes wide.

"Yes, please explain," a regal voice demanded.

Ari gave a half bow. "Your Majesty, I have the pleasure of introducing my mate Deputy Brie

Wilson and her father Doctor Chris Wilson. As you know Brie was an enormous help this afternoon. Brie, this is Queen Aleksandra Vi' ÉirDan and her consort Brennus Eirlea."

"You have my thanks once again Brie," the queen replied in greeting. Brie gave a half bow copying Ari.

"Aunt Aleks, are you feeling better?" Meryn asked.

"As well as I can possibly be. Now, what's this about you and the government?"

Meryn winced. "Well…"

"It's an entertaining story," Brie added. She accepted her glass of wine from Cord and took a sip.

Aiden placed his large hand over his mate's head, covering it completely. He bopped it around. "Meryn."

"Fine! Remember how I told you I used to help Law kill people?"

Aiden frowned but nodded, so she continued. "So, after college, I ran a bit wild on the interwebs. One day, there was a knock on the door, and a bunch of suits were there to take me in. They drove me to this huge building and sat me down in the middle of this sort of office to await processing. Evidently, I skipped normal jail and went right to federal 'they check in, but they don't check out' kinda establishment." Brie watched as the color in Aiden's face drained away. She took another sip of wine. She knew the story after all.

"So, I was like, freaking out and kinda mad,

because they didn't stop to grab food on the way to the office, when I heard a bunch of raised voices down the hall. The giant they had watching me was looking away, so, I slipped past him to go in the direction where I heard people yelling and panicking.

"The door to this high-security room opened, and this guy ran out, so I snagged the door and went in, thinking I could hide from the Sasquatch guarding me. I went to the corner and looked up. They had all of these monitoring stations mounted everywhere. At first, I thought they were watching some kick ass action movie, but then I realized that it was real life. The reason why they were freaking out was because one of their teams was stuck behind enemy lines in this huge corporate high rise.

"I wasn't going to do anything, I mean these guys were about to send me up the river, but then I saw the sleeve of one of the soldiers. It had a battered looking US flag on it, and on his vest was a patch showing one of my favorite comic book character logos. I couldn't let him go down, ya know?

"So, I walked up behind one of the useless pencil necks and kinda shoved him away from his workstation and got busy. I grabbed his headset and turned on the mic and said..."

A tall man walked up behind her. "Yo, Deadpool, this is Red Queen, follow my instructions, and you'll live."

Meryn beamed up at him. "Yup!" She jerked her thumb backward to her friend. "I hacked the

company's security and basically guided them
out. After that, the suits wanted to make a deal.
If I continued to help their teams, all charges
would be dropped, and I could live my life doing
whatever I wanted as long as I didn't steal or
commit treason. So, I worked for the government for a few years, mostly with Law's team
and then got out."

Brie chuckled. "She didn't just work for the
government. The base that she operated out of
was ground zero for some of the most insane
and successful missions the US never officially
pulled off. At her insistence, she convinced high
command that she should be taught how to carry
and shoot a weapon. When they argued that the
only ones allowed to carry weapons on base
were Black Ops, she just shrugged and said,
'Well, make me Black Ops.' And they did."

Brie smiled sweetly at Aiden. "Your mate has
one of the best shooting records amongst the
most dangerous men on the planet."

Aiden stared down at his petite mate, aghast.
"You were Black Ops?!"

"Sort of."

"You were trained to shoot?"

"Yeah."

His eyes narrowed. "And you accidentally
shot me?"

Meryn blinked. "Uhhhh."

Law, then most of the men, began to laugh at
the large commander's chagrin.

Meryn turned to her. "What about you? My

exploits wouldn't have been mentioned in a normal training class."

Her father turned to Meryn. "You'd be right. You're looking at one of the few individuals to attain a perfect score on every single test to get into Quantico."

"You're a Feebee?"

Brie shook her head. "I had to quit the program before I could finish. But, like you, I would help out when I could, unofficially of course."

"Computers?" Meryn asked.

"No, profiling. My first degree was in Abnormal Psych, so I would read case after case after case to study trends and patterns."

"Kickass," Meryn whispered.

"Why did you quit?" Ari asked.

"My mother was diagnosed with cancer, so I dropped out to return home to take care of her."

Ari wrapped an arm around her shoulder as her father chuckled. "Your mother was so furious that you quit, but also so thankful you were there."

Meryn tilted her head at her. Brie answered the unspoken question. "My mother and my mother's mother as far back as we can trace were all law enforcement. My mother was FBI, one of the first Black females to serve, which is why she wanted me to stay in the program."

"Why not go back?" Meryn asked.

Brie gave a half shrug. "After my mother died, I lost the passion for it. Rathais approached me on campus after I finished my second degree and asked if I would be interested in becoming one of his deputies. It wasn't as prestigious as the FBI, but it felt right."

Gage laughed. "And he is so pissed that you will probably be moving here. He will have to find someone else to replace him now."

Brie frowned. "I was looking forward to becoming Sheriff."

Ari gave her a gentle squeeze. "Nothing has to be decided right now. We have enough on our plates as it is."

Meryn blinked. "Oh yeah, the dead people."

Brie had to hold back a smile at her statement. It was horribly insensitive and blunt, but somehow the small woman pulled it off.

Cord simply kissed the top of Meryn's head. "How about you all adjourn to the dining room. We'll continue drinks, but at least everyone will be seated."

Brie was seated between Ari and Rex. She recognized a few faces from this afternoon, but not all. Rex caught her looking from person to person and leaned down. One by one he began to put names to faces with small bits of information about each person.

Meryn overheard what he was doing and whipped out a tablet. "What's your email?"

Brie gave it to her and watched as Meryn's small fingers tapped rapidly. "Why?"

"Gonna forward you the information packet that Kari created that we compiled regarding all the problems we've been facing. That way you can read it later and ask questions at your own pace."

Brie exhaled in relief. "Thank you."

"Thank Kari. She's the one that color coded this thing. She said my notes read as if an over-sugared kindergartner was rambling off facts to his mom after school."

The woman Rex had introduced as Amelia winced, but nodded. "Everyone has their own strengths," she said soothingly.

The queen turned to her. "Brie, I know I put you on the spot at the processing center, but I really would like for you to take charge of this entire disaster. Your clear-headed suggestions have created the start of processes that will least traumatize my people."

"Your Majesty…"

"You can call me Aleksandra, if you wish. Your mate, Ari, is one of my most dedicated warriors, and I have a feeling you and I will be communicating quite a bit in the weeks to come, and 'Your Majesty' is such a mouthful."

Brie inclined her head. "Thank you. Aleksandra, I know that this isn't what you want to hear, but unless River uncovers something substantial that was overlooked by the killer, there was nothing at the scene to give us a direction to go."

The queen's face fell. "But you said…"

Brie nodded. "I know. I was standing in front of over a hundred grieving family members; that isn't exactly the time or place to admit that we've very little to go on."

"There'll be more," Meryn whispered.

All heads swung to face her as the queen gasped. "A premonition?"

Meryn shook her head. "No, facts. We're missing more than the seventy-eight found in the warehouse in Monroe. I'm willing to bet tomorrow's scones that there are multiple processing warehouses across the country, probably centered on where fae congregated while living outside Éire Danu."

"What can we do?" the queen asked, reaching for her mate's hand.

Meryn lightly tapped her butter knife against the side of her plate distractedly. "Look for large buildings that may be housing kidnapped fae, I guess, but..." the knife stilled. "Something isn't quite right. Like the timing of it. I saw some of the photos that were taken at the scene; they hadn't been dead that long. So why wait? What was the determining factor to kill them? Was it all in one go?"

"Meryn!" Amelia whispered.

Meryn ignored her cousin. "Yeah, that's the first thing we need to determine. How and when they died."

Brie held out her hand, and Meryn passed her tablet down the table. Brie began to skim the notes that were beautifully organized by this Kari individual. If Meryn was focusing on cause of death, there had to be a reason.

Brennus, the queen's consort, changed the subject as the first course was brought out. The squire introduced as Leo took one look at the tablet in her hand and changed her food selection. Instead of soup, she received some of the easier to eat hors d'oeuvres. "Thank you," she whispered. He winked at her and also filled her wine glass. The man was simply amazing.

As everyone engaged in small talk, she continued to read. Every once in a while, she would look up to find that Meryn was watching her intently. It was almost as if she was hoping that Brie would be able to follow her train of thought.

As they were about to transition to the entrée, she read something that stopped her in her tracks. She must have gasped, because the conversations around the table ceased.

Meryn leaned forward. "See anything?"

"Hold on." She pulled out her phone and dialed River.

"Hey, Wilson."

"Hey, can you forward me the crime scene photos that I took?"

"Sure." He paused. "Did you catch something?"

"Not sure yet, I need to see the photos. Also, shift your focus to method and time of death."

"You got it. The photos are on their way. Call me back if you find something concrete," he replied, before disconnecting.

"What photos?" Meryn asked.

"Once we got back from getting Ari patched up, I needed a distraction, so I helped photograph the scene."

Meryn scowled. "I didn't see those."

"River is probably pulling them from the memory card now. We did have a lot going on."

"Patched up?" Rex asked.

She nodded as she scrolled through her phone.

"Yeah, I shot him when he shifted into a lion and roared at me, then my dad accidentally neutered him."

Gasps were heard around the table.

"What!" Rex and Jedrek roared in unison.

"My baby!" Catherine, clutched at her chest.

Ari simply growled at her side. Gage, Priest, and Kincaid were laughing their asses off, and her father was sinking in his chair.

She looked up at Ari. "Still think it's funny?"

"Brie, you do not need Ari, become my mate," Gage offered.

Ari hissed at his friend.

"Will someone please tell me what in the hell is going on?" Jedrek demanded.

Ari, looking sheepish, told everyone about his earlier prank. Around the table, everyone began to laugh, including the queen.

She wiped at the corner of her eyes with a napkin. Though she smiled, Brie could tell half her tears were from mirth, the other half grief. "After today's horror, I thought I'd never laugh again, yet here I am, mere hours later, enjoying myself as my children lay cold and dead."

"If everyone stopped laughing because of the loss of a loved one, this world would be no place for the living," her father said softly. "After I lost my Brianna, I felt angry every time I saw someone else smiling, until I realized that because of how I was reacting to others, my own baby girl had stopped smiling altogether. I knew that Brianna would never want us to live like that. In fact, I bet I have an ass beating waiting for me in the hereafter due to how I behaved after her passing."

Brie nodded. "Probably," she agreed as she went through the photos sent to her.

He turned to the queen. "If you give up your joy, then the ones that took your people from you gain another victory."

The queen gave a timorous smile. "We can't have that."

"Now, what'd you find?" Meryn asked.

Brie held up a finger and continued to scroll through the photos. There. That was the one she was looking for. She passed her phone over to Meryn and sat back.

Meryn quickly turned the phone in her hands and looked down at the picture. She scrolled forward a few pictures then back. Brie knew exactly what she was looking for.

The queen looked from her to Meryn then back. "Please tell me you found something."

"I think we found something."

Meryn sat back. "I was right."

"You were right."

"Right about what?" Aiden asked explosively.

"Catherine has only just filled me in on what's been happening in your world, so when Meryn said what she did, it sounded similar to something Catherine had told me." She glanced over at Amelia. "When Amelia was kidnapped, she was also taken to a processing type center. In the report, it said that had Keelan Ashwood not blocked the spell that targeted the unit warriors, they would have been stripped of their souls."

She nodded at Meryn, who held up the phone.

"There's threaded holes in the support beams of the warehouse and scrapes on the floor."

Amelia covered her mouth with a trembling hand. "That crystal machine."

Meryn nodded. "Brie and I are only guessing at this point, but I think that the medical examiner will come back with the same time of death for all the fae."

"We go from knowing nothing to having a solid lead, just like that?" Justice asked.

Aiden beamed down at his mate. "My baby is a genius."

Ari rested his arm on the back of her chair and rubbed her back. "As is mine."

Meryn smiled, but her eyes went back to the pictures. "It's just…"

"Meryn, you should have been in law enforcement," Brie said, leaning back against Ari's warm hand.

Meryn scrunched up her nose. "No way." She then looked at Brie. "Do you know what I'm going to say?"

"I have an idea, because it's the one thing bothering me too about our theory."

"On three," Meryn challenged.

"One, two, three…"

"The pile," Brie said.

"The bodies," Meryn replied at the same time. "Well damn."

"What about the bodies?" Law asked.

Kendrick exhaled and leaned back. "Brilliant. Simply, brilliant."

Meryn held out a thumbs up to the man. "Good for you."

He gave her a flat expression. "So glad I can keep up."

Ari squeezed her shoulder, and she looked up into his questioning face. She took a deep breath. "If the killers used a machine to kill them all at once, the bodies should have been more spread out; they would have been found where they had fallen, but they weren't. The killers took a lot of extra time and effort to dehumanize the dead. They were piled in such a way to make a statement, which is more terrifying than the act itself."

"You think that is scarier than killing people?" Amelia asked incredulously.

Both she and Meryn nodded. Brie looked at Amelia. "People die every day. They don't happen often, but mass murders do happen, lately in the form of mass shootings. In those instances, think about what happens to the people. They are shot, and the killer moves on. The killer is usually acting out of rage or a perceived injustice. They shoot, then they keep going. It's tragic, but the dead in a way keep their dignity. These killers didn't stop their terror after their victims had died. Their torment followed these people into death. They were stacked up like things, not people." She paused. "You see, when killers stop seeing people and start seeing objects, true horrors begin."

"I think I kinda miss dealing with ferals," Meryn said softly.

Aiden pulled her into his lap as did most of the men with mates. She looked up at Ari then down to his clenched fist. "I didn't want to assume," he admitted.

Her heart melted a bit. "It's okay to assume this time." She knew he needed this almost as much as she did. The moment he wrapped both arms around her, she sighed and relaxed against him. "You're like my own snuggie blankie," she whispered. Ari chuckled and kissed the top of her head. "Anytime."

"What are our next steps?" Anne asked from Kendrick's lap.

"It's my turn," Meryn said, reaching for a roll. Ryuu stepped forward and handed her one. "I'm going to run the locations of the missing through my database, then look in a twenty-mile radius for hits of possible buildings being used."

Brie turned just enough so she faced the table, but stayed relaxed against Ari. "I'll be working with River to determine cause and time of death and we'll go from there."

"I'll be heading up security of Éire Danu and Ben will be taking point in assigning out Old Guard and warriors to assist in getting the deceased claimed and laid to rest," Aiden said before he leaned forward and took a massive bite out of Meryn's roll. Meryn's shocked expression had Brie giggling.

"Dude!" Meryn protested.

Aiden just smiled as he chewed.

"Thank the gods for you, Meryn," Brennus said quietly, as he smiled.

Ryuu simply handed his charge another roll and sighed heavily when she shoved the entire thing in her mouth so that Aiden couldn't steal any more.

"Meryn," Aiden chided gently.

She smiled wide, showing off a glob of white dough as a smile. Brie stared but her attention was soon diverted to the queen who began to laugh so hard it sounded as though she was having a hard time catching her breath.

"Gods, I love you, Meryn."

"Ruv oo ooo," Meryn mumbled.

Brennus grinned broadly at his mate's laughter. The heaviness of the evening seemed to lift a bit. Brie could hardly believe that the bane of her director's existence was a goofy little nut. "Meryn, do you have a space I can work at tomorrow?"

Meryn swallowed and nodded. "Yup, first thing I did was work with Cord in setting up my Batcave."

"You have an extra station or should I head back for my laptop?"

"It might be easier to get your own laptop. I mean I can totally hack into whatever systems you're privy to, but it'd be faster to do it the 'legal' way."

She looked up at Ari. "Can someone take me to the station in Monroe tomorrow? While I'm there, I can meet up with River to see if he found anything."

Darian lifted a hand with a silver ring. "I can

take you. I'm going to be working with Cam in getting the deceased's property sorted."

Amelia clapped her hands together. "Okay, enough depressing talk. For the rest of our dinner, only happy topics. I'll go first." She turned to Darian who was sipping his wine. "I'm pregnant, by the way."

Darian spewed wine all over the table. "What! How!"

Amelia tilted her head, a confused expression on her face. "You were there."

He scowled. "I know that." Then her words truly seemed to sink in. "A baby?"

The queen scrambled from Brennus' lap and practically collided with Cord and Oron as they raced over to Darian's chair. The queen hugged her son tightly and Oron nuzzled the top of Amelia's head.

"You should have told us sooner!" the queen cried, as she switched from Darian to Amelia.

Amelia blushed. "It happened recently. I had planned on telling you tomorrow, but other things made it more important to announce tonight."

"Cord! More wine!" Brennus shouted, as he held up empty glasses. Thane, Justice, and Law began conjuring balloons out of nothingness, laughing all the while.

Cord was dashing away tears as he began to pour. "A baby! Finally, a baby!" he sniffled.

Kendrick stood and made his way over to his goddaughter. He placed a hand on the top of her head then smiled. "Perfectly healthy," he announced. "Good job, crybaby," he said, a sheen to his eyes.

Amelia dabbed at her own eyes. "Mother, Father, and my brothers know. I called them this afternoon." She looked over to Meryn. "They're on their way. Mother wants to watch that orb of Aunt Violet."

Meryn was grinning from ear to ear. "Almost all my family will be together."

"We'll get the boys here soon enough," Aiden promised.

"When Pip is ready," Meryn added.

"What exciting news! And just what we all needed," Catherine said, sitting back in her chair, holding her wine glass.

"It seems like only yesterday Brie was pretending to do press conferences with her hair brush microphone in the mirror," her father said, winking at her.

Jedrek nodded. "I know what you mean. I swear Ari was just in diapers, then I turn around and he's a warrior for our city."

"Father!" Ari hissed.

Rex laughed. "You were, without a doubt the most adorable baby I've ever seen." Then he paused. "But we do have Baby Lionhart on the way in Noctem Falls, they may end up being cuter."

Ari smiled. "I bet they will be! I'm hoping for a niece."

"What's all the commotion?" A tall man that looked similar to Brennus and Celyn asked as he walked through the door.

The queen turned to him, beaming. "You're going to be an uncle!" she crowed.

He looked at Meryn and frowned. "Again?"

Brennus laughed. "No, Doran. Amelia is with child!"

Doran's eyes lit up. "That news was sorely needed tonight!" He strode over to where Amelia was being showered with affection and dropped a kiss of his own to the top of her head. "A thousand blessings on the future King or Queen of Éire Danu," he said, his voice ringing.

Amelia blinked. "Oh gods, I never even thought about that."

Darian cupped her face. "I won't be taking over for my mother for thousands of years, and our little one may be geriatric before they take over from me. Don't let it worry you; you have our little prince or princess to think of."

The queen spun to face her son. "Thousands of years?"

Darian and Oron nodded. "Yes, you are our queen."

Aleksandra sat down in the chair next to her son. "Now I know how Magnus felt. An around the world cruise sounds heavenly right about now."

Doran laughed at the way his brother scowled at the mention of the vampire prince, however, his laughter was cut short as he looked across the table. "Mine," he growled. Faster than she could track, he had rounded the table and pulled her father up into his arms. When they kissed, she felt her chin drop.

"What!" the word echoed around the table.

Brennus began to hop around the room in a joy filled jig. "Finally!" he crowed.

Meryn stared. "So, more of the butt sex, huh?"

Aiden's hand went up to cover her mouth.

Ari spun her around to face him. "Brie? Are you okay?"

She felt tears fill her eyes at the sight of her father's happiness. "I will be as soon as my father stops embarrassing me by being molested at the damn dinner table."

Doran stepped away from her father, breathing hard. Both men looked dazed. Doran recovered first and eased her father back into his chair before sitting down beside him. He looked at her. "Father?"

"Yes. You had the honor of kissing my father, Chris Wilson, the most wonderful dad in the world," she announced proudly.

"Oh, baby girl." Her dad was smiling, but there was a hesitation in his eyes. She knew she had to nip his worry in the bud before he blew up into an anxiety-ridden mess.

"Don't you for one moment think you are betraying mother. You know for a fact that she'd only want you to be happy."

Her father's face cleared. "You're right. She'd probably try to talk both of us into the bedroom."

"La la la la la la," she yelled, covering her ears. Everyone laughed at her antics. She knew both of her parents had been free spirits when they met; having her hadn't changed that fact.

Doran looked from her, to her father, to his

brother, then back to her. He clutched at his chest. "I'm a father," he whispered. He smiled at her. "I swear I will do everything in my power to ensure your happiness."

Her father inhaled, his lower lip trembling at Doran's declaration. He then stood. "Dinner was amazing, thank you for inviting me." He looked down at Doran. "We're leaving." She groaned at her father's obvious intentions.

Doran shot out of his chair like a jack in a box. "We will, of course, see you in the morning."

"Maybe," her father murmured.

"Gods above," Doran whispered, before both men practically ran from the room.

"Never. Never in all my years have I ever seen him so flustered." Brennus howled his laughter.

Meryn's expression became thoughtful. "So, if Ari is mated to Brie, and Brie's dad is mated to Uncle Doran, what's that make me and Ari?"

Ari looked at his brother. "Cousins?"

Rex beamed out at the room. "The adorable menace is my baby cousin!"

"I can still call you hot right?" Meryn asked.

Rex nodded as Aiden growled the word, 'No!'

"Much better," Amelia murmured as she sat back.

Brie realized she was right. This was much better than wallowing in despair. She stood and held out her hand to Ari. "Like father, like daughter." She raised an eyebrow at him.

Ari, much like Doran, shot out of his chair.

"Goodnight," he said simply. He scooped her up in his arms and ran from the room, leaving catcalls and whistles in their wake.

CHAPTER SIX

❧

ONCE THEY WERE OUTSIDE, ARI set her down on her feet. "We have a couple options."

"For what?" Because there was only one thing she was thinking of, and if that's what he was referring to, options were always good.

"We can return to my rooms at the Lionhart estate or head to the Unit Warrior villa."

Oh, that's what he meant.

"Since I've already seen the Lionhart estate, we can go to the Warrior villa. I just need to grab my clothes from your parent's place."

"That won't be a problem," Ari smiled, then reached down and took her hand. "Why the shift in attitude. Wasn't I your 'supposed' mate?"

"I'm not sure. Earlier, when I was feeling like my head was about to explode, just being in your arms made everything feel safer. That kind of comfort can be an aphrodisiac, and I found myself craving you more. If Fate, or whatever, feels like we'd be a perfect match, I'm going to throw caution to the wind and just try this out. I mean, Fate can't choose worse than I've chosen for myself over the years."

Ari frowned. "I'm ecstatic that you have accepted our mating, but I'm not sure how I feel regarding the 'it can't get any worse' mentality."

"I'm a cop, Ari, we're pessimists by nature."

"Warriors aren't much better." He gently tugged on her hand, and they slowly made their way through the golden city until they were back at his parents' home. He opened the door and they stepped into the foyer. "You run up to the bathroom and grab your stuff; I'm going to my room to grab my fatigues, duffel, and your gun from the safe."

"Fatigues?"

"Yeah, tomorrow Tau unit is training, so our fatigues serve as our workout gear."

"Hmmm."

He flashed her a boyish grin. "I'll model them for you tomorrow."

She laughed and began to jog up the stairs. "Damn right, you will."

Once in the large bathroom, she discovered that someone had laundered and delivered her clothes. They sat folded neatly in a pile on the counter. The travel toiletry kit sitting on top made her smile. She scooped everything up and went to Ari's room. He was waiting for her by the closet. "Come here," he asked.

She followed him into the closet and he led her to one side where the wall was covered in different mirrors. He had her place her hand on the center mirror. "Now, you have access as well."

She stared as the mirror slid aside to reveal a massive gun safe. "This is so damn sexy."

He chuckled and retrieved her gun. He showed her that it was loaded and handed it to her. She tucked it away with her things and he closed the safe.

"Your squire is a miracle," she said, holding up the kit. He handed her a small travel bag and she dropped her things in.

Ari's face brightened. "Leo has been taking care of us since before I was born. He's just as much a parent to me as my mother and father."

"So, what Meryn said about them being like Super Moms is true?"

"Very much so, in fact, it's probably one of the best descriptions I've heard for a squire. Granted, not all squires are the same. Most strive to become even a fraction as good as Sei Ryuu, Cord Danuthal, and Sebastian Hearthstone."

"So, we're just lucky?"

"Pretty much."

This time she didn't wait for him. She reached down and took his hand, earning her a bright smile. "I wasn't kidding when I said I was all in," she reminded him. They walked downstairs and into the warm evening air.

"Once you make up your mind, that's it, huh?"

She gave a half shrug. "I've always been that way."

Together, they walked through the streets, past the splendor of the Upper City, until they came upon a brightly lit building amongst some of the older homes on the street. The windows were thrown open, and male laughter could be heard from the walkway. Rising from the center of the large building, a towering holly tree created a dark green canopy overhead. She pointed to the evergreen. "Why a holly?"

Ari held open a simple iron gate. "We didn't always have one. But when Darian became a unit warrior, he donated a cutting from his family's tree so that us poor warriors would have someone looking over us. In return, we try to keep things as lively as possible for the Alina guardian."

Brie remembered what she learned about how Darian's entire family was murdered. "I think any guardian would like it here." She pointed to where the amber glow from the lights inside seemed to beckon them forward.

"We do our best." He opened the door, and the male voices were even louder.

"Ari! Welcome home! Done being important at the Lionhart estate?" a warrior teased as he walked down the stairs toward them.

"Ari's back?" another voice called out.

Soon, the foyer was filled with warriors. More than one reached out to ruffle Ari's hair in a brotherly fashion. Ari smiled at them all.

"Guys, I have someone important I want you to meet. This is my mate, Brie Wilson. Brie, these men are my fellow unit brothers." He puffed out his chest. "Isn't she wonderful?"

"Too good for a baby boy like you!"

"I'll run your things up," another volunteered. She handed off her small bag, as did Ari.

"A thousand blessings on your mating!"

"Welcome!" All around them the men called out their greetings.

"I thought you were attending the palace dinner?" the dark-haired warrior asked.

Ari gave them a shit-eating grin. "We were, but then my mate decided we should retire early."

The men groaned, and a set of hands gently pulled her from Ari. "You know what that means?"

She felt a moment of panic before she realized she was being steered toward the kitchen. "Late night snack party!"

"No! We're going to bed early!" Ari argued.

The men ignored him and sat her down at the long island in the middle of the expansive kitchen. The men worked together like a well-oiled machine, pulling out snacks and components to make munchies. She smiled at Ari's chagrin, but knew he wasn't too upset by the way he kept sneaking chips and salsa.

"There he is!" a familiar voice said accusingly.

Ari winced. "Sorry guys, but my mate wanted to leave. What was I supposed to do?"

Kincaid walked in and placed his hands on his hips. "Take us with you for gods sake! My delicate nerves can't handle all the royalty!"

"Yeah, because us all leaving wouldn't have looked weird after my mate gave me a come-hither look."

Kincaid glared at him. "Don't care."

"Besides, you know she likes us more," Gage

said, breezing past Kincaid to kiss her cheek. He looked over to the counters. "Snack party!"

Kincaid looked a bit mollified. "Snack party?"

Priest sat down next to her. "Has the idiot even made introductions yet?"

She shook her head. "I may request everyone wear name tags the next few days. Between the warriors and the palace, my brain hurts."

Ari sat down on the stool on her other side. "I'm sure the guys won't mind doing that for you."

"Oh! I actually have name tags, hold on!" A blond warrior ran out of the kitchen.

"Leave it to Balder to have name tags," Ari smiled as he shook his head.

The dark-haired warrior placed a bowl of chips in front of her. "In the meantime, I'll start. I'm Bastien Géroux. My uncle is Simon Géroux, Founding Family head in Noctem Falls. I serve in the Phi unit along with Nerius Li'Meiner, fae. Kael Lyon, lion shifter. Jace Frazier, wolf shifter, and Ian Angelica, witch."

Priest nudged her. "We call him Angel."

Bastien leveled a look at Priest. "You really want to go there, Meredith?"

Priest scowled. "I hate that you guys know my name."

Bastien and most of the men belly laughed. "Know? We were at your naming ceremony, eaglet."

Priest sighed. "Yeah, yeah, we know. We're the kids around here."

The blond that had run from the room raced

back in holding up a small plastic package. "I have these from when we volunteered at the children's hospital." He began passing stacks of sticker tags and pens to the warriors who sighed and wrote their names before slapping them on their chests. When she saw the first one, she laughed, now she knew why they were sighing. All the name tags had adorable baby animals on them.

"No! Give me the lion one!" one of the warriors protested. Laughing, his friend handed him the name tag with the baby lion on it. He wrote his name down and smiled at her. "Hey, cuz! My name is Broden Lionhart. I serve in the Upsilon unit with Balder Ri'Ilindra." He pointed to the warrior who had passed out the name tags. "Tiergan Faulkner, tiger shifter." He nodded to the warrior who was drawing stripes on the ginger kitten on his own name tag. "Caleb LaVoie, vampire. And Heath Clover, witch."

He high-fived another warrior that looked as though he could be his twin. "This is my older brother Ramsey Lionhart, he serves in the Chi unit."

Ramsey winked at her. "First Kari and now Brie, the Lionharts are truly blessed to have such beautiful ladies join our pride."

"Ramsey," Ari growled.

"Just as snarly as your brother," Ramsey teased.

Ari grinned. "I'll take that as a compliment."

Broden laughed. "You would."

Ramsey stood on tiptoe to look around the

room, then pointed to the warrior pouring different drinks. "Aeson Vi'Liordon leads my unit."

A fae with strawberry blond hair waved at her. "He's currently planning revenge on Zach for locking him in his room on the day he was supposed to escort The Menace to the palace."

"Damn right," Aeson muttered.

Ramsey continued. "Matthieu Lucien, vampire. Leon March, fox shifter. And Carson Elderberry, witch." His finger went down the line pointing out the men making nachos. The Psi and Omega units are currently running patrols, so we'll leave out name tags for them for tomorrow."

"I really appreciate that, guys," she said, dipping her chip into what looked to be homemade pico. She took a bit and sighed happily. "This is so good."

Ari gently bumped her shoulder. "It's a weakness of mine. I had Leo show me how to make it."

"You made this?" she asked.

"Yup."

"All kinds of favors will be given for the pico if you add a margarita on the rocks to the combo," she offered.

Ari stood and immediately went to the sideboard that held familiar liquor bottles.

"Lucky bastard," Ramsey said.

Ari returned with a glass with a salted rim. "For you, my lady."

"You make my mouth happy, my mouth will make you happy."

Ari practically whimpered as he sat back down next to her.

"Lucky ass bastard," Broden repeated.

Ari turned to them, smiling wide. "Don't make me tell my father you were calling me a bastard."

Both Broden and Ramsey rolled their eyes. "Your father doesn't scare us; it's your mother that I would never want to cross."

Ari thought about that a moment. "True."

"Catherine? Your sweet as pie mother?"

Ari nodded. "You mean my lioness mother who is the Alpha of the huntresses of the Lionhart pride? Hell yeah."

Broden pointed between himself and his brother. "She's our mother's older sister."

She looked at them. "But you're Lionharts, doesn't that mean your fathers are related?"

Ramsey nodded. "Our mothers are sisters, and our fathers are brothers. Basically, two families completely merged together after those two matings."

Ari stole a chip from her bowl. "Our mother's maiden name was Eliana, which means 'daughter of the sun'. A matriarchal line as old and revered as Lionhart. Eliana's Daughters are known for being the best huntresses, so naturally when paired with the just as powerful Lionharts you get a generation of cubs that can do no wrong."

Broden nodded. "We are terribly spoiled, on both sides of the family. Ari, even more so being the baby."

"If the two of you end up having a baby girl,

our aunts will probably lose their minds. So far, only males have been born from our parents," Ramsey added.

"Kari is pregnant. I bet you anything she's having a girl." Ari sat back. "Gods, a baby girl with our strength and her mother's intelligence would be unstoppable."

Ramsey suddenly frowned. "She'll need all her uncles to keep the boys away."

Suddenly he, Broden, and Ari were growling low.

Brie rolled her eyes. "Or you could teach her to defend herself."

Ari pointed to her badge. "Auntie Brie could teach her how to shoot."

She sipped her margarita. Damn, the man had made it perfectly. "Of course, but I was thinking more along the lines of judo."

Ari blinked. "You know judo?"

"Yup. Had dad sign me up when I was four. Typical school yard bully kept pushing me down so he could look up my skirt. I asked my mom to show me how to fight big boys, and she suggested judo."

"Your parents didn't do anything to the little bastard?" Ari asked.

She shook her head. "I told them not to. I wanted to handle it myself. So, I took lessons, and it didn't take long for me to get really good at throwing his ass around. He left me alone after that. I hit a growth spurt in middle school and most bullies left me alone after that."

"Why?" Ari asked.

She dragged her hand up and down in front of her body. "My mom was six-foot one, I'm six-feet even. I towered over most of the guys through high school."

Ari blinked. "Is that tall for humans?"

Brie was about to answer, then looked around the room. She was actually way shorter than most of them. Meryn suddenly popped into her head; the woman was easily at least eight to nine inches shorter than she was.

"To answer your questions, yes, amongst humans I'm tall. Poor Meryn, her neck must absolutely kill her from having to look up all the time."

Balder opened his mouth, then closed it. "You know, I never really thought about how much she can't see." He dropped to his knees. "She's about this short right?"

Brie nodded. "There about."

"This is awful! I can't even reach the counter!"

"It looks like it was built for you warriors, so that makes sense," Brie pointed out.

More than one warrior dropped to their knees to see what Balder was talking about.

"This is bullshit!" Jace exclaimed.

"Can she even reach the toilet?" Ian asked.

Brie held her sides, laughing as she watched a group of grown men walk around on their knees in the kitchen, discovering what they couldn't reach.

"I mean, this impacts daily life, right?" Jace asked, trying to reach a bowl of chips.

The men stood shaking their heads.

"No wonder our commander carries her around so much. I thought they were just in a honeymoon stage, but maybe it's a survival mechanism that he's subconsciously adopted," Balder suggested.

"And she's pregnant," Ramsey added.

Bastien rubbed his chin. "You know, men, I believe it is our duty to assist our commander. While he and his tiny mate are in Éire Danu, we should do everything possible to ensure that Meryn's stay is not only safe but enjoyable."

Priest clapped his friend on the back. "You are a fine example of what it means to be a warrior. I am proud to call you my brother."

"Annnnd Leana threatened him over the phone when he did his weekly check in with his uncle. She said that Meryn had the love and support of Noctem Falls, and Éire Danu would do well to follow their example," Kael said, ducking out of the way when Bastien stepped toward him.

Bastien let Kael skip out of reach. "Magnus presented her with a Regalis card. You know how rare it is for one to be given out. That alone should make her everyone's priority."

"I think she's fine where she is. At the palace, she has not only her mate and her squire, but also the queen and uncles every which way she turns," Ari said.

Bastien thought about it a moment then nodded. "Agreed, however, if she ever has to leave the palace, I'd like to volunteer for guard duty."

Ari reached across the counter for a nacho.

"I'll pass that on to Aiden. I know that man will not turn down guards for his mate."

Brie sat back and was surprised to find that she was truly enjoying herself. Being in a male dominated profession, she was used to being the only female in the room. The men joked, played pranks, teased mercilessly, and puttered around the kitchen, creating a laid-back atmosphere.

Around midnight, she was introduced to the Psi and Omega units as they came in from patrol duty. Balder leading Upsilon and Nerius leading Phi headed out the door to take over patrols. Ari took her hand and started saying goodnight to the men.

"A thousand blessings on your mating, Ari," Ramsey called as they walked out of the kitchen.

"Sleep tight!"

"I doubt they will be sleeping," Aeson said, causing the men to laugh.

When they were at the top of the stairs, Brie noticed that Ari had gone quiet. She peeked up, and to her delight, his cheeks were pink. He caught her staring, and with his other hand, rubbed the back of his neck. "Sorry about the guys."

"Don't be. I think they're wonderful. Yes, they're a bit boisterous, but at no point did they say anything that made me uncomfortable. I felt like I was in a room full of brothers."

Ari's smile to her statement was bright. "They are. Like brothers, I mean."

She rubbed his arm as they resumed walking. "I know. They watched you like a hawk while we were down there. Every time your drink got low, someone walked by and filled it. You mentioned you loved tangerines, and suddenly there was a bowl on the counter. It's clear how loved you Priest, Gage, and Kincaid are."

Ari stopped dead in his tracks and looked down at her. "What?"

"You didn't notice?"

"No. Wait. Seriously?" She could tell he was mentally going through the entire evening.

She pulled on his arm to get them walking again. Her third margarita had her wanting to strip down and face plant into bed.

Absently, he walked a few more feet then placed his hand on the center of the door before him. She heard a faint click, and he swung it open for them. She stepped inside and looked around. The room was clean and tidy. He had decorated it in shades of blue, and while everything looked nice, it felt empty.

"Where's your stuff?" she asked, figuring out what was missing. There were no personal affects here.

"At home," he answered and pulled his shirt over his head.

"Home?" She looked at him confused.

Ari turned to her, and she looked her fill. His broad chest was nothing but compact and defined muscles. When she saw the way his hips dipped into his slacks in a 'v', she almost groaned. Was there ever a more beautiful man?

"I maintain quarters here and split my time between the warrior villa and the Lionhart estate. It's somewhat unorthodox given the way other units are run, but considering my family plays major roles in the city's politics, it works better for everyone. I get updates from my father and pass them on to the units so that Brennus doesn't have to."

"So, you come here when you want to be pampered," she teased.

Ari shook his head. "Until you said something, I never even noticed they did that." He frowned. "I wonder if Gage, Priest, or Kincaid knows." He sighed. "Sometimes it's hard being the youngest in a city of paranormals that can lives for thousands and thousands of years."

"It may not be a paranormal thing. In Monroe, the firehouse is across the street from our station. I've watched the older firemen coddle their probies. Don't get me wrong, they torture the hell outta them too, but yeah, the probies are treated like baby brothers."

"Probie?"

"Probationer, someone whose performance is evaluated before acceptance."

"We don't have those. Once you're moved up to serve as a unit warrior, that's it."

"You don't have any form of training?"

"We used to have an academy, but Meryn made a suggestion last year to move all trainees to stay and train with the units to allow for more cadets to move up. In theory, it was supposed to increase the number of trained men that could assist. However, many Founding and Noble families pointed out that if the trainees were moved up, then only one academy was needed. So, Adair McKenzie is in charge of all cadets now in Lycaonia's academy."

"I bet you Meryn was pissed."

"You have no idea."

She pulled off her robe, then paused. "Are we having sex tonight?"

Ari, who was in the process of stepping out of his slacks, turned to face her and tripped, falling against the mattress before bouncing onto the floor.

"Are you okay?"

"Don't mind me. I'll be sleeping with my tattered pride here on the floor," Ari said, sounding disgusted with himself.

"Don't be silly. Now, sex, yes or no? Because to be honest, I'm tired and not sure I can muster up the enthusiasm despite how incredibly hot you are."

He grinned. "You think I'm hot?"

She let her robe fall to the floor and began walking toward him completely nude. She put a little sway in her step, causing her breasts to bounce. She watched in fascination as his eyes turned the color of honey. "I think you're so incredibly hot that we need to invest in birth control, because I plan on jumping your fine ass every chance I get." She yawned wide, then blinked down at him.

His expression softened, and his eyes returned to their normal shade of gold. He stood and held out his hand. "You can jump me tomorrow, after we both get a good night's rest."

She took his hand, and they both crawled into bed. He immediately curved his body around hers, tucking her head under his chin. Her body relaxed almost instantly in response to his touch.

"Goodnight, my 'supposed' soul mate," she said, yawning again.

Her yawn was cut short when he nipped the back of her neck. "Goodnight, my mate," he countered.

And for the first time in her life, she fell asleep within moments of her head hitting the pillow.

CHAPTER SEVEN

❦

THE NEXT MORNING, SHE WENT to stretch and realized she was still completely cocooned in her own li'l Ari nest. As they were lying on their right side, his right arm curled under the pillow to cradle her head, and his left hand was latched onto her breast. She could feel puffs of air on her neck and found that she didn't mind it.

She eased out of bed, placing a pillow in Ari's arms so that he continued to sleep. Her hand flew to her lips to keep her laughter contained as he squeezed the pillow and grinned lecherously. Shaking her head, she quietly gathered up her real clothes and went to the bathroom to freshen up. She made quick work of her hair and make-up, then, not for the first time, sent up a prayer of thanks to Rathais, who required his deputies to wear only the uniformed shirt. Instead of hot polyester slacks, she pulled on her favorite pair of jeans. She belted on her holster and instead of repining her badge to her shirt, she slipped the sash on that held her new broach.

She tiptoed out the door and headed downstairs. She found a handful of men in the kitchen prepping breakfast. Outside the window, the world brightened slowly.

"Morning, fellas," she said, in greeting.

Aeson and Matthieu waved, and Aeson pointed to the frying pan. "Early birds get to pick their egg style."

"Scrambled for me and thanks. Any coffee?" she asked, looking around.

Matthieu pointed to the small alcove where multiple industrial coffee urns burbled. "Just finished."

She went over, poured a cup of black ambrosia, added sweetener, and took a sip. She sighed, leaning one hip against the wall. "This is amazing."

"Thank Izzy. She is setting up a small coffee shop in Dav's pub and offered to order us coffee from her wholesaler account. We could never get beans this good otherwise," Aeson explained

Ramsey came around the island, holding a small pitcher. "You should try with half-n-half. I had Leo show me how to get the milk to cream ratios right."

Normally, she didn't take cream in her coffee, just a bit of sweetener, but he looked so excited, she found herself holding out her cup. He poured then stopped, eyed the swirling brew then added a bit more. He went to the coffee station and grabbed a spoon and stirred for her. "Try now."

She took a sip, fully expecting to hate it, but found for once, the cream didn't overtake the taste of coffee, just added a smoothness to the experience. "That's freaking amazing!"

Ramsey beamed. "I know, right!"

She looked at the guys in the room. "Okay, what's the catch?"

The exchanged confused expressions. "What do you mean?" Ramsey asked.

She pointed first to Aeson then to Ramsey. "You guys are just too perfect. Last night, you did everything you could to welcome me for Ari's sake." She raised a brow. "And don't think I didn't notice how you spoil him and the Tau unit." Ramsey winced, and she continued. "Creating name tags was freaking adorable, and you're all so domestic, my ovaries are spiraling in shame, so what gives?"

Aeson laughed at her last statement then went back to his frying pan. "Unlike the other pillar cities, until very recently, the units of Éire Danu really didn't have much to do. Patrols were pointless in a city that had no borders. It's true that we still trained and did drills, but there was no urgency behind it."

Ramsey set down the cream pitcher by the coffee bar. "Éire Danu is known amongst the warriors as the transition city. We are a pretty evenly split between older warriors about to enter inactive status or turn Vanguard and recently promoted warriors. It makes for a very nurturing environment where we, the younger warriors are treated like baby brothers, and our estate has a less military vibe."

Matthieu smiled. "As for Ari, well, he is the baby. He is the youngest here by almost a hundred years. He was born and raised right here in Éire Danu, so we all watched him grow up. It is hard not to spoil him, and by extension, the nearly as young Tau unit."

"I never even noticed," Ari said, stepping into the room. He went to her, tilting her head back for a kiss. "I woke up molesting a pillow. Your work?"

She giggled. "You looked like a cat kneading his blanket."

He leered down at her. "I'll knead something later," he promised.

"Later?"

"Later. I had a few texts waiting for me on my phone this morning. Tau and Chi have been summoned to the palace. Tyrien Ri'Aileanach has declared a case of No Confidence in the way the murders are being handled."

Aeson whistled low. "From what I heard, that goes directly against the queen's decree to allow Brie to handle things."

Ari nodded. "It's the first time in Éire Danu's history that a case has been filed countering the ruling king or queen directly." He went to the coffee bar then opened the cabinet above the urns pulling out six travel mugs. "Thank the gods Rex is home. He was at the palace at the crack of dawn, scraping Brennus off the ceiling. Brennus wanted to challenge the pissant directly."

Leon walked in and went right to the fridge. He pulled out a small container of yogurt and an apple. "I would pay a hefty sum to watch that."

Aeson turned to Ramsey. "Go flip Carson's mattress. If we start now, he might be fully awake by the time he reaches the palace."

Ramsey nodded, then jogged out of the room. A few moments later, a loud thud followed by shouts were heard. She turned to Ari, who held up a finger. "Wait for it."

Seconds later a resounding boom shook the walls of the villa. "What on earth?" she asked, as the vibrations in the floor drifted away.

"Carson's a fire witch. I wonder if Ramsey avoided the fireball this time?" Ari poured coffee into one of the travel mugs then began to doctor it.

She heard footsteps on the stairs before Ramsey flew into the room. "I always forget he can do that!" The hair on one side of his head looked a bit singed.

Aeson smiled and slid her eggs on to a plate. "Which is exactly why I keep asking you to wake him."

Gage and Priest were the next to walk in, Kincaid behind them. Gage held up his phone. "Did you see this?" he asked Ari.

Ari nodded, then pointed down to the travel cups. "Grab your coffee."

Brie picked up her fork and began to inhale her eggs. She loved her morning coffee, but she needed fuel to face the day. Ari looked at her plate longingly, and she held up a fork. He leaned down and took a bite. "Thank you." He took her cup and poured it into one of the mugs.

He added fresh hot coffee then pointed down. "How do you take yours?"

"An extra sweetener and some of the cream. Ramsey has made me a fan." He nodded, then fixed her to-go cup before handing it back to her.

Kincaid whimpered, staring at Brie's plate, and Ari winked. "I'm sure if we look pitiful enough, Cord will feed us."

Kincaid brightened. "That's worth having to attend the meeting."

They all heard loud footsteps before a dark-haired warrior thumped into the kitchen, glaring at Ramsey. Before he could lay into the lion shifter, Ari held out a travel mug. "Tau and Chi have been summoned to the palace; grab your coffee." The warrior stopped mid-snarl then marched over to the coffee bar. Now the six mugs made sense.

Aeson removed his apron and handed the spatula over to the warrior that had been working the toaster. "Saxon, can you take over?"

"Sure thing." Saxon took Aeson's place at the stove, and the men headed toward the door.

Brie shoveled the last of her eggs into her mouth and washed them down with some coffee. She took Ari's hand, and they followed the guys to the palace.

⟐

The difference between the laid-back, fun, warrior kitchen and the tension-filled queen's chambers was drastic. No wonder Kincaid felt nervous coming here.

"I want to gouge out my eyeballs with that

prissy, silver, sugar spoon," Meryn complained, pushing her fruit around on her plate.

"Normally, I'd say you may be feeling a bit anti-social, but it's almost oppressive in here," Amelia agreed, closing her eyes and sitting back in her chair. Darian wrapped an arm around her and pulled her into his body. "Do you need to lay back down?"

She opened her eyes long enough to glare at him before closing them again. "Just because I'm pregnant doesn't mean I should be treated any differently."

Nearly every man at the table snorted.

Aiden actually nodded in agreement with Amelia. "Pregnant women are incredibly strong and very fierce."

Meryn beamed at those seated around the table. "Grrrrrr."

On her other side, Kincaid let out a breath he had been holding. Slowly, he began to relax. Across the table, Kendrick tilted his head, then stood. He walked around the table until he was behind Kincaid, who now looked petrified.

"Sir?" he asked.

Kendrick ignored him and simply placed his hand on Kincaid's head. When he lifted it, he was smiling. "I think being around Meryn has made me somewhat an expert with empaths."

"What?" Ari asked, sitting up straighter.

Kendrick smiled down at Kincaid before returning to his seat. "You hate political meetings, never go to the Upper City, and avoid the palace like the plague. You looked like you were two seconds from being ill at out last meeting here, and just now, when the tension broke, you looked like you could finally breathe. Kincaid, you're an empath."

"Is that why my magic never works right?" he asked, eyes wide.

Kendrick frowned. "It shouldn't affect your magic."

Meryn turned to Kincaid. "You are my people. If you ever need to escape, you are welcome to use my Batcave."

Kincaid turned to Meryn. "Thank you. That helps more than you know."

Brie pointed to Carson. "Is he an empath too? Is that why he is barely functioning?"

Ari and Aeson laughed. "No, he's a night owl and detests mornings. He's not even fully awake right now."

Meryn pretended like she was wiping a tear. "Another peep for me." She turned to Izzy. "Can you fix him that black eye thing?"

Izzy popped up. "Absolutely, this makes him one of my people too."

"While my mate is whipping up some caffeine, Portia, will you recap the events that transpired first thing this morning?" Oron asked, nodding to the very put together female holding a quill.

Portia nodded. "This morning, right at dawn, Tyrien Ri'Aileanach along with several members of Founding Families arrived at the palace to register a case of No Confidence regarding the handling of the investigation into the murders of our people." Her eyes cut to the queen before she continued. "Though a case has not been submitted, many have voiced the question of the timing of this atrocity."

Brie couldn't imagine why that'd be a major concern. "What am I missing?"

"Motherfuckers," Meryn growled.

The queen, looking pale and wan, turned to her. "They are implying that my lack of action in the past seven days could have led to the deaths of my people, and had I acted quicker, their loved ones might still be alive."

Brie just laughed. Everyone—except Meryn—was staring at her as if she had lost her mind. "Your Majesty, no offense to you, but you're not a god. From the reports and timelines I have read, you acted very quickly when presented with possible threat to the city."

"But I…"

Brie continued. "You may not have directly had a hand in anything for the first seven days, but Aiden, as Unit Commander, arranged for improved unit training and updated patrols within minutes of the first confirmed sighting of a feral in the city."

"But…"

Brie gentled her tone. "Aleksandra, I'm no expert on paranormal decay, but from the report I read over last night at dinner, in regards to Dr. Rheia Bradley's findings about cellular degradation and how it is slower due to each races' regeneration abilities, I think it's safe to say your people were killed right about the time the shad ows began to appear. There was nothing you could have done."

The queen practically collapsed back in her chair. "Gods, you're right."

Izzy breezed through the door with a tall mug, Cord at her side, carrying a platter of bacon. She immediately went to Carson. "Try this." She set it down in front of him.

Carson blinked up at her and lifted the mug to his lips. He took a sip, shuddered, then began to down the contents of the cup. When he was finished, he looked up at Izzy. "I love you."

Oron stood, growling at the witch. Izzy, however, just nodded. "I know."

"Coffee Goddess has a new acolyte. The empire of Merytopia grows!" Meryn crowed from her seat.

Amelia turned to Meryn. "Empire? I thought you were your own religion now."

Meryn shrugged. "Izzy is a better religion. I will be an Empress instead."

Izzy high-fived Meryn as she walked by, then pulled her mate back down into his chair. "I created a new place of worship at Dav's pub."

Aeson just stared slack-jawed at the women. "How did we go from mass murder, to cellular decay, to Merytopia?"

Aiden shrugged. "Welcome to my world."

Anne pointed to the table. "Meals are kinda always like this."

The queen had a bit more color to her cheeks. "And thank the gods that it is. You girls have given me so much strength," she turned to Brie.

"And your level-headedness has saved me much turmoil."

Meryn snapped her fingers. "If we got Kari and Beth here, we could probably take over the world."

Aiden just nodded and grabbed more bacon.

Even Portia looked a bit more steady on her feet. "If we could get evidence that time of death occurred weeks ago, most of the concerns centering around the case of No Confidence would evaporate."

"I'll call River. He is a vampire that has been working as a Vanguard in Monroe. He is currently heading up the forensic side of this case. I'll see if he has an update," Brie volunteered.

Portia winced. "Could you do it in the next thirty minutes? That's when we go to Tribunal."

Brie pulled out her phone. "Calling now." She sent off a text first, to make River aware she was calling from the queen's chambers and that he would be on speaker. He sent back the devil emoji and answered his phone.

"Hello, Wilson."

"Got anything?"

"Not much, but I do have some information I can pass along."

"Shoot."

"After you requested method and time of death, you piqued my curiosity. I spent all last night running panels."

"Please tell me you got some sleep."

"I will be fine. Anyway, you are on to something. Now, my equipment is nowhere sensitive enough to track rate of decay down to the hour, but I can tell you that, for sure, they all died the same day."

"Any idea when?" That was the big question.

"That is a little more tricky."

"Why?"

"The dead fae look weird under the microscope."

"Is that the technical term?"

He exhaled. "Look, science and the paranormal world are not the best bedfellows. If I had to determine when a human died, I could easily give you a time, down to almost the minute, because humans decompose the same across the board. Circumstances and environment may change up the numbers, but for the most part, they are identical. Paranormals, on the other hand, are a shake-n-bake bag full of different herbs and spices."

"I like him," Meryn whispered.

River laughed and continued. "If it were a group of vampires, I would just tell you that it was a lost cause. Vampire decomposition times are wildly different due to varying levels of transition. We are in luck since the group was all one race, and they were fae. Now, here is where it gets weird, like I told you. They are decomposing way slower than a human, but faster than any fae I have seen under a microscope."

"How?" she asked.

"You tell me," he countered.

She looked around and saw varying degrees

of confusion and consternation. "Shit. Can you give me a ballpark for time of death?"

"Over a week for sure. Any more detailed than that, I am not going to be able to help you without brand new equipment."

Meryn leaned forward. "What kind of equipment?"

"Oh, gee, I do not know, how about the XB540?"

"The one with nanoscale and 3D imaging?" Meryn asked.

"How in the hell do you know that?" River demanded.

"Muwahahaha! I just arranged for some of those to be delivered to Noctem Falls for Magnus' center of healing. How quick can you pack a bag?"

"Fuck clothes! Get me to that workstation," River begged.

"Only if you promise to loop Dr. Rheia Bradley-Albright in on your findings. She has been working on a project documenting different rates of decay regarding ferals and reapers."

"Seriously? There's an existing project working on that?" Brennus asked, looking impressed.

Meryn turned to her uncle. "Unit warrior mates aren't slacking."

"Please, get me to Noctem Falls! I am packing specimens now," River's voice had taken on a desperate tone.

"I will personally call Magnus and request you be given any and all materials you need to get as much information regarding these murders as possible," the queen promised.

"Your Majesty, you could bend me over and spank my ass as long as I got a chance at that microscope," River said, then went quiet. "Let us all forget I said that; I have been alone in my lab too long."

Meryn was laughing hysterically at her aunt's expression. "That was awesome!"

Darian was chuckling as he used his ring to open a portal. "Keep your pants on, River, I'm on my way," he teased.

"Gods above, shoot me now," River whispered.

"Update me the second you get something," Brie said, putting the man out of his misery.

"Sure thing, Wilson. Gotta go." River disconnected before she could say anything. She turned to the queen. "He didn't mean anything by it."

The queen simply waved off her concerns. "Being around Meryn, I have learned to value individuality that leads to genius over manners that lead nowhere."

Meryn thought about it. "That's good, right?"

The queen smiled at her niece. "It's a very good thing, especially at my age. The older paranormals get, the more we tend to get set in our ways. I swear just being around you for a week or so has helped me so much."

"Will he be able to submit an official report so that we can present it to the Tribunal?" Portia asked.

Brie nodded. "If I know him, he's already sent

the Sheriff his findings. I'll have Rathais forward them to me." She sent a text off to her boss requesting the official preliminary report.

Portia exhaled slightly. "That alone should quiet most concerns."

"I want a list of names of those who are 'concerned'," Meryn requested, her eyes narrowing.

Around the table a chorus of "No, Meryn," was heard from nearly everyone. Brie caught it, only because she was still looking at Portia, but the prim fae inclined her head slightly to Meryn, before turning to the queen. "I will get everyone seated. We should have this wrapped before lunch."

Brie's phone pinged. "Portia, can I forward this to you?"

Portia nodded. "That would be greatly appreciated. I can print and have these documents ready in twenty minutes." Brie handed the fae her phone so that she could input her email and then forwarded the reports on to her. Portia opened the document on her phone, scrolled, then nodded. "I will see you all at Tribunal."

"We shouldn't have to go at all," Brennus grumbled, his arm wrapped around his mate.

Brie shrugged. "They are scared and hurting. I would have been surprised if we didn't receive pushback of some kind."

"They are pulling us away from getting any work done," Ari countered.

"True, but you can't change emotions. It's actually a blessing in disguise that they acted so quickly in bringing their concerns forward.

We can address each item, reiterate what we're doing, and send them on their way. Moving forward, you can always say, 'as we previously discussed', and squash incidents before they blow up."

Meryn tapped her lips with her finger. "So, basically, we're pre-telling them fuck off?"

Brie winked. "Something like that."

"Me likey. I wonder if Beth knows about pre-emptive fuck offs."

The queen chuckled. "That child was raised in Noctem Falls; she can do that in multiple languages, my dear."

"Then why hasn't she told me about that method yet?"

"Probably because you're still learning subtlety and finesse," Law suggested.

Meryn sighed. "It'd be so much easier if we could just shoot people."

"You'll get there, baby," Aiden said encouragingly.

Ari turned to Cord. "We hate to bother you, but we left the warrior villa before breakfast. Is there anything pre-made we could have?"

Cord stared at Ari in horror. "Pre-made? You mean like those small meals wrapped in plastic?" he shuddered. "Give me five minutes." He raced toward the kitchen.

Meryn looked at her plate and sighed. "I bet he brings you fruit."

Ari grinned. "Shifters get served more eggs and bacon," he pointed to Aiden's plate.

Meryn stared, looking shocked. "It's so simple.

Why didn't I think of it?" She reached over and dragged Aiden's plate in front of her, causing his mouth to drop. "Real food." Meryn lifted two pieces of bacon and shoved them in her mouth.

When Aiden reached for a piece of bacon, she picked up a blueberry and flicked it at him, hitting his forehead. "You eat that and be 'healthy for the baby'."

"Meryn," he said, reaching for the bacon again.

Meryn hunched over her plate and growled at her mate. "My bacon!"

Cord walked into the room, chuckling as he pushed a service cart behind Ari. "Little Meryn, if you didn't want any more fruit, all you had to do was tell me," he chided

Meryn shrugged. "I didn't want to appear non-fae cuz I wasn't raised here."

Cord just melted on the spot. "You order whatever you are craving for you and your baby, and I will make it, and if anyone has the audacity to say anything because of your food choices, I'll see to it personally."

Meryn smiled shyly. "Then can I have a huge burger for lunch?"

Cord nodded. "Of course. I will have one waiting for you when you get back."

"Kickass!"

Aiden turned to Ryuu. "Why didn't you serve her meat? Don't tell me you didn't know that she was sick of fruit."

Ryuu looked down at Aiden, a slightly disgruntled look on his face. "Don't be ridiculous, of course I knew. The reason I didn't serve her anything different was because she didn't ask for it."

In that moment, Brie understood squires a bit more. Had Ryuu simply given Meryn what she wanted, he would have overridden and ignored Meryn's wish to fit in. He respected her enough to give her the space to figure things out on her own.

Aiden sighed. "No matter how important one gets or how high one climbs in our world, there will always be a squire right behind us that is smarter, more capable, and sarcastic prodding us along like toddlers at recess."

The queen laughed. "I'm not too arrogant to say I could have never made it this far without Cord."

Aiden smiled. "Marius practically raised me and my brothers."

Ryuu's expression was priceless, as he realized that Aiden basically just admitted to everyone that he saw the squire as smarter and more capable than himself. "It is our duty, and mostly our delight, to serve those that make a difference." He looked down at his charge smiling softly. "Even if they do need to be nudged here and there like a toddler at recess."

Meryn shrugged. "Nudge away, just keep feeding me."

Ryuu inclined his head. "Yes, *denka*."

Brie turned as she saw Kincaid lean toward Ari. "Do we really have to attend the Tribunal?"

Ari sighed then nodded. "Unfortunately. As Tau has close ties to the palace, we have witnessed every aspect of the unfolding investigation." He eyed his unit brother in sympathy. "I will speak for us as much as I can."

Kincaid slumped back. "I hate this."

Kendrick sipped his water. "With River's report, it should move quickly. It will mostly be Aleksandra along with Darian and Meryn, reassuring the Founding Family members."

Meryn blinked. "Wait, I hafta go too?"

Everyone nodded as the queen turned to her. "Yes, my dear. You're a princess now."

Brie watched as all color drained from Meryn's face. Meryn looked up at Ryuu. "I can't do this," she whispered, as she began to shake.

Ryuu blinked, then his eyebrows shot up. "Meryn, calm down." He quickly snatched up her wrist as both Thane and Kendrick jumped to their feet.

Kendrick rounded the table. "Ryuu? What's wrong?"

"Her heart is racing out of control."

Kendrick pulled Meryn's chair away from the table, and Ryuu stepped back with it, still keeping one hand around her wrist. On Meryn's other side, Aiden held her free hand and rubbed it soothingly.

"Meryn, you need to take a deep breath in and let it out slowly. On my count," Thane said, kneeling in front of her.

Meryn's eyes were wide as she shook her head. "I can't."

"You can," he repeated softly.

"What is wrong with her?" Brie heard Gage ask Ari.

She turned to them. "A serious panic attack."

Brennus and the queen looked on, both looking distraught. The queen looked up at her mate. "I didn't mean to upset her."

Brennus kissed the top of her head. "I don't believe it was you, dearest heart. I think she only just realized that she is now a princess."

"But we've been saying that she's second in line for the throne. Hell, she even threatened to take over. How could she not know?" Justice asked, looking upset at Meryn's distress.

"Because to Meryn, becoming second in line to the throne just meant she had family now," Amelia whispered. "That's all she cared about."

Brie turned her attention back to Meryn as the blue light began to grow brighter. Ryuu leaned down. "Listen to me, *denka*, I swear it on my life, that you will never be forced to do anything that you don't wish to do. If you do choose to take an active role as princess, I will be with you every step of the way. I will not let you fail," he promised.

Meryn finally took a deep breath and slumped backward. It was as if her body had been waiting on Ryuu's assurances to finally relax.

Meryn rotated both of her hands and clutched at her mate and squire. "Please don't let me embarrass anyone," she begged in a small voice.

Kendrick stood, his face etched in anger. "Embarrass anyone and everyone, Meryn, whether intentionally or not. I have spells no one has seen in thousands of years to deal with any puffed up self-important Muppet that tries to hurt you because of it."

"The things I will be doing to him later," Anne murmured. She blushed furiously when she realized everyone turning to look her way had heard what she said.

Meryn's face had a ghost of a smile. "That was seriously cool," she agreed. She let go of Ryuu's sleeve, then practically climbed into Aiden's lap. The large shifter wrapped his arms around her, until only her face and legs were somewhat visible. "Kendrick will only be able to play with whatever scraps remain after I deal with any who hurts my mate."

"That's if Aiden gets to them before me," Thane threatened.

Meryn was now grinning at the absurdity of the testosterone in the room. "I love you guys," she said, looking from Kendrick to Thane. Both witches looked as if you could knock them over with a feather.

Thane cleared his throat. "I love you too," he said gruffly. "After all, you're my godsdaughter."

"She loved me first as her big-brother cousin," Kendrick pointed out.

Thane turned until they were bumping chests. "Don't strain yourself, old man."

Kendrick began to sputter in indignation. "Old man!"

Behind them, Anne was laughing with Just

ice and Law. He wheeled on his mate. "Don't encourage him."

"Cradle robber," she teased.

Kendrick tried to keep up the offended façade, but Meryn's giggles had his mouth twitching. "I am overly abused."

"You like it, mannequin," Meryn said, causing the Ashleigh brothers to abandon any pretense of decorum and laugh loudly.

"Anne, quit telling Meryn our bedroom secrets," Kendrick exclaimed, causing his mate to choke on her drink.

The door opened, and Portia walked in. She looked at the scene before her and simply sighed. "They're ready for you."

Meryn hopped off Aiden's lap. "We got this," she said, before looking back at her squire.

He nodded. "Yes, we do."

CHAPTER EIGHT

A S THEY WALKED TOWARD THE large assembly hall, Brie watched as Meryn's sweats and hoodie become a gorgeous set of golden robes. Her normally whacky curls were slicked back, and crown of silver and gold encircled her head. Meryn really was worried about causing trouble for her family.

The entire group waited at the large set of ivory doors until trumpets echoed through the halls, heralding the queen's arrival. Two by two, their party entered the room and took seats along one side of a raised dais where the queen and Brennus' thrones sat front and center. Flanking them on either side were two smaller thrones. Darian accepted Meryn's hand from Aiden and escorted her to one throne, before returning to his own. To Brennus' left, a panel of four men sat, including Jedrek. She could only assume it was the city's council. They all sat when the queen did.

Portia stepped forward. "Her Majesty, Queen Aleksandra Vi' ÉirDan will now hear the concerns brought forward by Tyrien Ri'Aileanach and Seluden Li'Loudain from our Founding Families." She nodded to Tyrien. "You may approach the throne."

There was nothing in her voice that was rude. In fact, she sounded extremely neutral, but the way Tyrien flinched, you'd think she was calling him out on an embarrassing accident in front of the class. He strode forward.

"Your Majesty, thank you for seeing us today. Having only just returned to our fair city, I myself and others are incredibly concerned over recent changes in regards to your succession decree. We feel as if such changes are indicative of more deeply rooted problems that may have led to many of our people being murdered senselessly."

Brennus raised a brow. "Are you saying that by decreeing that our son is the next rightful heir, my mate caused the deaths of her beloved children?"

"Of course not. Our concerns lie not with the decree itself, just the timing. Mayhap, she was distracted by events surrounding her son and missed evidence of a growing hostile faction." His eyes darted to where Meryn sat. "After all, discovering that you have human niece could bewilder anyone."

Meryn smiled. "Tyrien, have you met Portia Kilardin or Cord Danual?"

Tyrien sneered up at her. "I haven't had the pleasure."

Meryn giggled, throwing Brie for a loop, Meryn was not a giggler. "How silly of me, besides this Tribunal, why would you have reason to enter the Royal Palace." She waved her hand in front of her. "If you had the chance to meet either of these amazing individuals, you would have known how inane your concerns were. Neither Portia or Cord would ever allow my aunt to become distracted to the point of negligence." She gasped as her small hands went to her mouth. "Is it because you don't have a squire that you didn't realize how marvelous they truly are?" She turned to the queen and, in a whisper that could clearly be heard by everyone, she asked. "Do Founding Families not use squires here?"

The queen's face was a mask of politeness, but having spent time with her, Brie knew she had to be laughing on the inside. She turned to her niece. "Many Founding Families employ squires here in Éire Danu, Meryn."

Meryn face screwed up in confusion. "Then I don't see why he was so concerned."

Despite the severity of the situation, small titters were heard around the room as Tyrien's face darkened to an unhealthy shade of red.

"Whether or not my house employs a squire is irrelevant."

Meryn tilted her head. "You missed the point, didn't you?"

Brennus chuckled. "He did, sweet Meryn, but the others have not."

"Oh. Good." She sat back, smiling.

Portia's cheeks were still glowing from Meryn's praise when she turned to the room. "To speed things along, I will ask that Deputy Brie Wilson, mate to Ari Lionhart of House Lionhart, step forward and present what we currently know as fact in regards to our peoples' deaths."

Brie froze. Had she known she was going to be presenting she would have worn her own robes. Standing, she walked over to where Portia stood; the woman handed her a portfolio and stepped back. Inside were most of the notes they had gone over the night before.

"Ladies and gentleman, as Portia said, my name is Brie Wilson. Until very recently, I worked under Cameron Rathais, a Vanguard warrior, serving as Sheriff in Monroe." Brie knew that Rathais being a paranormal would carry weight here. "Yesterday afternoon, Sheriff Rathais received a call from the Unit Commander to immediately come to a warehouse to secure and process the scene of a gruesome mass murder. As there are family members in attendance, I will spare you the more grisly details, but from the multiple conversations I overheard from the warriors there, it was one of the worst things they had ever seen, and considering their mission is to hunt and kill ferals, their statements brought home just how terrible the scene was." She prayed she was using all these new terms correctly. She flipped open the portfolio as if she were reviewing the notes. In actuality, she was trying to organize her thoughts.

"I will only present what we know to be fact. Seventy-two bodies of varying ages were recovered. The bodies were all placed together in the warehouse that had been spelled so that the deaths of the individuals didn't register with family trees in Éire Danu. The medical examiner, River Carlisle, a vampire and also a member of the Vanguard, was the one who worked meticulously in gathering every piece of evidence he could. He has determined that the time of death for these poor souls was well over a week ago and prior to the emergence of the shadow portal that appeared outside the Border City." She looked up from the notes to peer out at the crowd. "I haven't been in your world long, but I can tell you unequivocally that Queen Aleksandra would never become so engrossed in something that she would lose sight of her children."

Tyrien pointed to her. "Another point made by the lady herself. She hasn't even been in Éire Danu twenty-four hours. How could she possibly know what is best for us." He looked over to where her mate sat with the Tau and Chi units. "Her own mate is the youngest warrior to serve in Éire Danu. That was fine as the warriors played soldier, but now that we have a *real* threat looming against us, we need *real* warriors to stand in defense of our people."

Brie shifted her hand to her gun's hilt and felt a small surge of satisfaction when he stepped back. "I am the least qualified to respond to that drivel." She turned to Aiden. "Unit Commander, would you like to address these fine people?"

Aiden stood, his face a large scowl. He stepped up beside her and faced the crowd. "As you all know, I am the Unit Commander and have been for hundreds of years. I take my duty seriously, so if anyone believes that I have no idea what I am doing and that the men I train are useless, please see me after the Tribunal," he said, in short clipped tones. "Every single warrior that serves, has my complete confidence, regardless of age." He eyed Tyrien. "Some things such as loyalty, sacrifice, and skill cannot be bought."

Ouch! That one had to sting, she thought gleefully.

She looked at the crowd, who was visibly shrinking back from the angered commander and smiled. "What it boils down to folks is this: Either you believe your queen to be a flake that lets her children die and that your Unit Commander is an incompetent fool that has no idea what he is doing, or you can believe that these two leaders with impeccable track records are doing the very best they can, in the first twenty-four hours of a tragedy. A case of No Confidence is positively ridiculous when the persons you're stating you have no confidence in hasn't had a chance to do anything yet." As Aiden took his seat, Brie was certain she could have heard a pin drop, then low murmurs filled the room.

Portia raised her hand, and everyone quieted. "As usual, everyone here has a voice and will be heard. If you truly feel as if your concerns have not been addressed please stand. It's why we're all here today."

No one stood, which left Tyrien the only one on his feet as he was the one addressing the Tribunal. "Well, Tyrien Ri'Aileanach, have you anything else to bring forward?" Portia asked sweetly.

"Not at this time," he answered, through clenched teeth.

"Very well." She turned to Jedrek. "If you would?"

Her father-in-law stood. "I declare this case of No Confidence to be resolved and the Tribunal session closed." As one, the queen and Brennus stood, followed by Meryn and Darian and everyone began to file out.

Aiden held out his arm, and he escorted her back to Ari's side. Ari placed her hand in his elbow, and they followed the party back to the queen's personal chambers.

☾

Upon walking in, Brie didn't expect to find Amelia holding Meryn in a headlock, raking her knuckles across her scalp. "Were you trying to kill us?! Do you have any idea how hard it was not to laugh?"

"Get offa me, Amelia. I was just doing politics," Meryn complained, pushing at her cousin.

The queen collapsed into a chair. "I thought for sure I wasn't going to make it." She eyed her niece. "And she just kept going."

Brennus just sat back, a huge smile on his face. "Gods, she reminds me of Eamon."

Celyn nodded. "He lived to see assholes squirm."

Meryn pushed a final time at Amelia. "See! It's in my DNA."

Brie looked around. "Speaking of fathers, where's mine?"

Brennus and Celyn both turned a bit pink in the cheeks. Finally, Brennus spoke up. "Doran has been waiting thousands of years to meet his mate. We may not see them for a while."

Cord cleared his throat. "Doran placed several standing orders for food for the next couple days."

"Days!" Brie exclaimed.

"I learned about the butt sex in Noctem Falls; you better send lube, too, Cord," Meryn added.

Cord gave a short nod. "You have a valid point, Meryn. I'll see to it they have everything they need."

"Eww! Blalalalalalalala!" Brie yelled, toppling to one side on the chaise lounge, pulling a pillow over her head.

Beside her, she could feel Ari laughing at her distress. She popped back up. "It's not funny."

"Their souls have become one and neither are alone anymore. I don't think there's anything wrong with that."

"I love the fact that they're not alone anymore, but I don't need to hear about the becoming one stuff."

Meryn turned in her chair to face the queen. "Did that seem too easy?"

The queen thought about it a moment. "Yes and no. You took the wind out of Tyrien's sails regarding the 'no confidence' in me. The proof that those poor people died before things started happening here in the city was just icing on the cake after your little show." She eyed Meryn. "I never would have thought to use Portia and Cord as a type of defense. Truly amazing, Meryn."

Meryn shrugged. "I had just had a mini meltdown, and Ryuu helped me. I figured had you truly been up shits creek, Portia and Cord could easily run stuff for ya, even if we weren't here." She picked up her laptop and powered it on.

"So eloquent and so true," Portia said dryly.

"Brie was just as amazing," Jedrek bragged. "My daughter, with one play, eliminated every doubt the people may have had about my son and the other warriors." The look of pride on his face warmed her. "That was a power play, my dear, a very effective one."

"It was partially calculated. Honestly, I was trying not to shoot the bastard, and I wanted to give Aiden the advantage in case he had to reach out and love tap someone," Brie admitted.

"I'm an expert at accidental brilliance too," Meryn said, giving her a thumbs up.

Aiden just smiled at her. "I *was* trying to figure out how close I had to be to reach that mouthy sycophant."

"We can always summon him back," Brennus offered. "Then you and Ari could show him personally how well trained Éire Danu's warriors are."

"Don't tempt me," Aiden said sourly.

"Hey, babe," Meryn said, turning to her grumbling mate.

His face brightened. "Yeah?"

She pointed down to her laptop. "I think I may have a second location."

The room quieted. Aiden stood to look over her shoulder. "Where?"

"Georgetown. It's about four-hundred miles south of here, close to Dover, Delaware."

Aiden looked at Ari, then at her. "Gear up."

Ari turned and looked down at her. At first, she thought he would argue for her to stay behind, but his expression was thoughtful. "Kincaid, see if she fits any of your Kevlar."

"You got it," Kincaid said, rising from his chair to stand next to the other warriors.

Kendrick turned to Thane. "I'll go. You stay behind and manage the portal and transport."

Thane shook his head. "No can do. You're staying behind and managing the portal while Justice and I tag along." Kendrick scowled and opened his mouth to argue when Thane looked at Anne. "Tell him to sit and stay."

Anne was smiling. "Darling, let the boys handle this one."

Kendrick looked at his mate incredulously. "What?"

She just smiled sweetly. "You know why you shouldn't go, now sit tight and let them do their job."

Kendrick's mouth just dropped as he looked around the room for some measure of support. Finally, the queen pointed to the chair across from her. "Welcome to my hell. Maybe, if you get frustrated enough with not knowing what is going on, you'll create a way for us to monitor our loved ones from here."

Brie felt like she was missing something huge. Of anyone, Kendrick seemed like the obvious choice to go. She watched the large witch as he basically threw himself into the chair. "If I am to stay behind, I require treats and snacks."

Anne sighed. "What are you, five?"

Meryn looked up at her squire. "Actually, snacks are a good idea. I'm going to be paving the way for them, so I needs foods."

Ryuu met Cord's eye, and they both nodded. Ryuu looked down at his charge. "Anything in particular you need, *denka*?"

"Meat kebobs," was the immediate answer.

"Bobs!!" A tiny voice shouted excitedly. Brie's heart melted every time she saw the tiny brownie. When she was first introduced to Creelee and Meryn's sprites, she decided right then and there, that no matter what evil she faced in the paranormal world, meeting those adorable beings made it worth it the danger.

Izzy rubbed his curls with her finger. "I'm sure Meryn will share Creelee."

Meryn winked. "Of course, he's my eating buddy."

Ryuu placed a gloved hand over his chest. "I will contact Sebastian immediately."

Darian glanced from Aiden to Ryuu, looking torn.

"I am fully capable of opening a portal to Noctem Falls, son, you go with your commander and help our people," the queen said to Darian.

He stood then walked over to her chair. He bent down and placed a kiss on her forehead. "Thank you, Mother."

"Aiden," Ari called out, getting the commander's attention. When Aiden turned, he continued. "We're heading to the warrior villa to get our gear. Did you want to roll out with Tau and Chi?"

"Sounds good. You all were slated to attend the Tribunal through this afternoon, so the other units are already covering for your absence."

"We can trade with Upsilon, if you'd prefer an older unit," Kincaid offered quietly.

Aiden frowned. "Older doesn't necessarily mean better. My mate is the youngest amongst us, but it's because she's so young that she sees things from a fresh perspective, without which, we would have probably lost Lycaonia and Noctem Falls. To be honest, I'm seriously thinking about finding ways to incorporate younger trainees into the units so that we get a jolt of curiosity and questioning that older warriors have lost."

With each word Aiden spoke, Brie could see the change in the Tau unit, including Ari. Each man stood a bit straighter and held his head up a bit more. "Youth is about all I have going for me with my spells going sideways all the time. But I'll do whatever is needed to help my brothers," Kincaid offered.

Aiden nodded. "Good man!"

Ari turned to the Tau and Chi units before taking her hand. "Let's go get our gear." He looked over his shoulder at Thane and Aiden. "We'll meet you at the official portal."

Feeling excited and a bit nervous, Brie walked out with the other warriors.

Ari couldn't believe what Aiden had said. He viewed their age as an advantage?

"Wow," Kincaid breathed.

"I know," Ari replied.

"What?" Brie asked, looking up at him with her warm brown eyes.

"In the paranormal world, especially in Éire Danu, age means a lot. For Aiden to have that mindset, is a drastic turn from our normal," he explained.

"Don't forget, Aiden is considered young himself at only seven-hundred and change. Many forget that fact since he's been leading the units since he was practically an infant," Aeson reminded them.

"Infant?" Brie asked.

"He was one-hundred years old when he took over the units, that's when a paranormal is considered an adult."

"Yikes! I see what you mean about ages playing a role in your society."

"I think his own experiences and mating with Meryn, who has made changes left and right, has reshaped his way of thinking." Ari felt excitement and a bit of hope begin to flicker in his chest. Things were changing and changing for the better. He had so many ideas to improve the units. Prior to Aiden visiting Éire Danu, he never would have dreamed he could approach Aiden and voice them. Now, especially after what was just said, he felt like he would be heard and taken seriously despite his age.

Brie lightly kicked Aeson in the ass. "Is infant a derogatory term here in Éire Danu?"

Aeson looked back, surprised. "Of course not, but young is young. We may baby Ari and the Tau unit, but we respect them too. They are the ranking unit in the city because of how good they are. We follow Ari's lead because he has proven he can think outside the box and moves us all forward."

Ramsey chuckled. "Being a Lionhart helps too."

Aeson shrugged. "It gives him a slight edge that he understands the city's politics, but even before the shadows appeared Ari was creating new drills and training methods, that has nothing to do with his family's politics."

Ari was flabbergasted. All these years he assumed they were humoring him, to hear that they actually respected his hard work was humbling. "I just want us to be the best we can."

Ramsey reached out and ruffled his hair. "Which is why we follow you."

Ari exchanged glances with Gage, Priest, and Kincaid. He could see the visible changes in them already in response to Aeson's words. There was no hesitancy in their steps now. They had received a major dose of confidence, and it showed.

"Let's grab our gear and go, gentlemen. Our Unit Commander is waiting."

"Yes, sir," his brothers responded, and they hurried through the Border City to the warrior villa.

CHAPTER NINE

❡

STANDING NEXT TO THEIR VEHICLE, in the human realm, Ari had to admit his mate looked hot. Her jeans hugged her ass perfectly, and when you added the Kevlar vest and tactical gear, she morphed into a warrior goddess.

"Stop that," she complained, her cheeks bright red.

"What?" he asked.

"Ari, you keep staring at her like you're about to make her your next meal and growling non-stop," Priest advised him, amusement in his voice.

Ari paused. "I am?"

"You are," the men around him replied.

"I can't help it; look at her." He motioned to Brie. When the men turned to look at his mate, his lion roared. He growled loudly. The men just looked at him and rolled their eyes.

"Sorry," he said sighing.

Brie, on the other hand, was laughing into her hand.

"You find my caveman routine funny?"

"I like that you find me attractive decked out

in SWAT gear, are proud enough to show me off, possessive enough to warn them away, yet secure enough in your masculinity to apologize for such a display."

Ari narrowed his eyes. "So, a good thing, right?"

She walked over and wrapped her arms around his neck. "A very good thing."

Ari heard many of the men mutter 'lucky fuck' and 'bastard', and he couldn't help grinning. "Fate has truly blessed me with such a beautiful and fierce woman."

Brie pulled his head down for a kiss, and he happily obliged. One of the things he had noticed about his mate yesterday was that her plump lips were soft every time he kissed her. He couldn't get enough.

A throat cleared. "Brie, when you're done scrambling Ari's brain, can you huddle in for orders?" Aiden asked, walking up to where the units waited by the portal. Ari noticed that Micah, Darian, Oron, Thane, and Justice were with him.

His mate pulled back and winked up at him. "Yes, sir," she said and walked over to receive orders.

Ari felt like he was stuck on stupid. Why were they leaving again? He felt hands on his back as Gage steered him over to the meeting.

Aiden looked at the group. "We'll do a three-prong attack again. Tau, you're assigned the back. Chi, the westerly side exit, and my group will go in the front." He tapped his earpiece.

"Were you able to hack the closed camera surveillance circuit yet?" he asked.

Meryn's voice responded in their ears. "Yup, I have good news and bad news."

Aiden rolled his eyes. "Good news first, Menace."

"Good news is I don't see anyone in the building."

Aiden exhaled. "That's great. What's the bad news?"

"Bad news is that the camera mounted in the main storage room is black. Not staticky. Black. With a faint glow around the edges. I'm willing to bet it's been painted."

Every single person in their group began to cuss, including his mate.

"Sonofabitch," she murmured.

"We're heading in, baby. Let me know if our situation changes."

"Will do. By the way, I overrode their security system, so all the doors should be unlocked, and no alarms will sound," she added.

"You take such good care of me," Aiden said.

"It's because you're really good with your penis," she answered, causing more than one of men to choke on their own spit as they inhaled a laugh.

Aiden closed his eyes as a flush worked up the back of his neck. "Thank you, babe."

"Menace is out," Meryn replied.

Aiden opened his eyes. "Move out."

Ari led his men around to the back of the building. Knowing that Meryn was monitoring their advancement and suppressing any alarms was huge. He reached forward and pulled on the door; it opened with ease. He looked back at his unit, and they grinned back at him. He could really get used to this. Quietly, they made their way through the halls that smelled like lemon disinfectant. He heard movement to their right as Aeson, leading Chi, appeared in the hallway, coming in from the west.

They had almost made it to the main storage room when they heard a deafening roar. He and Aeson took point and ran to the door that led to the front of building. Despite wanting to run through, he held up his fist. He pointed to Aeson who peeked through the cracked doorway. When the older fae spun around and slid down the hallway wall, Ari knew what they'd find.

"Gage, stay with Aeson, the rest of you are with me," he ordered.

He opened the door and led them into the large, mostly empty room. Along one wall, Aiden's team formed a semi-circle around a stack of bodies. They walked up. "Sir, did you need me to call Rathais?" Brie asked.

Aiden nodded. "He and River will need to head thru the portal, then on to the palace…"

"I'll get them," Darian said quietly, walking away from the pile. "If I go, I can bring them directly back here, and they can start processing the scene sooner."

Ari had never seen Darian look so broken. Oron walked up behind his brother. "I'll go with them. Darian can drop me off at the palace so I can update the queen in person, then he can pick me up to bring me back here."

Darian shook his head. "No. I'll drop you off, but you need to stay with the queen. This is going to kill her."

Oron looked torn. Every warrior knew that there were no two people that Oron loved more than his mother and baby brother. "Are you sure, Dari?"

Darian took a deep breath. "Yes. It's time we started protecting her for a change."

Oron looked around the room. "Where's Aeson?"

"I'm here," the warrior said, walking in with Gage.

Oron looked over at Darian then back. "I'm leaving him in your care."

"I give you my word that nothing will happen to our prince," Aeson promised.

Aiden scowled at Oron but didn't say anything. Ari knew that the commander wanted to add that he wouldn't let anything happen to his own unit brother, but by not saying anything, he acknowledged that the request was just as much to help Aeson as it was to protect Darian.

Brie approached, tucking her phone back into her vest. "He said they'd be ready by the time you got there."

Aiden waved Thane over. "I'm assuming there's a barrier."

Thane nodded. "It's identical to the one we saw in Monroe."

Aiden looked over at the pile. "Considering the reaction we got in Éire Danu last time, let's wait until we have processed the scene and transported the bodies before we take it down."

Thane eyed the walls. "That works. I want to study this a bit more as well."

Ari and Brie stared down at the dead. He immediately noticed a difference. "They haven't been dead long," he observed.

Brie pointed to one arm. "There's barely any bloating."

"The sooner River can get here and begin documentation, the better," Aiden said, sounding tired.

As soon as River arrived, he began to bark out orders, getting the men organized. He, along with the rest of the warriors in gloved hands, began to unstack the dead. It took them hours to get the bodies photographed and into the black body bags. Every once in a while, his mate would pass by wielding an impressive looking camera. She took pictures of everything, paying special attention to the ceiling and the marks on the floor.

When they were done, all but Aiden's group and the Tau unit had made their way back through the portal to Éire Danu. Ari stayed behind because he wanted Kincaid to watch Thane and Justice in action. He might not be a witch, but he knew that opportunities to work with these legends didn't happen all that often.

A few seconds after the barrier went down, Aiden's phone rang.

"It happened again," Meryn reported in a small voice.

Ari couldn't even fathom the confusion and pain that would be running rampant in the city tonight. He sent up his prayer of thanks that his family was alive and safe.

Aiden turned to Darian. "Let's head back."

Darian was already using his signet ring to open a portal. They stepped through, and Ari felt a wave of relief that he had brought them directly to the palace. He didn't want to walk through the streets tonight.

"Where's Mother?" Darian asked, glancing around the room the moment they walked through.

Brennus looked up at them from where he sat in an oversized chair holding a goblet of gold liquid. "Anne, Amelia, Meryn, and Izzy took over the bedroom. They have Aleks cocooned in blankets, eating chocolate and watching some sort of cartoons to help her feel better."

Aiden accepted a similar goblet from Cord. "That method has proven to be very effective in helping females recover from traumatic situations."

Ari sat next to his brother. He pulled Brie down to sit on his other side. "How'd it go in the city?" he asked.

"The queen did a general announcement prior to the barrier going down, so the people weren't completely blindsided again. Though it did nothing to lessen the grief of the family members of the recently discovered." Rex leaned back to squeeze Brie's shoulder. "How are you holding up?"

Brie placed her hand over his and smiled. "Actually, I'm much better today than I was yesterday…was it yesterday? God, it feels like we've been handling this for weeks."

Rex gave a final squeeze then sat up. "I know what you mean. The past forty-eight hours has aged us all."

Ari looked at his mate. "Not that I'm not ecstatic that you're doing well, but how?"

Brie shrugged. "Part of the job mostly. Yesterday threw me for a loop because I wasn't expecting to walk in on a mass murder scene. Today, I was kinda expecting it." She nodded her head to Darian, Brennus, and Oron. "Plus, I have some distance from the situation. I didn't even knew fae existed yesterday morning, and I have no loved ones amongst the dead. It helps me to process."

Brennus turned to his mate. "You all should head home and get some rest. We start assigning warriors tomorrow to help process the dead. You won't be missing anything by having dinner at home." He grinned sadly. "Besides, Leo has all but threatened to come here and drag the two of you back by the ear if you don't show up."

Ari exchanged quick glances with his brother, and they both stood. "We'll take our leave," Rex said, inclining his head.

Once standing, Ari wrapped an arm around Brie. "We'll swing by the warrior villa to get your robes. Leo will ensure your clothes get washed tonight."

Brie laid her head against his shoulder. "I could use another bath," she said, rubbing her face on his arm.

Gods, she was adorable!

"Of course, sweetheart." None of them had actually handled the dead, that had been the other units, but being in the same room with those poor souls made him want to wash away the cloud of sadness that followed them back from the warehouse.

Walking back to the estate, Ari wondered how many confrontations they avoided by having his brother with them. As a unit warrior, the citizens were used to walking up to him and the other warriors to start conversations, but an Elder wasn't as approachable.

At the warrior villa, the men gave them some space while Brie ran up the stairs to grab their things.

"Thank you for waiting for us," he said to his brother.

Rex bumped his shoulder. "I figured it was the least I could do to help. You and Brie have done so much to organize and investigate these horrors. Truth be told, I'm feeling quite useless."

Ari stared at his older brother. To him, Rex could do no wrong. "Rex, simply having you home and assisting helps more than you know. Our people and the fae adore you."

Rex smiled warmly. "I'm just glad I could be here for you."

Ari ducked his head. "Thanks." It was no secret to anyone that Rex was his hero.

As Brie was coming down the stairs, Balder walked up from the back of the villa where the kitchen was. He handed him a flat pan. "Broden made these for you this morning when we came off shift and heard what was going on. You can leave your gear in the foyer, I'll get it put away," he offered.

Ari sniffed, and his mouth began to water. In all their family, only Broden had managed to master their great-grandmother's recipe for Sun Brownies—a mix between a lemon bar and a blondie; they were the best of both of them in one pan.

"Gods love my cousin."

Rex whimpered and Ari smiled. "Of course, I'll share with you."

His brother smiled at him. "I have the best baby brothers in the whole world."

"What smells amazing?" Brie practically had her dainty nose against the foil.

"Sun Brownies, family specialty. We'll have them after dinner."

Brie licked her lips. "Maybe a small piece…"

Ari hugged the pan to his chest. "No. After dinner."

Rex sighed. "Might as well give up, Brie, he's an absolute stickler when it comes to food. To him dessert is after a meal."

Brie leveled a look at him. "He can do whatever he wants, but if I make or buy dessert and want them before dinner or even as dinner, that's what's gonna happen."

Ari stared at his mate. "But, that's not right."

"I'll even have popcorn for dinner," Brie continued.

He stared at his mate in horror. "No, you need a balanced meal."

Rex chuckled. "Let's go see what balanced meal Leo has whipped up."

Ari nodded. His brother was a genius. Once Brie saw the amazing meal Leo had made for them, she'd understand how important eating a nutritious meal is. "Excellent idea."

He carefully carried his pan of precious brownies on the other side of his body from where Brie held his hand. He was so preoccupied with his dessert, the walk to the Lionhart estate was over before he realized it.

Leo greeted them at the door. "Thank the gods you boys and little Brie are home." He held out his hands to his mate. She looked up at him, and he nodded to her bag of clothes. She handed them off to him. "I'll get these washed up for you in no time." He leveled a look in his direction. "Though, it may be best if she were able to get a few of her things and change of clothes from her home so that she isn't stuck wearing the same thing for days on end."

She smiled. "I'm used to wearing a uniform everyday, so it hasn't really bothered me."

Ari winced. "We'll head back to Monroe in the morning," he promised.

"Excellent. Now, boys, your mother and father

are waiting for you in their antechamber. Miss Brie, I have taken the liberty of running you another bath. I hope I wasn't presumptuous, but Lady Catherine did say you thoroughly enjoyed the one you had last night."

"I did. That sounds so wonderful. Thank you, for thinking of me. I hope it didn't put you out," she said, biting her lower lip.

Ari just stared at where her teeth were nibbling. Rex elbowed him, and he realized he had been growling again.

Laughing, she stood on tiptoe to kiss Leo on the cheek before heading up the stairs for her bath.

Ari sighed happily as he watched her ass all the way up the stairs.

"The way you keep looking at her, you may want to invest in either a contraceptive amulet or baby clothes," Leo said, smirking. "Personally, I'm hoping for baby clothes. It's been much too long since you were a baby, Ari," he said, before turning to head back toward the kitchen.

Ari's brain was still processing the words 'baby clothes'. He looked up at Rex, unable to formulate words to express how his brain was imploding.

"Let us go find you a drink. Calm down, Ari, you haven't even claimed her yet. You have plenty of time to discuss such things," Rex said soothingly, steering him toward their parents' antechamber.

"Right. Time. Right," he repeated.

"Father, Leo was feeling mischievous and

short circuited Ari's brain with talk of baby clothes. Can you pour him a small glass of Forbidden Fruit?" Rex said, sitting him down in one of the wingback chairs.

"Baby!" his mother exclaimed. "It's much too soon. Isn't it?"

Ari blushed. "We haven't…" he trailed off. They had only just cleared the twenty-four hour mark in knowing each other. Much too soon to be thinking of baby clothes.

"Not that I'm opposed mind you," his mother added slyly.

His father simply walked over and handed him a glass. "This should help."

Without thinking, he downed the liquid. His throat seized, and he began to cough. His father pounded on his back. "It's not meant to be gulped."

"Leave the poor boy be, Jedrek. Baby talk notwithstanding, he and Brie have had a long day. Don't forget it started with a Tribunal at the palace and ended with another murder scene." She shuddered. "What is our world coming to?"

His father looked contrite as he went over to pour him a second glass. "Sip this one," he said when he handed it off.

He nodded and took a sip. Since the first glass had burned his mouth, throat, and esophagus, this glass was actually pleasant.

He sat back as Rex and his father discussed the newly discovered bodies. The liquor did its job in relaxing the tension he hadn't known he was carrying, and before he knew it, he could smell his mate coming toward him.

He stood when his brother and father did. When his mate came into view, he felt his mouth drop. Instead of the emerald green dress robes that he had purchased her, she now wore a pale pink dressing gown and robe. Her skin glowed, and her normally thick, brown curls were braided and hanging to one side.

Blushing, she pointed at her attire. "I hope this is appropriate. Leo left it out for me."

Ari walked over to her and simply pulled her into his arms and bent down to devour those plump lips of hers. When she sagged against him, he heard his father cough. He pulled back and looked down into the face of his flushed mate. "Gods, you're beautiful," he whispered.

When she leaned forward to nuzzle his jaw with her nose, he about came unglued. How could such an innocent act turn him inside out. "Only you think I'm pretty," she replied, looking up at him.

"Good. No one else needs to think you're beautiful but me." Ari suddenly didn't want anyone else to see his mate.

"Like father, like son," his mother said, walking up behind them with his father. "Come along, children, it's time for dinner."

He held out his elbow, and his mate placed her hand on his arm. They made their way to the small dining room they used for family meals. He pulled out her chair and scooted it in for her when she sat. He took a seat on one side, and Rex took the seat between Brie and their mother.

Leo came in from the kitchen, pushing a serving cart laden with food. "I thought something light would be best tonight, so I have prepared a lemon chicken orzo soup to start. After soup, we have grilled white fish and garden salad, and for dessert, I'll serve some of the brownies that Broden made for Ari."

Ari was about to protest but saw the way both of his parents perked up. There was no way he could deny them.

"Can't we just have the brownies for dinner?" Brie asked.

His mother nodded, but Leo frowned at them both. "No. You need to eat a healthy meal so that you can appreciate the decadence of the dessert."

Rex lifted his wine glass to Brie "Told you."

Brie sighed then shrugged. "Oh well, had to try." She sniffed the air. "That soup smells amazing."

Leo puffed out his chest. "It's a new recipe to me, so I hope you like it." He started with his mother, before serving Brie and making his way around the table.

Ari lifted his spoon and stared down at the soup. He was more of a meat and potatoes guy. He lifted a spoonful and was surprised at the explosion of flavor. "Gods, Leo! This is beyond amazing," he exclaimed. He couldn't seem to eat it quick enough with his spoon, but he finally finished his bowl. "Leo, could I have some more please?"

"Me too!" his mate added, holding up her own empty bowl.

"Of course!" Leo quickly served them again.

After the second bowl, he found himself still craving the incredible soup.

"Just a bit more," Brie asked.

"Ditto."

Leo looked at the two of them. "Is it really that good?"

He exchanged looks with his mate, and they both nodded. "I don't know what it is, but it's hitting the spot."

Rex and both of his parents were looking at them strangely. His mother looked down at her half-eaten bowl. "It's okay, but not a favorite." Both his brother and father nodded their agreement.

"I bet it's the cilantro," Brie said, watching Leo carefully, as he ladled out their third bowl.

Everyone stared. "Why do you think that, baby?" Ari asked.

"It's a controversial herb in the human world. Scientists have discovered a portion of the population taste soap when eating cilantro, everyone else tastes yumminess."

Catherine snapped her fingers. "That's it exactly. I thought there might have been residual soap on the bowl."

Ari smiled at his mate. "So, our house will be Team Cilantro?"

"Absolutely."

Leo simply stared at them. "There's science in

existence now that links your DNA to what you taste?"

Brie swallowed her latest bite. "Some. Then again, most cooking is a mixture of chemistry, alchemy, and witchcraft to me."

"We're so perfect for one another," Ari said, tackling his soup.

"If neither of you can cook, how will you eat?" Rex asked.

Ari looked at Brie, and they both shrugged before looking at Leo. "Leo," they said in unison.

"Of course I'll feed you two! They're the babies of the family until Kari has her little one. Plus, they are dealing with those gruesome murders, why should they have to worry about cooking?"

Brie turned to Ari. "Can we marry him?"

"As he practically raised me, no, that would be weird. But I agree with the sentiment a thousand percent."

"Will you be getting your own squire like Kari and Declan when you establish your home?" Rex asked.

Brie lowered her spoon. "Ari, where do we live?"

His lion purred at her question. She was already referring to them as a unit, which meant they were one step closer to being a true mated pair. Then her question sunk in. "Shit. I have no idea."

"Brie, darling, don't you want your own space outside the unit estate? When I mated with

Jedrek, I couldn't wait to leave my parents estate so that I could finally set up my kitchen the way I wanted," his mother asked.

Brie gave a one shoulder shrug. "I'm not really domestic. I live with my dad, so he's the one that cooks and does laundry." She smiled. "I kinda liked waking up at the warrior villa. The guys are great."

Leo looked crestfallen. "I was looking forward to cooking for you."

Brie turned to Ari. "What if we made your quarters at the warrior villa our work space. It's where we'll keep our guns, gear, and investigation notes. But on the weekends we leave all that behind and come here. You could maintain your connection with House Lionhart, and we get to eat Leo's food every weekend."

Her words seemed to resonate within him. He knew that she had just laid out exactly what would work best for them. "If Mother and Father don't mind us invading every weekend," he looked over at his parents.

"Of course, we don't mind!" His mother practically screeched before sniffling a little. "I thought we'd lose you for sure once you mated." She dabbed at her eyes with her napkin. "We not only get to keep seeing you, but it was your mate that suggested it."

Brie smiled at her. "You're family now." She paused. "We also need to work in some time to spend with my dad and my new dad."

Rex's mouth dropped. "I completely forgot

you're Doran's daughter now, making you the queen's niece."

"I don't begrudge my dad finding a mate, but I do not want to be there for their honeymoon phase. Trust me. My dad has little to no filter; the less I hear the better," she shuddered at the thought of too much information.

"My poor mate," Ari laughed. He thought back to the way her dad came up with the prank to tell everyone he was neutered. "It might be best to give them some space," he agreed.

"Mother was the serious one of the two," she said, finishing her soup.

"How long has it been?" his mother asked gently.

"Coming up on fifteen years, but some days, I pick up my phone excited to tell her something only to realize all over again that she's gone." Brie stared into her lap.

"You said she got sick," Ari said, reaching over to take one of her hands.

She nodded. "Yup. Cancer. It spread like a forest fire in high winds. It seemed like one day she was fine and the next she wasn't."

"I'm sure she's looking out for you even now. I mean, what are the odds that both you and your father found happiness here in Éire Danu?" his mother pointed out.

Brie seemed to brighten at his mother's words. "You really think so?"

"Absolutely. Those that move on ahead of us are never truly gone. Just a bit out of touch for a while," his father said gently.

"Think of all the things you'll get to tell her the next time you see her," Leo added, bringing out their main course.

"It would take years to go over everything," Brie said smiling.

"At that point, darling, you'll have all the time in the world," his mother said.

Leo placed a plate of perfectly grilled fish down in front of them. By this time, his lion wanted a bit more than soup. He cut the filet in half and shoved the other half in his mouth. He sighed happily at the flavor.

"Ari! That was half a damn fish!" Brie exclaimed.

"Hmm umm," he agreed.

Leo placed a hand on her shoulder. "I always cook at least triple the amount for Ari."

"He's a growing boy," his mother added.

Brie looked his way, and her eyes raked him up and down. "Yum."

Ari winked at her and continued to eat his fish.

"Mayhap we should expect another grandchild sooner rather than later," his mother said, sounding excited.

Brie shook her head. "Not anytime soon."

Ari couldn't help but agree. "As much as I love kids, I want to enjoy getting to know my mate more. Maybe after the initial mating heat dies down in a century or two, we can try for one."

Catherine arched a brow. "What makes you think it dies down?" She looked at Jedrek, who winked back at her.

Ari stared. "I knew that there would always be a pull, but you're telling me that this clawing need never goes away? That it's not some 'honeymoon' period?"

Rex, Jedrek, Leo, and Catherine shook their heads.

Brie turned to him. "We need some sort of birth control. If this heat or whatever doesn't die down, I'll be pregnant for the next century." She looked up and down his body. "Because I'll probably be jumping you every chance I get," she admitted.

Rex and Jedrek dropped their forks, and Catherine raised her napkin to hide her smile.

Ari simply stared into her chocolate-brown eyes. She wanted him that badly? "I'm yours Brie, mind, body, and soul. Just let me know when and where, and I'm there," he promised.

Leo came up behind them and ladled extra-large portions of pasta on to both of their plates. "For energy," he said, winking.

She pointed her fork at him. "See what I mean! We need some sort of contraceptive; I only have so many eggs."

Catherine smiled openly. "I'll arrange for an amulet to be delivered tomorrow. It will halt your ovulation so that you will be able to have children centuries from now."

Brie exhaled. "Good." She perked up. "Does that mean no cycles while I'm wearing it?"

His mother nodded. Brie smiled wide. "That's amazing." She wiggled happily in her chair.

"You have to keep it on for it to work," he reminded her.

She gave him a flat expression. "If that amulet keeps cramps away, I'll have it welded to my arm."

Ari stared. "Are human female cycles that bad?"

She nodded emphatically. "Medical science has yet to accurately gauge how painful women's cramps can be. Some women say that their monthly cramps were worse than childbirth."

His mother shuddered. "I cannot imagine."

Jedrek rubbed his chin. "No wonder little Meryn is able to keep up with her mate. She must be extraordinarily strong."

"She is half-fae," Rex reminded him.

Jedrek nodded at him. "Yes, but I think that the reproductive side of things must be human, since she became pregnant out of season."

Catherine turned to her mate. "She's not some sort of robot made of specific parts, Jedrek, honestly."

His father had the grace to blush. "We had three sons, my dear. I'm lucky I know the very little I do regarding cycles."

Catherine sipped her wine. "You might want to pick up a book or two. We have daughters now and a possible grand-daughter on the way. You wouldn't want to be ignorant of any pain they may experience would you?"

Jedrek scowled. "I won't allow them to be in pain."

Brie chuckled. "Nature doesn't give us a choice."

Jedrek huffed. "That isn't acceptable."

Brie looked between Jedrek and Rex. "I see where he gets it from."

Ari nodded. "Only Rex seemed to inherit father's indomitable will. Declan and I are too laid back to truly pull it off."

"Where did you get your super lion from?" she asked.

Ari winced. He had been hoping that wouldn't come up.

Both his mother and father leaned forward. "What's this?" his father asked.

Rex sat back with his wine glass, smiling. "Ari shifted to third form when Tyrien insulted House Lionhart."

His mother gasped and covered her mouth with both her hands—his father simply stared. He shook his head in wonder. "Ever since you were a cub, you'd attack anyone that insulted your family, but you've never shifted to third form before."

Leo buzzed around the table, happily refilling wine glasses. "The Lionhart line is truly blessed! Once this gets around, no one will be able to question his strength or capabilities again."

"Family? It wasn't insulting the Lionharts that had him angry." Brie clarified. "He lost his shit when Tyrien insulted his brothers. It was sexy as hell too."

Catherine turned to him. "What changed?"

Ari glanced down at Brie and his mother nodded. "Of course. Any insult to your family would be perceived as a threat to your home and mate. As you were always sensitive to such things, having a mate at your side would escalate the scenario." She dabbed at her eyes. "What a marvelous discovery."

Brie turned to him. "Why wouldn't anyone question you now? How come Tyrien still brought up your age at Tribunal?"

Ari gave a half shrug. "He's fae, not a shifter, so he may not be aware of the implications surrounding such a thing." He chuckled. "I imagine he ignored the entire scene where I shifted, since it resulted in him running for his life. As for Tribunal..." He looked from his father to his brother for assistance.

Rex cleared his throat. "In our world, amongst shifters especially, shifting to third form is seen as a blessed event. For the shifter to have the strength and will to house both his human and animal emotions with equal intensity to the point both are able to merge as one, well, it's said to be a blessing from the gods and a sign that their house is meant for great things. Ari shifting to third form will more than likely secure him an Elder seat later in life, if he so chooses." He grinned at him. "Possibly at a younger age than me."

Ari groaned. "No, thank you. Two Elders in the family are plenty." He lifted his fork. "Now, if that 'blessing' could secure me my current unit leader position for centuries to come, that'd be a different story."

"Oh, so that third form isn't all the time?" Brie asked, sounding disappointed.

Ari swung to her. "Didn't I terrify you?"

A shudder swept through her body as she stared up at him. Her tongue darted out and licked her lower lip. "I knew you wouldn't hurt me." She swallowed. "You were radiating pure power. It was…"

Her cheeks tinted pink, and she looked back down at her plate.

No man alive would be able to resist this. His mate was looking at him like he was some sort of god on earth. He stood. "Mother, Father, Rex, Leo. Goodnight." He reached down and took her hand.

Her mouth formed a little 'o' before she stood, smiling. "Goodnight, everyone."

He swept her up into his arms, causing her to giggle.

Behind them, he heard his father and brother laughing uproariously. Ignoring them, his mother called out.

"I'll look into getting that amulet first thing tomorrow!"

❦

He carried her up the stairs. Each step seemed to take an eternity.

"I can't believe you just did that."

He paused at the top of the stairs. "Did I go too far?"

She shook her head. "No, it's just…" She pointed to the way he was carrying her. "No other guy I've dated has ever treated me like you do. You respect my job and trust in my abilities, yet, still know when to treat me like a woman."

Ari walked over to his door and somehow managed to swing it open. "I think I understand what you're saying, Brie, but I feel like I have to correct something." He kicked the door shut and set her down on the bed. She looked so vulnerable looking up at him. "I think in your world women are treated like men when they do a 'man's' job, which somehow translates into treating them like men as the standard. You're not a man, Brie; you're a beautiful woman. A strong woman. Why would I treat you like a man?" He couldn't fathom treating her any differently.

He wanted to gut himself when he saw tears begin to spill down her cheeks. "I am a woman," she repeated softly.

He blinked, unsure of what to do. "Yes, you are." She was repeating the obvious.

She wiped away her tears and smiled up at him. "If the men in my life didn't know how to accept that, then that's on them."

"Damn right," he agreed.

She took his hand. "I'm a woman," she said again. He gave her hand a squeeze. "An amazing one."

"I'm your woman," she repeated softly.

"Godsdamn right you are!" He pulled her to her feet and went to the hem of her robe. In one fluid motion he pulled it off over her head. "What does my woman want?" he asked as she stood in her silken underthings before him.

"I trust you, Ari." She exhaled and removed the rest of her clothes. "I trust you with my body." She hesitated before voicing her desires. "I don't want to be in charge anymore. I don't want you to assume that because I'm capable that I don't need your strength." She twisted her hands before her.

Ari knew exactly what she needed, and he was the perfect one to give it to her. She was his mate, and he would fulfill her in ways she only dreamed of.

"Get on the bed, kitten. Hand and knees," he ordered.

She looked so relieved he thought she'd faint. She quickly climbed onto the bed and crawled to the center on all fours. "Like this?" she asked.

He stared at the exquisite picture she had created. Her heart shaped ass curved perfectly, and at the center, a small, dark slit beckoned to him.

He removed his shirt, then his shoes. "Stay just like that, kitten. Do you like being on display for me?"

"Ari," she whimpered.

"Do you?"

"Yes."

"Good girl."

He stilled so that the sound of his belt clearing the loops echoed through the room. He was shocked to see the effect on his sweet mate. Clear liquid began to seep down one thigh.

He quickly removed the rest of his clothes but kept his belt in hand. When he climbed on the bed, her heart rate increased.

Slowly, he knelt behind her. He placed a hand at the small of her back before tracing a finger across her beautifully rounded ass to tease her opening.

"Ari!"she yelled.

"Shush, baby, we've barely started."

She lowered her chest to the mattress, further presenting herself to him. "Good girl."

Using the belt in his right hand, he swung, placing the leather across her cheeks and grazing her slit. He paused, gauging her reaction.

"Oh god!"

He swung twice more, leaving a pretty pink stripe across her bottom. "Good girls get treats."

He scooted back and leaned down. Using his thumbs, he opened her like a flower, parting her petals. Without warning, he shoved his tongue as deep as he could inside of her. He alternated between tongue fucking her and thrusting two fingers deep inside.

She cried out in ecstasy as he lapped up her sweetness.

"Please!" she cried.

He sat back on his knees. "Please, what?"

He was curious. Would she say? Sir, master? What would she choose for the next part of their game?

"Please, my mate!" she wailed.

Ari felt something inside of him snap at her begging. She had called out to him as her mate!

He reached down and lined up his cock with her opening and plunged deep.

"Yes!"

"Mine, my mate!" he growled. No one would take her from him. Her beauty and strength belonged to him alone.

Over and over again, he thrust and thrust deep. He would leave no inch of her untouched.

Within, he felt his lion pacing restlessly. It was past time to make her his. Leaning down, he covered her body with his and pulled her up so that her back was flush against his chest. He eyed her neck before sinking his canines into her tender flesh.

"Ari!" Brie screamed his name as she shuddered under him.

His lip nicked his canine as he threw his head back. He and his lion roared in unison. Her unshakeable strength wrapped around his heart. He could feel her surrounding his lion and his soul, soothing them both.

He thrust a final time before filling her with his seed. Neither wanted children just yet, but his lion demanded they claim her in this way, and he agreed. He wanted to be inside her every way possible.

Breathing heavily, he reached down and gently tilted her head back to look up at him. Her eyes were unfocused, and she smiled softly.

He kissed her. The flavors of her sweetness and their mixed blood created a heady combination. When he pulled back, he could tell she was on the verge of sleep.

"I love you, Brie. I always will," he promised. Her answering exhale was long, as if she was finally able to relax after years of struggle.

He carefully pulled from her body and shuddered at the painful pleasure it caused after such an intense experience. On wobbly legs, he made it to the bathroom and returned with a warm wash cloth. He gently cleaned his mate then felt around the bed. They had lucked out. Her being on all fours had kept the mess to a minimum.

He aimed and threw the cloth at the bathroom door. He'd pick it up in the morning. Right now, all he wanted was to sleep with his mate.

CHAPTER TEN

❦

T HE NEXT MORNING, BRIE STRETCHED
and felt tiny aches that reminded her of the
night before. She vaguely remembered Ari kissing her forehead and saying something about
checking in with the men earlier this morning.
She had grunted, then gone back to sleep. He
had thoroughly worn her out. Blinking drowsily,
she took inventory of her body. Never before had
sex been so hot and fulfilling. In the moment, it
had felt liberating handing over control, but now
she was nervous that he would think less of her.
It seemed like he was changing everything, and
her world was topsy turvy.

She rolled over until she lay on her back, staring up at the ceiling. Ari was a part of her now;
she could feel him in her soul. She was equal
parts happy that she had found someone so perfect for her and terrified at how much he meant
to her.

Both of their professions were dangerous ones,
and she knew there was a real possibility that
she could lose him. She swung her legs over and
climbed out of bed. She quickly freshened up

then looked around for her clothes. She slipped on the soft, pink robe that Leo had left her the night before and opened the door to Ari's quarters.

Hanging outside the door on a rolling clothing rack was her uniform. It had been laundered and pressed to perfection.

"I freaking love having a squire," she whispered to herself and grabbed the clothes. Once inside, she got dressed, took her weapon out of the safe Ari had shown her, and headed downstairs. Following her nose, she found Ari's parents sitting at the small table in a sunny parlor.

"Good morning," she said in greeting. Jedrek stood and motioned to the empty chair.

Catherine smirked. "Don't you mean good afternoon?"

Brie reached for her phone. Sure enough, it was after eleven. "Why didn't anyone wake me?"

Leo walked up behind her and got her seated, pushing her chair in. "Would you prefer a late breakfast or an early lunch?" he asked.

"A cup of coffee to start, then maybe an omelet and a Diet Coke for breakfast?"

Leo nodded. "Would you like toast with your breakfast?"

"No, just the omelet should be fine."

He flipped over the mug in front of her and poured a cup of coffee. "I'll be out in a few minutes with your breakfast."

"I have coffee, take your time."

Leo nodded then headed toward the kitchen.

She fixed her coffee and eyed the cream. Didn't Ramsey say he learned the cream ratios from Leo? She added some and took a sip. "Ahhhh, perfect." She sat back, holding the mug to her chest. "I really should have gotten up when Ari did."

"Nonsense. You've had a great deal thrown at you over the past two days, and you've only just been claimed. If anyone deserves some rest, it's you, darling," Catherine explained.

What she said stuck with her. It had only been two days, and everything was different. Her entire world had been turned upside down and shaken like a snow globe. Maybe she had earned a few extra hours to sleep in. She turned to Jedrek. "Do we have any idea what the guys did this morning?" She pushed back a growing sense of guilt. The queen had trusted her to head up the investigations and, she had let a really, *really* good romp in bed lay her out.

Jedrek sipped his own coffee. "Ari went to the warrior villa first thing this morning to ask for volunteers to work with you in getting the dead identified. Evidently, there was much arguing, then a brawl broke out as they competed to see who would help. Finally, Ari just had them draw straws. He sent the lucky five on to meet up with Rex and Ben at the storage facility. They divided up the dead amongst them, and their first task was to photograph each person and create a file for them. That's what they have been working on all morning," he explained.

"That was exactly what I would have done." She smiled. "They must have really wanted to get out of patrols," she added.

Both Catherine and Jedrek laughed before Catherine shook her head. "They wanted to be the ones to help you, dear," she replied.

Brie stared. "Really?"

Jedrek gave a single nod. "Really."

She lifted her mug to hide her smile. "Do you know which five were tapped?"

Jedrek rolled his eyes. "Both of my brother's silly cubs, Bastien Géroux from Phi, Saxon Wright from Psi, and Colin Althea from the Omega unit. The men decided that one from each unit would be fair. Tau performs daily with only four warriors, so the men argued that the other units in Éire Danu were no less capable. Which is how you ended up with five volunteers instead of the initial three requested."

She couldn't have asked for more. The men that she'd be working with were the ones she knew the best so far. "I'll head over there right after breakfast. I want to be on site when we start working with the families. Once the men have been assigned and I've met with all the deceased's loved ones, then I will concentrate on the investigation. River had all day to get settled in Noctem Falls; I want to know if he discovered anything more with their nifty microscopes."

Jedrek sipped his orange juice and set the glass down. "Don't hesitate to lean on Rex. We have him on permanent loan from Noctem Falls to assist here in the city. If you find yourself unsure of what to do or who to contact, go to him."

Brie felt a lot more confident knowing Rex would be at her side for the initial interviews. "That makes me feel so much better. Rex exudes confidence and dependability that I don't think I'd ever feel nervous with him in my corner," she admitted. Both of Ari's parents smiled at one another at the praise for their firstborn.

"Rex was a born leader," Leo said, coming up behind her. He set down a plate with a huge omelet on it. "Even when he was a cub, others looked to him."

She stared at the monster omelet, then looked up at Leo, then back down at her breakfast.

Catherine coughed delicately. "Leo, I think you made her an Ari-sized portion."

Brie looked up Leo whose eyes widened. "I'm so sorry! Ari is the only other one in the family who requests omelets, so I was somewhat on autopilot when I was cooking it."

"It's fine! I just didn't want you to get mad if I couldn't finish it," she said, picking up her fork.

"I could never get mad at you, my dear. You've made Ari the happiest we have ever seen him. A tiny uneaten portion won't change that," Leo said pointing to her plate.

"It won't be a tiny portion, Leo. You'll probably be getting half this back."

Catherine turned to her squire. "Could you wrap it up for Ari? You know he'll be getting hungry by the time he catches up to her."

Leo snapped his fingers. "Just the thing. Brie,

let me know when you're full, and I'll put this
between two slices of buttered toast for Ari's
snack. I'll go prepare a bag now." He turned and
headed back toward the kitchen.

Brie took a bite of her fluffy omelet and
sighed. The man was a true genius in the kitchen.
"Maybe, three day weekends here," she murmured to herself.

Both Catherine and Jedrek laughed. Jedrek
winked at her. "Sounds like a perfect plan to us."

As she tried to make a dent in her delicious
breakfast, she wondered if it would be a serious
faux pas to bring her laundry with her when she
visited.

❦

Once she was done, Leo whisked her uneaten
portion away and returned with what looked like
a medium size cooler. "Here's Ari's snack."

"Snack?" How much did her mate eat? "Leo,
you have me really worried about how I'm going
to feed him when we're not visiting. Neither of
us can cook."

Catherine stood by her mate at the door.
"Never you worry; the boys at the warrior villa
have been cooking for Ari for over a century
now. They're used to his bottomless stomach."

"Good, because I really don't want us to
starve."

Leo handed over the cooler, his expression
thoughtful. "I'm sure I could manage mid-week
snacks for the both of you."

She accepted the cooler and pulled him down

so she could kiss his cheek. "I'd marry you in a heartbeat," she teased.

"Go on with you now," he said, sounding flustered.

Jedrek laughed and pulled her aside to kiss her own cheek. "I mean it, young lady. If you need anything, go to Rex."

She made a face at him causing him to laugh. "Yes, Dad."

He blinked. "Dad?"

She froze. Was she not supposed to call him that?

"Jedrek, stop that! You're scaring her to death." Catherine turned to her. "It's perfectly fine to call us mom and dad. You surprised my dear mate because the boys have only ever called us 'mother' and 'father'," she explained.

"Good, because using 'mother' and 'father' sounds way too stiff for me."

"Dad is perfect," Jedrek grinned. "I can't wait to call Byron and tell him that Brie calls me dad."

"Why is that a thing?" Brie asked Catherine who was rolling her eyes.

"Because Byron McKenzie was a bit insufferable after Aiden found Meryn. He bragged to the other council members that she called him 'dad'."

Brie laughed. She imagined that the men of Jedrek's generation were probably just as big of goofballs as the warriors that walked around on their knees to simulate Meryn's height. She doubted they ever truly grew up. If her dad was any indicator, the same could be said for human men too.

"Try not to do too much, dear," Catherine called out as she walked away

"I will," she yelled back, laughing. She wasn't about to lie. She knew the next couple days were going to be flat out hard.

She lugged the cooler down Maple street until she saw the familiar building where she had arrived in the city. Warriors were standing outside, forming a barrier between the gate and the concerned citizens milling about out front. When they saw her approaching, two warriors stepped forward to flank her and escort her inside. The one on her left relieved her of her cooler, and she flexed her hand. The damn thing was heavy.

"What's going on, fellas?"

"Tyrien was out here this morning, stirring up the crowd. One of his cohorts threw a brick and hit Bastien in the head. Ari had to hold Gage back since he and Bastien are close as their families are tied together. Molvan and Malcom from the palace escorted Tyrien and his brick-slinging friend to the palace to face Brennus," the warrior with her cooler explained.

She looked at his chest and smiled. The men were still wearing name tags—it was Corrin Li'Loudain from Psi who had spoken.

Balder chuckled evilly. "Ari released the fae unit warriors, in addition to those assisting here at the facility, from patrols. We're to act as guards to dissuade others from getting violent."

She looked over to him. "Does that leave enough for patrols?"

Balder gave a short nod. "Aiden called in the rest of the Gamma unit to assist in patrols," he smiled wide. "Aiden said something about separating Sascha and Colton to keep them both breathing."

"Meryn filled me in on their shenanigans. They sound fun."

"I don't know how they manage to stir up so much mischief and still manage to stay the highest ranking units between the four pillar cities," Corrin shook his head.

Balder held the door open for her. "I think that just proves how good they actually are."

She nodded and stepped inside. It was eerily quiet.

"Hello?" she called out.

Ramsey poked his head out from the back hallway that led to the larger main office. "Hey, you made it. Ari's been like a lion cub with a thorn in his wittle paw all morning waiting for you."

"I evidently needed to catch up on my sleep? Where is my lion?" she asked. She turned and reclaimed the cooler from Corrin.

"In the office. We had just sat down to re-group, so perfect timing," he explained as he led her down a dimly lit hallway. When they walked into the office, the men stood, and she went right to her mate. Ignoring the men around them, she pulled his head down for a kiss. As usual, he completely took over, leaving her to wonder what planet she was on. Sighing, she pulled back. "Good morning," she said a little breathlessly.

He nuzzled her neck then straightened. "I missed you."

"I could tell." She set the cooler on the table with a thud. "I brought you snacks from Leo."

The men were practically pouting. Balder scowled at Ari. "I hate you."

Ari just laughed. "I have the perfect mate who brings me food, I'd hate me too." He blew air kisses to the men who just groaned and threw wadded up paper balls at him.

Ari opened the cooler then turned to her. "Did mother tell him I might be hungry?"

"Yup. Half my omelet is in there somewhere on toast. Find it for me? Walking down here has me getting peckish."

Ari rooted around the cooler and held up a wax paper square. "I think this is it."

He handed it to her, and she sat down in the empty chair next to him. Ari looked around the room. "Dig in, guys, Leo packed for a small army."

The guys were all smiles now as they reached for food, which made sense since it was approaching lunch time. Once everyone had something, she turned to Ari. "I heard about Bastien's assault, is he okay?"

The men all growled as Ari's eyes darkened. "Yes, but that incident had us changing how we were going to start this process."

"We're no longer going to allow them to line

them up and take them first come first served, huh?" she guessed.

"Exactly. We're waiting on an announcement from Portia that asks each family that has lost someone to send a single representative to the palace first to create a file on their loved one." He grimaced. "One of the things we noticed right away is that most of the dead look the same."

Brie licked a bit of butter off her fingers. "Like, de-comping the same?"

Gage shook his head. "No, literally. They are all fae. They are all tall and blond. Fae tend not to get tattoos and do not need dental work. Take a generic look and distort it from bloat, now you have over a hundred corpses that will be nigh impossible to identify."

Brie sat back with a thump. "Shit. I never even thought of that."

Ari rubbed across her shoulders. "Neither did we. We have requested additional assistance from Noctem Falls."

"Their microscopes?" she asked.

Ari shook his head. "No, their hematologist. Vivian Vi'Aerlin, mate to Etain Vi'Aerlin, is a renowned scientist. We're hoping she will be able to help us match bodies to family members using DNA."

"I guess we don't need the guys assigned to this huh?"

Ari shook his head. "We absolutely do. The men have been assigned roughly fifteen bodies each. They will be working with Anne Ashwood in getting samples organized and labeled for shipment. As we receive information back about each person, the warrior will confirm with the families and make the arrangements to release the bodies for final arrangements."

"So, we're on hold for now?"

Ari and the men nodded. Her mate squeezed her shoulder. "Once Portia makes the announcement, the crowd will disperse. Anne should be here soon to gather samples. We'll maintain guard duty on the building to avoid anyone disturbing the dead. After that, we're waiting on matches from Vivian in Noctem Falls."

She crumpled up the now empty wax paper, and she was surprisingly still a bit hungry. She was going to gain weight if she kept stress eating. "I'll forward Portia the form we use to file a missing persons. She can tweak it as needed, but it should give her a jumping off point."

Ari stood and looked at the table full of empty containers. "Ben, you stay here as point of contact for the facility. Gage, you check up on Bastien. Priest, work with Sascha Baberiov in getting the rest of Gamma settled in. Kincaid, can you act as escort for Anne?" His unit all stood and nodded. Ari turned to the rest of the warriors. "Add in a rotation to guard this facility then head back to the villa. Rest up for your next patrol."

The rest of the men stood. "Yes, sir."

Priest eyed his unit leader. "And what will you be doing?"

"Heading to the palace to see if Cord is serving lunch," Ari replied, not looking the least bit ashamed.

Kincaid laughed. "I'll tag along so I can pick up Anne."

"Unbelievable," Gage muttered as everyone moved for the door.

Ari held a hand down to her. "Are you okay with heading to the palace?"

She grinned up at him. "Yes, because I'm still hungry too."

Laughing he wrapped an arm around her and they walked up the hill toward the palace.

CHAPTER ELEVEN

W HEN THEY GOT TO THE palace, Brie was surprised to see the atmosphere was surprisingly light. She looked up at Ari, who nodded his head toward where Meryn sat, bouncing in her chair.

"Ari, Brie, Kincaid, welcome. Just in time for lunch. Please join us," the queen said, motioning to the table.

They sat down in three empty chairs as Brie continued to watch Meryn. "Did someone over-caffeinate her?" she asked.

Aiden placed his large hand on his mate's head and pushed up and down causing her to laugh. "Darian got a call from Noctem Falls today. He went to get the collection vials for ViThreePO, and Sebastian said he's forwarding on my meat kebobs!"

"Meat bobs! Meat bobs!" Creelee chanted from Izzy's shoulder.

"In the meantime, can I interest you in a garden salad?" Cord asked.

Meryn shook her head emphatically. "No, thank you, Cord. Every square millimeter in my stomach is reserved for meat kebobs and pudding today."

Cord eyed the empty plate in front of Meryn as if it were an enemy. "How about a piece of fruit? It'll be digested before Darian returns." The poor squire simply couldn't stand that someone at the table he was serving wasn't eating.

Meryn saw his face and relented. "Okay, maybe something small though. Oh! Those baby oranges would be great."

Amelia sighed. "They're called tangerines, Meryn."

"Whatever, he knew what I meant."

"I did, and I will be right back with some for you." He looked at them. "What can I get the two of you?" he asked.

"Technically, I've had two breakfasts, but I'm still kinda hungry. But I don't think I need a full meal," she explained.

Kincaid smiled. "Any kind of soup would be perfect for me."

Ari shrugged. "Double of whatever is easiest," he said simply.

Rex smiled. "You better watch out, Cord, Ari is like a stray house cat. If he knows that you'll feed him, he'll keep turning up."

Cord shrugged. "That's perfectly fine by me. I'll be right back with your lunches," he said, heading toward the kitchen.

Aleksandra turned to Brie. "Thank you for sending Portia that form. She said it was exactly what was needed and saved her hours of work."

Brie felt better knowing she helped. "I wasn't

sure how much of it could be used, but I figured it would be better than starting from scratch."

Beside her, she felt Ari turn until he was facing Brennus. "How'd their hearing go?"

Brennus smirked. "They will both be assisting House Liordon in providing support to the warriors in the form of cleaning and laundry duties. Tyrien tried to weasel out of it, protesting that he had not thrown anything, but I cited testimonies from the warriors who were there, saying he was inciting violence. Neither was very happy with me to say the least."

"Uncle Bren kicked ass. When Tyrien tried to argue, he just did this murder face, and the douchebag shut right up."

"Murder face?" Brennus chided gently.

"Yup. Murder. Face. It was awesome. I want to be able to do that someday," Meryn scowled at her cousin. "How's that?"

Amelia smiled but Kendrick shook his head. "You look like you're constipated."

Meryn stuck her tongue out at him. "That's how you always look," she retorted.

Anne laughed and took another bite of her salad.

Kendrick sighed. "It's like raising Serenity all over again. Sisters are more vicious than brothers. Keelan never said I had a god complex or that I looked constipated," he complained.

"God complex?" Brie asked, looking at Serenity, who laughed. "He gets so insufferable when he's lecturing. There were many times I wanted to throw a book or two at him."

"You did throw a book or fifty at me," Kendrick pointed out.

"And you deserved it every time," she replied.

"I haven't shot you yet," Meryn added smiling.

"Thank the gods for small favors," the witch murmured.

"Are you feeling better, Aleksandra? When we came by the day before, we heard you had gone to bed with Meryn, Amelia, and Anne to watch cartoons and eat chocolate. Did it help?" Brie asked, taking in the queen's pale complexion.

Aleksandra smiled softly. "The girls did everything they could think of to make me feel better. And I wouldn't necessarily call them cartoons; they seemed like so much more. Especially that delightful romance between Yuri and Tezuka, I couldn't get enough."

Anne threw her fist in the air. "Another convert!"

Brie had no idea what they had watched, but if it made Aleksandra smile, it was worth it.

Cord walked in from the kitchen, a mysterious smile on his face. He placed down plates in front of her, Ari, and Kincaid. "You all need to keep up your strength."

Meryn frowned. "Where are my baby oranges…" She sniffed the air. "My meat kebobs are here!"

Cord looked over at her astonished. "How on earth did you smell them from here? You're half-fae not half-shifter."

"Never underestimate my spiritual bond

with my meat kebobs and magic pudding," she informed him.

Cord shook his head. "Darian opened a portal to the kitchen to surprise you." He laughed. "Darian, she knows the meat kebobs have arrived, you can bring them out," he called out in a loud voice.

Meryn immediately turned and sat straight in her chair. She picked up her napkin and placed it in her lap. "Meat kebobs, just for me.." she paused. "And Creelee," she continued her little song.

Brie watched as three young men emerged from the kitchen. Two carried platters and the third a huge bowl. The kitchen staff approached Meryn's chair and set down the food in front of her before stepping back to linger behind her.

Brie didn't know what to think as they continued to watch Meryn eye her food.

"I hope you're sharing, Meryn. We had to smell the pudding Sebastian was making all morning," one of the men said.

Meryn froze, she turned to her right and looked up before bursting into magnificent tears. "You're here!" she sobbed.

The men pulled her chair back and cuddled her from all sides.

"Of course, we're here! You're in a strange city, you find out about your parents, people start dying...again. Where else would we be?" the other man said.

"About time you three got here," Aiden said gruffly.

Around the table, Anne, Amelia, and Serenity dabbed at their eyes.

"Who are they?" she whispered to Ari.

Her mate shrugged. "I think the twins are Nigel and Neil Morninglory."

Micah just smiled as he rubbed his mate's back. "You're correct. The red-headed trouble-makers are Nigel Morninglory from Theta and Neil Morninglory from Kappa. The dark-haired adorable one is Pip Maverick. All three have been adopted by Meryn as her brothers."

The queen gasped as Brennus smiled wide. "We have nephews!" she exclaimed.

The one introduced as Pip looked up from where he had been rubbing his cheek against Meryn's curls. "Huh?"

Nigel and Neil exchanged confused glances. "What now?"

Kendrick held up a hand and whispered low. Suddenly, the air around them pulsed and Brie opened and closed her mouth trying to get her ears to pop. "What the hell was that?"

Kendrick lowered his hand. "A soundproofing spell. We have some things to go over." He eyed her, Ari, and Kincaid. "Things will be revealed that could change our world. If you stay, you will be asked to swear an oath of silence."

Ari's eyes darted to Aiden, then to his brother. Both men nodded. He turned back to Kendrick. "So do I swear." Kincaid echoed Ari's oath.

Brie had no flipping clue what was going on. "I'll swear to whatever."

Kendrick stood and went to the twins. Thane

and Justice had already pulled up chairs for them to sit to one side of Meryn. Oron had retrieved a chair for Pip, who sat on Meryn's other side.

Nigel and Neil looked from Kendrick to Meryn and back. "What?"

Kendrick knelt down in front of the two red-heads and began to tell a story. When he stood and stepped back, confessing to being their king, the young men slid from their chairs to their knees on the floor in front of Kendrick, both sobbing silently.

Brie turned to Ari to get confirmation that they were hearing this correctly and saw that Kincaid had tears streaming down his face.

"This is big, right?"

Meryn rubbed Neil's back while Pip rubbed Nigel's. She nodded. "They've been without a king for about five-thousand years."

Kendrick knelt back down and lifted the twins so they stood on their feet. "You do not bow to me. As my cousins, you need only incline your heads."

Neil sniffled. "We're your cousins because of Meryn, does that count?" he asked as he and his brother stood.

Kendrick placed one hand on each auburn head. "No, boys. Where do you think this red hair came from?"

Nigel simply started wheezing. Neil took a step back and fell onto his chair. Kendrick helped Nigel sit. Meryn glared at him. "You could have told them in another way."

"They're my baby cousins; if I don't torture

them out of love, who will?" Kendrick asked flippantly, though his eyes were shiny.

Neil looked up. "How?"

Kendrick shrugged. "When a boy likes a girl..." His explanation halted as his mate popped him upside the head and kept walking until she could cuddle the twins with Meryn. "Way back when someone had a mistress," she explained, before turning to Nigel to get his breathing under control.

Beside Ari, Kincaid stood and walked over to where Kendrick and the twins were. He knelt down on one knee. "Your Majesty, I swear fealty here and now. I, Kincaid Bayberry, do solemnly swear to defend and uphold the reigning line of Stormhart, for as long as there is breath in my body. Command me as you will."

"Well, damn. He beat me to it," Micah groused.

Serenity smirked at her mate's chagrin. "You had plenty of time to make your pledge. Kincaid is the only one smart enough to make it official."

Kendrick looked taken aback. "Please rise, Kincaid. As the first to pledge your fealty to me, I offer this boon." He placed a hand on Kincaid's shoulder then stepped back, frowning. "That should have worked."

Thane stepped up. "What were you trying to do?"

"Bring a new element online."

Thane's mouth dropped. "You can do that?"

Kendrick nodded absently as he rubbed his chin. "Only on rare occasions" He eyed Kincaid. "What was your magic again?"

Kincaid exhaled as his shoulders sagged. "Broken.

Ari stood and walked over to his unit brother. "Not broken. So far we've seen Earth and Fire."

Kendrick's brows shot to his hairline. "Those are not complementary elements."

Ari nodded. "We think that's why he's having a hard time."

"Newbie in the room, feeling super lost over here. What does he mean not complementary?" Brie asked, trying to follow the conversation.

Nigel inhaled, then exhaled. "There are four elements. Earth, Air, Fire, and Water. Air strengthens Fire, Water liberates Earth. Those elements work together well. For him to have Fire and Earth," he winced. "It must be frustrating."

Neil was also starting to get some color to his cheeks. "But, it's amazing that he has two elements at a young age. We only have Earth."

Kendrick looked over at his cousins. "And you're barely one-hundred years old." He eyed Kincaid. "Not that he's much older. Two-twenty five?" he guessed.

Kincaid shook his head. "One-fifty-three."

Kendrick, Thane, Justice, and Law stared. Kendrick began to pace back and forth. "I know the council sends out young witches to fulfill warrior obligations, but this is getting ridiculous. The only reason I let Keelan go was because I had been following Aiden's career for centuries and knew he'd take care of my brother. To just send these babies out with no support in place…" Kendrick kept pacing back and forth muttering about self-important Muppets.

Meryn grinned. "I love when he calls them Muppets."

Ari scowled at Kendrick. "He has support. He has his warrior brothers."

Kendrick wheeled on him. "I understand that, but can you teach him to channel his magic into roots to ground himself? Can you create a wall of earth or air to buffer him against himself when his fire magic goes awry?"

Ari shook his head. "No, I can't. But Heath Clover and Riley Redwood can. Heath served as Beta's witch for centuries before coming here. He's managed to stay one step ahead of the Witches' Council, and I trust him with Kincaid's training. We've reached out to Storm Keep for more training materials, but haven't gotten any response from the Academy."

Thane turned to Ari. "Please tell me you didn't reveal that he has two elements."

Ari just stared at the witch. "I may be a unit warrior, but I am also a Lionhart. I know how the Storm Keep Witches Council runs the Academy. We kept the request very generic and didn't mention Kincaid at all."

Kendrick stopped his manic pacing. "I have books I can give him. If the Academy reaches out, tell them never mind."

"Your Majesty, I'm not really a baby," Kincaid protested.

Kendrick waved his hand to point at the group

of them, his own mate included. "You're all babies."

Aiden grinned. "Dirty old man," he teased.

Kendrick stopped in his tracks then looked at Aiden before bursting out in laughter. He was joined by most of those who had recently come from Noctem Falls. Kendrick wiped at his eyes. "You've just been waiting to say that to someone else, haven't you?" he asked Aiden.

Aiden gave him a shit eating grin. "Of course."

Brennus looked to Aiden. "Did someone say that to you?" he asked.

Aiden exhaled. "Young Stefan, on many occasions."

The queen tapped her fingers to her lips. "Kendrick, can you take down the soundproofing spell. Unless you have any other secrets to divulge."

Kendrick released the spell. "I'm fresh out of secrets." He fiddled with a pouch at his belt and began rummaging through it. When he had both arms in, up to his elbow, Brie realized that there was more to his bag than met the eye. He pulled out two heavy tomes and handed them to Kincaid. "Start with those."

Kincaid stared down. "Yes, You…you're awesome," he corrected quickly.

Neil turned to Meryn. "So, what are we working on?"

"Trying to find warehouses that may have dead peeps in them," she said bluntly.

"Noah and Jaxon?" Nigel asked.

"Pulling and scanning maps into the database.

I have a Batcave set up. Did y'all bring your laptops?" Meryn asked.

Neil grinned. "Of course, and *Sugar Free Red Bull.*"

"No," was Kendrick's immediate response.

Nigel simply smiled up at him as he lay his head shamelessly on Anne's shoulder. "You wouldn't hurt us, would you?" he asked innocently.

"You're so fucked," Serenity whispered, under her breath, causing Micah to stare at her. "You cussed again."

Serenity pointed to the twins. "They can literally get away with anything now."

Meryn sat up, a devilish smile taking over her face. "We can do anything."

Nigel smiled then stared at Meryn's shoulder where Finley was staring back just as enraptured.

"Meryn, who are they?"

Meryn slapped her hand to her forehead. "I completely forgot to introduce you. This is Feris and Finley, Felix's baby brothers."

Nigel held out his hand palm up and Finley floated over to him. "You two," the sprite said pointing.

"Us too?" Neil asked.

Meryn shook her head. "I think he means, there's two of you too."

Feris flew over to Neil and landed on the table in front of him.

Meryn brightened. "You guys can carry them! I was worried since Felix takes up all the room in my boob pocket. They have to keep warm, and I only have so much room. But if they're with you, that's perfect."

"Us—"

"Together," the tiny sprites said in unison.

Nigel and Neil lifted the sprites to their shoulders.

"Gods they are still identical," Amelia breathed.

Brie nodded. "Both sets."

"We're the dynamic duos," Nigel announced.

"Duos!" the smaller sprites crowed.

The queen sipped her tea with a satisfied expression as Kendrick's face paled even further. She leaned over and tapped a crystal. A moment later, Portia entered. "Your Majesty?"

"Could you arrange for robes in varying shades of green to be delivered from Baba for the twins? From my understanding, she is one of the best merchants we have. Also," she eyed Pip. "Robes in blues for young Master Pip."

"Anything else?"

"Make sure the robes bear at least Founding Family emblems; they are to be treated as such."

Portia just nodded. "I am beyond being surprised. I will see it done. The young masters should have robes and dress robes by this evening. I will ensure they are self-fitting and cleaning."

"You are simply a marvel," the queen gushed.

"I do try," Portia replied dryly, then left.

Pip practically glued himself to Meryn's side. "The pretty queen said I was to be treated like a

Founding Family member, but I am a nobody," he whispered. "What do I do?"

Meryn wrapped an arm around him. "You're my brother," she said firmly. "And she is my aunt. And she's the Queen of all the Fae and is like ten-thousand years old, Pip. If this amazing, smart woman who has seen so much says you're to be treated at the very least like a Founding Family member, then don't you think you're actually something very special?"

Pip stared at Meryn. "Just being your brother is special."

"I freaking love you, Pip," Meryn exploded.

Pip sat up straighter. "And I freaking love you too. And I am special because the pretty queen thinks I am."

Aiden ruffled Pip's hair. "We all think you're special, kiddo."

Neil snagged a meat kebob and handed it to Meryn. "What do you want us working on?"

"Foreclosures and past due property taxes using a four-hundred grid matrix," Meryn replied immediately.

Brie shook her head. "Little genius."

Meryn winked at her. Pip bumped Meryn's shoulder. "What about me?"

"Pip, you're in charge of cuddles," she replied, biting into her meat kebob.

Pip saluted. "Roger!"

"Creelee, you have to try this." Meryn waved an entire skewer at the small brownie.

Creelee flew over, eyes wide. "So much bob."

Izzy watched, concern written all over her

face. "Creelee, did you want me to take it off the skewer for you?"

Oron waved off her concern. "He'll be fine."

Creelee sat down and lined up the meat kebob.

Meryn turned to her brothers. "Watch this."

Creelee pulled one chunk of meat off after another, practically inhaling them. "More bob!" he chirped.

"Whoa," the twins said in awe.

Pip handed him another skewer. "Here you go."

Once again the tiny brownie decimated the small pieces of meat. Meryn continued to eat hers as Brie watched the huge pile of kebobs dwindle down to sticks.

Meryn sat back rubbing her stomach. "Now time for Magic Pudding."

"Pud-ding," Creelee repeated, his stomach engorged.

Cord set down a stack of bowls in front of Meryn and scooped out some for her, then Creelee, then the small sprites.

Creelee eyed the pudding then climbed up on the rim of the bowl.

"No!" Izzy rounded the table and caught him before he dived in.

Creelee pouted up at Izzy. "Pud-ding! Peaz!"

Izzy rubbed her cheek against him. "Of course, you can have some, but you can't jump into it like you did your pie."

Meryn held out what looked like a small cracker. "Here's some graham cracker from the side of the bowl. Maybe he can break off crumbs and use that to scoop up the pudding."

Izzy handed the cracker to Creelee, who did exactly as Meryn suggested. He broke off a small piece then thrust the entire thing up to his forearm into the pudding. He gulped and licked, before repeating. Despite his size, he finished about the same time Meryn did. Both were now groaning and rubbing their bellies.

"Come on, li'l mama. Show us your Batcave, and you can nap while we run financials," Neil said, helping Meryn to stand.

Meryn tugged on his hand. "Y'all okay?" she asked, her eyes cutting to Kendrick.

Neil exchanged looks with Nigel, and they both nodded. Nigel kissed Meryn on the forehead. "Our lives changed so much when you adopted us. We suddenly knew what it was like to be loved and cared for. To have family." He looked at Kendrick. "That's just icing on the cake, but you're the cake, Meryn." He frowned. "Did that make sense?"

Meryn nodded her eyes shining. "Cord, can you bring my Magic Pudding to the Batcave for the boys?"

"Of course, my dear."

"Do you want to get started now?" Neil asked Meryn.

"Yup, I can connect you to the network, and then we can dive into databases. Jaxon uploaded more coastal maps, so we should be able to start looking farther south."

Pip popped up, then went over to the queen.

He bent down slightly and hugged her fiercely. "Meryn said I am in charge of cuddles, and you looked like you needed one."

Brie thought he was the cutest thing ever.

The queen's eyes went wide before she pulled him back down for a hug and to kiss his cheek. "Thank you, Pip. You can give me cuddles whenever you want. It's been a long time since we had a baby boy in the palace."

"Roger!" Pip said, giving another salute, then hurried back over to Meryn.

Aleksandra turned to Brennus. "That boy is to be spoiled shamelessly."

Brennus just nodded. "I was thinking the same thing, my dear. Your aura brightened so much from such a small gesture; he is a treasure worth protecting."

"How can one person be so adorable?" the queen mused.

"Come on, guys, let's boogie." Meryn, along with the boys, headed for the door.

As they were walking away, Brie heard Neil ask who Pierce was and why was he following them.

"He's after Ryuu's butt, so we have to protect him."

"Right!" The twins said, glaring at Pierce.

"No butt sex for you!" Pip declared, his voice ringing through the chambers as he shook a finger up at the huge shifter.

Pierce couldn't hold in his laughter. "It gets better and better," he chuckled.

When the young quartet had left the room,

Kendrick, Brennus, and surprisingly, the queen herself burst into laughter. Law was coughing as he tried to get some air.

Brennus just smiled at his mate, a bit of relief in his eyes. Laughter for the queen was a good thing right now. "Gods bless those four," he whispered.

Kendrick exhaled and looked at Anne. "Quit spoiling them. How can I be the Big Bad if they hide behind you?"

Anne stood and patted his cheek. "You're so very clever; I'm sure you'll figure it out."

Kendrick looked heavenward. "Gods above, give me strength."

Aiden sipped his wine. "No offense, Kendrick, but they're probably laughing at you too."

Justice turned to his brother. "You and Law have laid claim to Meryn, so I get dibs on the boys. They will be like my godsbrothers."

Thane stared. "You can't invent words like that."

Aiden shrugged. "Meryn does it all the time."

Justice grinned wickedly at his older brother. "She already approved of another term I came up with. *Brothair*. Means brother of my *athair*. This way I get to spoil her too."

Thane literally growled. "She's my godsdaughter!"

Law rubbed his chin. "Justice, you're a genius. I am her *brothair* as well."

"No, you're not," Thane argued.

"Don't be greedy," Justice refuted.

"You can't be anyone's anything if I bury you two idiots," Thane threatened.

"Mother won't let you kill us," Law pointed out.

"She'll be fine with me as her only son—you two are just back-ups," Thane said, pointing to his brothers. Justice and Law eyed each other then jumped their elder brother.

Kendrick whispered a few words, and the brawling trio was moved to the open area by a set of double doors. "There, now they won't hit the table."

Ari and Kincaid edged toward the fight, watching it entranced. "Twenty on Thane," Ari said.

"Deal," Kincaid agreed.

"Oh, I need in on this," Micah jumped to his feet and raced to where Ari and Kincaid stood. "Fifty on Justice. He'll use Law to get the advantage on Thane, then trounce his younger brother."

Brie walked over to her mate. "Twenty on Thane for me. He won't let his younger brothers show him up." They watched as the fight raged on.

A loud crash had everyone else in the room looking over to the Ashleigh brothers. Thane stood over his two younger brothers who were shaking their heads. "My godsdaughter," he repeated.

Both Justice and Law stayed silent, but it was clear that this argument wasn't over. Micah and Kincaid handed over their money. Brie held up her winnings. "Where can we spend all this loot?"

Ari smiled. "I know just the place." He smiled down at her. "We could use a bit of downtime while blood samples are being compiled. I would like to show you that this world isn't all death and horror."

"Dav's?" Izzy asked.

"What's Dav's?" Brie asked.

"Only the best pub ever. He's serving coffee now, and I'm helping him get set up," Izzy replied.

"Yup. You two coming?"

Izzy nodded and Oron shook his head. Brie laughed. "Looks like you're coming along."

Oron sighed. "Fine, but just for a little bit."

Izzy ran off toward the kitchen, and moments later, she returned carrying three glass bottles. "Okay, ready to go."

Brie waved to Kincaid, who was staying behind to later escort Anne to the storage facility. Together with Izzy and Oron, they headed toward the supposedly best pub ever.

CHAPTER TWELVE

W HEN THEY WALKED INTO THE pub, a chorus of greetings went up all around. Ari raised an eyebrow at Priest. The shifter was sitting at a table with four other men. When they saw Oron, the men jumped up and pounded him on the back.

"I am just running to Éire Danu to help The Menace settle, be back before you know it," the dark-haired man said in a mockingly high-pitched voice.

Oron punched his shoulder. "I do not sound like that, Christoff. I don't know why Aiden thought you lot would be useful." His smile turned gentle as he looked down at Izzy. "Izzy, these idiots are the men of my unit. Sascha Baberiov, tiger-shifter and unit leader for Gamma. Christoff Du'Prince, vampire. Ben McKenzie, Aiden's baby brother, you already met him. And Quinn Foxglove, witch."

Ben waved at them. "Corrin took over at the facility so I could catch up with these jokers."

Izzy beamed at the men. "I've heard so many wonderful things about you. Oron is always saying how he'd feel so much better if he had his unit with him."

The men all tried to hide how touched they were, failing miserably. One by one, they gave a half bow to Izzy. Oron rubbed the back of his neck. "Way to put me out there, Iz. Being away from these meatheads has been nothing but a relief. A vacation."

"I'll tell you what's a vacation. Being away from Colton Albright and enjoying this fine cold beer," the white-haired, barrel chested warrior said, sipping at his tankard.

Brie nudged her mate then looked at the men. Ari wrapped his arm around her shoulders. "Gentleman, I have the honor in introducing my mate, Brie Wilson. She is a Deputy Sheriff out of Monroe and has been instrumental in moving our investigation forward." He paused. "Also, she can probably kick all your asses."

Brie pinched the skin between her eyebrows in exasperation, but secretly she was pleased by her mate's introduction. The men in turn surprised her further. Sascha stuck out his hand. At first, she thought he wanted a handshake, but his hand grasped her forearm instead. She looked up at Ari, who beamed. "That's a warriors' greeting, Brie."

She felt tears start to prickle her eyes but fought them back. These men had accepted her as an equal right from the start. There was no way she was going to undo that with a silly display of emotion. The other men greeted her in the same fashion. They ended up pulling over two more tables so they could all sit together.

"Now, who is this stunning creature?" a deep voice asked from behind them.

Ari simply placed an arm around her shoulders. "She's my mate, Dav. Brie Wilson, Dav Li'Filrien, he owns the pub."

Dav took her hand and kissed it. "All of you ugly bastards keep getting gorgeous mates; it doesn't seem fair," he teased.

"Hey, people," a warrior called out before he and his companion sat at their table.

Sascha pointed to the man. "Brie, this is Lorcan, lion shifter. He's the unit leader for Beta. The shaggy one is Graham Armstrong, bearshifter and the Delta unit leader."

Ari frowned. "If we're all here, who's doing patrols?"

Lorcan grinned and pointed to the walkie talkie at his waist. "Aiden said that the Old Guard here volunteered to take perimeter and city patrols for a bit so we could focus on the murders and defending the storage facility. Aiden about came unglued when he heard that Bastien had been struck by one of the citizens. He was two seconds away from challenging the idiot."

Oron sat back, grinning. "You mean like he challenged all of Noctem Falls?"

"Wait? That was true?" More warriors crowded in. The one that spoke looked down at Brie, he pointed to his chest then to his friend. "My name is Bryok Vi'Erdolin, this is Casek Li'Velen." He turned to Oron. "That's right, you're just back from Noctem Falls. Please tell me that rumor is true."

Oron looked around and saw he had an audience. Just as he was about to start his story, Brie held up her hand. "Before you get started, can I get a beer? I have a feeling this story would go better with alcohol and snacks."

Dav gave a booming laugh. "Give me a few moments, and I'll get everyone sorted, because, honestly I want to hear this too." He hurried to the back to get their drinks.

"Snacks? Gods, the Éire Danu warriors have already corrupted her," Lorcan teased.

"Wait, is that a thing?" she asked.

The men all nodded. "They are known for their addiction to snacks. They actually have contacts all around the world for imported munchies," Oron explained.

"Snack Party," she whispered. Ari just winked and nodded.

"There are worse things units could be doing. Like super-gluing one of their unit leaders to a bell tower," Sascha griped. The men all laughed as Dav came back with trays of beers. Once everyone was settled, Oron launched into the story of how a tunnel escort had hurt Meryn and how Aiden responded. The bear-shifter had gone from level to level, challenging thousands of people to ensure that no one hurt his mate again.

"Etain said that Aiden eyed one of the Noble family sons as if gauging his weight. Then bent down and grabbed the mouthy shit by the ankles, causing him to slam his head on the ground. He then swung him to the left and used him to knock his equally offensive older brother into the wall. Etain had tears in his eyes as he told the story." Oron sighed. "Gods, I am so glad I serve under him."

The men all around the room echoed his sentiment.

Ben raised his tankard. "To Aiden McKenzie the surprisingly amazing leader who is completely ruled by his pint-sized terror of a mate who entertains us all."

"To Aiden McKenzie!" The men cheered and laughed at Ben's toast.

Brie turned to Lorcan. "If the Old Guard are doing patrols, two-thirds of the units are freed up, assuming the other third is still maintaining drills and training. Two men were left behind at the storage facility for guard duty, and five were tapped to help the families in identifying the dead. If we include Oron, seven unit warriors were brought in to help here in Éire Danu, in addition to the four already here including Aiden, Micah, Darian, and Kendrick. That brings the grand total of warriors freed up for orders to twenty-nine. I'm not counting Nigel and Neil since they just arrived, nor the Ashleigh brothers since it was explained to me that they weren't unit warriors." She locked eyes with Lorcan. "So what is Aiden planning on doing with the nearly six units at his disposal?"

Around her the men quieted in stunned silence. Oron whistled and nodded at Ari. "She put that together before any other warrior. You should be proud."

Ari blinked. "What?"

Lorcan and the other warriors from Lycaonia just grinned and sipped their beers.

Dav sat back, holding his own tankard. "That sly bastard."

"Mother and Father were mated when they had Aiden, thank you very much," Ben said, sniffing dramatically.

Ari collapsed back, rubbing his hand over his mouth. "Not even the council has noticed." He looked around.

Quinn waved his hand. "I cast a soundproofing spell on this place the second we got here."

Dav shook his head. "We may need to think about getting a permanent one installed if we keep having meetings here."

Bryok looked from her to Ari and back. "What are we missing?"

Ari half turned to face him. "Aiden managed to bring in and free up six units of warriors without anyone noticing."

Casek frowned. "Why would he do that?"

Brie sat back. "He definitely has a more modern mindset than I expected."

"What?" Bryok repeated.

Brie shrugged. "I can't say for sure, but Aiden is organizing the men the same way the SWAT commander back home organizes his men before raids. You get everyone together, review intel, then go in. If he's quick enough and sends half the men out before everyone realizes how many warriors are milling about, no one may notice for a while."

Quinn pointed to Ari while looking at Brie. "You say six units, but Tau is only a four man team."

"I'll be going out with them, " she said, deliberately not looking at her mate.

Quinn turned to Sascha. "Can she do that?"

Sascha exhaled. "You know, thanks to Menace electrocuting me on multiple occasions, I find that very little surprises me anymore. I just go with the flow now."

"She did say she missed you," Izzy added, then frowned. "Though she did say that after Ryuu upped the charge on her screwdriver thing."

Sascha whimpered and proceeded to empty his tankard as even his own unit laughed at his plight.

Brie snuck a look up at her mate. He looked down at her and shrugged. "You keep expecting me to get mad that you're taking an active role in the investigation. That won't happen. In the wild, it's the lionesses that hunt to feed the pride. I come from a home with strong females, so you being in law enforcement doesn't faze me one bit."

Oron turned to Ari. "You should introduce her to your aunts."

"Aunts?" she asked.

Ari cracked his back. "Yeah, on my mother's side, Eliana's Daughters. My mother has six sisters, and they're all incredibly strong. Remember, we spoke about them back at the warrior villa. " She nodded, and he continued. "They're all warriors in their own right but don't serve in units. They currently exist to protect other lion-shifters. It's not needed as much now that most paranormals live in or around pillar cities, but back before the cities were created, the lionesses were known as Protectors of the Weak."

"Kinda like old school beat cops that knew their neighborhoods inside and out. The lionesses would patrol and keep the stronger shifters from dominating communal spaces," Oron added.

Brie turned and grabbed Ari's arm. "I have to meet them."

"Do you really?" he asked, in a strained voice.

"Why? Are you ashamed of me?" she demanded.

"Hell no. It's just that…they're…they…" Ari floundered.

"They baby him like no other, and they'll probably challenge you on the spot," Oron finished.

She laced her fingers together then cracked her knuckles. "Sounds like fun.

"No, it sounds like a quick way into a body cast," Ari refuted.

"If they're that good, Ari, they'll be able to adjust their strength used." She felt a tremor of excitement. She rarely got to face off against other females.

"Gods, look at her face," Lorcan said, pointing.

Ari just pounded his forehead on the table, before simply letting it rest there. "Healers. I want every witch healer we have on standby," he said in muffled tones.

She stood pushing her chair back. "Ari, let's head to the warrior villa, I owe you at least two blow jobs for backing me up and believing in me."

Ari sat up straight in his chair, looked up at her, drained his tankard, then stood. "Good day, gentlemen."

"I hate you!" Sascha called out to their backs as they left the pub.

"Don't care!" Ari yelled back.

Brie had to practically run to keep up with Ari's long strides. She couldn't help the bubbling laughter from erupting at his enthusiasm. They had almost made it to the villa when Aiden along with Kendrick, Micah, and the Ashleigh brothers caught up with them. Behind the men, Meryn and the twins followed at a leisurely pace, her squire and Pierce accompanying them.

"Good. Glad we ran into you," Aiden said. He raised his arm and pointed toward Dav's and the direction they had just come from. "We need you in a meeting to discuss our next mission."

"Nooo," Ari whimpered.

Brie could barely keep a straight face.

Ari's expression was tragic. "Can't we catch up to you?"

Aiden gave him a shit-eating grin. "We must all make sacrifices as unit warriors." He clapped her mate on the back, then wrapped an arm around his shoulders to steer him away from the villa.

Brie followed. Every once in a while, she made mouth noises that would make Ari turn and glare at her.

Meryn fell in step beside her. "You're kinda evil. I like that."

Brie without even thinking held up her fist, which Meryn promptly bumped. "Where's your cousin?"

"She went with Anne and Kincaid to the facility to get samples. Darian is also acting as escort so he can pop the vials or baggies or whatever over to ViThreePO in Noctem Falls."

"You're just a goofy little geek, aren't you?" Brie asked, amazed that this small woman made so many of the men she knew at Quantico curse and cross themselves.

Meryn held up her fingers in a 'V'. "My kung fu is strong."

"So is mine," Brie said, then paused in their walking. She leaned back and held a kick way over Meryn's head before relaxing back to resume standing on both feet.

"That was so freaking awesome," Meryn whispered. She went to lean back but Ryuu placed a hand on her shoulder. "I would not try, *denka*, you are at a disadvantage due to the baby throwing off your balance."

Meryn sighed. "No ninja kick for me."

"It's okay, Meryn, you're kick ass in other ways," Neil said, pointing to her bag.

"So very true, short stuff. You've made grown men weep with that thing."

Meryn brightened. "Really?"

"Yes, you sadistic little shit."

Meryn just laughed outright. "That totally makes Aiden my mannequin."

"Huh?" Brie asked.

"She always means masochist when she says mannequin," Nigel informed her.

"Good to know."

Brie saw that they, were, once again back at Dav's.

When Aiden opened the door to pub, there was silence then rowdy men's laughter. Brie couldn't help laughing herself. Ari's expression was sure to be priceless.

They made their way back to where they had just left as more table and chairs were scooted over. Wordlessly, yet with a smirk, Dav handed Ari a fresh pint and a small shot glass.

"Thank you, Dav," Ari said, downing the shot and taking a hearty drink from his tankard.

Aiden finished clasping forearms with the warriors from Lycaonia when looked around and winced. "Dav, we're gonna need to take over your pub for a bit."

"One step ahead of you, Commander," Dav said, as he walked back from where he flipped around the closed sign.

A few minutes later, the unit warriors of Éire Danu filed in and sat down. The only ones missing were Corrin and Balder, who were standing guard at the storage facility and Darian and Kincaid, who were escorting Anne and Amelia.

The men from Gamma kept throwing coasters at Ari and teasing him over his misfortune. Brie watched as Bryok leaned over and explained what was happening to newly arrived Bastien, who still sported a white bandage around his head. Bastien leaned over and whispered to Ian who turned to face the Gamma unit, his eyes narrowing. A moment later, each warrior that had been teasing Ari jumped from their chairs, cussing as blue sparks popped around each man.

Ian just grinned. "Still want to play?"

Sascha sat back down. "Menace, did you teach them that?" he asked the small woman, who was still in fits of giggles.

"Nope, but that was very awesome. Keelan would be proud," she said, holding up her hand to Ian for an 'air' high-five. He obliged and turned to Ari. "The way you Lionhart men are, you'd need more time anyway," he said, clapping him on the shoulder.

Ari straightened. "You know it," he said, sounding a bit less depressed.

"I'll make it up to you, baby," she promised.

Ari brightened at that, then gave each man around them that was scowling a shit-eating grin. "I win," he said.

Aiden cleared his throat. "All right, men, let's get started. Kendrick?"

Kendrick shook his head. "One's already in place."

Quinn raised his hand. "I did it earlier, sir."

Aiden gave a short nod. "As you may have noticed, quite a few warriors have suddenly found themselves without standing orders." All of the men nodded. Lorcan pointed at Brie. "Brie spelled it out for some of us slow ones earlier."

Aiden gave her an appraising look. "Very good." He turned to the men. "My mate has identified two more possible warehouse locations here on the East Coast. I'd like to use every warrior in Éire Danu to hit both at once."

Bastien, along with the other fae warriors, placed their fists over their hearts in a silent show of gratitude and respect.

Brie eyed Meryn. She knew the woman was a genius, so her information wasn't wrong, but could they all be missing something. She raised her hand before Aiden started in on the mission details.

Aiden looked surprised. "Yes, Brie?"

She turned back to Meryn. "Why the Coast?"

Meryn blinked. "It's what's closest."

Brie pointed to the fae. "But we have portals, couldn't we go anywhere?"

"I suppose."

"Meryn, I don't know if you've had a chance to look at the reports from the second site, but in mine, I made mention that it felt staged. The people hadn't been dead that long, hell, we could still smell the lemon disinfectant in the hallways."

"Go on," Meryn said, looking intrigued.

"What if you run the same search parameters, but farther out, say, around Noctem Falls. If this is a cat and mouse game, I'd rather catch the cat unawares. It'd be nice to save people for a change instead of recovering bodies." She frowned.

"The only downside is if we disrupt their plans, it may change whatever game they're playing, and they may become more aggressive. It could lead to others getting killed faster."

Meryn was already reaching for her laptop, which had the twins reaching for theirs. "I think the risk is warranted. If we catch the bad guys actually in the warehouse, that would give my mate someone to torture for more info, which could actually lead to saving everyone. Give us a few minutes, I'll see what we can come up with."

Aiden just stared at her. "We have been so blessed in our mates."

The men all raised their tankards and drank deeply.

Smiling, Ari handed her his pint. He nipped her neck as she drank. "You're so damn sexy when you talk cop."

"You want to get arrested later?" she whispered.

"I'll even let you strip search me," he teased.

Aiden looked over the papers they had brought. "I'd still like to hit one of these targets," he said, placing a map on the table. He pointed to a circle around a town in southern Virginia. "This is a little too close to home for us.

"The plan is relatively simple. We'll be dividing into two groups." He held up his hand, which now sported a silver ring. "This is on loan from the queen. It works similarly to the one Darian has and will allow me to open a portal anywhere as long as I work in tandem with a fae. I will be leading the group heading to the Virginia site," he looked around the room. "Brie, I'd like you to head up the group going to the secondary site."

Brie felt her mouth drop. The men around her literally had thousands of years more experience. "Sir, I'd be honored, but, are you sure?"

"I had Meryn hack your file and looked at your test scores. You're the best suited to lead a more modern SWAT style mission. As we speak, updated gear is being secured by Marius, Sebastian, and Cord. It will be gear you'll be familiar with."

Ari's arm came to rest across the back of her chair. "I can't think of anyone who would be better," he admitted.

She looked at Aiden. "Who's opening our portal?"

"Darian, so Oron will also be going with you. Do you have a preference for your team," he asked. There was a curious expression on his face. His question wasn't a test, more like a gauge.

"I'd like Tau, of course, Gamma, Phi along with whatever Superwitch would like to tag along."

Aiden pointed to Bastien. "Why Phi and Gamma?"

"I feel like I know Bastien and his unit well from the limited time I've spent here. Gamma because if Darian and Oron are assigned to the secondary site, it makes sense for Oron to have his unit with him."

"Any preference on the Superwitch," Aiden asked, his mouth twitching.

"Thane."

"Why?"

"It increases the likelihood that one of his brothers will tag along, securing me two Super-witches," she explained.

"Damn good job," Aiden said.

Ari pointed to his chest. "You didn't ask why she wanted Tau along."

Brie just stared. "You didn't assume I wanted you there because you're my mate?"

Ari snorted. "If anything that'd be a deterrent to you. You know damn well our attention may become divided."

"I love how you get me."

Aiden pointed to Ari. "Wait, he's right?"

"Would Meryn choose you because you were her mate?" she asked.

Aiden shook his head. "No. She's actually a quick thinker on the field and a crack shot. I'd be wasted in a perch with her."

"I chose Tau because of all the men, I know them best, but more than that, I feel like they know me best. They won't hesitate when I give an order, and that may make a difference later."

"Brie, I felt like I knew how good you were, then your mate proves I was underestimating you. It won't happen again," Aiden promised.

"No problem, sir."

"Okay, I may have something," Meryn called out, looking up from her laptop.

"Where, baby?" Aiden asked.

"It's gonna cost ya."

Aiden frowned. "You know I'd deny you nothing. What would you like?"

Meryn pointed to her. "Can I have a broach like that? But all your stuff and your tartan sash."

Aiden scooped up his mate. "I'll happily get you a representation of my warrior status to wear. That way the whole world will know you're mine."

Meryn peppered his face with kisses before wiggling about for him to set her back down. "You won't let me get a tattoo, so I figured this would be the next best thing."

Aiden turned to Ari. "Is the jeweler local?"

"Yes, sir. He owns a small shop here in the Border City," Ari answered.

"Perfect. Baby, I promise to commission one immediately. Can you tell us the secondary site now?"

Meryn scrunched up her face. "It's a long shot. Only a few people's homes have missed payments, but I think it's because the late payments haven't hit the systems yet."

Balder sat forward. "That may mean they're still alive."

Meryn shrugged. "It's possible." She flipped her laptop around. "It's about fifty-miles north of Noctem Falls. I already sent a text to Eva; she said that the Eta unit is grabbing their shit and will rendezvous here." She pointed to a large parking lot. "This mall was shut down last year, so you won't have anyone bugging ya."

Brie looked up at Aiden. "Sir, with your permission I'd like to hit that location this evening. Sunset is around six pm here on the East Coast for your team, which means we'll be hitting our location around four. Darkness will help you remain hidden, but it still being light out may give us the advantage of surprise, no one expects these type of things to happen in the middle of the day."

"Agreed." He looked around. "Tau, Phi, Gamma, you're with Brie. Thane are you okay with heading out to New Mexico?" Aiden asked.

Thane nodded. "It's old stomping grounds for me. Cristo liked to stay close to home, so whenever we had downtime, we lingered in the southwest." He looked at Justice. "You're with me. Law, you babysit the commander."

Aiden gave him a flat expression. "I'm standing right here."

Brie stood, and the units assigned to her stood as well. "Can you update Darian and send him to the warrior villa?"

Aiden nodded. "Good luck. Gods willing, this may be over tonight."

Brie didn't say a word. Situations like this were never easily resolved. "Meryn, do you have anyone that can guide us in?"

Meryn jerked her thumb to the twins. "It's buy one, get one free. I've been training them along with Noah and Jaxon to be eyes in the sky."

Brie looked at the twins. "We'll be counting on you."

Neil gulped. "We'll do our best."

"Come on, guys, I have phone calls to make," Brie said, already heading toward the door.

"After, right?" Ari called out from behind her.

She just chuckled and kept walking.

CHAPTER THIRTEEN

❧

"ARE YOU MAD?" SHE ASKED, as they began laying out their gear.

Ari looked over at her, surprised. "What, because my blow jobs got postponed? No. I know your head needs to be in the game for this to work."

She walked over and hugged him from behind. "How are you so perfect?"

Ari rubbed her hands where they rested at his waist. "I'm not, but I think I am perfect for you."

In truth, Ari wanted to scream. He didn't want her within one-thousand miles of this entire mess, but she had been chosen and recognized by his commander. There was no way he'd take that from her. He'd just have to ignore her orders and guard every step she took. He sighed.

"Thank you," she whispered. "I know this has to be hard for you."

Ari turned in her arms and pulled her close. "It is. It's very hard. I want to wrap you in cotton and keep you safe, but that's not who you are here." He tapped her chest.

"I'm assigning you my six."

He grunted.

"You were totally going to do that anyway, weren't you?" she asked, amusement dancing in her eyes.

"Absolutely." He saw no reason to lie.

"I knew it." She laughed. "I suppose having you act as my back up is a small price to pay." She tilted her head back, and he practically sagged in relief. Any action where he touched her felt like heaven. He kept things light and simply nibbled and tugged on her lower lip. When her phone rang, they stepped apart.

She answered it. "Wilson, here."

"Hey, Brie, I asked our boys for what you wanted, and they were more than happy to donate. I'm at the portal now; where should I drop your stuff?" Ari wondered what Brie had asked Cam for.

"I'm at the warrior villa, we're mobilizing for tonight."

"That soon? Need help?"

"Think you can keep up, old man?" she teased.

"Old man? Wait until I see you, young lady," he groused before he hung up.

"What'd ya ask for?"

"Some SWAT tactical gear. I helped nearly every team member study for their advancement tests, they *so* owed me."

"We have gear," Ari protested. It was unit gear; it was the best. Right?

"And it's solid equipment, but what I asked for is part of the reason why Aiden chose me for this mission. It's all new tech gear that you and your fellow unit brothers may not have been exposed to yet."

"I guess, if it's so important."

"Are you pouting right now?"

"No. Maybe."

"God, I love you," she said, then froze. His heart practically stopped. They turned to face one another. She covered her mouth with her hand. "God, I do. I love you. This is bad."

"Wait. What? This is in no way bad!" he protested, pulling her close. His mate loved him! He wanted to shout it from the palace walls.

"Yes, it is, because I can't lose you and live," she struggled in his arms.

"Baby, I'm a lion-shifter. I'm close friends with witches that can do shit like make it snow and create tornadoes. I'm not going anywhere."

She calmed down but still clung to him. "I can't lose you, Ari. I just can't."

"You won't," he reiterated.

She looked over at their bed and sighed. "We don't have time."

"Normally, I'd see that as a challenge, but as we just admitted our love for one another, the next time we're in that bed, we're going to spend all night making love, and I'm reclaiming you. I don't want to be rushed."

Brie gave him the stink eye. "I didn't hear you admit shit. I'm the one dangling out here in vulnerability land."

Ari stared. She was right. He cupped her face. "Brie Wilson, I have loved you from the moment I first saw you. I loved you even more when you shot me. Every day that love grows. From now until the day we pass from this world, I will be yours and you will be mine."

She rubbed her cheek against his hand. "You would say something about me shooting you in your love confession."

He kissed her nose and let his hands drop. "Of course."

They heard a doorbell chime. "That's probably Cam with your stuff." He grabbed the last of his own gear, and they headed downstairs where Bastien was greeting Cam.

Cam eyed his mate. "I heard y'all were having a party. Feel like letting this poor, bored Vanguard join in?" He held out an impressively large duffel to Brie. She stepped forward took it, then headed off to one side of the foyer to rummage through it like a kid in a candy bowl.

Bastien pointed to Cam's attire. The man had come completely decked out in black gear, an automatic weapon slung across his back. "And if we said no?"

Cam shrugged. "I already bribed Meryn with an Apple watch to get the locations of both sites. I could just meet you there."

"Damn," Bastien muttered.

On the floor, Brie just chuckled. "Oh, they remembered. Awesome." She started attaching, buckling, clipping, and even velcroing items to her body. When she stood, she looked like his own personal wet dream. "Damn, baby," he breathed, taking her in.

"Ari, you're doing that growl thing again," Priest said, nudging him.

"I don't even care anymore," Ari said.

His saucy mate winked at him and looked down at her watch. "It's almost time to go. Is everyone ready?"

The men that had crowded the foyer with the doorbell's chime all chorused, 'yes'.

"Is Darian here?"

"I'm here. Just arrived though. I've been arguing with my brother for him to stay at the palace with our mother, but he's being stubborn," Darian complained.

"Don't be like that, Dari. It's been ages since I've had a mission with Gamma; let me have some fun," Oron pointed out.

Brie tapped her watch then looked at Darian. "You know where we're going?"

He nodded. "I went out there a bit earlier to get my bearings for the portal and to scope the place out. Menace did a good job picking a rendezvous point."

"Why do you call her Menace. I mean it suits her, but isn't that kinda mean?"

"She's the one that started these call signs, she's stuck with it," Sascha growled.

"What's yours?" Brie asked.

Sascha turned pink. "Gamma Kitten One," he muttered lowly.

"I'm Foxy Boy," Quinn added.

"I'm Adonis," Ben said smirking at his unit leader.

Ari turned to Christoff and Oron. "You two?" He was dying to see what the rest of the unit got. The warriors of the Tau and Phi units were laughing their asses off.

Christoff gave a modest shrug. "Prince."

Oron beamed. "Oreo."

Sascha scowled at the warriors. "Yuk it up. You'll probably be getting christened tonight. And from what I heard from Aiden, she's hungry and stressed, so I don't think you'll fair as well as we did."

Ari chuckled to himself as his brothers stopped laughing almost immediately.

Nerius turned to Sascha. "They're not real call signs, right?"

Sascha gave him a flat look. "We're about to go on a council sanctioned two prong mission with coordination from three of the four pillar cities." He pointed to their walkie talkie. "I can guarantee you at some point tonight, Meryn's chirpy voice will be calling out to Gamma Kitten One. Real? Maybe. Permanent. Absolutely."

Bastien turned to Oron. "Why are you so happy with Oreo?"

"Because it's one of her favorite cookies, which means she loves me and because those cookies are freaking amazing," Oron explained.

"Double stuff?" Kincaid asked.

Oron nodded. "Evidently, according to Meryn, double stuff are regular Oreos. Regular Oreos are diet Oreos and those thin ones are abominations."

Kael's head bobbed as he agreed. "Exactly. We need to invite Meryn to a Snack Party. It sounds like she knows her stuff."

Brie tapped the comms piece at her ear. "Menace, you set up?"

"Ready to rock 'n' roll, NinjaGaiden."

Brie grinned at the guys at her call sign. "Who will we be working with?"

"I have you set up with Gemini. They'll be taking over comms when you meet up with Professor."

"Roger that, Menace. Over."

"Werd. Over."

Brie motioned to Darian. "Anytime you're ready."

"As you say, NinjaGaiden," Darian shook his head and opened a portal in their foyer.

Ari made sure he was right behind his mate as they walked through.

Once on the other side, they saw another group of men standing by a black SUV. A tall dark-haired warrior stepped forward, his arm out. Brie clasped forearms with the man, and the others waved their greetings.

"Welcome to New Mexico," the warrior said. "I'm Adriel Aristaios. This is Declan Lionhart, my second. Grant Douglas, wolf-shifter, Etain Vi'Aerlin, and of course, you've already met Micah. Darian dropped him off with us when he checked out the warehouse for portal placement," Adriel said, by way of introductions.

Ari never even saw it coming. One moment he was standing with his mate, the next he was wrapped up in the arms of his older brother, being swung around.

"Ari!" Declan laughed, his eyes bright.

"Put me down, Dec!" Ari protested. His mate was watching for goodness sake.

Declan set him down, and he was pulled in for an immediate hug. "Gods! It's good to see you. I wish that it were under better circumstances though."

Ari gave his brother a sour look. "That's rich coming from the brother that never visits, mates, and gets a baby Lionhart started without calling." He crossed his arms over his chest.

"Ahh, Ari don't be like that." Declan's eyes narrowed. "Wait, didn't you mate recently as well without calling?"

Ari grinned. "Yup."

"Do you have a picture of her on your phone?" Declan asked, pulling his own out. "I have a ton of Kari."

Ari pointed to where Brie stood, wide eyed, taking everything in. "Brie Wilson, squad leader for this mission."

Declan froze then turned to stare at Brie. "That's my baby sister?"

"Yup."

"Oh, hell no!" Declan threw his arms in the air.

Brie's face crumpled, and Ari took a step forward, about to knock some sense into his brother.

"She's too gorgeous for a little brat like you." He looked at her gear. "So, I guess I'll be guarding you, huh?"

Brie's expression turned from hurt, to pleased, to resigned. She covered her face with her hand. "Well, considering I'm mated to your brother, have met your father, your other older brother and cousins, I know that it would be an absolute waste of time to argue with you."

"So very, very true," Declan admitted shamelessly.

Ari breathed a secret sigh of relief. With his older brother at his side, nothing was getting to his mate.

Adriel placed a hand on Brie's shoulder. "It does not get any easier. Trust me, I have been trying to beat sense into Declan for centuries. It is a lost cause."

Brie just shook her head and checked her watch. "Okay, men, listen up."

The men huddled around Brie for orders.

"We'll be running this a bit differently than Aiden's mission in Virginia. We're hoping to catch actual perps on site and live hostages. Which means we'll have to be very precise when it comes to timing." She looked down at her watch again. "In four minutes, we'll be linking up with Gemini—the twins. They have hacked the building's security and cameras and will be guiding us in. Our goal is painfully simple. If the hostages are alive, they take priority." She leveled her eyes at the men. "Éire Danu needs this win. The queen needs this win, so we're going to do our best to give it to them. Second priority will be securing any hostiles alive. Let me repeat that, gentleman: the more we take alive, the more chances we have at getting the locations of more warehouses in time to save people."

"Yes, sir," the men said, followed by an awkward pause.

Brie grinned and waved off the gaff. "Sir is fine. Now, according to what Meryn showed us earlier, this building has one entrance in the front. It's double doors, no windows. The back has a single door, but a window to the side. Anyone have any ideas of how we can obscure it?"

Quinn raised his hand. "I'm an Earth witch. I can sling mud up on the lower panes."

Brie nodded and kept going. "From the second we hit the door, we have less than thirty seconds to secure the building. If we give them any more time, we could lose hostages or face hostiles and their reinforcements. We'll have to hit and hit hard." She held up a small tablet with a schematic. "Gamma, Phi, we'll give you a twenty count, can you secure the back?"

"Consider it done," Sascha promised, and Nerius bumped forearms with the tiger-shifter.

"Good. That means Tau, Eta you're with me. According to the map, the double doors lead into a very small front office with an interior door leading to the warehouse storage floor. Adriel, Gage, once those double doors are open, I'd like either of you to flank the entrance and watch our six." Adriel and Gage nodded. "Thane, I'm not sure what you're capable of, so please don't get mad if I ask a question that paints you in a childish or poor light. I'm not used to working with people that can use the elements."

Thane smiled. "Ask away, you won't upset me."

"Can you open locked doors?"

Thane blinked. "Easily."

"Good. You and Justice have the following three orders. Open the front and interior door. Locate and defend the hostages, and if possible, prevent the perps from escaping."

"Dibs on securing the perps," Justice said quickly with a wolfish expression.

Thane just nodded. "If I don't let you do real work every once in a while, you'll become useless like Kendrick."

"I'm gonna tell him you said that," Justice threatened.

"I'll embroider it on a throw pillow for him," Thane replied.

Brie shook her head at their bickering. "That means the rest of Tau and Eta will divide their efforts between hostages and perps. You all have been running missions for more years than I can even imagine; you're experienced enough to act accordingly." The men nodded.

Her watch pinged, and she tapped her comms piece. "Gemini, men are briefed, and we're ready to go in."

"We hear you loud and clear. Move out whenever you're ready. Over."

"Darian?"

Darian stepped forward and opened a portal. Unlike most that Ari had seen, this one did not glow in a golden light. In fact, he could barely see the shimmer of the air in the center of the portal at all. He looked over at them.

He looked around. "Seriously, guys? Did you think I was going to open a glowing beacon right outside their door?"

"New?" Thane asked.

Darian grinned at him. "The useless mage helped me craft it."

"We're running silent. Keep comms open unless you are calling out for positioning or back up."

The men nodded.

"Gods above, guide and protect us. Please, let there be someone to save," Kincaid whispered.

As usual, his witch brother knew just the thing to say. Around them, the men whispered, "So mote it be." And they crossed through the portal.

Once on the other side, Brie tapped her ear. "Gemini, night, night."

"Cameras and security offline," one of the twins responded.

Gamma and Phi peeled off to go around to the back. Brie started a countdown on her watch. They got in position around the front entrance and waited. Ari looked over at his brother and met his eyes. Declan looked over at Brie, then nodded. The men might have their assigned priorities, but he had only one. Keeping his mate safe.

Brie held up a hand and began the five second count down. When she got to one, Thane released a spell and burst the front doors open. Immediately, everyone was moving.

Adriel and Gage took up positions on either side of the door, and they made their way inside. A moment later, there was a second boom, and Thane practically dissolved the interior door. The men fanned out, taking in the situation. Off to one side, a large group of fae were huddled in a corner. They were alive!

"Thane, Justice!" Brie called out, pointing.

The witches moved quicker than he could follow, and a moment later, a shimmering silver barrier stood between the ongoing battle and the scared hostages.

"They've gone invisible!" Sascha called out over the comms.

"Got two!"

Ari turned to see who had shouted out. To his surprise, Kincaid stood, breathing hard, next to a large clay box.

In front of them gunfire rang out as first Kael, then Quinn went down.

"Man down!" Ari called out over the comms.

"Palace is prepared to receive injured," one of the twins relayed.

"Face me, you cowards!" Sascha snarled, standing over the bodies of his unit brothers, defending them with his life.

Ari and Declan moved with Brie, acting as shields.

"Rathais, you in position?" his mate called out.

"Ready to go," he replied.

Brie tapped her ear piece. "Everybody down!" she ordered.

Every single unit warrior dropped to the floor. He and his brother stayed standing by Brie.

She pulled out a pair of goggles and adjusted them as gunfire continued to echo throughout the room. Ari watched in amazement as pools of blood appeared on the floor all around them.

Brie brought up her firearm and began to fire rapidly. She would no sooner aim, then another pool of blood would appear. She was moving almost as quickly as the warriors. After what seemed like forever, the gunfire stopped. She tapped her ear piece. "Clear! Resume operation."

The warriors jumped to their feet and fanned out. Once the invisible defenders were down, ferals emerged from behind each stacked crate.

Sascha bared his canines at them. "Come get this!"

Brie's hand went to her ear. "Darian, we need to get Quinn and Kael treatment."

"On it," he replied. He motioned Bastien to the small front office they had entered from. They each lifted a warrior then retreated to get the wounded back to the palace.

Ari heard a snarl only moments before a weight crashed into them from the right. A feral straddled him, snarling and spitting in his face. Both of his hands gripped the monster's vest to keep his teeth away from his neck.

An ear splitting roar reverberated through him. Seconds later, the feral was lifted and thrown across the room into a concrete wall. "You dare hurt my brother!" Declan hissed, then shifted both hands into claws as he proceeded to shred the feral that had waylaid him.

Brie bent over, holding out her hand. He took it, and she helped him up. "You good?" she asked.

"Golden."

"Report!" she called out to the men.

"Nothing new on thermal," Cam replied.

"Back secure," Ben added.

"Quinn and Kael have been transferred to Éire Danu. Darian is on his way back. Brennus will maintain the portal here in the office as a fall back point," Adriel reported.

"Ferals are down," Christoff reported. "For gods sake Sascha, he's dead," they all heard him mutter.

He and Brie turned to see Sascha jumping up and down on what looked to be a body.

Brie just shook her head. "We clear?"

"Clear!" the men rang out.

"Justice, Thane, report," she barked out.

"Alive," Thane came back. "Thank all the gods, we have over one-hundred people here and they're all alive."

A cheer went up, and Ari swept his mate up in his arms. "You did it!"

She wrapped her arms around his neck. "We all did it."

"No, baby. You did it. Coming this far out was your idea. You and Cam took down every reaper, leaving us free to take out the ferals." He set her down. "How'd you do that?"

She pointed to the goggles. "I wasn't sure if

they'd work. I didn't see anything in the report about using thermal to track those invisible. I was scared to death that something in the neck-laces blocked it."

"Aiden is gonna have a fit," Ben whispered gleefully. "Please let me be the one to tell him."

Sascha pulled his goggles out. "We only have night vision. When did they start making ther-mal imaging goggles?"

Brie patted hers. "They're not new technol-ogy, but it's a lot easier to get it in the form of tactical gear now."

Sascha grinned evilly. "They can't hide from us anymore."

Nerius pointed to Brie. "We'll have to employ some new methodology. She had us drop to avoid mixing us up with hostiles."

"So brilliant, my mate," Ari whispered into her hair.

Brie looked around. "Where are the hostages?"

"Right here," a female voice answered.

They turned to see many smiling faces looking at them. "My name is Elissa Elian. We cannot thank you enough." She wiped at her eyes. "They would play the screams of others for us and said we would soon be next. Had you not come, we would have died for sure."

Jace and Ian stepped forward. "If you'll fol-low us, we have a portal set up that will take you directly to Éire Danu. There's a very anx-ious queen waiting to see her children," Ian said, pointing to the front.

His statement brought on more tears as the

people immediately began moving toward the place where their queen awaited their return.

Darian passed many of them as he re-entered the warehouse. One of them saw his ring and gasped. "Your highness," the man breathed in a timorous whisper. The crowd halted, and as one, they dropped to one knee.

Darian quickly went to the side of the man who had recognized the signet ring. "Please, stand, all of you. Don't worry about deportment now of all times. Let's get you home and looked after."

They stood, some on wobbly legs. The man looked at Darian. "You came for us?"

Darian clenched his jaw. "I will always come for my people when they need me, this I do swear."

His quiet promise had the rest of the crowd dissolving into quiet sobs. Darian looked around, and Oron went to his side. "We'll go with you. The queen is insisting on making sure you're all well, and her squire is cooking up a storm," he said, smiling.

One of the women looked at him fearfully. "An Eirson," she whispered, backing away.

Darian slung his arm around his brother's shoulders. "You're wrong. Much has been celebrated in Éire Danu as of late. For example, the queen's consort Brennus has passed on head of household to Oron, he is now Oron Vi'Eirlea."

The people gasped and stared at Oron in wonder.

Oron rubbed the back of his neck. "My uncle Eamon also had a daughter, Meryn. She is mated to the Unit Commander. She's the most adorable little thing."

"Gamma Kitten One, if you don't update me, I'm going to shock you till your nuts fall off!" an irate female voice yelled. Her threat echoed from the walkie talkie through the empty warehouse.

Oron grinned. "Speaking of my little sister," he said, winking at the crowd.

The people began to chuckle as Sascha frantically tried to unclip his walkie talkie. "Dammit, someone tell that pint-sized menace I'm trying!"

Ben lifted his walkie talkie. "Menace, Gamma Kitten One says there's no way your screwdriver can do that and to watch your mouth or he'll tell BooBear on you."

Sascha froze, his mouth hanging wide. Abandoning all modesty he pulled his pants off and lifted the walkie talkie to his face. "Menace, I said no such thing. My walkie talkie was stuck on my belt loop!"

"I will see you when you return," she said ominously. "Over."

Sascha dropped his pants and reached for Ben who was laughing manically as he ran from his unit leader.

Darian jerked his thumb at their shenanigans. "As you can see, they have serious and important work to do. If you all could head through the portal and meet up with Portia and the queen, we'd be helping them enormously." The once somber people were now chuckling and moving once again.

Once the warehouse was clear and they had pried Sascha's fingers from around Ben's neck, they walked over to the strange box Kincaid had created.

Thane and Justice were examining it with excitement. Thane looked over at Kincaid. "Do you know what you did?"

Kincaid looked confused. "I made a box."

"You made more than a box. Kincaid, this is porcelain," Thane explained, running his hand over the wall.

"And?" he asked.

Justice shook his head. "He doesn't get it."

"Porcelain is created when clay is heated in a kiln to over two-thousand six-hundred degrees Fahrenheit," Thane shook his head. "I've never seen anything like this before."

"Thane! There are traces of steel and diamond in the clay!" Justice exclaimed, pulling his hands from the side of the box. "Kincaid, how'd you do this?"

"I have no idea! It just happened," Kincaid exploded.

Ari walked over and stood by his unit brother. "This is really good work, Kaid. Damn good work."

Thane nodded. "I agree. Now, let's open it and 'greet' our new friends."

Kincaid paled. "I don't know how. I was kinda hoping you would."

Thane and Justice both blinked. "What?" they asked, in unison.

Kincaid pointed to the cube. "I knew I had to stop them, so it just kinda happened."

Thane closed his eyes. "You didn't use any form of a spell, did you?"

"Umm. Nope."

"Justice, you do it," Thane exhaled and walked away.

"I screwed up again," Kincaid said morosely.

"You're the only one that was able to secure prisoners, Kincaid. I'm calling that a huge win," Brie pointed out.

"Really?"

"Yeah. Who knows, maybe staying in a completely dark box for a few days with no food will loosen their tongues," she added winking at him.

"Yeah. Let's go with that," he agreed.

Justice pulled out his cell. "Hey, Kendrick, my brother can't figure something out and is begging for your help."

"Lies!" Thane shouted from across the room.

"On my way," Kendrick replied.

Ari pulled Brie so that her back was against his chest. He knew he had done the right thing when she leaned against him.

After a few minutes, Kendrick, looking tired, walked in from the front office.

"The other site?" Ari asked.

Kendrick shook his head. "No, and there were more bodies this time. Close to three hundred." He shook his head. "Livor mortis had set in, but there was no sign of bloating. We missed saving them by less than twenty-four hours."

"Gods," the men whispered around them.

Kendrick pulled Brie from his arms to give her a hug. "Thank the gods for you. The people you saved tonight will go a long, long way in keeping the city from falling into complete despair. You have proved that we can out think them and fight back. You have no idea how vital this was." He released her then gently nudged her back into Ari's arms.

"The queen?" she asked.

Kendrick grimaced. "She's focusing on the living." He smiled softly. "There were children and a newborn amongst the survivors."

Brie gasped. "I didn't see them."

Kendrick pulled off her black skull cap so he could ruffle her dark brown curls. "I imagine you were busy." He cracked his knuckles. "Now, what simple, easy to figure out thing did Thane beg me to come here for?"

"Asshole," Thane growled and pointed to Kincaid's cube. "Have at it."

Kendrick blinked. "It's an earthen box Thane."

Thane gave him an evil smile. "Open it, then."

Kendrick placed a hand on the wall. Ari felt a pulse, then nothing. Kendrick frowned. "That should have worked."

"You've been saying that a lot lately," Thane teased.

"Only when it comes to me," Kincaid interjected.

Kendrick wheeled around to face Kincaid. "You did this?"

Kincaid nodded miserably. "I don't know how to undo it."

Kendrick placed a hand on the wall. "This is porcelain," he announced excitedly.

Thane rolled his eyes. "We went over that already."

Kendrick eyed Thane. "I don't think you get it."

"Oh, no. We do. He used both his elements," Thane replied.

Kendrick pinched the bridge of his nose. "He used both of his elemental powers at the same time with the exact amount of intensity. If there had been more earth magic, it wouldn't have hardened; if there had been more fire magic, it would have crumbled at the first touch."

Thane and Justice paled, but poor Kincaid still looked clueless.

"What'd I do?" he asked.

Kendrick lowered his hand. "Kincaid, you performed the impossible."

Kincaid was now looking panicked. "We can open it, right? I finally was able to help with my magic, but it won't mean anything if we can't get those guys outta there."

Kendrick eyed the cube, a downright fright-ening look in his eye. "The ones responsible are within?"

"Yes," Kincaid replied.

Kendrick rubbed his jaw. "We need to secure

this warehouse from any human intervention, buy the damn building if we have to."

Ari pulled out his phone. "I'll handle that," he volunteered. This was something his family could do.

Kendrick looked at Thane and Justice. "Later, once the survivors are sorted and the new bodies have been processed and added to our depressingly growing list of deceased, we, along with Law and the twins, will try to crack this nut."

Justice's eyebrows snapped together in a frown. "Those two?"

"First off, they are my cousins, so watch what you say. Second, yes, those two. They rival me in earth magic," Kendrick explained pleasantly.

Thane's head dropped back. "Those two seriously have that much magic?"

Kendrick smiled. "Runs in the family," he boasted.

Brie eyed the earthen cube. "We leave it?"

Kendrick nodded. "Unfortunately."

Ari dropped a kiss to the back of his mate's neck and smirked when she shivered. "I'll be right over there, love," he said, pointing across the room.

"Miss you already," she replied, as she adjusted her vest.

Ari jogged over to where Declan stood talking with Etain. "Hey, big brother. Got a minute?"

"For you, of course," Declan said.

"Kendrick can't figure out how to crack that nut, so we have to buy the building," he explained.

Declan whistled low. "If Kendrick can't figure it out, it must be serious magic."

"Kincaid threw it around our feral friends with no clue how to bring it down." He looked over his shoulder at his unit brother. "With Kendrick and the Ashleigh brothers seeing his magic first hand, hopefully, he'll finally get the help he needs."

Declan laced his fingers behind his head. "If he's done something Kendrick can't figure out, he officially has their attention," he said laughing.

"I'm going to call Rex and get him to start on the purchase. Would you or your unit be able to maintain twenty-four hour watch?"

Declan nodded. "Easily. We can also ask Noctem Fall's wolves if they'd like to assist. Now that the virus is over, some are feeling a bit on edge over how helpless they were. Guarding a prison where the enemy is entombed may actually help quite a bit."

Ari was about to call Rex when he looked up at his brother. "You know, with the portal being open here to Éire Danu and with Noctem Falls volunteering for guard duty, you could visit every day if you wanted," he pointed out.

Declan's face became unreadable, and Ari continued. "Come home tonight, Dec, let's surprise mother by having us all home."

Declan nodded slowly at first then smiled. "After everything we've seen lately, I would say that is not only wanted, but very needed. We need to celebrate and appreciate our family now more than ever."

Ari felt his eyes begin to water, so he turned back to face his mate. "I'll give Leo a heads up. You craving anything?"

"Gods yes! I'd do anything for Leo's London Broil, like five cows worth," Declan said in a breathy voice. "And mashed potatoes and his vegetable medley that he does with whatever witchcraft seasonings he adds to it. Oh! Oh! And his fruit tart!"

Ari turned back and couldn't help laughing; his brother had a look of pure rapture on his face. "Consider it done, big brother."

He dialed Rex and wasn't at all surprised when he answered on the first ring.

"Ari, are you okay?"

"Yup, barely a scratch on me. Declan pretty much eviscerated the feral that tried to rip my throat out."

"What! Where's the damn portal?!"

"Rex! I'm fine! I need you there anyway."

"Why? What's going on?"

"Long story short, we trapped the bad guys in a box we can't open. So we now need to buy the warehouse so Kendrick and the Superwitches can play with it," he explained.

From across the room, Justice called out. "I'm living for the term Superwitch!"

Ari ignored him. "Also, can you secretly let Leo know that Declan and Kari are coming home for a visit. We'll need a late night dinner of London Broil, mashed potatoes, vegetable medley, and a fruit tart."

"Dec is coming home," Rex whispered.

"Yeah, he is," Ari felt his heart swell. It had been way too long since they had all been in the same room.

"Consider the purchase done. What about guards?"

"Noctem Falls has it covered. Just let the queen know we'll need two temporary portals from here in the warehouse to Noctem Falls for the guards to get back and forth. And, of course, we'll need one from here to Éire Danu."

"If Lionharts own the warehouse and I persuade the queen to make the portals permanent, Declan can visit whenever he likes," Rex said excitedly.

"Exactly."

"Hanging up now. I'll work with Leo to make everything perfect," he promised.

"Everything you do is perfect, Rex."

"No, not everything. But I'm working on it. See you soon." Rex hung up, and Ari could just imagine him issuing decrees at the speed of light.

Declan scuffed his foot on the hard concrete. "He really does care, doesn't he?"

Ari frowned then punched Declan as hard as he could in the upper arm. He smiled in satisfaction when his older brother howled. "We both do, you big dorkus."

Declan was primed to pounce on him when they heard Brie. "Ari! Time to go! We have reports to give at the palace!"

Declan narrowed his eyes. "Saved by your mate."

Ari looked around to make sure no one was watching, and he stuck his tongue out at his brother.

Declan's booming laughter filled the warehouse. "See you in a little bit," he said.

Ari waved. "See ya real soon, big brother."

He jogged back over to Brie and looked at the collection of stumped witches. "The Lionharts will be purchasing the warehouse outright. Declan and the Noctem Falls' wolves will be providing guards around the clock, and Rex is arranging for portals so transportation to and from the warehouse is easier."

Thane clapped a hand on his back. "Excellent work."

Ari shrugged. It wasn't like he was doing any of the actual work himself, just setting things in motion. "We won't be able to stay at the palace long. Declan and Kari are going to take advantage of the portal and will be coming to dinner." He licked his lips. "Leo is making his famous London Broil for Declan, I can't wait."

Brie eyed him. "To visit with your brother or to eat?"

Ari shrugged. "Both."

"London Broil?" she asked, swallowing hard.

"Oh, yeah."

"What are we waiting for?" she asked, marching toward the front office where the portal shimmered just out of view.

Ari watched her ass as she walked away. "What are we waiting for indeed?"

CHAPTER FOURTEEN

WHEN THEY STEPPED THROUGH THE portal, the first thing Brie noticed was the noise. It seemed there was more people in the queen's outer meeting room than the room could accommodate. Everywhere she turned, fae were weeping and holding tight to their loved ones.

"There she is!" a voice called out. All at once, she and Ari were surrounded.

"Thank the gods for you!"

"Gods blessings on you both!" The voices were full of gratitude and warmth.

The crowd soon parted as the queen made her way over to them. She first went to Ari, pulling him into a tight hug. Moments later, the queen did the same to her. Before the queen pulled away, she whispered in her ear. "Thank you! Thank all the gods for you." The queen stepped back and nodded. "Is there anything I can do for you? A favor I could grant?"

Ari shook his head. "You never have to reward a warrior for doing his job," he answered.

The queen turned to Brie. "You are new to our world and not a unit warrior. What can I do for you, as a show of thanks, for the lives of my people?"

Brie thought about the offer. If she refused it might seem like she didn't value the lives of the fae. She looked around the room where the warriors beamed in her direction. "Tonight, one of the most invaluable pieces of equipment was a set of thermal imaging goggles I had on loan from the Monroe SWAT team. Is there any way you could secure these goggles for every unit warrior and Vanguard that may be facing these invisible perps?"

The queen blinked. "You mean to tell me there is a way for our warriors to see these invisible wretches, and they don't have the equipment they need?"

Aiden stepped forward. "Your Majesty, as you know, personal wealth cannot be used to supply items for public use. It was a major point of contention my brother faced when updating our clinic. The same holds true for the warriors. We are not able to purchase items with our own funds to add to our armory." He rubbed the back of his neck. "Though, to be honest, we didn't know these goggles existed. We have night-vision goggles, but had no idea thermal imaging technology was now available in tactical gear. That is my fault and mine alone." He hung his head low.

The queen actually snorted. "And when exactly, Aiden McKenzie, did you have time to re-evaluate the men's gear? It's been less than six months since the first reaper appeared, and in those months, your warriors managed to save and secure Lycaonia, uncover a device that can strip a witch of their magic, discovered what their damned necklaces do and what they are, revealed treachery at the committee level, defended Noctem Falls from an internal incursion, and cured a magic-made virus. You managed to do all this despite not having these special goggles, so what does that actually say about your leadership skills?" she asked.

"It says he is a blessing from the gods and that we are lucky to have him," Bastien announced loudly.

"Gods all bless the McKenzie!" a cheer went up.

Aiden looked shocked as the multiple voices reverberated around the room.

"And he's an amazing mate!" Meryn yelled, standing on one of the tables, both Ryuu and Pierce at her side, ensuring she didn't just topple off.

Aiden's eyes became shiny. "Only because you're so easy to love," he said as he walked over to her and plucked her off the table.

"And we have the next generation Commander on the way," one of the fae shouted.

"And they will be part fae and tied to our queen!"

Meryn scowled. "My li'l nugget is gonna be a hacker."

The queen blew a kiss to her niece. "Considering you used your hacker skills to find my people, I would say that would be amazing too."

"The little one found us?"

"What do you mean tied to the queen?"

"Is she Eamon's daughter?"

The fae started throwing out questions at the speed of light. Meryn wiggled until Aiden put her down, and she immediately retreated behind Ryuu and Pierce.

Aiden was about to say something when the portal glowed again, and Declan, along with a beautiful woman, walked through.

"Kari! Simba!" Meryn ran to where Declan stood smiling. He opened his arms and she jumped right into them. Despite being pregnant, he easily lifted her up and swung her around, causing her to laugh.

Kari just shook her head. "It has not even been two weeks, Meryn."

Declan set Meryn down and the small woman grabbed Kari's hand and dragged her over to Portia. "Kari, Portia needs your superpowers getting this mess organized."

Meryn turned to Portia. "You're going to love Kari. She's all neat lines and boxes like you."

Kari nodded to the fae. "Pleased to meet you."

Portia just stared down at Meryn's exuberance. "We may need to add deportment to your daily schedule." She looked at Kari. "Any assistance at all would be greatly appreciated. I do feel a bit out of my depth as of late and everyone here has been singing your praises."

Kari blushed and ruffled Meryn's curls. "What has the little monster been saying?"

"She said you live and breathe forms, Power

Point, and highlighters," the queen answered, walking up to them.

She and Ari followed behind Declan as he made his way over to his mate. "My Kari is an invaluable asset to Prince Magnus. He regards her as nothing less than his right-hand person and implicitly trusts her in the day to day running of Noctem Falls," Declan announced, keeping his tone neutral.

Brie didn't have a lot of experience when it came to the political side of the force, but she knew a power play when she saw one. In a single statement, Declan let it be known that his mate was valued highly by Prince Magnus, and impertinence to her would be dealt with swiftly.

"And while she is here, she will be treated as a close friend of the throne," the queen confirmed.

Kari eyed Portia's quill and scroll, and her eye began to twitch. "We are expected for dinner at the Lionhart estate, but perhaps tomorrow, you can show me what you have thus far?"

Portia nodded. "Many thanks."

"Dinner?" Meryn asked, piping up. "Whatcha havin'?"

"Leo's London Broil," Rex answered, smiling as he walked up from behind them.

"Hell yeah!" Meryn danced around excitedly.

"Meryn, no," Aiden chided.

"You both would be more than welcome. In fact, I insist," Rex said as he placed a brotherly hand on each of his brother's shoulders.

Brie watched as both Declan and Ari tensed a bit, then relaxed just as quickly.

"Leo would love to feed you again, Meryn," Ari added.

Rex turned to Kendrick. "In fact, I'd like to extend that invitation to you and your mate as well."

Kendrick simply nodded. "We'd be honored."

Meryn tugged on her mate's hand. "Come on! They're having London Broil!"

Aiden frowned down at his mate. "When did you become such a little carnivore?"

She stopped tugging and pointed to her belly. "Blame your kid."

His eyes softened. "Of course," he conceded.

Meryn turned to Rex. "If I'm going, the boys are going."

Rex nodded. "I already took that into consideration when I texted Leo our updated numbers. In fact, we're expecting two more. They'll be meeting us there."

"Yes!" the twins threw their fists in the air.

Pip gulped. "I can do this. I can do this. I have my special umbrella." He ran off to the other room.

Meryn looked at the twins. "Say what now?"

Neil shrugged. "It worked."

"What worked?"

"Well, Nigel and I realized that as long as Pip didn't see the sky he was fine."

Meryn put her hands on her hips and pointed up. "How can you avoid the freaking sky?"

"With this!" Pip said excitedly, as he returned in a flash.

"They made me my own special umbrella.

This is the night time version." He opened what looked to be a parasol and pointed to the underside. "Nigel and Neil painted it for me."

Brie caught a glimpse and marveled at the art work. Swirling constellations and shooting stars were meticulously painted on the fabric of the parasol.

He showed Meryn who looked from the twins to the parasol and back. "You could have let him get used to the sky more, so he didn't need this."

Pip shook his head adamantly. "No. We needed to come to you. It will probably take me months, even years to be fully comfortable with the sky. You needed us now."

Meryn swallowed hard. "It's a gorgeous umbrella, Pip."

He stood up straight. "Neil added the stars, and Avery found some silver paint." He hugged it to his chest. "It is my first present, well, besides getting you as a sister."

Aiden wrapped an arm around each twin. "Good job, boys."

"Yes, sir," they answered together.

Pip opened the parasol all the way and held it over his head. "I am ready to go outside now."

Brie had to admit the parasol added a certain flare to the delicate vampire.

Meryn looped her arm through Pip's. "Let's go eat lion-squire food."

Brie cracked her back. "I'm starving, and my back is killing me."

Meryn chuckled. "It should; you're wearing like fifty pounds of gear."

Brie gave a half shrug. "Comes with the job."

Meryn bent down and hoisted a laptop bag to her shoulder, which Aiden immediately stepped forward to take. "I only have to worry about my laptop."

Ari rubbed her shoulders. "Come on, my warrior, let's head home and get you in the shower and into comfortable clothes."

She whimpered. "That sounds amazing right now."

"I expect to see you all in the morning for breakfast," the queen said.

"Yes, Auntie!" Meryn called back as she and Pip headed out the door.

Brie caught the queen's expression. "Auntie?" the queen questioned as she blinked.

Brennus kissed the back of his mate's neck. "It suits you."

The queen just shook her head. "I suppose." She then turned to move toward the crowd of survivors. Brie felt sorry for the fae queen; her night was only just beginning. Her expression must have shown her concern, because a moment later Ari kissed the back of her neck as well. "Let's go home."

𝕮

The closer they got to the Lionhart estate, the more the three Lionhart brothers seemed to vibrate with anticipation. Brie could feel the excitement emanating from her mate.

Meryn was making Aiden a nervous wreck as she and Pip walked backward so she could talk with Rex. "So, when you say legendary London Broil, do you actually mean it?"

Rex rubbed the side of his nose. "Meryn, most squires become known for one or two dishes. For example, Sebastian has his Vanilla Parfait…"

"Magic Pudding," Meryn interrupted.

Rex inclined his head at her correction. "My apologies, Magic Pudding. Cord has two specialties. His Cinnamon Scones and his Vegetable Medley, which consists of grilled garden vegetables and vegetable tempura. Leo, on the other hand, is known for his meat based dishes. Being a lion and serving a lion household, that makes a lot of sense. One is his London Broil, the other is his Venison Stew."

Meryn licked her lips and stumbled a bit, causing both Ryuu and Aiden to lurch forward to steady her. "Damn, they both sound good." She looked up at her squire. "What do you do?"

Ryuu's eyes widened, his cheeks turned pink, and he coughed into his fist. "I do it all, *denka*."

Meryn came to a complete stop. "Ex-squeeze me?"

Ryuu sighed. "Meryn, I can cook anything."

She nodded. "Yeah, I knew that, but what's your specialty?"

Rex stared. "Meryn, I think what he's saying is that whatever he cooks, it is to the level that most squires aspire to master when they use the term specialty."

"So, I totally lucked out when I got you as my squire, huh?" She rubbed her hands together evilly. "I get to eat all da foods."

Ryuu's eyes softened. "I have the power to submerge this world in chaos and ruin, and all she cares about is food."

Kendrick clapped his friend on the back. "That's our Meryn."

"My Meryn," Aiden growled.

Ryuu eyed the commander. "She's my charge."

"And my baby sister-cousin," Kendrick pointed out.

"And our sister!" Nigel and Neil added.

Meryn blushed and resumed her backward march. "I have lots of family now."

Ari nudged Brie's side. "Five bucks Aiden won't be able to eat when we get there; his stomach will be in knots from watching her walk backward."

Brie shook her head. She knew better. She had watched men like Aiden eat their weight in food when they were nervous. "I bet you ten he puts a serious dent into whatever meat platter Leo puts out."

Ari grinned. "Deal."

Declan looped his arm through hers. On his other side Kari walked with her phone in her hand as she scrolled with her thumb. "You both speak to each other like fellow unit brothers," Declan observed.

Brie exchanged looks with Ari who shrugged before she turned back to Declan. "Ari is my mate, both are close bonds, of course it would sound similar."

Ari squeezed her hand. "Fate gave me some

one that would walk beside me, and I couldn't be more thankful," he said, nuzzling her temple.

Brie swallowed hard. "I got someone that accepted me no matter what. To me, that's priceless."

Declan pointed to his mate. "She tells me what to do and keeps us moving forward. Without her, I didn't have much of a life at all."

Kari looked up from her phone. "He became the home I always craved, a place to come back to."

Aiden, his face somewhat pinched, smiled. "Meryn gave my life purpose and helped me to see things differently, expanding my world."

Meryn stared up into Pip's parasol. "Aiden is my world. I had nothing before him, and I'd have nothing without him."

Brie heard a curse then a muffled exclamation. They all turned to see that at Meryn's declaration, Aiden had stumbled, taking out Ryuu and Pierce when he went down.

Meryn smiled down at her mate. "Remember how you feel right now, because whenever you get that expression, my world gets thoroughly rocked that night in bed."

Laughing, Kendrick, Rex, and Ari helped the other men stand. Aiden immediately swept Meryn up in his arms. The second he turned like he was going to head back to the palace, her little fists bopped him about the chest.

"Hell no! Food first, then sex. I need that London Broil in my life!"

Aiden pouted. "But baby…"

For a moment, Meryn looked like she was about to relent.

"It's not just London Broil," Ari said, looking down at the small woman. "He also serves it with the most delicately prepared caramelized onions on earth," Ari added, a wicked look in his eye. "The potatoes have just enough garlic, and I think he makes the butter himself," he continued.

Meryn licked her lips. "Definitely food first."

Aiden shot Ari a death glare, and her mate only laughed. "Serves you right."

Aiden blinked then looked at Brie before he got a sheepish expression. "I suppose so."

Brie couldn't help but laugh. Ari had cockblocked his commander for getting in the way of his blow jobs earlier.

Meryn wiggled out of Aiden's arms and caught up to the boys. "I need foods for energy!" she announced to the world.

Aiden brightened. "Sounds like a great idea, baby," he said walking behind her.

Ryuu shook his head. "I better get with Leo so I can make sure I have the seasonings at home for this meal. I have a feeling they both will request it."

Rex walked next to Kari. "How the units get anything done is a miracle to me."

She held up her phone. "Counteroffer on the warehouse," she said, handing it over to him.

Rex took her phone and scrolled quickly. "Offer two-percent more if they leave the building as is and if we can have access to it immediately. Tell them we have merchandise we need to store and time is of the essence."

"I figured as much," Kari took back the phone then pressed a few buttons. "I had a counter-offer prepared. We offered three-percent though."

Rex nodded. "That's acceptable."

Brie leaned across Rex to eye the phone. "You got all that done since he called?"

Kari smiled. "It is what I do."

"I shoot shit," Brie said, pointing to her tac belt.

Kari eyed her guns. "I would love to be able to shoot. Could you teach me?"

Declan and Rex paled. Declan wrapped an arm around his mate's shoulders. "Babe, you don't have to worry about that. You have me."

Kari just met Brie's eye, and Brie understood. She couldn't imagine living in this world, with a warrior as a mate and not know how to shoot. The desire to help Ari was overwhelming at times. Plus, with a baby on the way, Kari would have a driving need to protect her baby. "Anytime you want, come see me. I'll start you with a Glock. It's a bit heavier, but that helps with kickback."

Kari's relief was visible. "Thanks."

Declan looked hurt. "Why didn't you ask me?"

Kari wheeled on her mate. "Because by the time you would actually let me touch a gun, our son or daughter would be grown." She shuddered. "Gods, I cannot even imagine you and me at a range."

Ari grinned. "Don't worry, little sister, we have

a shooting range at the Lionhart estate, Brie can show you as early as tomorrow."

"I wanna shoot shit!" Meryn added.

"Meryn, no."

"Come on, you know I was black ops now. I can shoot," Meryn protested.

Aiden's eyes narrowed. "That's right, we haven't talked about that yet. Someone distracted me." He gave her a flat look.

"Shit," she exhaled.

The twins and Pip stared. Neil spoke first. "Black ops?"

Meryn brightened. "Yup! From when I worked with Law."

"Badass," Nigel whispered.

"Badass," Pip echoed.

"You'll have to save that conversation for later," Rex said smiling. He pointed up. "Welcome to the Lionhart estate."

They made their way inside, and Brie could see from the coy expressions Meryn was shooting her mate that the li'l shit was trying to talk her way out of that covert ops discussion.

Just as Brie was about to take a step toward the stairs, a jubilant screech bounced off the walls around them.

"Declan!" Catherine launched herself at her second born who caught her easily and held her tight. "Good evening, Mother."

Catherine looked from Declan, to Ari, then to Rex before she simply burst into tears. "Oh! Oh!" she said over and over again.

Jedrek stormed in at the sound of his mate's

tears only to be brought up short at the sight of his three sons standing shoulder to shoulder in the foyer. "Declan," his father whispered.

"I hope you don't mind me stopping in?" Declan said gruffly.

"We may have some dinner prepared for you, boy," his father replied in a similarly gruff tone.

Catherine had one arm wrapped around Declan's neck, and she was reaching for Ari with her other hand. Both Ari and Rex stepped close enough to hug their mother between the three of them.

"They really love their boys," a voice observed, coming up behind her.

"Dad!" she ran to her father and buried her face in his shoulder. "I missed you."

"I know, baby girl, I know. You've had a rough couple days, haven't you?" he asked.

She looked up and sniffled. "Yeah."

A strong arm pulled them both close. She looked up into Doran's face. "We should have been there for you," he said contritely.

She shook her head. "No, you both needed time to yourselves." She wiped her nose on her sleeve. "I'm a grown woman, after all."

Her father eyed her sleeve. "A grown woman that hasn't learned how to use a tissue?"

"There's been no time, Dad."

His face fell, and he pulled her close again. "I would give anything to save you from the horrors you've seen over the past few days."

She sagged against her father, knowing Doran was supporting them both. "I wouldn't change a thing," she murmured. "Yes, I saw some truly horrible things, but I found Ari, and he's perfect for me. He has this light about him that helps me face the dark. I wouldn't trade finding his love for anything."

Doran rubbed her back soothingly. "You have us now. My brother filled us in on everything we've missed. I'm so proud of you, baby girl. I know your mother would be too."

Brie pulled back in surprise. "He told you about Momma?"

Doran looked confused. "Of course he did. She played a huge part in both of your lives; I owe her much."

"I ran home since Doran could open a portal for us. I packed us both quite a few things and I brought your laptop bag and work duffel." Her father pointed to the second floor. "Leo had everything put into Ari's room."

"Leo! We have to make Declan's favorite!" Catherine called out.

"It's ready to be served, my dear," the squire responded.

She eyed her squire. "You knew?"

He simply placed his fist over his chest. "Dinner will be served within the hour. Boys, your rooms have been prepared for you." He smiled at Aiden. "We have also arranged for guest rooms and baths for the Alpha members," he said, indicating Aiden and Kendrick. He sighed and looked at Catherine. "Might I suggest you release your stranglehold and let the poor boys freshen up. They did participate in an important mission today."

Catherine huffed. "I finally have all my boys home; I don't want to let them go."

Jedrek peeled her away from Declan. "Go ahead, boys, we'll be waiting for you in your mother's parlor."

"Jedrek! Honestly!" Catherine protested.

Jedrek winced. "Do make it quick," he added.

Ryuu looked to Meryn. "I will assist in the kitchen. Is there anything else you're craving?"

"Those mushy, smelly, soggy green leaves Cord served the other night. When you added vinegar, they were amazing."

He nodded then turned to Leo. "Have you any collards I could prepare?"

Leo raised his arm, pointing the way to the kitchen. "As luck would have it, I have some cleaned and cooking. All you have to do is season them to her tastes."

Ryuu bowed. "My thanks."

"Yes!" Meryn said excitedly.

Catherine looked past Jedrek and noticed the twins and Pip hanging back. "Who are these adorable boys?"

Meryn pulled them forward. "These are my brothers! Nigel and Neil Morninglory are warriors from Noctem Falls. And Pip Maverick, he is super important because he helps me smile."

Catherine clucked and pulled the boys toward the parlor. "Leo, I think these boys look hungry. Is there anything we can serve them before dinner?"

Obviously having her own boys home had awakened every maternal instinct in the lioness.

Nigel gave Meryn a thumbs up as they were led away.

"I don't know about the rest of you, but I'm ready for a shower." Brie stepped away from her dads and kissed each on the cheek, causing her dad to smile and Doran to blush. "We'll see you in just a bit," she promised, before she took Ari's hand to lead him up the stairs. The other couples trailed behind them with Rex bringing up the rear.

"Meat and soggy leaves!" Meryn eyed her mate. "If we could manage shower sex without breaking my leg, this could be a perfect night."

Aiden's eyes darkened. "I'm sure we'll be all right."

"First door on the right," Rex advised. He turned to Kendrick. "Third door on the right."

Giggling, Meryn bolted from her mate, causing him to give chase.

Kendrick eyed his mate, who shook her head. "If I run, I won't have any energy for sex."

Kendrick frowned and scooped her up so she didn't have to walk. "We can't have that." They too disappeared down the hall.

"Here's where we get off," Ari said pointing to his door. "See you at dinner."

Declan leered at his mate, then winked at him. "See you at dinner."

They walked into the room, and she started stripping off her gear. She wanted to let it drop to the floor but knew the weapons needed to be secured. When faced with all she had to do, she felt tears spring to her eyes, she was becoming overwhelmed and quickly.

"Start from the top and hand me your stuff," Ari said, pushing her toward the closet.

Exhaustion and the high emotions she had felt at seeing her father had tears leaking down her cheeks. "I'm sorry," she whispered.

Ari nipped her lips. "Why?"

She just waved her hand about, indicating to what he was doing.

"Love, if I didn't do this for you, who would?"

"No one," she responded. There hadn't been anyone there for her, except for her dad in so long. But not even her dad saw her like this; it would worry him.

"Now, you have me." Ari pulled her into the walk-in closet and sat her down on a long white leather bench. He went to one wall and placed his hand on the side mirror. The wall slid to one side, revealing the huge gun safe. He walked back to her. "You'll get your own side of course," he pointed to the dark cherry wood shelves and gleaming silver accents. Slowly, piece by piece she took off her gear. With each item she handed him, he kissed her softly and told her how much he loved her and how proud he was to be her mate.

Once they were both naked, and the clothing part of their uniform in the hamper for Leo to take care of, he closed up the safe.

He had undone her with his absolute acceptance of who and what she was. It was less the words of love and more his actions that shattered the tiny pieces of the wall around her heart. He stored her gear, emptied her gun, gave her space in his gun safe as if every man on earth did the same for the woman in their life.

"Ari, I love you so much it actually hurts," she whispered, clutching her chest.

Ari scooped her up, much in the same way Aiden had Meryn, but she was no Meryn. She was probably twice the woman's size, yet her mate held her with no problem. "The moment I saw you, you were branded to my soul, Brie. Every day, looking at you, breathing in your scent, it simply carves that brand deeper into my being. It's a pain I welcome, because it ties me to you."

Brie laid her head on his shoulder. "Do you think we could have shower sex without breaking my leg?"

Ari laughed and kissed the top of her head. "As athletic as we both are, I'm sure that it won't be a problem."

She leaned back to look up at him. "Trade you those two blow jobs for a savage pounding under your rain head."

"Deal!" he accepted eagerly.

He practically ran for the bathroom and set her down gently on the counter. She yelped a bit when her ass hit the cold marble, but watching her naked mate walk around the bathroom had her distracted soon enough. Unlike both of his brothers, he wore his hair short. She stared, entranced at the muscles of his neck as they transitioned into his wide shoulders. Everything from his square jawline to his perfectly tight ass screamed of strength and power, and it was all hers.

She hopped off the counter and walked up behind him as he held a hand under the water stream testing its warmth. Wordlessly, she stepped up behind him and pressed her breasts to his back and wrapped her arms around his torso. He inhaled sharply but let her hands roam. Grinning, she trailed a finger down either side of his hips and was rewarded with a throaty groan. She peeked around his body to see that his cock was straining against his stomach, clear glistening liquid already seeping from the head. "My poor baby has been wanting this all day, hasn't he?" she whispered, moving her right hand into the water. It felt warm enough to her.

"Gods, yes," he whispered.

She stepped around him and let the water sluice down her body. Reaching up, she placed her hand over his heart, marveling at their different skin tones. Hers gleamed like darkened bronze, and his glowed like gold. Side by side, they were beautiful.

"Join me."

He took a step and bent slightly in front of her. She had no idea what he was doing until both of his hands came up to cup her ass. Moments later he had her lifted and wrapped around his body. With her full weight supported by him, her hands were free. She ran them over the tightened tendons of his neck and shoulders before she leaned down and captured his lips with her own.

They took their time. Each of them exploring and memorizing the other. Ari leaned back, breathing heavily. "Gods, I hate to admit this, but if we keep going, the show will be over before it starts," he warned.

"You could come, just from kissing me?" she asked, feeling like a goddess.

"Brie, baby, I could come just looking at you," he admitted.

"Then this will be even better," she said, using her thighs to support some of her weight as she lifted herself up. Reaching down, she searched for him and wasn't disappointed to find he was hot and hard for her. Ever so slowly, she lowered herself down until he was seated inside of her. They both exhaled in physical relief at being connected once again. And that's what it felt like to her. In the long hours since he had last been inside of her, she felt as if she had been dying of thirst. Only now, being joined with him, could she drink deeply.

She placed her hands on his shoulders and rose up, feeling him slide from her, before relaxing her legs and dropping down on him again. As she rode him, she realized that her legs weren't even straining. She felt like she could easily do this for hours. Groaning at the thought, she rocked her hips, enjoying how he felt deep inside her.

She liked to think that her stamina was due to long hours in the gym, but she knew she would never have been able to do this before being claimed by Ari. He had not only soothed her battered heart, but also strengthened her body.

She set a slow pace. Unlike before, she was able to see his face and the effect she was clearly having on him. His head was thrown back, and his eyes were closed. When he licked his lips, she leaned in and reclaimed them. He lowered his head and opened his eyes at the first touch of her lips. Never breaking eye contact, they teased and tormented one another. He pulled back, grinning. "There's no part of you that doesn't flat out do it for me, baby," he admitted. "I could spend the rest of eternity kissing you."

She wrapped her arms around his neck and pulled him close. "You're the only one who has ever touched my heart," she confessed. "You scare me to death, Ari."

His low growl was her only warning as his hands wrapped around her waist. He stepped forward and used the wall to pin her in place, which allowed the snapping of his hips to increase the pace.

"Mine!" he snarled and buried his teeth in her shoulder.

The moment her body registered the pain, everything tightened low in her body, causing him to repeatedly plunge over that elusive spot she could never quite get to on her own.

She screamed out her ecstasy as his body spun hers out of control. He pulled away from her shoulder and thrust into her one final time. Breathing heavily, he rested his forehead on her shoulder.

"Gods above, I love you," he whispered with ragged breath.

"And I you," she said, holding him as close to her body as she could. She'd have to get Rathais to order more weapons for her, because there was no way in hell she was losing this man.

CHAPTER FIFTEEN

❧

MUCH TO BRIE'S EMBARRASSMENT THEY were the last to arrive to dinner. Leo simply gave her a wink and held out her chair for her. She kissed his cheek. "I love this dressing gown as well. You have impeccable tastes."

Leo looked pleased as he flushed at her praise. "It was a simple thing really."

"Is that comfy?" Meryn asked.

She nodded. "It feels like a nightgown, but looks fancy."

Meryn closed her eyes, and a moment later her sweats and tee changed to a gown similar to hers but in shades of gold. She opened her eyes. "I could get used to this. They're even better than the dress robes, and I thought those were good for being formal."

"Leo?" Rex said.

Leo nodded. "Ryuu and I have brought all the food to the sideboard, which will eliminate running back and forth to the kitchen. You're free to secure the room."

Rex looked at Kendrick. A moment later there

was a familiar pulse, and Brie knew the room had been soundproofed.

Meryn was shaping her mashed potatoes on her plate to act as a barrier between her collards and her meat. "So what'dja need us for?"

Aiden looked at his mate, surprised. "How did you know?"

She pointed to Rex with her fork. "He asked me to invite myself. I was gonna pass, but then he said they were having London Broil, so it was a no-brainer to come."

Brie lifted her wine glass, and Leo was at her side in a moment. "Red, white, or rosé?"

"Red, please." She turned to Rex. "And I saw you silence Declan and Ari in the queen's chambers when you placed your hand on their shoulders."

Rex exhaled. "We may have a tiny problem."

Jedrek snorted, then growled low.

Meryn pointed to him with her fork. "I know that growl. Council or Committee?"

Jedrek gave a short nod. "Both, in a way."

Meryn picked up a roll and pulled the insides out of it before stuffing it with collards and mashed potatoes. "Most of the council are good peeps. So it has to be the Committee."

Jedrek looked exhausted. "You're absolutely right, Meryn. Most that serve as Elders are good men, however, we do answer to our people, mostly the Founding and Noble families. We may have personal opinions on things, but we still have to represent the general consensus of those we stand for."

Meryn blinked. "Douchebag by proxy?"

Rex covered his face with his hand chuckling as Jedrek turned to his mate. "I don't know how to respond to that."

Catherine rolled her eyes. "Actually, Meryn, that is a perfect term."

Aiden lifted his wine glass. "For example, after the last attack on Lycaonia, nearly every member of the council was being pressured to secure Keelan's body for observation, to determine that he wasn't a threat." He gritted his teeth. "Father had a hard time going against the Witches' Council that wanted him shipped back to Storm Keep. If Kendrick hadn't shown up, he may have had to capitulate."

Rex looked to Meryn. "We'll take it one step further. Founding and Noble families speak for the people that look to them. So, if a large majority of people are pressuring their Founding and Noble Family Heads, they in turn pressure the Elders, who bring up issues in council. For issues impacting all four pillar cities, all four councils weigh in and so on."

Meryn winced. "Sounds too complicated to me."

Kari sipped her water then turned to Jedrek. "What exactly is being said, Father?"

Jedrek straightened a little and was suddenly all smiles at Kari calling him 'Father'. "The Gods must have known we'd need you here, little one." He eyed Declan. "You're welcome as well." Catherine whacked her mate's shoulder as he smiled at his son. Declan smiled back.

"Father, I've missed your dry sense of humor."

Kari reached under the table and pulled out a tablet from her bag. Seeing this, Meryn also reached down under her seat and grabbed her laptop, setting it in her lap. Kari held up her digital pen. "Start with the most pressing issue, and we will go from there."

Jedrek nodded. "The council heard about the vote of No Confidence, and they are calling for a review of actions leading up to the murders." He eyed Aiden. "The unit warriors are also under review. The Committee stepped forward and brought up the fact they themselves had questions in how things were being done back when Lycaonia was attacked."

Aiden began to growl low in his throat. Jedrek smiled and shook his head. "Like father, like son. I believe your father is hosting a similar dinner right now with Lycaonia's council members trying to line up arguments for what happened within the city."

Meryn blinked. "Is that why Uncle Celyn wasn't at the palace?"

Rex nodded. "He was needed to keep your father from exploding."

Aiden snarled. "I'm stuck here and cannot be there to answer for my own actions."

Rex held up a finger. "That's where we come in." He looked at Kari. "Magnus and I feel it best I stay here. Dagda and Alastair have both assured Magnus that after what happened in Noctem Falls, Aiden and Meryn could do no

ALANEA ALDER

wrong in their peoples' eyes, so I can remain here to assist."

Kari covered her mouth as she smiled. "I feel sorry for anyone that says something even slightly bad about Meryn in Noctem Falls."

Meryn blushed furiously as she began to sculpt shapes in her potatoes.

Kari tapped on her tablet. "That leaves Lycaonia, Èire Danu, and Storm Keep. Let us start with Èire Danu. In addition to the No Confidence, what else is being said?"

Rex sat back. "Until tonight, most of the citizens did not want Brie involved in the search for their people." He tilted his head. "Though that may change drastically after this evening. They weren't anticipating that your heroic efforts would save over one hundred fae lives, all who are currently singing your praises, Meryn too. The queen didn't disclose Meryn's efforts without reason; we'll need the survivors support in the days to come."

"Who are the council members here?" Meryn asked.

Jedrek pointed to his chest. "There's myself, Godwyn Vi'Aileanach, Frederic Géroux, and Lucius Hollyhock."

Kendrick snarled at the witch's name. "Hollyhock was a born bootlicker. He doesn't have two brain cells to rub together. If he says anything it's because that's what he was programed to say by the Witches' Council."

Rex nodded. "We know."

Brie looked to her mate. "Aileanach and Géroux sound familiar."

Ari gave a half nod. "Géroux should sound familiar because that's Bastien's family. Gage comes from the Noble family that serves under Géroux. Aileanach is Tyrien's surname."

Meryn winced. "Are they mad because of me?"

Jedrek shook his head. "Quite the contrary, Godwyn is very much a fan of yours, Meryn. He feels that his younger brother needs to grow up, and his actions that led to Bastien's assault was the last straw as far as he was concerned." He looked at Brie. "He was very grateful for how you spoke to his mate. He said your clear statements regarding what was being done made it possible for her to move forward in her grief. He was stuck in Lycaonia when the trees screamed their pain and couldn't be at her side. He supports all your efforts."

"That's a welcome surprise," she admitted.

"Would we be remiss in assuming we have Frederic's support?" Aiden asked.

"You would not. Even if it weren't for the direct orders from his prince, the Géroux's have always supported the warriors. They, more than any other vampiric line has had the most sons become warriors. You sealed their support when you brought Jean-Marc home," Jedrek said, admiration in his voice.

Aiden stared down into his wine. "That was so long ago. I can't believe that single action carries so much weight."

Jedrek along with Catherine, Rex, Kendrick, and even Leo simply stared. Rex started to say something, but Jedrek help up a hand. "Aiden, son. I feel like I have to address this as your father isn't here to explain. I know you feel as though most respect you because of your father, and that's understandable, they are some mighty shoes to fill." He waved at his sons. "It's something I am aware of as a father. But what you don't understand is that it is your own actions that have led to the towering esteem the warriors feel for you."

He paused. "What do you remember of feral attacks before you took over as Unit Commander?"

Aiden shook his head. "Not much. Just that they were like wild animals, not to let them corner you, and some grew in strength after turning."

Jedrek shook his head. "This should have been explained, but I can see why it wasn't. You were so young when you took over." He took a long sip of his wine, then sighed. He looked at Leo. Instantly, the squire pulled a small bottle from the sideboard cabinet and hurried to the Elder's side. The first splash of golden liquid filled the room with the faint scent of apples. He continued. "Before you took over as Unit Commander. Before that fateful day where we lost an entire unit, things were different for the warriors. Yes, they ran patrols and yes, they did drills, but unlike now, their deaths were very different. Before you, Aiden, any warrior that fell to a feral had their mutilated bodies impaled and put on display. Retrieving them was impossible, as each body was essentially a deadly ambush or trap."

Brie felt bile crawl up the back of her throat. Ari handed her some water. She drank some gratefully. Every younger person at the table looked shocked.

Aiden looked furious. "They don't do that now! Why was it accepted before?!" he demanded.

Jedrek held up a single finger. "They don't do that now because of you, my boy."

Aiden's mouth open and closed repeatedly.

"Aiden, you went back for the dead. Do you remember the night you killed over twenty ferals single handedly? For once, they were the ones being ripped apart as your bear defended his brothers." Jedrek smiled sadly. "Darren was one of the warriors that was assigned feral clean up. They found your broken sword stabbed through a feral and buried so deep into a tree it took him and another warrior to remove it. When your sword broke, you evidently started using feral body parts to kill the others. You inadvertently did to them what they had been doing to warriors for centuries, and you scared the hell out of them. Those that survived spread their terror of you to the next animal-like creature until ferals stopped their barbaric practices out of sheer fear of you."

"Oh my god," Meryn whispered.

Aiden turned to her, panicked that his bloody rampage may have upset her. "Baby…"

She looked up at him, her eyes bright. "You're so hot."

"Huh?"

"Sooooo hot," she sighed as she eyed him up and down.

"Baby, your kittenish ways after hearing about bloodshed is equal parts disturbing and arousing," Aiden admitted.

Jedrek chuckled. "She's a perfect match for the Unit Commander that scared decency into every feral in existence."

"Do you understand now, Aiden? It wasn't just that you fought. You brought back your fallen brothers safely. They were the first to receive a warriors funeral since the Great War. Before your rampage, a killed warrior would receive a small ceremony, but nobody was laid to rest. For someone your age, you probably never questioned the closed caskets.

Today, the warriors, and by extension the Géroux's, follow you without question because if they have to die, they are going to die at your side, where they know they'll be safe, even in death."

Aiden bowed his head and rested his forehead on steepled fingers in front of him. "I never knew," he whispered.

"Neither did we," Ari admitted, his eyes shining bright.

Rex looked at his younger brother. "We did. The older generation, we made sure you took your direction from us. Aiden McKenzie was to be supported at every turn. It practically became an unspoken vow amongst the warriors."

"How do you know of it?" Ari asked.

"I told him," Declan admitted softly. "Adriel relayed to me a similar story when I became a member of Eta. Evidently, that story has been passed to every warrior after Aiden became Unit Commander."

Meryn stood and ducked down so she could wedge her head under Aiden's arm and climb into his lap. Aiden pressed his fingers to his eyes to manfully wipe his tears and kissed Meryn's head. "I don't deserve my brothers."

"You deserve every ounce of support you've gotten and more," Jedrek refuted. "Your sheer strength of character and will radiated from that horrible event. You not only cemented your own position, but also your father's. By stepping up as Unit Commander, Byron could concentrate his efforts on the council level and your two older brothers could finally start the programs they had been dreaming of to further support the units. Everything comes back to you." Jedrek eyed his own sons. "It'd be nice to see a Lionhart excel in a similar fashion."

Rex, Declan, and Ari rolled their eyes in unison. Brie smiled, she had seen Catherine do the exact same thing multiple times now, she knew exactly where they had gotten it from.

"You'll just have to settle for one of us becoming the youngest Elder since the pillar cities' inception," Rex drawled.

"Or a son who is the right hand to both the

ranking unit leader of Noctem Falls and the Prince himself," Declan continued.

Ari remained silent at her side. "And then there's Ari who manages to do all of that and more in Èire Danu," she added.

Ari swung to her. "I do not."

Brie scowled up at her own mate and started ticking off everything he was responsible for. "Even Brennus admits that you are the unit leader here and the men agree. You manage your unit with four men instead of five, allowing Brennus to function as the queen's Consort. The men have told me that you are like Aiden in updating and improving drills. Every time someone needs something done that concerns the Lionharts, they come to you, and you arrange everything." She crossed her arms in front of her. "You are like a combination of Aiden, Rex, and Declan and it's time you and others realize that."

Ari rubbed the top of his head. "I'm just..."

"Amazing," she finished.

"Of course he is. I tell him that all the time," Rex interjected.

"Yeah, Ari may be the baby, but the only thing that signifies is exactly how incredible he is. I hadn't accomplish half as much at his age," Declan admitted.

Ari looked from one brother to the other. Aiden cuddled his mate. "Not easy to hear, is it?" he asked.

Ari shook his head. "I always felt like I scattered my efforts and fell short constantly."

Jedrek coughed to hide his embarrassment. "I

know I give you boys grief, but it's because I know you're capable of so much." He smiled and wrapped his arm around his mate. "I mean, look who you have for a mother."

Ari and his brothers nodded, agreeing. "True," they echoed.

"Oh, really!" Catherine shook her head. "That's enough gloom and doom at the table. Let's fill them in on the rest so we can eat this wonderful meal in peace." She smiled around the table, then frowned as her eyes went from place setting to place setting. Declan, Ari, and Meryn had food-smeared empty plates. Both Nigel and Neil looked up, cheeks pouched out like chipmunks, their forks laden with meat frozen in front of their faces and Ryuu and Leo were in the process of adding meat slices to Meryn and Declan's plates. "Oh, dear."

Jedrek simply threw his head back and laughed. "Let the kids eat, Catherine."

Kari turned to the Lionhart matriarch. "Please continue, Mother."

"Humph!" She punched Jedrek's leg as he continued to chuckle. "At council level, Elders are obligated to review concerns sent in by their citizens. With so many worried about the breach in Éire Danu, the Committee has officially gotten involved."

Kendrick turned to Catherine. "Are they the same members that visited Lycaonia?"

She nodded. "They are, of course without the treacherous Adalwin. He was replaced by Grier Larkspur."

"Oh yeah, I forgot he literally shriveled up and died," Meryn snort laughed.

"Meryn," Aiden chided gently.

"What do you feel the Committee is after?" Kari asked.

Catherine tapped her lips. "Power, pure and simple. If they crumble the foundation that supports the unit warriors, they could then move in their own personal guards that report only to them. We'd return to the way of life we had before the Great War. People would have to walk the line or you'd face the ferals because the guards that are meant to keep you safe report to those pulling the strings. The creation of the unit warriors was the single greatest thing to come from such a horrible war. Whoever came up with the idea of mixed race units to achieve true neutrality was a genius."

"I'll let him know you think so," Kendrick said absently, as he swirled his wine.

Catherine turned to him. "What?"

Kendrick blinked. "What?" He looked like she startled him into paying attention.

"You know who designed the units?" Jedrek asked.

"Oh. That. Yes, it was the Dark Prince of Noctem Falls. By the end of the war, I heard his patience snapped, and he wanted to wash his hands of the entire thing. His suggestions carried weight, and the rest is history. With unit warriors guarding the pillar cities, they didn't need a single Dark Prince anymore," he explained.

"He did it to be lazy?" Meryn asked. "I aspire to be that lazy."

Kendrick shrugged. "I think he deserved a break at that point."

Rex looked at his parents. "In order to maintain peace in the city when Magnus was laid low, Gavriel Ambrosios claimed his heritage."

Jedrek nodded. "We heard that he was confirmed as a true Ambrosios."

Rex nodded slowly. "Yes, however, he isn't just a member of the line, he is the Gavriel Ambrosios from legend. He's *the* Dark Prince."

Both Jedrek and Catherine reached for Jedrek's glass at the same time. Jedrek allowed his mate to drink of the liquid first. She passed it to him. "*The* Dark Prince?" Catherine asked hoarsely.

Declan winced. "Yes, Mother."

Jedrek eyed his sons. "You both knew?"

"Yes, Father," they replied together.

"They were sworn to secrecy," Aiden said, then sighed. "We have too much going on to deal with that damn Committee now."

"The Dark Prince is a unit warrior?" Catherine asked.

Aiden brightened. "He's my second-in-command."

Between Catherine, Amelia, Anne, and Meryn, Brie had gotten pretty much caught up on what was going on. But in seeing Ari's parents' reactions, she wondered how much of that was common knowledge. "Can I just assume everything I've heard in the past few days are secrets?"

Kendrick nodded. "Probably a good idea," he said, leveling his gaze at her.

"No problem," she gave him a mock salute.

"There's more?" Jedrek demanded.

"Yes, much more. But in light of certain events, it's probably not wise to divulge such things to the council," Kendrick responded.

"So we need a way to sabotage or kill the Committee?" Meryn asked, opening up her laptop.

"Meryn, let's give Jedrek the ability to say he has no idea what's going on later, shall we?" Kendrick advised.

"Oh, yeah." Meryn closed her laptop and put it away.

Jedrek stared at the small woman in horror. "You can't do that." He looked from Aiden to Kendrick. "She can't do that."

"Do what?" Meryn asked brightly, her face full of innocence.

Leo refilled Jedrek's goblet.

Smiling slyly, Kari also put her tablet away. "We will figure something out, Father. Do not worry about it."

"They're vicious. I love it," a female voice said from the doorway. Brie turned and stared. Growing up, her mother had read countless bedtime stories to her all revolving around female warriors, but her personal favorite had been the Valkyries.

That's what the group of women standing behind Declan embodied, with their long, blonde braids hanging over varying degrees of undercuts and visible arm tattoos. "God," she whispered.

Her father laughed. "Baby girl, you should see your face. You remind me so much of your mother right now."

"Aunt Elysa, what are you all doing here?" Declan asked, as he and the men stood to greet the women.

"We knew Ari had mated, but we didn't know Declan and his mate were visiting." She rotated her finger, pointing to the room. "We heard silence when doing our rounds and got worried." They frowned at Catherine. "All our baby boys are home, and you didn't tell us?"

The tall, built, blonde women converged on the Lionhart sons. They were passed around until each son had received his own hug from each aunt.

Once the women had hugged their nephews, they looked around the table. "Which ones are our baby girls now?" Elysa asked.

She and Kari exchanged worried looks and slowly they raised their hands. The women pulled up chairs and surrounded them. "We've heard a lot about Kari from Rex. He says that she practically runs Noctem Falls. I'd say that's good enough to be mated to Declan," the one with braids at each temple said, pointing to Kari.

Kari sat back. "Excuse me?" Her eyes began to bleed to red.

The women laughed. "She's so proper."

"Look, bizsnatches, you don't upset Kari on my watch," Meryn said, hopping from her chair.

"Oh gods, look how tiny she is," one breathed.

"She's getting so snarly; isn't she adorable!"

"Is she actually standing?"

Meryn's face flushed red. "I have a gun, you know!" she threatened.

"Can you not insult and threaten the strongest group of female warriors in existence," Aiden pleaded, grappling his mate. He froze. "When did you get your gun back!"

"She's fierce. I like her," Elysa said. It was as if that statement cemented the entire group's opinion. She then turned to her. "What about you? Are you good enough for our baby Ari? Strong enough?"

Brie simply chuckled and stood. "Let's go." She had been thinking of this since Ari had described his aunts.

"Is she serious?" one of them whispered.

Brie unlaced her gown and let it fall. She turned, facing the room in her silk chemise and leggings. "Whenever you're ready, Blondie," she said, pulling her arm back to stretch.

"Hot damn, girls!" the women exited toward the front of the house, leaving Elysa standing by Brie.

"Oh Gods," Rex, Declan, and Jedrek whispered.

Catherine shrugged. "I saw this coming."

Ari was already on his phone. "Kincaid, I need you and Ian at the Lionhart estate. Brie just challenged my aunts. What? No! We're not waiting for them to make snacks! Get your asses over here!" he hung up his phone.

"Ryuu, I need beatdown-watching food!" Meryn pleaded, her eyes bright with excitement.

Ryuu gave a half bow. "I spotted some chips and M&M's in the pantry, will they suffice?"

"Hell yeah!" Meryn bounced toward the foyer, throwing jabs in the air and humming the Rocky theme song.

Brie smiled. "I love that little terror."

"Aunt Elysa," Ari started.

She held up her hand. "You will respect your mate and say no more. She trusts us to do the right thing, as should you."

"She's my mate, Auntie El," he whispered.

"Which is why we're going to enjoy this, Ari. Now go grab a seat so you can watch your mate. I have a feeling your unit brothers will be here soon."

"Sonofabitch!"

Ari turned like he was about to head to the door, then swung back to kiss Brie. "Don't get permanently maimed, okay?"

"I'll do my best," she compromised.

Her dad and Doran both kissed her cheek. "I've got a hundred on you, baby girl," her dad called back as he walked away.

Once the room was empty, Elysa turned to her. "Parameters?"

Brie bent at the waist to stretch her legs. "I know you're shifters so our strength and speed will be wildly different." She stood up straight. "How would you adjust your abilities when fighting a new warrior amongst you?"

Elysa had her arms crossed over her chest. She

began tapping her finger on her forearm. "For the cubs, you mean?"

Brie grimaced at the term. "Would you equate a human's strength and speed to that of a cub?"

Elysa nodded. "Absolutely."

"Even the men?"

The tall warrior burst into laughter. "Especially the men. My girls can out-perform the unit warriors any day of the week, and they know it."

"Why aren't you unit warriors then?" she asked curiously.

"Why tie ourselves to that political headache? We answer to no man."

"That's so cool."

Elysa uncrossed her arms and placed a hand on her shoulder. "I'll hold back, but will adjust to your capabilities."

"I'm counting on it," she said, her insides shaking in excitement.

"Look at you. Poor baby girl has never had a good sparring session," Elysa murmured in sympathy.

"You have no idea! The guys back home either come at me like I need to be put down or they pull their punches. I can't get a square fight out of any of them."

"Let's go see what you can do," Elysa held up her arm, inviting her to walk outside.

Once through the front door, her mouth dropped. The squires had set up seating, and it looked like a mini arena.

"Kick her ass, NinjaGaiden!" Meryn yelled.

Elysa chuckled. "The men probably think she's

cute." She paused and tilted her head. "But she's the most dangerous one here, and with Eliana's Daughters present, that's saying something."

They stepped into the ring that someone had burned into the lawn. "Rules?" she asked.

"Nothing that would cause permanent harm. No unnecessary violence. If you're down, I won't continue. Good?"

"Perfect."

They separated to either side of the circle. Around them the females roared in unison, signaling the start of the fight.

Quicker than she could track, Elysa was on her. Brie grabbed her wrist and jerked forward, shifting her own weight. The lioness went down, but didn't stay down. They circled one another once, and Elysa burst forward again. Brie tensed her abdomen muscles and took multiple blows. With her arms protecting her head, she did a half-body twist to flip backward and put distance between her and the lioness.

Elysa's eyes widened, and she gave her a wicked grin. "Kitten has surprises."

"Come find out if I have any more," she replied.

Brie lost track of the exchange of strikes after that. She had never moved so fast in her life. No sooner had the thought entered her mind to block, her arm or leg was already there. After a few minutes, they were both breathing hard.

Brie laughed from the sheer thrill of it all. "Come on!" she roared, and Elysa responded.

The lioness landed a solid hit to her stomach,

causing her to gasp for air. Closing her eyes, she pivoted on her back leg and brought her foot up. She connected to Elysa's jaw, causing her to step back, shaking her head. Brie let out a flurry of blows to further disorient her opponent.

Barely able to draw breath, Brie knew that if she hesitated, she would lose the chance to gain the upper-hand. She darted forward, and as she predicted, Elysa saw her incoming and threw her entire body into a punch aimed at her mid-section.

Brie grabbed her arm and literally threw her over her head and into the air. She heard and felt the vibrations of Elysa hitting the ground before she spun to face her. Brie immediately took a defensive stance.

Elysa held up a hand. "Yield," she croaked.

All around them the lionesses roared loudly—to the point where Brie wanted to cover her ears. They flooded the ring, some stepping over Elysa to congratulate her. "Welcome to the pride!" they cheered.

"Huh?" she asked, still trying to catch her breath from that punch to the gut.

"You defeated our acting Alpha Female, that makes you the newest member of our pride. Welcome to Eliana's Daughters," one of them explained, wiping her eyes.

"I'm sorry," she said, thoroughly confused.

The female looked shocked. "Don't be sorry; these are happy tears! Jubilant tears! It's been centuries since an outside female has joined our ranks."

"But, she was adjusting her strength and speed, it shouldn't count," she protested.

Two females helped Elysa to stand. She made her way over to them, and she thrust her arm out to her. Brie knew what to do now and grasped it in a warrior's clasp.

"Brie, I stopped having to make adjustments after you challenged me. I faced you with everything I had. Your training, in addition to whatever boost you received from mating with Ari, has you nearly equal to one of us."

Brie could only smile. Throwing her head back, she bellowed out her victory. Answering her raw guttural cry, a deep, male, lion roar shattered the night from the stands. The men sitting around her mate released victory cries of their own. The unit warriors of Èire Danu had witnessed her triumph.

Elysa clapped her on the shoulder. "You're more than worthy of our Ari," she said, pointing to where her mate's once short hair now flowed about his head like a mane. In front of him, both Declan and Rex vibrated with the same energy.

"I told you they puffed up like house cats," Meryn said to Aiden, pointing at Ari.

Ari stood and stalked toward her. His eyes glowed golden. "Mine," he growled.

She smiled coyly before sweeping her leg and knocking him to the ground and straddling him. "And you're mine."

The men whistled from the crowd, and the female warriors laughed at Ari's stunned expression.

"I could get behind this," he agreed.

A piercing whistle had everyone looking at Catherine. "Elysa, you girls head back to the manor and get the gun prepared for Brie for tomorrow." She eyed the unit warriors. "You boys head back to the villa." She smiled at her. "Let's head back inside and allow Brie some time to freshen before we continue our dinner."

Elysa shook her head. "Better listen, she's the oldest." She leaned down to Brie. "And the strongest of us."

Brie eyed Catherine. "Well, she did have three sons, so there is that."

Her dad and Doran walked by, both grinning. Her dad held up a wad of cash. "This is going toward your birthday present."

CHAPTER SIXTEEN

❦

BRIE CHUCKLED, THEN STOOD. SHE reached down and pulled her mate to his feet. The crowd dispersed, and they, once again, were heading upstairs so she could freshen up.

When they walked into their bedroom, Brie noticed that Leo had placed her gown across the bed with new underthings. That reminded her to look for the things her father had brought for her.

She went to the dresser and started opening drawers. Her things were perfectly folded and put away in the third drawer down. She shook her head. Squires were amazing.

She pulled off the sweaty silk and walked to the bathroom. She turned at Ari's low growls. "We don't have time. Your mother will hold dinner for us, and you know it."

Ari's eyes dimmed a bit, but his hair remained long. She pointed to his head. "I love it. Why didn't it grow when you became your lion-man?"

He brought his hand up and ran it over his hair. "Third form was a knee jerk reaction out of anger." He pointed to his head. "This was a primal, soul level response from my lion." He sighed. "I'll have to have it cut."

"Do you have to?"

"No, but I've always worn it short. Why?"

"Gives me more to grab later," she explained, stepping so just her body was getting wet under the shower head. She quickly soaped up and rinsed off, carefully keeping her curls dry.

"I'm feeling the long hair," Ari mused out-loud.

She laughed and dried off. He handed Brie her clothes and they walked downstairs. As she predicted, the squires had pulled out small hors d'oeuvres to serve along with celebratory drinks. When she walked in, cheers and glasses went up. The men stood until she sat down.

"Have a good time, baby girl?" her father asked.

She smiled wide. "It was so much fun! I've never been able to face someone that allowed me to go all out before."

"I made eighty bucks betting on you!" Meryn exclaimed. "That's a lot of chicken tenders."

Brie turned to Ari. "Who bet against me?"

Ari chuckled wickedly. "Nearly all the guys. They respect the hell out of you, but none of them thought you'd hold your own against Aunt Elysa."

"Why?"

"Because that woman has been putting us all on our asses for decades. She's one of the changes I made as unit leader. I asked her to help with drills. Each warrior probably as a low key form of PTSD when it comes to that woman," he explained.

"Dude, she's hot," Brie said, then noticed Leo had refilled her wine glass. She lifted it and took a healthy drink.

"Brie!" Ari shuddered. "That's my aunt!"

"Well, she's not mine, not by blood anyway. Most of those women caused me to question my sexuality. They were so powerfully sexy."

"Ditto," Meryn agreed.

Aiden looked down at his mate in shock. "Really?"

Meryn glanced up. "Did you see their arms? I bet that's where Rex gets it from."

"Like I said: just like her mother." Her dad winked at her.

"What do you mean?" Ari asked.

"When I met Brianna, she was dating a woman, and I was dating a man. We saw one another from across the room and pretty much abandoned our dates. The first thing she said to me was, 'I'm going to have your baby,' and she did."

"Mom and Dad were best friends first and foremost," she added.

Her dad smiled wistfully, and Doran wrapped his arm around him. "She was like a soul mate, but not like a fated mate. I think we were meant to be together."

Meryn snorted. "Yeah, so you could make Brie," she said flippantly. Everyone around them paused at her words.

Ari pulled her close. "I don't care how or why, she's here and she's mine."

"Ryuu, can I have more meat, please?" Meryn asked.

Ryuu moved to add more slices to her plate from the platter. "Thank the gods Leo cooked so much. Meryn, I think you've eaten a cows' worth."

Meryn pouted, then looked up at Leo. "Am I eating too much?"

Leo practically tripped over himself to take the platter from Ryuu. He generously loaded up her plate. "Of course not. Here, take some more. Oh, and some onions."

Ryuu eyed his charge who was smiling up at the other squire shamelessly. He shook his head, smiling. "Simply adorable."

Brie got the feeling he was referring to her manipulation and not the smile.

"She's totally playing you, Leo," Declan pointed out, trying to spear pieces of meat off the platter.

Leo blinked. "Of course she is." He pointed down. "Look at that devious little smile. How could I say no to that?"

Jedrek looked from Meryn to Leo and then to his mate. "Thank you for having boys. They're so much simpler."

Catherine raised a brow. "You have two daughters now, remember."

Brie flashed him a peace sign, and Kari smiled sweetly. Jedrek reached for his drink again.

"So, if we follow the trickle down path of bullshit concerns, then we really need to start with the people, not the council, right?" Meryn asked. She now held a fork in each hand, with beef on each fork.

Kendrick snapped his fingers. "Exactly. Meryn, as usual, you're a genius."

"I knooow," she said with a mouth full of food.

"If we do something similar to what we did in Lycaonia, it may work," Kendrick continued. "I know a journalist that submits to the Chronicle."

Jedrek sat back. "That's impressive. They like to keep their names secret to avoid outside pressure. It lends credibility to their neutrality. You contacting them is exactly what they try to avoid."

Kendrick gave a half shrug. "I won't tell them what to write. I'll just give them all of the facts as I know them and let them decided what to do. The Chronicle is the only newspaper that is distributed to all four pillar cities. It would be the fastest way to sway public sentiment."

"It could backfire. They could reveal that you tried to color what would be written," Rex pointed out.

"It may be a chance we have to take," Kendrick said. He tapped his lips with his finger. "Storm Keep will be the hardest sell. Meryn and Aiden have almost no ties to the city."

"Her uncle is an Elder there," Anne pointed out.

Kendrick shook his head. "That doesn't carry much weight in Storm Keep. The Witches' Council runs the city."

"Yeah, and I may be responsible for a murder there soon," Meryn admitted casually.

Nearly everyone choked.

Aiden and Kendrick whirled on her. "What!"

Meryn's eyes darted to the twins then down to her plate. "The guy that runs the orphanage may be expiring due to unforeseen circumstances." She grabbed her forehead. "It must be a premonition."

Kendrick sputtered, laughed, sputtered again, then finally he shook his head and sat back. "Is there any way this premonition could possibly be from a much more distant future? Like much, much more distant future?"

Meryn shrugged with one shoulder. "Maybe."

"Meryn," Aiden growled.

"Fiiiiine!" she pulled out her phone and sent a text. "There. Happy now?"

Rex closed his mouth. "You know what? I don't really need to know." He looked up at Leo. "Wonderful meal as always."

Leo held up a bowl. "More potatoes?"

"Yes, please." Rex sat back to give him more room to serve.

Brie looked up at Ari. "Are we gonna ignore that?"

Ari pointed to his brother. "I have been following his lead since I was in diapers. He hasn't steered me wrong yet." He held up his plate. "More potatoes for me as well, Leo."

"Alrighty then," Brie picked up her fork and dug into her meal. After the fight, she was crav ing protein, and the London Broil really was cooked to perfection.

Across the table, the twins were sniffling and squeezing Meryn between them while Pip kissed all three heads repeatedly.

Aiden held up his glass, and this time it was Ryuu pulling out the small bottle of apple scented amber liquid. He filled the glass once, which Aiden promptly emptied and then filled it again. "Just a premonition," he muttered.

Kendrick turned to Aiden. "Did you need Micah back here?"

Aiden blinked then shook his head. "What?"

"Micah? He rejoined Eta for the mission; did you need him back here?"

Aiden rubbed his chin. "No. I'd rather he work with his unit in guarding the warehouse."

Declan sighed in relief. "Don't tell him I said this, but we all missed him at home. He kinda made the day go by faster."

"When will you be going back?" his mother asked.

"Tomorrow. We'll spend the night here then go back," Declan said.

"Oh," Catherine sighed.

"Mother, as long as the portal is open, I can come home every day for lunch." Declan's eyes widened as he realized what he said. "Hot damn! I can come home for lunch."

Catherine turned to her squire. "Leo, starting tomorrow let's make lunch our bigger meal of the day. If that's the meal where all my boys will be able to be together at once, let's make it a good one. They need their energy."

Leo was already nodding. "I can easily adjust our menus." He eyed first Ari, then Declan. "We'll need to order higher quantities though."

Both Declan and Ari looked pleased at his assessment instead of offended.

"So Kendrick calls this Clark Kent, then a story goes out about how awesome I am, hopefully swaying the public. If that doesn't work, then we target the Committee?" Meryn asked.

"Meryn, no," Aiden repeated, sounding exasperated.

"What? It's not like we have a lot of choices. They're creating new rules. How'd the Committee get so much power anyway? One day, some peeps just said, 'hey, you have to do as we say,' and everyone just hopped to? That's bullshit," Meryn groused.

Kendrick inhaled his wine and started choking. Anne immediately began to rub his back. "Gods!" he gasped. "All these long centuries, I blamed the people. I just couldn't fathom how one day we had a king and queen and then the next a council." He turned deathly pale. "But it's happening again, isn't it?"

Kendrick stood, causing his chair to tip. "Aiden, we need to head to the palace." He looked around the room. "Rex, Ari, Declan, you'll all be needed. Rex, you can filter what you know to the council; you'll know what to leave out. Declan, you'll need to be included to help Magnus and likewise Ari to assist Aiden and Brennus." He threw his napkin on his plate. "Leo, Catherine, thank you for a lovely meal, but we really do have to go."

Catherine, looking flustered, stood. "Of course."

Jedrek didn't look at all pleased at being excluded. Rex placed a hand on his shoulder. "Trust us," was all he said.

"You boys help one another, and don't forget that I'm here if you need me," Jedrek said, nodding at his eldest.

Brie looked at her dad. He held up his hand that was twined around Doran's. "We'll be staying here. Brennus will update us later."

Doran looked worried. "Tell my brother to call me if I'm needed."

Brie gave his arm a squeeze. "We will," she promised.

Everyone was almost to the foyer when Kendrick looked around. When his eyes landed on something back at the table, his eyes softened. "Meryn, come on."

Meryn hadn't stopped eating as everyone was getting ready to go. She was still at the table, plowing through some beef. Leo placed a hand on her back. "I'll send up a midnight snack for you, okay?"

Meryn sighed, then stood. She picked up two rolls and crammed slices of beef in each. "Thanks, Leo, you rock."

Ari turned to Brie. "You can stay if you wish. You have to be tired after that fight."

She shook her head. There was no way she

was going to miss whatever that witch had to say. "I'm staying with you." She bit her lower lip. "Leo, about that midnight snack?" She pouted, giving him the best 'boo boo' face she could muster.

"Please, Leo?" Both Ari and Declan wore similar pouty faces, which ruined her efforts because she was now laughing.

Leo beamed. "It feels so good to be cooking large meals again."

"Come on, you three," Rex called out.

Together they headed out and back up the golden street toward the palace.

€

When they arrived, it was eerily quiet compared to the chaos they had left.

The marble halls had an ominous feel after Kendrick's scary observation.

"I feel like a masked murderer is about to pop out with a butcher knife," Meryn said, sticking close to Aiden.

"It does feel empty, doesn't it?" Anne agreed, inching closer to Kendrick.

"And darker," Brie added, and it did seem darker to her.

When they approached the queen's personal chambers, the door swung open, and Darian greeted them. "What's this about an emergency meeting?" he asked, holding up his phone.

"Were you able to contact Magnus?" Kendrick asked, walking past the prince.

"Nice to see you, too, Kendrick," Darian

drawled. "And yes, he arrived a few minutes ago via the warehouse portal."

"Magnus is here?" Meryn demanded, then flew past Darian as well. "Sebastian!" she called out.

"I thought she asked about Magnus?" Brie observed out-loud.

Ari pointed to Ryuu, who hurried after his charge. "Usually squires follow their charges. Sebastian would of course be with Magnus."

The twins and Pip ran after Meryn. "Sebastian!" they hollered.

Declan smiled. "Sebastian became like a pseudo-mom for them," he explained. "They must have missed him."

When they entered, Brie saw that Meryn, the twins, and Pip were gathered around a tall man who looked just as happy to see the younger people bouncing around him as they were to see him. "Level One has been so very empty without you!" Sebastian pulled Meryn into a hug then held her out at arms' length. "Look at you, Princess Meryn."

Meryn waved her hands in front of her. "None of that stuff. Just Meryn for you, Sebastian." She surprised the squire when she wrapped her tiny arms around his waist. "Missed you," she mumbled.

"And I have missed you too," he admitted.

"Princess Meryn, I bring you greetings from the City of the Night," a deep voice declared.

"Magnus!" Meryn turned from Sebastian and

hurried over to the gorgeous dark-haired man. "I got my flame-thrower!"

Magnus chuckled. "You will have to show me later."

"Like hell she will. When did you get it?" Aiden demanded.

Meryn looked up to the ceiling. "I don't know."

The queen shook her head at Aiden's distress and turned to Kendrick. "What was so important that you called a meeting tonight, of all nights?" Brie had to admit the queen looked absolutely exhausted.

Kendrick went to the queen and pulled her in for a hug. When he kissed her forehead, Brennus was there in an instant. "Keep your lips off my mate."

The queen sighed. "That bad?"

Kendrick simply leaned down and rested his forehead on Brennus' shoulder, much to everyone's shock. "Gods, I'm tired," he admitted.

Anne went to her mate and wrapped an arm around his waist. She pulled him back so she could hold him close. She then shot a look at Thane. Instantly, the Ashleigh brothers were there. They each laid a hand on Kendrick's back, which soon began to glow in different colors.

Kendrick exhaled and stood a little straighter. "Thank you, my friends."

Brie realized that he had not only assisted Aiden in his mission this evening, but he had also been called to help them as well. He was probably at his limits as much as the queen.

Sebastian turned to Cord. "Let us get everyone

settled. Does the queen have an antechamber?"

Cord shook his head. "We've been using the outer rooms of her personal chambers. We have plenty of seating there."

Sebastian nodded, then turned to where everyone was standing—looking spooked at both the queen's statement and Kendrick's admission. "It is late, and everyone has had a very long day from what I have heard. Let us adjourn to these outer rooms and get comfortable for the evening. Ryuu, Cord, and I will serve late night cocktails and desserts."

"Magic Pudding?" Meryn asked immediately.

"Of course, darling."

Slowly, everyone began to claim either loveseats or sofas. Oron, Darian, along with their mates, sat close to their mother and Brennus. Brie sat with Ari and the Lionharts to their right. Magnus sat with Meryn and Aiden to the queen's left along with the twins and Pip. Which left Kendrick and Anne with the Ashleighs sitting across from the queen.

Kendrick looked at Thane. "Can you cast a sound proofing spell, the strongest you can?"

Thane didn't argue for once, and he and his brothers cast the spell that had everyone popping their ears.

Kendrick looked over at Meryn. "Meryn, can you repeat what you said about the Committee, so that the queen and Magnus knows what I'm referring to?"

Meryn's face scrunched up. "The douchebag by proxy?"

"No."

"The kill first, ask questions later, plan?"

By this time Kendrick was smiling. "No."

Meryn scratched her head. "Was it how we're all being gaslit into accepting their trumped up power plays?"

"Yes." Kendrick turned to the queen and Magnus. "You both are the sovereign leaders of your people; why are you listening to the dictates of the Committee?"

"Because they are the Committee," both Magnus and the queen said at once, in unison.

Kendrick pointed. "That's a conditioned response."

The queen held a shaking hand to her mouth. "When?"

Magnus grit his teeth. "How?"

The squires began walking around with trays holding varying cocktails and treats. Brie looked the tray over until she saw something pink. "Cosmo?"

Sebastian nodded. "A wee bit strong too."

"Perfect," she whispered and lifted it from the tray.

Brie looked around the room and shook her head. Aiden, bless his heart had a drink in each hand, and Meryn had a serving size bowl in her lap with two spoons. Aiden sipped from one of his drinks. "It had to have started around the time the perimeter went up. That's when they first appeared in Lycaonia."

"Let me text René Evreux. He is the Commit

tee member for Lycaonia," Magnus said, lifting his phone.

Meryn growled. "No. He's a huge jerk."

Magnus gave a half nod. "He is not the best when dealing with others, which is why I made him the Elder for Lycaonia, the most diverse of the four pillar cities. Of all people, Meryn, I thought you would see that about him."

Meryn's lips were pressed in a straight line. "He said that my baby and Penny made him sick."

Magnus scrubbed his hands over his face. "It is his gift, Meryn. He can see the true nature of a person. We now know that you were missing your light. It was normal for you, but how do you think that registered to him? Also, you are carrying a mixed race child, similar to Penny. He has admitted to me on more than one occasion that he sees both essences, and it gives him motion sickness. He is rude, crass, and tends to despise anyone not a vampire, but he is learning."

Meryn's mouth dropped. "He's not a douchebag?"

Magnus winked. "He absolutely is, but he is not evil."

"Meryn, I believe that it was René that snuck me the necklaces for testing. He was also the one that saw through Rowan's deceit and freed me to save the Alpha Unit," Kendrick admitted.

Meryn held up a hand. "I will need time to realign him in my brain."

"Understandable," Magnus said, looking down at his phone. "He said he was one of the last ones to be approached. Jourdain Régis put his name forth as a candidate last August, and he was officially asked to join in September."

Meryn frowned. "That was months before I even moved."

Aiden sat back. "You're right, baby, this was before you." He looked around. "But it lines up perfectly to when the spell was cast to bring the warriors their mates."

"That spell's reach has yet to be determined," Thane said.

"What if that wasn't the only thing the spell did?" Meryn hypothesized.

Kendrick leaned forward. "Go on, Meryn, this is where you usually shine."

Meryn scooped up another spoonful of pudding. "Well, it's kinda like when you send out a massive update to multiple computers. You have to make sure everyone has turned on their systems, they have to leave them on overnight, you have to push the packets. Pain. In. The. Ass. So, usually, higher ups and tech supervisors are like, if we're going to dedicate this much manpower for this update, let's get a lot of other stuff knocked out at the same time, like OS updates, removing certain installed games, adding VPNs, the whole ball of wax, so that when they're done, they're good for a while." She looked around. "What if this spell had some huge component that had to be obtained, and they just made sure that they got their money's worth."

"Sonofabitch," Justice whispered, collapsing back into his chair.

Law shook his head at his brother's disbelief and pointed to Meryn. "I told you she's a genius."

Kendrick held up a finger. "So, what was the intended spell and what was added on? Was the primary purpose of the spell to seamlessly add the Committee to our society without question or was it to bring the warriors their mates for culling?"

Anne smacked her mate. "Did you have to word it like that?"

He shrugged. "Either way, it's terrifying."

"I wonder if it's neither," Meryn said, eating another spoonful of pudding.

Even Kendrick looked ill at her statement. "What do you mean?"

She held up her spoon. "Remember the demon guy?" She smiled. "Dude was seriously hot, by the way. Ouch!" Meryn rubbed her shoulder where Aiden nipped her. "Anyway. He said that the necklaces were just a means to an end. What if everything is moving us toward an endgame we don't even know about?"

"Meryn, please don't take this the wrong way, but I hate you right now," Kendrick growled.

She shrugged. "We don't have all the pieces, so trying to nail everything down and make sense of it all is pointless. All we can do is address what is right in front of us and do what we can to mitigate the damage."

"The damage is our people being murdered, Meryn," the queen reminded her softly.

Meryn nodded. "And back in November, it was pregnant shifters. In February, it was the citizens of Noctem Falls. At each turn, we have thwarted them in some way, shape, or form. They didn't get Lycaonia, Keelan saw to that. They didn't destroy Noctem Falls, Vivi, Ellie and the healers blocked them there. Yes, they have killed fae, but we surprised them tonight. We're one step closer to figuring out what the grand scheme is." She grinned. "We'll be even closer when we figure out how to open Kincaid's dirt box."

"Porcelain," both Kendrick and Thane corrected in unison.

Meryn shrugged. "So they've used some crazy mind stuff to install this Committee. Paranoia is a powerful thing. Just start rumors that the Committee is trying to secure property in each pillar city for an elite neighborhood or something. The demand for housing in the pillar cities is at an all-time high due to all the murders. If people suspect, for even a second, that the Committee is acting out of greed, they won't listen to a word they say."

Magnus looked at Meryn as if he was seeing her for the first time. "That is brilliant." His eyes narrowed. "You are actually a born leader, are you not?"

"Yeah, fuck that. I was born to eat pudding and watch Netflix." Meryn dug into her treat again.

Brie mulled over what she said. "It's basic human nature."

Meryn licked her spoon. "Yup. Their stupid Committee is rendered useless if no one listens to them. Even if that was the 'add on' to the mate spell, it doesn't matter. We haven't lost a warrior mate yet; we're all too kick ass. Especially Brie. So like, if they counted on this being a huge power play, we kinda got it covered."

Kendrick growled. "I don't like it."

Anne kissed his arm. "That's because you don't like anyone telling you what to do, much less what to think."

"That's it exactly. It makes me doubt my own mind, because before Meryn's cavalier statement, I never even noticed I was being influenced," Kendrick ranted.

Magnus looked to Meryn. "I wonder why it did not affect her?"

Ryuu smirked. "Meryn, stand up," he ordered.

Meryn scowled up at him. "Why?"

Ryuu pointed down at his charge. "Meryn loves me and trusts me to provide even the most basic necessities for her. But the very fabric of who she is questions everything. If someone told her to do something, her knee jerk reaction is to do the opposite."

Meryn nodded emphatically. "Yeah. What he said."

Brie looked at Ryuu and understood what he was saying. "We're not from here."

He nodded once sagely. "Exactly. From day one, Meryn has questioned why we, as para-normals, do certain things, because it was all foreign to her. I would imagine the same would extend to you, but to a lesser degree."

"Why to a lesser degree?" she asked.

"Because of your profession. You're used to a system that has a hierarchy that issues orders. You're trained to follow orders, and unless something crosses a hard line for you, you'd obey." He eyed Meryn, who was trying to ensure the same amount of pudding was on each spoon. "She was kept mostly to herself growing up, so she doesn't know or care about even the most basic social norms that act as the building blocks of rules and decorum in the human world. Her brain is constantly asking, 'why'."

Ryuu pointed to the others in the room. "Paranormals are raised following many rules and traditions. Some date back so far that even the queen would be hard pressed to answer the question, 'why' about many of our forms of etiquette."

The queen nodded. "It's true. I may have known the 'whys' at some point, but since I didn't have to think of it, routinely, I've forgotten much."

"I believe Meryn has said this before, but the spell to bring the warriors their mates may be their eventual downfall." He turned to Kendrick. "*Heika*, I know that this especially upsets someone like you, who has depended on their own mind and abilities for so long, but you have to remember that it only takes one person pointing out the truth for an illusion to fail." He nodded down at his charge.

Kendrick slumped back. "I don't like it, but you're right. There's not much we can do about it now except foul up their efforts."

Neil leaned in closer to Meryn. "Couldn't we let something slip on the message boards under a fake account? I don't think the Committee is tech savvy enough to figure that out."

Meryn nodded slowly before handing Neil her spoons and Nigel her bowl. She reached beside her to her ever-present bag and pulled out her laptop. "I can create a person in two seconds flat, hold on."

Ari frowned. "Isn't she already doing that?" He pointed to her distended belly.

Brie laughed. "No, she's creating a person online. When she's done, I bet they'll be real enough to owe taxes."

Meryn beamed at her. "You got it." She tapped away. "Let's see. The person shouldn't be from Éire Danu, too close to us at the moment. I'll make them from that other wolf pack where Eva's from. They haven't been accepted to a pillar city yet. We'll have her work in real estate, and she'll share that a packet came across her desk to secure land very close to Lycaonia. I would say Noctem Falls, but they have that national preserve." She licked her lips. "We'll have the name be something close to Adalwin Dulse; dude is dead so he'd make the perfect dummy account for this kind of thing. In fact, let me create a dummy account for him really quick."

"I have his financials up, Meryn," Neil said

from his laptop. "No one has touched his accounts since last year. Looks like everything is still open."

"Perfect," Meryn crowed gleefully. "Now, our poor scared girl from Texas will see someone named Alwin Dalse attempting to purchase land near Lycaonia. Which makes even more sense if you factor in they were there last year scoping things out. Now, considering this is the Committee she's posting about, she needs a fake account."

Aiden blinked. "Meryn, she is a fake account."

"Yeah, but my fake person isn't stupid enough to post under her own name. So, she has created a fake user name for the message boards I created last year, and she uploads a scan of Alwin's interest. She'll even create a fake Facebook account to lend credibility to her user name, that way even if someone from the Committee looks into this and discovers that the Facebook account is fake, they'll probably stop there, thinking they're geniuses." She chuckled. "What a bunch of poo brains." She typed for just a few moments more. "There, icing on the cake. She has an outstanding parking ticket outside the real estate office where she works and an active complaint on file with the building manager that someone keeps parking in her assigned space." She closed her laptop and cracked her back. When she looked around, everyone was staring at her. "What?"

Magnus leaned forward. "You did all of what you said as you were typing?"

"Yeah." She held out her hands, and the boys passed her back her pudding.

Brie looked over, and with her hand, she closed her mate's mouth. "You do remember me telling you all that she made grown men at a high security levels cry, right? I wasn't joking."

Ryuu practically glowed azure. "The world we currently live in is dictated by what people see, hear, and read online." He placed a hand on Meryn's curls. "And she dictates what they see, hear, and read."

"Oh gods above," Rex choked out in a strangled voice.

Brie chuckled. "Sounds like you're just now joining the program. Welcome to the digital age."

Chapter Seventeen

(

"IT'S IMPOSSIBLE. SHE CAN'T CREATE something out of nothing," Ari argued for the fifth time. "No matter what you say, that woman doesn't exist."

"She does if you don't have to touch her," Brie refuted.

"This is harder to understand than magic," he admitted, shaking his head.

She squeezed his hand as they passed the shops and eateries of the Upper City, now closed since it was basically the middle of the night. It didn't take long for the buildings around them to become familiar, as they turned onto the street leading to the Lionhart estate.

"I just want to go to bed and forget this night happened," Kari said, leaning against Declan as they walked.

Brie blinked, then blinked again. She noticed that the moments between blinks were getting longer. After a few more steps she was suddenly swept up into Ari's arms, and he snuggled her close. "You're dead on your feet. Next time there's a meeting after a major mission, we're skipping it."

She rested her eyes. "I don't think we'll get that option."

"You two take my baby sisters to bed; I will update father accordingly," Rex commanded.

She and Kari both laughed at his imperious order that placed more importance on them being his baby sisters, than mates to his brothers.

Rex opened the door and led them into the foyer.

"Goodnight, Baby Lionhart, your Uncle Rex loves you very much," Rex said. Brie opened one eye to see him leaning down to speak to Kari's belly.

"Are they well?" his mother asked.

"Yes, but tired. Is father still awake?" Rex asked.

"You should know better than to ask that; he's been pacing his office, waiting for your return. I had Leo make that Forbidden Fruit fruitcake you both love so much. Do try to get some sleep tonight," she chided.

"Goodnight," Ari called out and headed for the stairs.

A chorus of goodnights were said, and Ari carried her up toward their room. He set her down in the hall and opened the door. They entered the room illuminated only by the soft amber light of the glow stone on his nightstand. He shut the door behind them. Wordlessly, she quickly stripped from her dress robes and climbed into bed.

Ari turned off the light before joining her. He no sooner slid through the sheets before he was pulling her close.

When hands began to rub her shoulders, she snorted. "You're not getting lucky tonight Lionhart, I don't even know what planet I'm on."

He kissed her shoulder. "You go to sleep. I just wanted to rub some of these marks. Your gear left indentions in your skin; it can't feel good."

Brie reached up to where he was rubbing. Sure enough, she could feel ridges in her skin where her holster had dug in. "You're amazing, Ari."

"I know." She thought she'd be able to hang on a bit longer to enjoy his massage, but the second he started purring, it was lights out for her.

☾

Brie looked around, scowling. "Weren't we just here?"

Ari patted her leg. They had both risen early, then headed straight back to the palace. "Don't try to placate me. We're missing Leo's breakfast, and he was making pancakes!" she protested.

She sniffled a bit. She had woken up to the smell of them cooking. They hadn't even had time to grab coffee.

"Poor thing. I'm not making pancakes, but Sebastian prepared some waffle batter for little Meryn for breakfast before he and Magnus returned to Noctem Falls. I hear they're quite amazing," Cord said, filling her coffee cup.

Somewhat mollified, she fixed her cup and sat back. "Where is Tiny Toons?"

Aiden smiled. "Still sleeping, thank the gods.

She's had such weird sleeping patterns since Noctem Falls that I let her sleep whenever I can."

Brie looked around and saw that Ryuu was assisting Cord with breakfast, and the boys were huddled over their laptops. "It's quiet without her," she observed. Around the table, everyone nodded.

Brennus smiled. "I've noticed that myself on many occasions since she's come to visit. I always miss her when she's not about."

Next to Brennus, Rex was going over paperwork with the queen. "We were able to secure the warehouse with no problem. Declan will be overseeing the guard rotation in New Mexico, but will still need to be able to check in with us on a regular basis."

The queen held up a hand and smiled at him. "I had already planned on establishing a permanent portal there, so there's no need to sell the idea to me, Rex." She arched a brow. "Everyone knows that you spearheaded the project to secure a way for your brother to visit more easily."

Rex blushed when faced with the queen's teasing. "And of course to assist in bringing those foul ferals to justice," he countered.

She pointed down to his packet. "Molvan installed the portal to the warehouse this morning. I had him place it in the cold storage facility to keep traffic in the palace to a minimum." She looked at Declan. "Not that you can't visit whenever you like."

Declan nodded his head. "Thank you, Your Majesty."

The queen turned to Kari. "Based on the updated numbers you received from Beth, where do we stand?"

Kari hesitated then pulled out her tablet. "It does not look good, Aleksandra. According to Beth's update, there should be thirty-five thousand, seven-hundred and six fae. That is nearly three-thousand more than projected. Of that number, nine-thousand four-hundred and two were living outside of Éire Danu, which is good, it is lower than we thought. Of those roughly nine-thousand, five-thousand eight-hundred and three have responded to your summons."

The queen held up her hand. "I thought it was closer to fifty-seven hundred."

Kari nodded. "It was, until the murders began. That seemed to create a sense of urgency in responding." She looked up from her tablet. "Go figure," she said in a deadpan voice before continuing. "When we subtract the numbers of known dead and recovered, we have exactly three-thousand fae still unaccounted for."

Kendrick sat back. "Exactly three-thousand?"

Kari nodded solemnly. "Yes," she confirmed.

"What don't I get?" Amelia asked.

Brie turned to her. "It's nothing concrete, but it's harder to imagine that they're off on some remote island enjoying the sun and surf when you have an even number like that," she explained.

"Oh," Amelia replied in a small voice.

Brie couldn't stand the dejected look on her face. "Look on the bright side; once we torture the ferals in Kincaid's box, we'll be able to save everyone all in one go."

Ari rubbed her back. "I know that you meant to make her feel better, but it's probably not a good idea to use the word 'torture' with the empath."

"Shit." Brie shot Amelia an apologetic look.

Amelia shook her head, smiling wanly. "With Meryn around, I'm used to those kind of conversation bombs now."

The queen turned to Brie. "I would still very much like you to stay in charge of this investigation. You've proven time and again that your input is invaluable. I truly believe that I will only be able to save my children with you at the helm."

Brie sat straighter. "I will do everything I can to help. Though, it feels like we're at a standstill at the moment, until I get more information from River confirming what we suspect, or unless Meryn finds another warehouse."

The queen smiled. "I know you will. Even more so after your arm feels better."

Brie blinked. "My arm?"

Brennus chuckled. "Elysa came by first thing this morning to requisition fae enchanted ink for your tattoo."

"I'm getting a tattoo?" Brie looked up at her mate.

Ari beamed at her. "One of the rarest ones in our world. The tattoo for Eliana's Daughters isn't offered lightly. It's a symbol, much like our

warrior tattoos, that you have proven yourself."
He nuzzled her neck and whispered. "I'm so
proud of you."

Brie couldn't say no after her mate said something like that. In truth, she had never wanted a
tattoo before. They looked great on others, but
she hated needles. "I will require pampering
afterward," she informed him.

He frowned. "Why?"

Across the table, her father laughed. "Because
she hates, and I do mean hates needles. She
passed out when she had to get her tuberculosis
test for college."

"Dad!" she protested. "They're going to think
I'm a big baby."

Brennus placed another scone on her plate.
"After your bout with Elysa, I highly doubt anyone would think that."

"You heard about that?"

Brennus nodded. "My niece flattened the acting Alpha Female of Eliana's Daughters and was
offered acceptance in their ranks? Of course, I
heard about it." He nodded at Ari. "You'll learn
that the warriors are horrible gossips. Balder and
Bastien were waiting for me in the queen's outer
chambers this morning to be the ones to tell me."

"Why acting Alpha?" she asked Ari.

Ari lowered his coffee cup. "Mother is the
Alpha Female, she is the eldest and the strongest,
but her mating my father shifted some of her
focus away from her duties for Eliana's Daughters. My aunts refused anyone else as Alpha, so
they made Elysa acting Alpha Female. It frus-

trated Mother to no end that Elysa wouldn't actually be Alpha, but there was nothing she could do about it. Her sisters are just as stubborn as she is."

She dipped her scone in her cream and took a bite. She didn't think they were supposed to be eaten this way, but if everyone from the queen to Aiden dunked, then so would she.

It didn't take Ryuu and Cord long to whip up the waffles and soon everyone was enjoying the tasty breakfast.

Amelia turned to Aiden. "Should we wake her? If she hears we let her sleep through waffles, she'll be angry."

Aiden shook his head. "Let's let her sleep herself out. If she gets some good rest in now, she'll be good to go for a while."

It was early afternoon by the time she had finished her breakfast and received the update from Ben at the facility.

Groaning, Brie sat back patting her belly. "Those have to be the best waffles I've ever had."

"Ready for your tattoo?" Ari asked excitedly, standing.

"I guess. But remember, pampering and spoiling are required later."

"Spoiling you is no hardship."

"Ari, if you swing by around dinner time, Neil and I should have some more warehouses and buildings picked out for Meryn to review. We can give you both locations then so you can start planning," Nigel offered.

Ari looked at him. "Why around dinner?"

Nigel and Neil exchanged looks then turned back to him and shrugged. "That's when we always go over things."

Amelia laughed. "Meryn got us in the habit of doing all our meetings and updates over a meal. The reasoning was that we had to stop and eat anyway, honestly I think she just wanted to eat during our update sessions."

Ari took her hand. "We'll swing by, but I imagine Mother will want to have us home for dinner as long as Declan is in Éire Danu."

The queen looked from Oron to Darian. "That's understandable. Everything tastes better when both my sons are home."

They waved and walked out the door, into the halls of the palace. She went as slow as she thought she could get away with. If Ari noticed the snail's pace, he didn't mention it. Much quicker than she'd liked, they were at the Lionhart estate.

He opened the door and led her to the back. Down the middle of an expansive courtyard, a cobble path branched off in different directions.

"Mother put in a shooting range for me and Declan after we became warriors; my aunts use it all the time," he said, pointing toward the back left.

As they passed a large building on the right he smiled. "Dojo."

She perked up. "Maybe I can train later."

"Let's see how your arm feels first."

In the back right-hand corner was another stone building. Without knocking, he opened the door and led her inside. "Aunties! We're here."

The room looked to be some kind of training hall and gym. In the middle of the floor a reclined bench awaited her. Elysa picked up a tattoo gun from a small table next to the bench. "About time you two got here. Park it, missy."

Brie edged toward the seat and, finally facing the inevitable, sat down.

Elysa eyed her carefully. "You don't like needles, do you?"

She shook her head. "Not even a little bit."

Elysa gave a short nod then turned to Ari. "Go work out, she doesn't need you hovering. Battle ropes and chest presses until she's done."

Ari groaned before dropping a kiss on her forehead. "Good luck, baby."

Brie scowled at Elysa. "I could have squeezed his hand to death, you know."

Elysa just smiled. "Trust me, baby girl." She handed her a tank top. "Change into this real quick."

Without even thinking, she pulled off her shirt and changed right there. Once the tank was on, she looked around. Thankfully, she was surrounded by Ari's aunts, and they were the only ones in the building except for Ari.

"Now, lean back and go to your happy place," Elysa teased.

"Happy place, my ass," she grumbled.

At the first touch of the tattoo gun, she about

came unglued. It stung and burned all at the same time. She grit her teeth and looked up at the women watching her closely. There was no way in hell she would crumble in front of these amazingly strong female warriors.

It's just a tiny needle. Just a tiny needle. She repeated.

After the first few minutes, she was ready to say 'fuck it' and walk away. Happy place huh? She turned her head and saw Ari approaching the battle ropes. He whipped off his shirt overhead and threw it down on the mat before bending down to pick up the thick ropes. Adjusting his stance so that his feet were shoulder width apart, he began working the ropes. With his knees bent slightly, his normally perfect and firm ass ascended to divine status. She sighed and watched as his arms rose and fell as he easily made the impossibly heavy ropes dance to his tune. The slap of the rope on the mats provided a rhythmic staccato that had her mind drifting as she watched her god-like mate flex and move.

"Happy place," she whispered.

Elysa just chuckled, and Brie whipped around to look at her. The older lioness had planned this! "Can I be you when I grow up?" she whispered.

Elysa just winked. "Stick around, kid, there's a lot we can teach you. This"—she pointed to the tattoo—"is literally just the beginning."

Brie just gave a short nod then turned her attention back to Ari, because as she had been talking to Elysa, the burning in her arm had increased.

The entire process took six hours, of which

she had only had to have Elysa stop once to give her a minute to catch her breath.

By the time the tattoo was done, both she and Ari were whipped. The tattoo itself was an intricate band of knot work lions around her arm. Each panel was a different scene that told a story. Elysa said she'd teach her about later.

The tattoo wasn't very big, but using magical ink meant Elysa had to go slower than normal. Evidently, the ink was spelled to help her heal and link her to the pride. If her life were ever in danger, the tattoo would alert her new sisters.

"I heard I could find you here," a familiar voice called out.

She turned from watching her arm be wrapped in plastic to see her boss striding toward her. "Hello, sir."

He winced. "Can't you call me Cam? Sir, while work appropriate, doesn't really fit anymore, does it? Unless you're planning on staying my deputy and taking over for me," he asked hopefully.

"Sorry, Cam, the queen has put me in charge of the taskforce leading the nationwide search for her people." She looked at Ari's aunts, then to her tattoo. "Even once that is done, I have a feeling there's a lot these women can teach me. I'd rather focus on what I can learn, not punch the clock."

"Congratulations on becoming an Eliana's Daughter. When it became apparent you were Ari's mate, I had a feeling you'd end up here." He pointed to the training hall.

"What has you swinging by, Cam?" Ari asked, wiping his face with his shirt.

Cam pointed to her. "I just needed to get her official answer before I could process her paper-work. Seemed like something I should do in person, rather than over the phone."

Brie would miss working with Cam and River, but not enough to divide a large portion of her time away from her mate, especially with how delicious he was looking.

"Gonna miss you guys," she said, looking up at the man who had taught her everything she knew about investigating and working with the public.

"We're going to miss you too," Cam heaved a huge sigh. "Now, I have to find a replacement for you." He frowned down at her. "Do you know how lucky I felt when I found you? A brilliant mind that I didn't want to strangle three times a day?"

"Emerson," she said and gingerly pulled on her shirt.

His eyebrows shot up. "Emerson? Really? Does he even know how to talk?"

She threw a wadded up paper towel at him. "Of course, he knows how to talk. He's just quiet." She smiled. "But he's also very thorough and conscientious. Given some prodding, I think he'll make a perfect Sheriff."

Cam rubbed his jaw. "Emerson, hmm."

"Trust me on this. He'll be wonderful."

"I'll try him out and see what happens." He looked at his watch. "If I hurry, I might catch him before he leaves." He gave her a one-armed hug then jogged out the door.

Ari pulled her to her feet. "We have just enough time for a shower and maybe a quick nap before we have to head out to the palace."

She shook her head. "Let's head there now. If I take a shower and lay down, I'm not getting back up for anything less than Leo's cooking."

Ari thought about it a moment then nodded. "Good point." He leaned down and kissed Elysa on the cheek. "Thank you, Auntie."

Elysa stood then ruffled his hair. "Get on with you two. The sooner you can solve all these murders, the sooner I can start training Brie."

Brie gave a mock salute. "Marching orders received."

Hand in hand, they headed back toward the palace. When they had been on their way to the Lionhart estate to get her tattoo, she'd dragged her feet because she wasn't looking forward to the needle gun, now they were both meandering slowly because they were exhausted.

When Cord let them into the dining area, where it looked like a late lunch or early dinner, hors d'oeuvres were being served. At once, Brie noticed the heavy atmosphere.

"What now?" she asked, as they sat down.

Amelia turned to her. "Nothing really, well, yet."

"Huh?"

Amelia pointed to where Aiden scowled into his plate of french fries. "Meryn is still asleep," she explained.

"So, wake her," Brie suggested.

Aiden stabbed his french fry into his ketchup. "But she needs her rest."

"I no like," a tiny voice chirped. It was the sprite, Felix, that looked to Meryn. Brie had to suppress the urge to cuddle him every time he appeared.

Ryuu held out his hand, and Felix flew to him. "Why?" he asked.

Felix stood on Ryuu's large palm. "She too far away."

Ryuu looked at Aiden. "I'm waking her." With that decree, he spun and headed toward the bed-rooms.

Aiden, Brennus, Kendrick, Amelia, and Thane were hot on his heels.

The boys stood, looking torn. They looked from the direction of Meryn and Aiden's rooms to their laptops and back.

"Boys, go see what's going on with Meryn. She still needs to review the locations and to be honest, the only thing Ari and I are good for right now is a shower and dinner," Brie suggested.

"Right. Good idea. Come on, Pip, Neil," Nigel said, and all three boys quickly beelined it toward Meryn's room.

Ari snagged a croissant and stood. "We'll swing by tomorrow to catch up," he promised.

The queen nodded absently, distracted by her worry over her niece. "Of course."

Brie hated every step they took, trudging their back to the Lionhart estate for what seemed like the billionth time. "I hate this walk now," she growled.

"How about this?" He started when they reached the Lionhart front gate. "You head up for your shower, and I'll have Leo arrange for dinner to be delivered to our rooms. We'll eat and turn in early," he suggested.

"If I wasn't head over heels in love with you before," she said, tilting her head back.

"I know, I know," he said, smiling before kissing her softly.

Once inside, she went upstairs, and he headed for the kitchen. She was nearly done when he made it up to their room. After his shower, he turned on the television to the Discovery Channel to watch How Things are Made and they waited for dinner.

To her delight, Leo surprised them with a huge selection of finger foods and appetizers. When he offered her a choice between three types of beer she thought she'd cry.

She snuggled in close to Ari as they split a platter of nachos, mozzarella sticks, chicken wings, and sliders. The food was savory, the beer was cold, and Ari was spoiling her at every turn.

When they turned in for the night, and Ari once again pulled her into the curve of his body, she couldn't imagine a more perfect evening than the one they just enjoyed. None of the magical splendors of Éire Danu could come close to eating bar food with Ari on the floor of their room watching television. Her beautiful mate made even the most simple things treasures to be enjoyed, and she could no longer live without him.

CHAPTER EIGHTEEN

☙

MERYN BLINKED THEN LOOKED AROUND. The room was familiar with its stark white marble and glass.

"Hello again," a deep voice greeted her.

Meryn spun around and growled. "I better not be dying again. That shit hurt." Damn, he was just as beautiful as she remembered.

He shook his head. "There is no need for that method this time. When you called out before, stating that you wanted to meet me, the path was created. You, in essence, invited me in. Now, I can speak to you like this whenever I wish, especially on nights where you've thought of me."

"Can I uninvite you?"

He nodded. "You could, but, then we wouldn't be able to chat," he smiled slyly. "And something tells me you're too curious to do that."

She sighed then glanced around the room. "You got any chairs?"

The man waved his hand, and the room was suddenly completely furnished. "Please, make yourself comfortable."

Meryn hesitated. "Is this another, 'oh by the

way, bad shit is happening but by all means park your butt on my insanely expensive leather couch' kinda thing?"

"No, as I said before, I don't believe I will be killing you."

Meryn walked over and climbed up on the cream leather loveseat. At first it was cold, but soon her body heat had it quite comfortable. "So, what do I owe the pleasure of this visit?"

He sat down across from her. "To be perfectly honest, I was curious about you. What makes you so dangerous to me that multiple witches warned me of you?"

"Rowan said something about you being honest, that you never lied to him, but therein lies your treachery." Meryn noticed the slight change in his expression, before it went back to his carefully crafted mask.

"I never lie. Most of the people I work with lie to themselves; I don't have to."

Meryn had a moment of clarity. "You can't lie, can you?"

He flinched. "I'm starting to see what the witches were referring to. You see things others don't."

"But you can evade the question." She stared. "God, that has to absolutely suck."

He blinked in surprise. "You're the first to ever voice that opinion."

"I personally don't like to lie since I have this tendency to just blurt out whatever I'm thinking, so that makes remembering to edit what I say impossible, so I can kinda sympathize. Because, trust me, there were times I wish I could have lied and couldn't."

Meryn met his gaze. "How can I kill you?"

"Did you really think I was going to answer that? Besides, why kill me? I've been nothing but cordial with you."

She ground her teeth together. "Because you killed my parents, so I'm going to kill you."

He tilted his head. "I did no such thing."

Meryn jumped to her feet. "I saw the moment they died. Your warrior ferals with red tattoos were there. My mother had a premonition that she and my father died horribly at their hands and drank a poison to evade capture. But they wouldn't have had to do that if you hadn't sicced your reapers on them," she shouted. Every moment she had lived without her parents fueled her anger, which burned even fiercer now that she had had a glimpse at how wonderful they had been and how much they had truly loved her.

He stood and gently took both her hands in his. "Meryn, you have figured out my one true weakness. Look at me," he ordered.

She choked down her tears and stared up at him defiantly. "I had nothing to do with their deaths. I only asked that your father be brought in for a simple conversation. Unlike you, he had never opened a channel for me to speak to him, so it had to be done in person, as it were."

Meryn felt the fight in her evaporate. She knew without a shadow of a doubt that he was telling the simple truth without any trickery. "Why did you need him?" she whispered.

He steered her back to her couch and had her sit down before sitting on the coffee table in front of her. "Even for a fae, he was a man ahead of his time. His use of fae magic was extraordinary. In exchange for the information he sought, I wanted him to make me something. That is all, Meryn, I promise you."

His eyes began to blaze scarlet. "You have revealed a treachery I did not even know existed. The one I trusted to bring your father in reported to me that they came upon your parents' house as it was burning and that there were dead ferals in the yard indicative of a random attack." His eyes darkened to a deep crimson. "True, your parents didn't die at the hands of my men, but according to your mother, they would have. In my eyes, that is one and the same."

"Who was it?" she asked.

He met her eyes, and she couldn't look away. "I'll make you a deal," he started.

"No way. I've seen tons of movies, and I always think the person who makes the deal is an idiot for trusting the bad guy," Meryn shook her head.

"I swear to you there is no trick to my offer. It's an exchange, pure and simple. If you accept, you free me to do what I wish."

She pointed at him. "That right there, is the scary part, by the way."

His eyes faded back to scarlet. "Let me explain. Nearly all my actions are dictated by contracts. I cannot go forth and impale the lying bastard that killed your father, because I haven't been contracted to do so. If we make an arrangement, then I am free to do more."

Meryn hesitated, if Ryuu were here he'd have scooped her up and marched from the room by now. "What do you want in exchange?" She tried to ignore the ball of ice forming in her stomach.

He held up a finger. "A single memory. One that I can keep as my own and replay as I wish."

"Huh?"

He pointed to the room. "White marble and glass. Do you think I chose such an aesthetic?"

Meryn looked around. "You mean, I did this?"

He nodded. "I told you the last time we spoke, my environment is hot and dry." He smiled as he touched the coffee table. "It is a relief to be cool for a change." He eyed her. "Why white marble and glass?" he asked.

Meryn shrugged. "I think it's because you look like an angel to me," she admitted.

He simply stared then burst into laughter. "Never, in all my long, long millennia has any-one ever thought me an angel."

She tilted her head. "Why? I think you're the epitome of what an angel looks, sounds, and acts like."

"Every modern religion would call me a demon or devil."

"Yeah, but wasn't the devil once an angel?"

His laughter died. "You're serious."

"I think that you are doing horrible things. I think that you've caused tens of thousands to suffer," she paused. She couldn't put her finger on it. "But for some reason"—she pointed to her chest— "in here, you don't seem evil. Not truly evil."

"Well, I am. I offer men choices they cannot refuse and seal their fates. As I told you before, I kill people, you should remember that."

She snapped her fingers. "That's what I was missing. They have a choice, don't they? They could always choose to say no." She pointed to the room. "You're not forcing me to say yes."

"Is it really a choice when I deliberately offer them everything they desire?"

She blinked. "Yes."

He sighed. "You're so very young."

Meryn took in his exasperation and made up her mind. "I'll do it. Because I trust you to uphold your end of the bargain," she said, leaning back against the sofa. She ran her hand over the leather. If this was from her mind, she had damn good taste.

"Haven't we just gone over why you shouldn't trust me?"

"Yup."

"You realize that I may still kill you?"

"Yup."

"I don't get you."

"Join the club; Aiden is the president."

He sat up straight. "Here are the terms. I will arrange for the deaths of every creature involved with your parents' murder and will gift you the memory of their demise. In exchange, I want a single memory from you. Once you choose the memory and offer it to me, it will be gone for good. Do you agree?"

"I get to choose?"

"Yes."

"Deal," she paused. "I don't have to sign anything in blood right?"

"No, no blood. Your verbal agreement is binding."

She looked around. "What happens now?"

"Now, you think about the memory that you wish to offer."

"Can I ask you a question?"

"Yes."

"Why a memory?"

"Because through a memory I get to experience everything you saw, smelled, felt, heard or tasted."

"Because you're in that dry, hot box right?"

"Yes."

Meryn wrapped her arms around herself. She had experienced something similar growing up and wouldn't wish it on her greatest enemy. She looked across the room. Literally. As much as her brain wanted to avoid the memory of being in her grandmother's attic, it was tied to the one she wanted to give.

Those days in that attic had been hell on earth, but the days that followed had been some of the fewest happy childhood memories she had. "I think I have the one I want to exchange."

"Are you certain?"

"I am." She didn't know why she had chosen that particular memory, but it felt right. No matter how evil, no one deserved that kind of pain.

"I will place my hand on your head, you will

need to think of a starting point and an end point. Once you show me the memory in its entirety, it will be gone."

"Ready."

When he placed his hand on her head and she felt the heat coming off of him she knew she had made the right choice. She closed her eyes and thought back.

She had been five or six. Still young enough to want her grandmother's love. She was confused why she had been dragged to the attic. It was hot, so very, very hot. It was hard to breathe because of the heat.

"Stay here until I come for you. If you upset my weekend, you'll be in trouble," her grandmother ordered.

"Yes, Grandma."

"What did I say about calling me that! Call me Estelle."

"Yes, Estelle," she replied, meekly.

When the door shut, she felt panic begin to claw at her. She looked around the room. She had a blanket on the plywood floor and a bucket in the corner. She went to the window and tried to open it. It was nailed shut. Feeling weak she went to the blanket and laid down.

"Just a couple days," she whispered.

Her mind fast forwarded. "Start here," she said out loud.

She heard the door creak open and a bit of cool air floated toward her. "Get down here."

Slowly, she forced herself to stand. She'd do anything to get out of that attic. She hurried as fast as she could down the stairs. The air felt so good on her face.

"Go outside, stay out of my way."

She nodded then went to the back door. She just wanted fresh air; she'd do anything to inhale fresh air that hadn't been heated by dry wood and scented by aging boxes. She hit the back door at a run and kept running until she was in the neighbor's yard. Sometimes, when she didn't think they were home, she'd hide in their covered gazebo. It was like her own private oasis. Today, she didn't care if she was seen, she needed to feel the wet ground under her bare feet and smell the wonderful flowers.

She sat on the soft covered bench and breathed deeply.

"Finally caught our little rabbit," a rough male voice commented.

Scared, she looked up. It was her neighbor, Mr. Vesling. "I'm sorry." She hopped to her feet.

He held his gnarled hand to his ear. "What was that I hear?"

She frowned. "I said I was sorry," she repeated a bit louder.

He chuckled and shook his head before reaching into his pocket. "I hear the ice cream truck. Do you think you're quick enough to grab us a few?" He handed her a few dollars.

"For ice cream, I can be!" She took the money and darted down his driveway. She had to catch that truck!

She spotted the white van and waited until all

the other kids had their treats before approaching the window.

"What'll it be?"

She blinked. She didn't know. Mr. Vesling hadn't told her what he wanted. She sniffled. "I don't know, he didn't say."

The man's face softened. "How about vanilla ice cream in a cinnamon cone? My wife makes them, but they're not as popular with the other children as the cartoon ones," he suggested.

"Two please," she held out her money.

He nodded, counted out her change and dipped out two cones for her. Slowly, she made her way back to her neighbor's covered gazebo. Mr. Vesling waited for her in the shade.

"Thank you, Meryn. These old bones can't keep up with that truck anymore, and Mrs. Vesling says ice cream isn't good for me."

"Should you have it?" she asked, worried for him.

"Bah! A cone here and there is fine," he said, looking down, then smiled. "My favorite. How'd ya know?"

"I didn't but the nice man suggested these, so I got em."

She hopped up on the bench and licked her ice cream cone. The vanilla ice cream was cold and creamy. Outside the gazebo, a breeze whirled around them, bringing her the scent of freshly cut grass.

Yesterday, she had pleaded with God to take her to her mommy and daddy, but today she was outside enjoying the cool breeze and ice cream. It was the best day of her life.

"Okay, stop there."

Meryn exhaled, then shook her head. What had she been doing?"

She looked up to see the handsome demon staring at her. "When your memory began, I thought you were punishing me, but then…"

"Since you have it now, I have no idea what you're referring to," she reminded him.

"The day after you left the attic. Your ice cream with…"

"Mr. Vesling! I remember him," Meryn smiled.

"How? I took that memory."

"It's kinda fuzzy, but if you have the day I was released from the attic, I think I'm remembering the day after that. Mr. Vesling bought me ice cream that day too," she sighed. "I remember that day clearly because he died the day after that. I was on my own again for a while until I discovered the library."

"Why? Of any memory you could have given, why that one?"

Meryn shrugged. "Because I figured if I had to use a memory as payment it should be a good one, right?"

The demon looked lost in thought. "I never knew ice cream was so good."

Meryn snuggled against the arm of the sofa. "Don't forget our deal," she said, then yawned.

The demon straightened. "Of course. For a memory like that, you will be more than satisfied."

"Won't that mess up your plans?"

"No. The ones responsible have outlived their usefulness. They are acting recklessly in pursuing their own agenda. It is past time for them to leave this world."

Meryn found she could barely keep her eyes open. "Werd." She closed her eyes and felt herself begin to drift.

"I do apologize. I hadn't meant to keep you for so long. You may be a bit tired when you wake," he advised, his voice sounding more distant.

"That's why God made coffee," she replied.

For a moment, she relaxed before she heard a frantic voice.

"Meryn! Gods, baby, please wake up!"

Meryn opened her eyes to see Aiden and Ryuu staring down at her. "Dude, I'm tired."

"Thank all the gods," Ryuu whispered, clutching his chest. He sat at the edge of the bed.

"What?" she struggled to sit up. When she looked around the room, she saw the boys, Kendrick, Thane, Brennus, and Amelia staring at her, concern written all over their faces. "Can't a girl sleep around here?"

"Meryn, you've been sleeping for almost twenty-four hours!" Aiden practically yelled.

She gave him a flat expression. "You yell again, I will cut you."

He swallowed hard and simply scooped her up and placed her between his legs as he leaned against the headboard. She snuggled against his chest and closed her eyes.

"Meryn!" Aiden shook her awake.

"You wanna die?" she asked.

"You have to stay awake," he pleaded.

"Fuck my life right now," she groaned. "Where's Izzy? Where is my Coffee Goddess?" Felix stayed in her lap, holding tight to her finger, as if she would disappear.

Amelia brought her phone up and sent off a text. "She'll be here in a minute." She sniffled. "We were so worried."

"What happened, Meryn?" Kendrick asked, eyeing her intently.

Meryn closed her eyes and yawned, deliberately delaying her answer. She knew if she mentioned the demon, everyone would lose their shit, and she didn't really feel like confessing she had made a deal with the devil. "I didn't get to sleep until late; there was a lot swirling around in my head. Plus, the demon was on my mind since I mentioned him at dinner. I think I was just tired." It wasn't exactly a lie.

Ryuu took her wrist in his hand. "She's exhausted."

"We have asked so much of her lately," Brennus said, looking grim.

"I just need coffee," Meryn growled.

"I'm here!" Izzy called out, coming through the door with a tall glass and silver straw. "I made you a quad shot, bittersweet mocha with caramel drizzle."

"Gimme. Gimme!" Meryn held out her hands, causing Felix to take up his usual position on her shoulder.

Izzy smiled and handed over the glass.

Meryn took a sip and sighed. "Soooo good."

Aiden just kept nuzzling the top of her head. "You can't sleep anymore."

"Like ever? Do you know how dangerous that is for you?" Meryn looked up at her poor mate. He had hit new stress levels lately.

"Don't you mean that it would be dangerous for you, Meryn?" Amelia asked.

"No, I definitely mean it would be dangerous for Aiden. I love my mate and don't want to have to murder him because he pissed me off when I was sleep deprived," Meryn yawned, then sipped her coffee. "God, I love you, Izzy!"

"You had us freaking out. You just kept sleeping. At first everyone was like, just let her sleep, but then right before dinner we realized how long you'd been out," Izzy paused in her ramble. "Don't you have to pee?"

Meryn chuckled, then gasped as she became aware of the growing sense of urgency her bladder was presenting her. "Yes! Shit, yes, I have to pee! Aiden, let me go," Meryn wiggled until she slid down out of Aiden's arms. Ryuu helped her off the bed, and she beelined it to the bathroom.

The next time she chatted with the hot demon, they needed to set a damn timer!

CHAPTER NINETEEN

B RIE WATCHED AS AIDEN AND Ryuu both hovered around a drowsy Meryn, who kept growling at them while sipping on her coffee. Meryn's eyes turned toward her. "What'd I miss?"

Brie winced and flexed her arm. "Not much as far as the investigation goes. The warriors are still working with the families to get bodies identified."

"What happened to your arm?" Meryn asked, pointing to the plastic wrap sticking out from under her sleeve.

"I got a tattoo to symbolize that I'm an Eli-ana's Daughter now." She pulled up her sleeve to reveal the amazing tribal knotwork encircling her arm. "The under part of my arm hurts the worst, but I'm glad I have it."

Ari kissed her arm right above the markings. "It's so hot."

She felt herself blushing. She still wasn't used to being viewed as a desirable woman, but every day Ari showed her that she had just needed a strong enough man at her side.

"Badass," Meryn whispered. She looked up at her mate. "I want a tattoo."

"You have one. That freaky dragon one that keeps changing," Aiden pointed out.

"No, I want a warrior tattoo."

"You're not…" Aiden let his voice trail.

Meryn's eyes narrowed. "I'm not what?"

"Maybe you should design a sixth man tattoo?" he suggested quickly. "Take all the time you need to get it right. I mean it took years to get the unit warrior tattoo finalized."

Meryn's eyes widened. "Why didn't I think of that! A geek warrior tattoo!" She pulled out her laptop and began tapping away. "It's gonna be awesome. I want a magic one like yours and my dragon."

Aiden went from looking relieved to looking worried again.

"We had more people post on the message board grumbling about elitism," Nigel said, looking up from his tablet. "We don't have a lot of views yet though."

Meryn shrugged, her eyes still glued to her laptop. "These things need to grow organically. If it was a concern all of a sudden, then it would seem planted."

"It is planted," Neil pointed out.

"Yeah, but they don't know that."

Brie felt a hand on her shoulder she turned and smiled at her dad as he and Doran sat down on the sofa on her other side.

"How'd Cam take the news that you were officially quitting?" he asked.

She laughed. "I think he's still cussing. He really wanted me to take over as sheriff. Now, he needs to pick out and train a replacement before he can retire."

Ari scowled. "What did the man think would happen? That you were going to commute back and forth every day? Besides we need you here."

"Yeah, there's no way I'd pass up on Leo's food," she agreed.

Ari nodded then looked at her. "Is that the only reason?"

She leaned over and kissed along his jaw. She heard his swift inhale before she sat back. "And I'd miss you," she whispered.

"Maybe we should have lunch at home?" he suggested, his thumb lazily rubbing circles on the top of her hand.

"No can do, Ari," Aiden interrupted. "We are receiving those thermal imaging goggles from the queen today. You need to be at the briefing, and your mate needs to lead said briefing."

Ari's eyes turned a dark honey color as he began to growl at his commander.

Aiden's eyebrows shot up. "What'd I do?"

Brie was laughing so hard she collapsed against her dad. "That's like the third time," she howled.

"Nothing, sir," Ari grumbled. "But if you don't have a future generation of warriors to lead it's your own damn fault!"

"No little baby fruit baskets and NinjaGaidens," Meryn chortled.

Everyone stared. Finally, Thane asked the

question that most probably had. "Meryn, what do you mean fruit basket?"

She pointed to Ari. "It's what I saw for him."

Kendrick tilted his head. "Meryn, do you remember exactly what you saw when you looked at Ari?"

Meryn nodded. "Yeah, stars, bells, flowers, and berries. It reminded me of a festive fruit basket."

Kincaid lowered his mug frowning. "Why does that sound familiar?"

Kendrick stood and walked over to Meryn. "Do you think you can try something different? I'd like to see if you can recall the images."

Meryn scrunched up her face. "I can try, but no promises."

They both closed their eyes.

"See, flowers and stuff," Meryn said, pointing to her head.

A moment later, Kendrick stepped back, causing them both to open their eyes. He looked from her to Ari then back, before finally turning to stare at him. "What she's seeing is actually Deadly Nightshade," he informed them.

Kincaid snapped his fingers. "Belladonna, that's why it sounds familiar." Then he looked at Ari. "Oh."

Beside her, Ari flinched. "Is that a good thing?"

Kendrick looked down at Meryn. "Well?"

She shrugged. "I think it's pretty."

Kendrick walked back to his chair and sat down. "You know, I think this fits Ari exceptionally well."

"My brother is not a poison," Rex protested.

Kendrick's expression became sly. "To you, he wouldn't be. Belladonna had many applications, including medicinal and even cosmetic. I think what you get from Ari depends on how you approach him. A deceptively beautiful flower that is the essence of death. Simply fascinating."

Meryn typed for a moment. "Okay, you're in the system as Nightshade now."

Ari blinked. "Nightshade?"

Meryn pointed to her head. "I made your image for me, your call sign. I think it sounds like a comic book hero. Too cool."

Ari mulled it over. "Okay, I love it. Much better than a fruit basket."

Brie regained her composure. "Very cool," she agreed. She looked back over to her dad. "Will you live here? Ari and I have discussed our living arrangements, but I let him know, no matter what, we need to make sure we see you often."

"You and Doran are everything I need, and you both belong here. The house in Monroe is just four walls after all. We'll bring the memories we made there with us when we start our new lives here."

"What about your practice?"

Her dad laughed. "I'll be teaching the witches here all about lions. That way, they'll be able to heal them that much better. This will be especially helpful in Éire Danu, since it has such a large portion of lion shifters. In a way, I get to have my cake and eat it too."

Brie watched his face to see if he was fibbing.

They had a lot of memories tied to the house, but she understood how he felt. In such a short time, it no longer felt like 'home' anymore.

"As long as you're happy, I'm happy."

"Right back at ya, kiddo."

Aiden stood. "Come on, you two. I have a feeling the briefing and drills will run well into the evening," he said, oblivious of Ari's low growling.

She shook her head and stood pulling her mate to his feet. "The sooner we start, the sooner we finish."

On either side of them, Kincaid, Gage, and Priest also stood.

"Come on, 'oh deadly one'," Priest teased.

"Don't worry, Priest, I have a cool name for you too based on my image," Meryn smiled at him.

"It can't be any worse than Gamma Kitten One. Hit me, short stuff," he said, holding out his arms in invitation.

"Pandora."

He blinked. "Seriously?"

She winced. "I saw a box with a lock that I knew shouldn't be opened. All I got from that was Pandora."

Brie and Ari chuckled as they steered a pouting Priest from the room. "Come along, 'Dora'," Ari teased in retaliation.

Priest groaned. "You can't tell the guys."

Ari pushed his unit brother from the room so he fell in step with Gage and Kincaid. Shaking his head, he took her hand as the group made their way through the palace heading toward the warrior villa.

Brie shivered a bit. All her jackets were at the home she shared with her Dad in Monroe. Maybe they'd have something here in the city she could buy.

"Ari, can we stop in some shop? I'd like to get a jacket or a sweater."

"I guess it is still spring in Monroe." He smiled at her. "You may have better luck finding something like that there, we don't have much need for jackets here in Éire Danu," he waved his hand to the buildings. "Land of the Eternal Sun and all that."

Brie frowned and glanced around. It was dimmer here than when she arrived. She looked up; there was no cloud covering the sun. She squinted. Where was the sun anyway? As they hit the Border City, she noticed that some of the street lamps were flickering. She checked her watch; it was barely noon.

"Ari, if this is the Land of the Eternal Sun, should the street lamps be turning on at noon?" she asked, pointing to the lamps.

Ari stopped, turning slowly to stare at the lamps. When he faced her, he was milk white, and pure fear filled his eyes. "No, they shouldn't be."

EPILOGUE

G AGE KEPT PACE WITH ARI as they flat out ran back toward the palace. Between the murders and the city lights, he didn't want to know what the future held.

A flash of red as they ran past a clothing store had him shuddering. In his nightmares his mate turned and walked into a blazing inferno.

He could only pray that she was safe and that despite the chaos in their world, that he could keep her that way.

D EAR READER -
       Thank you for reading!
I hoped you enjoyed *My Warrior*.

   For a full listing of all my books please check
out my *www. alaneaalder.com*
   I love to hear from readers so please feel free
to follow me on Facebook , Twitter, Goodreads,
AmazonCentral or Pinterest.

SEND ALANEA A
HUG!

LEAVE A REVIEW

Hug me please!!

**If you liked this book please let others know.
Most people will trust a friend's opinion more
than any ad. Also make sure to leave a review.
I love to read what y'all have to say and find
out what your favorite parts were. I always
read your reviews.**

IMPORTANT!!
   As you know Facebook strictly controls what
shows up on your newsfeed. To ensure that you
are receiving all my latest news and teasers

you can to sign up for my newsletters so you will receive regular updates concerning release information, promotions, random giveaways and future Live events.

I typically send only 1-2 updates per month and won't flood your inbox, promise! ;)

Alanea

OTHER BOOKS BY ALANEA ALDER

KINDRED OF ARKADIA SERIES

This series is about a shifter only town coming together as pack, pride, and sloth to defend the ones they love. Each book tells the story of a new couple or triad coming together and the hardships they face not only in their own Fated mating, but also in keeping their town safe against an unknown threat that looms just out of sight.

Book 1- Fate Knows Best
Book 2- Fated to Be Family
Book 3- Fated For Forever
Book 4- Fated Forgiveness
Book 5- Fated Healing
Book 6- Fated Surrender
Book 7- Gifts of Fate
Book 8- Fated Redemption

BEWITCHED AND BEWILDERED SERIES

*S*he's been Bewitched and he's Bewildered...

When the topic of grandchildren comes up during a weekly sewing circle, the matriarchs of the founding families seek out the witch Elder to scry to see if their sons' have mates. They are shocked to discover that many of their sons' mates are out in the world and many are human!

Fearing that their future daughters-in-law will end up dead before being claimed and providing them with grandchildren to spoil, they convince their own mates that something must be done. After gathering all of the warriors together in a fake award ceremony, the witch Elder casts a spell to pull the warrior's mates to them, whether they want it or not.

Each book will revolve around a unit warrior member finding his destined mate, and the challenges and dangers they face in trying to uncover the reason why ferals are working together for the first time in their history to kill off members of the paranormal community.

Book 1- My Commander
Book 2- My Protector
Book 3- My Healer
Book 4- My Savior
Book 5- My Brother's Keeper
Book 6- My Guardian
Book 7- My Champion
Book 8- My Defender
Book 9- My Angel
Book 10- My One and Only
Book 11- My Solace
Book 12- My Warrior
Book 12.5- My Gifts at Christmas
Book 13- My Beacon
Book 14- My Salvation
Book 15- My Eternal Light

Coming Soon

THE VANGUARD

We Hold the Line.

Book 1- Inception

Made in the USA
Middletown, DE
06 July 2024

56965263R00236